Praise for *Menagerie*

"Well-paced, readable and imaginative."
—*New York Times* on *Menagerie*

"A dark tale of exploited and abused others, expertly told by Vincent."
—*Library Journal*, starred review

"Vincent summons bold and vivid imagery with her writing."
—*Kirkus Reviews*

"As depicted by Vincent, Delilah is magnificent in her defiance of injustice, and the well-wrought background for her world sets the stage for her future adventures in this captivating new fantasy series."
—*Publishers Weekly*

"Vincent creates a fantastic world that is destined to pique your curiosity... As Delilah Marlow slowly uncovers a side of herself that she never knew existed, you'll sympathize with her... desperate to see her succeed."
—*RT Book Reviews*

"The promising opener in a new series...a fast-paced story of vengeance and justice."
—*The Roanoke Times*

"Amazing world-building and a captivating cast of characters. My new favorite Rachel Vincent book."
—#1 *New York Times* bestselling author Kelley Armstrong

RACHEL VINCENT

SPECTACLE

mira

mira

Recycling programs
for this product may
not exist in your area.

ISBN-13: 978-0-7783-1820-0

Spectacle

Copyright © 2017 by Rachel Vincent

For questions and comments about the quality of this book, please contact us at CustomerService@Harlequin.com.

www.BookClubbish.com

Printed in U.S.A.

This is for everyone who followed me
down the dark and twisted tunnel that is *Menagerie*.

Welcome back.

PART ONE

DÉMASQUÉ

Twenty-seven years ago

A scream broke through the surface of Tabitha's dreams like an oar slicing through calm water, and she sat straight up in bed, still half-submerged in that other world. Heart pounding, she slid one small hand beneath her mattress, grasping for the handle of the knife her mother had hidden there.

Just in case.

Because if there were another reaping, parents could not be trusted. Children would have to protect themselves.

Tabitha's fingers found the blade of the knife instead, and the cut was a sharp, immediate pain. The clarity of the sting—not muddled like blunt blows that left bruises—drew her thoughts into focus and vanquished the fog of sleep. She sucked on the cut without truly noticing the familiar, coppery taste of blood. Then she slid off the bed and lifted her thin mattress, bedding and all, and seized the knife the proper way.

Just like her mother had shown her.

Another scream sliced through the night, startling crickets

and cicadas into silence, and Tabitha whirled toward the source of the sound. The open window over her nightstand.

She pushed the sheer curtain aside and bent to stare through the gap beneath the old, cloudy glass and the flaking windowsill.

Candlelight flickered in the barn.

Tabitha straightened her pale green nightgown, covering an old bruise on her leg, then headed for the hall clutching the knife. No one knew what a second reaping would look like, but Tabitha knew where to stab. Her mother had shown her which soft bits of flesh would be most vulnerable to her blade, should he come into her room at night, and Tabitha remembered every lesson.

What she did not remember was that the first lesson had come three years ago, almost a year before the reaping.

In the hall, Tabitha passed the bathroom and peeked into Isabelle's room on her way toward the stairs. Isabelle's bed was empty. Her sheet was thrown back and her slippers were missing.

Tabitha took the stairs one at a time, flinching with every creak of the wooden treads. Downstairs, her parents' bedroom door stood open. Their bed was empty too.

Barefoot, her stomach pitching with fear and dread, Tabitha pushed open the back door and descended three porch steps. The grass felt prickly against her bare feet, but the backyard was peppered with smooth patches of soft dirt. When she was halfway across the yard, another scream froze her in place. Her fist clenched around the knife handle.

But then she exhaled slowly and pushed forward. That wasn't her mother's scream. It was just Isabelle's.

Over the past two years, she had heard Isabelle cry a lot from her room down the hall. She'd heard Isabelle pray and beg in the middle of the night. But the screaming was new.

Was that why Tabitha's mother slept with earplugs? Had she known there would eventually be screaming?

Tabitha pushed open the barn door. The horses looked nervous, shuffling in their stalls and tossing their manes. Her father stood in the center aisle, clutching a thick-bottomed glass. In the light flickering from a candle stuck to the top of the nearest stall with melted wax, she could see that the glass was empty, but for a single melting ice cube.

The front stall was supposed to be empty too.

"Tabitha?" Her father's gaze struggled to focus as he stared at her, and she knew that was not his first glass of the night.

At the mention of her daughter's name, Tabitha's mother popped up from the nearest stall like Jack from his box. Her clear gaze was focused and hard. "Go back to bed. We'll talk in the morning."

"Let her stay," Tabitha's father said. "Nine is old enough to know how the world works."

Neither of them mentioned the knife their daughter held.

Tabitha's mother frowned, then sank onto her knees in the stall again. Her father waved her forward, and when she hesitated two feet away, he slapped one rough hand onto her shoulder and pulled her closer, positioning her in front of the open stall.

Tabitha flinched, but she forgot all about the unwanted hand when her gaze landed on the floor of the stall. There, propped up on both elbows in the strewn hay, lay Isabelle. Her face was crimson and streaked with tears. Her hair was sweaty and matted, odd strands of it clinging to her damp cheeks.

"Tabitha," Isabelle panted. "Help me."

But there was nothing Tabitha could do but watch.

Most of Isabelle's hair was dark, from the dye Tabitha's mother made her use, but the roots were a soft green. The very shade of the moss that grew along the edges of the stream running through the back acre of her father's farm. The acre that used to belong to Isabelle's family.

Isabelle had been fourteen when the soldiers had come for her parents after the reaping, when all the cryptids were being rounded up. Everyone knew it was coming. Isabelle's parents had begged Tabitha's mother to hide their daughter. To save her. But it was Tabitha's father who'd agreed. He was the one who'd thought of the dye—the same shade his wife used to cover her gray. The same shade of Tabitha's hair.

Tabitha and Isabelle could be like sisters, he'd said. And because he'd always been fond of his neighbors' daughter, he'd agreed not only to hide Isabelle, but to buy his neighbors' land after the state foreclosed on it and save it for her. For when she grew up.

Isabelle grew up real pretty. Tabitha's father always said that. But she'd had to quit school when she got fat. Tabitha's mother said people wouldn't understand. They'd figure out she wasn't human and they'd come for her too. So Tabitha kept the secret about pretty Isabelle, who cleaned the house and cried at night.

Nine years old was old enough to keep a secret, her father'd said.

But now, on the floor in the barn, Isabelle didn't look so pretty. And suddenly Tabitha understood.

"Is she having a baby?" That's what their mare had done when she'd lain down in the barn.

"It *might* be a baby." Tabitha's mother peered down at Isabelle, blocking Tabitha's view. "But it might be a monster. We'll know in a few minutes. It's time to push."

Tabitha's father's grip tightened on her shoulder. His other hand clutched his empty glass.

Tabitha watched, fascinated, as Isabelle gave birth, too tired now to scream. When it was over, the baby gave a hearty cry, and Tabitha's father sucked in a breath. Tabitha's mother pulled a rag from the pocket of her apron and wiped the infant's face. She stood and turned, holding the child closer to the candle-light to examine it.

"Please…" Isabelle begged from the ground. "Let me see him."

"Her," Tabitha's mother corrected. She folded the rag, then scrubbed it gently over the infant's head. Then she looked up at her husband, disappointment clenching her square jaw.

The baby's hair was a soft, pale green.

Tabitha's father threw his glass at the side of the barn. It shattered, raining shards all over the hay. She flinched. Her father stomped out of the barn, headed for the house.

Tabitha's mother spread the rag on the ground at Isabelle's feet, then laid the baby on top of it. She turned to her daughter as Isabelle cried.

"Give me your knife."

"While families all over the country are in mourning, a couple of local grandparents are counting their blessings. Two weeks ago, twelve-year-old Willem Henry Vandekamp survived what's become known as The Reaping because he was at a birthday party sleepover. He is Otto and Judith Vandekamp's only surviving grandchild."

—from a September 4, 1986, broadcast of the Channel 10 *Nightly News*, Poplar Bluff, Missouri

ROMMILY

The oracle wandered down the midway, her gaze flitting from one brightly striped tent to the next, her fingers reaching for each soft scrap of silk and scratchy patch of sequins she passed.

She had not forgotten the cages and chains and blood. No matter how fractured her mind might be, she could never erase the pain and terror of that night in the rain or overcome a lifetime spent in a four-by-six animal pen.

But those were distant horrors now, relegated to the realm of nightmares.

The daylight was for dreaming.

As she meandered in the afternoon sun, her eyes were bright and focused. Her thoughts—typically tangled like a knotted cord—were blissfully calm, because there were no customers yet, and her fellow carnies knew better than to touch or speak to her. Those she considered friends smiled or waved when she passed, and those she cared little for paid her little attention.

Rommily listened to the shifters count out beats under the big top as they rehearsed an addition to their hoop-jumping, ball-balancing act. She heard the soft shuffle of hooves from behind a heavy canvas flap as the centaurs played their afternoon game of poker with Abraxas, the young human roustabout who'd taught them when to hit and when to stand.

As she passed the next tent, Rommily heard a familiar snort, and the sound triggered a warmth that spread beneath the surface of her skin. She veered from the midway with no conscious intent. Her feet followed instructions from her heart without consulting her brain, and a minute later, she stood behind the equine tent, where a single broad tree spread limbs in all directions, and with them, cool patches of shadow.

The minotaur sat in the shade on a wide, sturdy bench most men couldn't have lifted. He stood when he saw Rommily, and the images that flashed behind her eyes were triggered not by premonition but by memory.

Strong hands tearing guilty flesh.

Blood spilled in the name of justice.

She said nothing as she crossed the patch of sparse grass separating them. Rommily only spoke in the grip of a vision, since that night in the rain, and without a human mouth, the bull couldn't speak at all. Their connection had developed without the luxury of unnecessary words.

The minotaur's arms spread as Rommily came closer. She reached out for him, her hand tiny and fragile against massive planes of muscle, her touch a delicate contrast to his raw power. The oracle trailed her fingers over the ridge of his human collarbone, just where dense, soft bovine fur began to grow. The top of her head didn't reach his shoulder, and three of her standing side by side couldn't have matched his width, yet she seemed to fit perfectly when she laid her head against his chest and wrapped her arms as far as they would go around his immense rib cage.

Check Out Receipt

Wapiti - Hudson Bay Public Library
(306) 865-3110
http://www.wapitilibrary.ca/

Friday, March 01, 2024 1:52:20 PM
33421

Item: 33292900157375
Title: Spectacle
Material: Book
Due: Mar-22-2024

Total items: 1

Thank you! If you would like to
update your library notification to
telephone, email or text message,
please contact your local library.

For several long minutes they stayed just like that, free from the burden of words. Safe from prying gazes.

When the pace of the day began to pick up—when footsteps fell hurriedly and voices began to sound tense—she reluctantly stepped back and squeezed the bull's hand, then made her way to the fortune-telling tent all on her own.

Her older sister, Mirela, was already dressed in the white flouncy blouse and long, colorful skirt of a fortune-teller—an oracle cursed by fate with the genes of a "cryptid" and cursed by law with the chains of captivity.

Once, the outfit and chains had been authentic. Their internment in the traveling menagerie had been reality. Now the clothes were a costume—the wool pulled over the eyes of an audience that wanted to believe what it was seeing.

Metzger's Menagerie—the institution that had once held her in bondage, half-starved and sometimes beaten where the bruises wouldn't show—had become her salvation. It was now the veil shielding her from the prying eyes and cruel hands the rest of the world seemed so eager to wield.

Lala, Rommily's younger sister, wore blue jeans and a red uniform shirt, which declared her name to be Louise. That was a lie Rommily found funny on some days and sad on others, but today she gave it little thought as she stepped behind the folding screen and exchanged her long white cotton dress for a blouse and skirt matching Mirela's. She wasn't fit to perform—not even the miracle of freedom could fix her shattered mind—but she had to wear the costume because the inability to control her visions meant she couldn't pass for a human employee.

Dressed, she let Lala secure her with chains and shackles that didn't really lock. Then when Mirela slid her paperback novel beneath the table and gave them a nod, Lala led Rommily out the tent onto the midway, where she would serve as a living advertisement for the wonder customers would find inside.

Overhead, static blared from a speaker mounted on a tall pole, then organ music poured forth, its playful notes dancing up and down the oracle's spine, spinning around and around in her head like the stylized mermaid and unicorn seats on the carousel. The music was calming, some nights, because it signified a routine she knew well. But tonight the notes made her dizzy.

The oracle's gaze lost focus. Her eyes closed as she chased the melody in her head, winding down mischievous paths and around dark corners. She didn't notice when the carnival gates opened or the crowd appeared. She didn't notice when Lala launched into her spiel.

The music felt odd tonight.

Laughter broke into the oracle's thoughts and her eyes flew open as a father passed by the fortune-teller's tent, tickling a toddler whose hair was fixed in blond pigtails.

"Cradle and all…" Rommily mumbled, her gaze glued to the child as terrifying images flickered deep in her mind. The crowd seemed to blur as her focus skipped from face to face, searching for another piece of a puzzle she would never be able to fully assemble.

Minutes later, a man and woman pushed a stroller down the midway. Rommily stared into it as it passed, and her eyes glazed into solid white orbs. "Out with the bathwater!" People turned toward the oracle and her petite female handler, intrigued by what they assumed to be part of the show. "Wednesday's child! From the cradle to the grave!"

Parents pulled their children closer. The crowd began to murmur, and the whispered word *reaping* met Rommily's ears.

Lala's sales pitch ended in midsentence as she tried to shush her sister. But Rommily's message—unclear as it was—could not go unheard.

"The hand that rocks the cradle rules the world!"

DELILAH

Calliope music shrieked from the speakers just off the mid-way, its grating notes bouncing around my head like the ricochet of a whimsical bullet. Night after night, the iconic circus music managed to overwhelm all the other sounds of the menagerie, no matter how loud the cries of the barkers and buzz of the crowd grew.

Not that there was much of a crowd on the midway, after 10:00 p.m. The main event drew most of the customers into the big top for the last two hours of every evening, leaving only stragglers to knock down mermaid-shaped cutouts with water guns and toss rings onto an inflatable minotaur's plastic horns. Or to visit the exhibits.

"Delilah!"

I turned toward the sound of my name to find Lala at her post in front of the fortune-teller's tent. Folding my arms over my clipboard, I crossed the sawdust-strewn path toward her, sidestepping a little boy eating a melting ice-cream cone while his father threw darts at the balloon breasts of a cartoon-style siren. My head throbbed from the music and my feet ached from another eighteen-hour workday, but I put on a smile for Lala.

She was living her dream.

"How'd we do?" the youngest of the three oracles asked, crossing her arms over a red Metzger's Menagerie polo. She'd filled out a bit with proper nutrition, since our coup of the menagerie, but the true source of her newfound confidence was the hours she spent watching television and listening to the radio while she worked, immersing herself in human culture. Despite her youth—she was barely nineteen—Lala had become one of our most self-assured and dependable liaisons with human society, and it certainly didn't hurt that she looked completely human when she wasn't in the grip of a vision.

"Um..." I checked the figure at the bottom of the form clipped to my clipboard. "Fifty-one thousand, two hundred seventy-two dollars." Gross. In one night.

"That's almost a thousand dollars more than last night." Lala's brown eyes shone in the light from a nearby pole. "That's good, right?"

"It's very good." That was nearly twice what I'd made in a year as a bank teller, before I was "exposed" and sold into the menagerie. I should have been thrilled, especially considering that at $104 per ticket, admission wasn't exactly affordable for the nine-to-fivers and minimum wagers who made up most of our customer base. Yet people kept paying night after night, in town after tiny, rural town.

"We'll be near Tucson in a couple of days, right? I know we have bills and things, but do we have enough?" Her wide-eyed optimism made me feel guilty for being the bearer of bad news.

"Lala, we don't have *any*. The money's spent before we even make it."

"What? All of it?" Unshed tears seem to magnify her eyes. "But we're going to be within a few miles of Gael's son."

Like most of us, Lala got invested in every cryptid we tried to buy from the other menageries, preserves and labs that owned them. But this one was personal for her. She was the one who'd found the berserker's son, in a vision.

"We have to buy him, Delilah. That's the whole point of this, right?" She spread her arms to take in the entire menagerie, and our perilous, secret possession of it. "So pay something late. We only need twelve thousand dollars."

Right after we'd taken over the menagerie, I would have paid it in a heartbeat to free one of our fellow cryptids from captivity. In fact, I'd done just that, before I had a handle on the menagerie's finances. Before I'd realized how dire our financial situation really was.

I'd handled tens of thousands of dollars in cash nearly every night since we took over the menagerie, but the vast majority of it went to paying our operating costs. Taxes. Licenses and permits in every single town. Fairground rental fees. Inspections. Food. Fuel. Maintenance. And insurance. That was the big one. Insurance alone cost Metzger's Menagerie more than a million a year. And we were only getting off that easily because Rudolph Metzger hadn't reported most of our recent "incidents" to the insurance company—some, because the old man was trying to cut corners, and some because he was no longer in a position of authority at the menagerie.

We'd shipped him south of the border in one of his own menagerie cages, as a peace offering to the *marid* sultan, whose only daughter had died during our revolt.

If the insurance company knew about everything Metzger had covered up, our coup of the menagerie would have been exposed long ago, not because a customer saw through our masquerade, but because of simple, stupid bankruptcy.

Even so, we sat on the verge of that very catastrophe on a nightly basis.

"Lala, we're already paying bills late. If that gets any worse, they'll start foreclosing on things." Old man Metzger had bought much of his equipment on credit. Ironically, we no longer needed most of it, since we were running our own show now and only selling the illusion of captivity. But we couldn't return any of it without explaining why our creatures and hybrids no longer needed to be restrained or sedated.

"There has to be a way," the young oracle insisted, heartbreak shining in her eyes.

"Maybe there is. I don't want everyone to get their hopes up, but I was thinking about asking Renata if she'd be willing to help."

"Oh!" Lala jumped and clenched her fists in excitement.

"Shhh!" I stepped in front of her, trying to shield her delight from the man running the funnel cake stand. The game booths and food stands—everything other than the actual menagerie—belonged to subcontractors who worked the seasonal carnival route. They had no idea Metzger's was being run by the very cryptids who made up its exhibits and performances, and if any of them ever found out, our ruse—and our freedom—would come to a violent end.

"Sorry," Lala whispered, as she recomposed herself into the role of tired carnival worker. "I just... I thought it was too dangerous to let the *encantados* play with people's minds."

"It is. But we don't have a lot of choice this time." I pulled my pen from the top of the clipboard while she tried to control her smile. "I have to go collect the stats. What was your head count?"

"Two hundred seven. We had a thirty-minute-long line late this afternoon."

"Mirela must be exhausted." The oldest of the three oracles was alone inside the tent, since it was Lala's turn to play carnival employee.

Lala shrugged. "Exhaustion makes the bed feel that much softer at the end of the night."

I gave her a smile as I moved on to the next tent. Her upbeat outlook never failed to amaze me. At the end of the day, as grateful as I was to have regained my freedom, I couldn't help missing the apartment and belongings I lost when I was arrested and sold. I resented the fact that even in freedom, I had to hide. But Lala lived for every minor liberty and moment of comfort, as if indulging in them might someday make up for everything she'd been denied in her sixteen years as a captive.

I continued down the sawdust path, taking head counts from the few tents that were still open until I got to the bestiary, where the nonhuman hybrids were on display in a series of vintage circus cage wagons. Ember, the phoenix, was easily my favorite. From her head down, her plumage graduated through shades of red, yellow and orange, ending in long, wide tail feathers that looked like living flames in the bright light thrown from high pole-mounted fixtures. But she could hardly even stretch those tail feathers in the confines of her cage.

Darkness shifted behind the next enclosure, a subtle blending of one shadow into another, and though I heard neither footsteps nor breathing, I knew I was no longer alone.

"This isn't fair to them." I tucked my clipboard under one arm and stared up at the phoenix.

"I know." Gallagher stepped out of the shadows, yet they seemed to cling to him, giving him a dangerous look that most humans would feel, yet be unable to truly understand. They would blame their instinctive fear on his towering height. On his massive musculature. But they wouldn't really grasp his destructive potential.

If they were lucky.

"I got a quote on bigger cages, but considering that our budget is around zero, it's not going to happen anytime soon." Three months after our coup, we had yet to come up with a solution for the beasts' confinement. Their enclosures were inhumanely small, but much like the lions in any zoo, the chimera, the griffin and the others were all far too dangerous to simply keep on leashes. "We're going to have to raise ticket prices."

Gallagher shook his head, and light shone on the red baseball cap covering most of his short, dark hair. "The menagerie's customer base is blue-collar. They're already paying more than they can afford. We need to be touring larger venues. Exhibition grounds. Amusement parks."

"No." I was already weary of the argument we'd been putting off for two months. "Bigger venues are too much of a risk."

"Eryx brings in five hundred people in every tiny town we visit. Imagine the thousands he'd attract in a larger venue. In bigger cities."

I turned to look up at him. "The cryptids… We're all still skittish, Gallagher. Most of them are terrified to deal with vendors and carny subcontractors, and with good reason. That would only be worse if we played larger venues, with more inspections and more invasive oversight."

His brows furrowed low over dark eyes. "It's September, Delilah. Schools are already back in session, and the county fair circuit will dry up in the next few weeks. If we're not prepared to step into the big interior venues—stadiums and concert halls—we won't make it through the winter, because we certainly can't raise funds the way old man Metzger did."

The very thought gave me chills.

During the off-season, when the carnival circuit shrank to

virtually nothing, Rudolph Metzger had rented the most exotic of his cryptids to various private collections, where they were exhibited in a more formal setting for high-dollar clientele who wouldn't frequent a sweaty, dirty, outdoor carnival.

"We're not renting anyone out, and we're not risking larger venues."

In our menagerie, we ran the shows and set our own limits. Except for the required inspections, there was no third-party oversight. Under Gallagher's plan, one suspicious stadium employee could blow our ruse wide-open, and we'd all be back in cages. We couldn't take that risk.

"We'll find another way," I assured him.

Our plan had been to take the entire menagerie south of the border. But when Sultan Bruhier's daughter, Adira, died during the coup, he'd closed his borders, leaving us trapped in the United States, where exposure would mean imprisonment, and in many cases, torture.

"We could send Bruhier another gift," Gallagher said. I shook my head, but he kept talking. "I could call one of the old handlers and offer him a job, then throw him in a cage and ship him down to the sultan."

"We gave him Metzger. If gifting him the owner didn't work, sending a mere menagerie employee won't either. And even if I were okay with sending someone else to be tortured to death at the hands of the sultan, it took forever for the *encantados* to make the old man's family think he ran off with an acrobat. We can't make another person disappear."

"We can't let everyone starve to death either."

"I know." I cleared my throat and took the pen from my clipboard again. "What was the bestiary's head count?"

"Four hundred sixty."

"Are we all set for takedown?"

"As soon as the gates close."

"Good." I turned to head to the hybrids' tent, but Gallagher took my hand before I made it two steps.

"Delilah." He tugged me closer, and when I looked up at him, I found his eyes shrouded by the shadow of his hat bill, in the light falling from overhead. "My oath to protect you includes protecting you from starvation. And from yourself. Buying the incubus nearly bankrupted us."

"I couldn't just leave him there—"

"But now we're rationing food. Something has to give."

I nodded. I knew that. "I have to get a head count from the big top. I'll think of something. I swear."

Gallagher frowned at my choice of words. Swearing meant something different to him than it did to the rest of the world because the *fae* can't go back on their word.

Nor can they lie.

Ever.

At eleven fifty, I stepped inside the massive striped tent and watched the big-top finale from the west entrance. Though I saw the show nearly every night, I was still awed by the strength and ingenuity of the performers. By their grace and beauty. By the pride they took in their performances, now that the show was truly theirs.

In the ring—we only assembled one of them, now that our show was smaller—Zyanya and her brother, Payat, had already completed their live shift into cheetah form. As I watched, Ignis, the draco, breathed fire over the first of two steel rings suspended from a sturdy steel frame, and the audience oohed as the ring burst into flames.

Ignis was a three-foot-long winged serpent whose fire-breathing range had been surgically reduced from over seven feet to a mere eighteen inches years before old man Metzger had bought me for his menagerie. Even with his surgical handicap, Ignis represented the biggest risk we were willing to take in the ring because he was difficult to communicate with and impossible to retrain without using the abusive tactics his previous trainers had employed.

Once Ignis had swooped to light the second steel ring, heralded by a crescendo in the soaring big-top sound track, Zyanya and Payat leapt through the blazing hoops in sync, still in cheetah form, and landed gracefully on the backs of a matching set of thickly muscled centaurs—part Belgian horse, part man.

Several minutes later, the orchestral sound track crescendoed with a crash of cymbals signaling the beginning of the finale. Eryx, the minotaur, took thundering steps toward the center of the ring, holding his thick arms out in the most graceful gesture we had managed to teach the former beast of burden. From their positions all around the huge ring, hybrid acrobats flipped and cartwheeled toward him. While I watched, as awed then as I'd been on the first night of their revamped performance, the acrobats climbed the minotaur like a tree, then each other like its branches until they stood on each others' arms and legs and shoulders. Eryx became the base of a diamond-shaped formation of hybrid and shifter acrobats stacked to within mere feet of the aviary net.

As the minotaur slowly turned, showing off the finale for the 360-degree audience around the ring, two harpies in glittering red costumes soared around the act, dropping steel rings from overhead. They landed around outstretched arms and legs, revolving like hula hoops. From one side of the ring, Zyanya's two young cubs pushed a large heavy ball toward the center with their small feline muzzles. When they had it in place, Eryx stepped up onto the ball, with one foot, then the other, lifting his graceful load as if it weighed no more than a bag of his own feed.

Through it all, Ignis swooped and glided through the air in and around the acrobats' limbs, dodging spinning rings and spitting small jets of fire. The music soared and the crowd stood on collapsible risers, stomping and clapping for a show they would credit to a huge staff of human handlers and trainers.

For nearly a minute, the performers remained frozen in their ending pose, breathing hard, basking in applause from spectators who would have run screaming if they'd known the truth about what they'd just seen.

Then the music faded and smoke machines fired a gray mist into the ring. Under the cover of smoke, the performers dismounted and jogged from the ring through a chain-link tunnel toward the back of the tent, while the audience climbed down from the bleachers and headed for marked exits in pairs and small clusters. Children clutched their parents' hands, chattering about the massive minotaur and the graceful leopard shifter. Adults recounted their favorite parts, from the berserker in bear form throwing glittering rings for the harpies to catch in their beaks, to the wolf and the cheetahs transforming from man into animal right in front of them.

I stood at my post, thanking them all for coming, directing them toward the main exit, past the closed ticket booth. I shook hands with fathers and high-fived young boys wearing souvenir Metzger's hats with minotaur horns sticking up from the sides and little girls who'd bought headbands with cat ears or fake teeth with wolf or cheetah incisors poking into their lower lips.

At exactly midnight, as I was ushering the crowd from the big top, Abraxas—one of our three human employees—turned off the calliope music and played a light instrumental intended to signal the night's end. The intercom crackled, then Lenore's smooth, siren voice spoke over the music, urging the audience members to make their way to the exit, then proceed directly to their cars.

I'd actually taken several steps in the same direction before I remembered—as I struggled to do every night—that Lenore was responsible for my sudden compulsion to leave the carnival and drive straight home. Even though I no longer had a car. Or a home outside the menagerie and the camper I shared with Gallagher.

Abraxas and Alyrose, our human costume mistress, still had to wear earplugs during the nightly farewell, but Lenore's human husband, Kevin, was used to it.

Caught in the siren's pull, the spectators headed for the exit as one, and as I watched, resisting that draw myself, an odd movement caught my eye. One tall man in the crowd had his hand over his ear, not cupped like he was covering it, but as if…he'd just put in an earplug. The light was too dim for me to see for sure, but the possibility set me on edge.

Everyone else was with a friend or a date or family, yet this man walked alone, amid the jostle and flow of the crowd. Watching. When his gaze met mine, he smiled, but the expression seemed localized to his lips, one of which was bisected by a thick line of scar tissue that hooked down and over the edge of his chin.

He looked familiar, but I couldn't quite place him, and the mental disconnect hovered on the edge of my thoughts like an itch that couldn't be reached.

When the crowd had gone and the smoke had cleared, Abraxas turned off the sound system. Gallagher locked the gates. All over the menagerie, creatures with scales and horns and tails shed their chains and emerged from their cages like monstrous butterflies from steel cocoons. They shook off the pretense of captivity and stretched muscles stiff from hours in confined spaces.

It was my favorite part of the evening.

Together, we closed things down and set up for the next day, our last night in this small southern town. While I swept the bleachers in the big top, I listened to Zyanya and Payat laughing as they broke down and stored the equipment in the ring. Zyanya's toddlers ran circles around their mother and uncle, and made the occasional mad dash into the stands, playing as children should. As they'd never been allowed to do before the coup.

I couldn't help smiling as I watched them. Even if we accomplished nothing else—even if we couldn't rescue a single other cryptid from captivity—we had done at least this little bit of good.

Afterward, I joined Gallagher as he fed the last of the beasts and nonhuman hybrids—the menagerie residents we couldn't simply let out of their cages, because of safety concerns.

As he bent to pluck a rabbit from a box of small rodents we'd bought at the local pet store that morning, I remembered the first time I'd ever seen him, standing beside a cage in the bestiary. Back before I knew what he was. Before either of us knew what *I* was.

Before he cast off his human disguise and the safety it brought in order to protect me.

Redcaps are *fae* soldiers from their birthing cries to their dying breath, but the few who survived their brutal civil war each swore to find and serve a noble cause. To fight a battle worthy of the blood they must spill to survive.

Gallagher chose to serve and protect me, an arrangement I still wasn't entirely comfortable with, because when fate saddled me with an inner beast driven to avenge injustice and corruption, it failed to give me a way to defend myself from those very things.

I chose to believe that the universe sent me Gallagher to

make up for what it took from me. My friends. My family. My property. My freedom.

Gallagher's oath to protect me at any cost was the driving force in his life. His oath was unbreakable. His word was his honor.

For the rest of my life, he would literally rip my enemies limb from limb to keep me safe.

Sometimes that knowledge felt reassuring. Sometimes it felt overwhelming. Sometimes it felt like the most natural thing in the world.

Those were the days when I truly understood how drastically my life had changed since my days as a bank teller.

"Did you see the man with the scar?" I asked, as Gallagher opened the feeding hatch on one side of the *wendigo*'s cage and tossed a live rabbit inside.

"No. Why?" Using the two-foot-long steel-clawed grabber, he plucked the last rabbit from the box.

"I think I saw him put plugs in his ears during Lenore's farewell message. And he was here alone. No one goes to the menagerie alone." I opened the feeding hatch on the *adlet*'s cage and Gallagher shoved the rabbit inside. The *adlet*—a wolf man stuck in a perpetual in-between state—ripped it nearly in half before it even hit the floor of the pen.

"You think he suspected something?"

"Maybe. But obviously we haven't heard any police sirens. I'm probably imagining it." I'd been living under a cloud of paranoia since the moment we'd locked Rudolph Metzger in one of his own cages.

"Maybe not." Gallagher shrugged. "The last time I had a feeling about one of our patrons was when you visited the menagerie, and that changed everything. For all of us. Tell me about this man," he said as he picked up the empty rabbit box. "What did his scar look like?"

"It ran through his lip and over the edge of his chin, and—"

Gallagher stopped walking so abruptly that I almost ran into him. His sudden tension made my pulse trip faster. "Which side of his chin?"

"The left."

He dropped the empty box, alarm darkening his eyes. "That's Willem Vandekamp."

"Vandekamp. Why do I know that name?" Why was his face familiar? If I'd seen him before, how could I possibly have forgotten that scar?

"He owns the Savage Spectacle." At my blank look, Gallagher explained, his words rushed and urgent. "It's a private cryptid collection catering to the extremely wealthy. But he also has a specialized tactical team. Vandekamp is who the police bring in when they need to capture a cryptid they're not equipped to handle. If he's here, he knows. And he's not alone. This is over."

Fear raced down my spine like lightning along a metal rod. "This? Over?"

Gallagher dug a set of keys from his pocket and pressed them into my palm. "Go straight to the fairground's main office and play the alarm tone over the intercom, then run back to our camper. We have to go."

A chill raced the length of my body. Everyone knew that if they heard an unbroken alarm tone they were to get in their designated vehicles and run. But our emergency procedure was so new we hadn't even practiced it yet.

Despite the risks, we hadn't really thought we'd need it.

"*Go*, Delilah. I'll get all the cash from the silver wagon, then meet you at the camper."

I nodded, but before I could take two steps, a man in a protective vest stepped out of the shadows, aiming a stun gun at Gallagher's chest. "Don't move." He had a regular handgun on his waistband, the snap on the holster already open. The name Brock was embroidered in shiny silver thread on the left side of his vest. Beneath that were the initials SS, stylized and intertwined, as if they belonged on an expensive hand towel or pillow case.

I eyed the soldier, my pulse racing.

"Put your hands up," Brock ordered. "Or I *will* taze you." He thought we were human.

Gallagher didn't move, but I could feel the tension emanating from him. Every muscle in his body was taut, ready to explode into motion. "Vandekamp deals in exotic fetishes. He'll rent them out by the hour," Gallagher said, trying to convince me of what needed to be done while he eyed the private soldier. "They'll die in captivity, Delilah. And in great pain."

Chains. Cages. Fists. Whips. Blood.

My heart ached at the memories. The terror. My lungs refused to expand. If Vandekamp knew about the coup, others knew, too. Gallagher was right. The menagerie was finished.

We had to sound the alarm and give people the chance to escape.

"Kill him." My words carried no sound, but Gallagher read them on my lips. He turned, impossibly fast, and ripped the stun gun from the soldier's hand. It broke apart in his grip like a child's toy.

Brock grunted and reached for his gun, his movements clumsy with shock. Gallagher grabbed his head in both hands and gave it a vicious twist.

I heard a distinct crack. The man's arms fell to his side, but to my surprise, his head remained attached to his body. Gallagher hadn't spilled a single drop of blood, even though he needed it to survive.

"You're not going to…?" I gestured to his faded red cap as the body fell to the ground at his feet.

"No time. We have to—"

Something whistled softly through the air, and Gallagher stumbled. He slapped one hand to his thick thigh and pulled out a dart attached to a tiny vial that had already nearly emptied into his flesh. He growled as he stepped in front of me, shielding me, and turned toward the direction the dart had come from. "Get down."

As I knelt behind him, I heard another soft whistle. He flinched, then fell onto his knees. "Gallagher!" My pulse racing, I pulled a second dart from his leg and stared into the dark, trying to spot the threat.

"Get the gun." Gallagher's voice was much too soft. His eyes were losing focus.

I spun toward Brock's corpse and was reaching for the pistol still in his holster when Gallagher fell to the ground with a heavy thud.

"No!" The gun forgotten, I dropped onto my knees to put one hand on his chest. It rose, then fell. He was completely unconscious, his hat still firmly seated on his head.

"Delilah Marlow."

Fear electrified every nerve ending in my body as I twisted to see the man with the scar staring down at me, his tranquilizer rifle aimed at my chest. I shoved my terror down to feed the rage burning out of control in my gut. "You have three seconds to get the hell out of my menagerie before I scramble your brain."

His brows rose in an insulting blend of fascination and amusement. "Do your worst."

My worst was already on its way.

Deep inside me, the *furiae* stretched as she woke up, intent on avenging Gallagher, and as her righteous anger rapidly filled me, my nails hardened and began to lengthen into needlelike points.

Vandekamp's gaze flicked to my hands, but his expression did not change.

I stood, and my vision zoomed into an extraordinary clarity and depth. My hair began to rise on its own, defying gravity as my rage mounted.

Vandekamp held his ground three feet away. He twisted a small knob on his rifle and aimed it at my thigh.

I lunged for him, my thin black claws grasping for his head. He pulled the trigger, and pain bit into my thigh. I gasped and stumbled sideways, then tripped over Gallagher's thick leg. The world rushed toward me. My shoulder slammed into the dirt path.

Gallagher lay a foot away, his eyes closed.

The dart burned fiercely in my thigh, and my vision blurred. My arms were too heavy to lift. I couldn't move my legs.

From somewhere in the fairgrounds, a scream rang out, then was suddenly silenced.

"Don't do this," I begged as a second scream split the night. But my voice was too soft. The world was starting to lose focus.

Vandekamp put his boot on my shoulder and pushed me onto my back. He knelt next to me, his rifle hanging from one shoulder, and stared into my eyes, apparently fascinated by the black-veined orbs they had become when the *furiae* awoke. "I've heard a lot about you, Delilah." He brushed hair back from my face and tucked it behind my ear. "My name is Willem Vandekamp."

I blinked, and his face blurred as darkness engulfed me.

"You belong to me now."

DELILAH

The squeal of metal ripped through my head like a chain saw through wood, and my eyes flew open. Bright, warm light turned the throbbing behind my eyes into a sharp pain that pulsed with my heartbeat, and at first I couldn't tell what I was looking at. My world seemed to be composed entirely of shiny steel slats and canvas.

My tongue felt like it was dried to the roof of my mouth, and my throat hurt when I swallowed. When I tried to sit up, I discovered my wrists were bound at my back with something that didn't rattle or clank like metal handcuffs, and they must have been bound for a while, because I couldn't feel my fingers. I was lying on my stomach in a long, subdivided steel cage, draped with a sheet of canvas thin enough to let light through. I blinked, trying to remember how I wound up shackled and caged, and…

Vandekamp.

With his name came the memory of his scarred face staring down at me. The iron weight of fear threatened to press all the air from my chest as understanding crashed over me.

The menagerie had been retaken.

I was a prisoner. Again.

For weeks, I'd battled nightmares about being recaptured. Recaged. But my dreams were pale shadows of the horrifying reality.

My lungs refused to expand. I gasped, trying to catch my breath as the steel slats seemed to be closing in on me. *I can't do this again.* I couldn't live in a cage and eat scraps. I couldn't wear rags and take orders. I couldn't "perform" in another menagerie, watching people I cared about suffer just to draw out my beast and its violent brand of justice.

Not again.

Motion to my left drew my eye, and I twisted on the cold steel floor to see Mirela lying in the next cell, unbound and evidently unconscious, still dressed in her fortune-teller costume. But I couldn't see into the cells beyond hers from my prone position.

Grunting with the effort, I tucked my legs beneath my stomach and pulled myself upright without the use of my hands. On my knees, I could see down the length of the steel cage into at least a dozen cells separated by steel-slat walls. I was in the very last one. And finally I understood.

We were in a cattle car—a long horse trailer modified to hold human-sized cryptids. Each pen had its own roll-up door and the whole thing was much cleaner and newer than anything we'd had at Metzger's. Much colder.

And much more expensive.

Mirela's sisters lay unmoving in the two narrow cells after hers, and beyond those were several more, each occupied by one of my fellow captives.

The light shining through the canvas strapped in place over the cattle car was too warm in tone to be anything but sunlight, and the canvas itself gave me no hint of our location. I closed my eyes and listened, trying to slow my racing heart.

I heard the rattle of a cage door rolling up on another cattle car and male voices, speaking too softly for me to understand. The only familiar sound was the breathing of the other captives.

"Where are we?" Lala whispered, and I turned to see her pushing herself upright in the middle of her cell. She blinked at me through eyes ringed in dark circles and drew her denim-clad knees to her chest.

"I don't—"

Heavy footsteps clomped toward us, and two shadowy silhouettes appeared through the thin canvas, starkly backlit, growing larger as they got closer. The shapes were male and bulky from whatever equipment they wore, and when one of them came to disconnect the canvas from the two rear corners of my cell, I could tell from his outline that he had a gun and some kind of baton.

When the canvas was unhooked, the men pulled it from the cattle car with practiced motions, then folded it with the same efficiency. Both men wore the Savage Spectacle's black tactical gear, including visored helmets, and each wore a pistol and a stun gun holstered on opposite sides of their waists. They worked in silence, and after an initial assessing glance into the trailer, they didn't leer, stare, laugh or point.

The soldiers' professional bearing was so unlike that of Metzger's rough-edged roustabouts and handlers that Lala and I seemed more interested in them than they were in us.

From my left, I heard and felt movement as the rest of the captives began to wake up, but I couldn't tear my searching gaze from the world outside the cattle car. Where were the rides and the booths? Where were the campers, trucks and trailers? Where was the fairground?

I saw nothing but a gray building and, behind that, a thick patch of forest.

"Where are we?" Lala asked again. "What's happening?"

I hardly even heard her questions over the chattering of my teeth, a nervous reaction I'd had since I was a kid. My mouth was dry and my hands were shaking in my bindings, which chafed my already-raw wrists.

"We've been captured, obviously," Zarah said from the other end of the trailer, where she was confined in the pen next to Trista, her twin and fellow succubus.

"But where's the menagerie?"

"Probably right where we left it," Mirela said to her sister, while she watched the black-clad men stack the folded canvas on top of at least two others. "It looks like we've been seized. They must know the old man is dead."

But how? Renata and Raul had done flawless work with Metzger's relatives. We'd hoped to get at least a year out of the ruse, which should have given us plenty of time to figure out how to get everyone south of the border.

"I think we're being sold," Lenore said, and for once, I didn't fight the calming pull of her voice. Instead, I let the sound relax my tense muscles and slow my racing heart, and finally my teeth stopped chattering. Clarity returned to my vision.

Our cattle trailer was parked in front of a squat gray brick building punctuated by a series of tall, narrow windows. Its resemblance to a prison was no doubt intentional. Two men stood guard at either side of the building's entrance, wearing padded bite suits similar to what K9 trainers used to condition attack dogs. Their utility belts each held a Taser and a baton, but no guns.

The trees visible behind and above the building were taller

than they typically grew in Oklahoma, my home state, and the flora was greener and more lush.

"We're *all* being sold?" Mahsa asked, and when I turned to follow the leopard shifter's gaze, relief flooded me. Two more cattle cars stood about fifty feet away, on the other side of the parking lot, but their occupants were still unconscious, and I wouldn't be able to identify them until they sat up.

"Mirela," I whispered as I watched the two tactical team members head for the building entrance. "Do you see Gallagher?"

She studied the other trailers, then shook her head. "But they might have put him in that last one, with Eryx and the centaurs. He's heavy enough."

I squinted, but the only thing I could tell about the third trailer, viewed through the one in the middle, was that its cells were larger and lower to the ground, and on the scale of horses and cows. More like an actual cattle car.

Even if all three of the trailers were full, they couldn't possibly hold even half the cryptids from Metzger's. Where were all the rest?

"Hey!" Lala shouted, and we both turned to her in surprise as one of the succubi tried to shush her. "Where the hell are we? Who are you people?"

"Lala!" Mirela scolded her softly, as the men continued to ignore us. "Don't make trouble."

I wasn't sure whether to applaud the young oracle or cry for us all. She'd grown bold and confident after months of relative freedom, and she seemed much less willing than the others to fall back into the trembling and quiet comportment of a captive.

Before the two soldiers made it to the building, the door opened and Willem Vandekamp stepped out. All four men— two in tactical gear, two in puffy, full-body bite suits—

snapped to attention as he marched past them, with another man on his heels, and I could only stare, trying to figure out what his presence meant.

Was this his building? Was Vandekamp storing us until... what? An auction? A bulk sale? Seizure by the government?

Vandekamp took up a position between our cattle car and the next and one of his men handed him a clipboard. "Okay, let's get them stored. Start over there." He pointed in our direction. "Individual cells. Give them uniforms, then start processing."

Murmurs rose the length of the trailer as the other ladies tried to figure out where we were and who the man obviously in charge was.

"The uniforms say 'SS,'" Lenore whispered, for those who couldn't read.

"The Savage Spectacle." I spoke just loudly enough for Mirela to hear, knowing she'd pass the information down. "That's Willem Vandekamp. The owner." But the gray brick building in front of us didn't look like someplace catering to wealthy, high-profile clients.

Most of the occupants of the next trailer had woken up, and I was relieved to see both cheetah shifters, Gael the berserker, and Drusus the incubus among its occupants. But I wasn't sure I *should* be relieved to find them confined alongside us.

"Let me know when it's done." Vandekamp let his assessing gaze wander over all three trailers, then he gave his clipboard to a man wearing a thick pair of brown cargo pants and a lightweight short-sleeved button-down shirt with a stylized set of overlapping *S*'s embroidered on his front left pocket. He carried a tranquilizer rifle just like the one Vandekamp had shot me with.

When his boss had gone back inside, the man with the clipboard turned to the other soldiers, who gathered around for their instructions. "Let's get this done right, boys. No mistakes. Start at the front and work your way back."

The other men nodded, then headed our way, and I didn't realize I was backing away from them until my bound hands hit the other end of my pen.

"I am Adrian Woodrow," the man with the clipboard said, in a loud, clear voice. "I am the gamekeeper here at the Savage Spectacle, which means I'm in charge of your daily lives."

Here at the Savage Spectacle? My stomach began to twist. The Spectacle was our final destination. Vandekamp wouldn't have to rent off-season menagerie acts anymore because he'd bought three trailers full of us.

"The Savage Spectacle does not travel, and it is not a zoo. We are a licensed private collection of exotic wildlife, catering exclusively to the cryptid-themed fetishes and fantasies of a select list of private clients."

"What's a fetish?" Lala whispered, her hands trembling as they gripped the side of her pen.

Trista snorted softly, and since my answer would only have further scared Lala, I kept it to myself.

"You're all about to be sorted into specific categories depending on your species and your position here at the Spectacle. You'll be issued clothing and given a complete physical exam to make sure you're bringing nothing infectious or transmissible into our community. It is in your best interest to cooperate fully. Consequences here at the Spectacle are swift and severe. Tolerances are nil. Orders will not be repeated."

The men reporting to Woodrow slid open the first cell in the cattle car, and the men in padded suits pulled Zarah out, while the one of the ones in tactical gear aimed his tranquilizer rifle at her. Zarah still wore only a red sequined bralette and matching bikini because the succubi worked—and lived—in as little clothing as possible. Her bright costume looked sad and absurd, removed from the carnival atmosphere, but none of the men even seemed to notice. They simply hauled her into the building by both arms.

While they were inside, another team of four came for her sister, Trista, and over the next hour, my stunned, scared friends were removed from their pens one at a time and led into the building. The men wasted no energy and overlooked no precaution. They answered no questions, and eventually the women stopped asking.

I took in every detail I could, trying to figure out how far we'd been shipped while we were unconscious, but the only clue I had, other than lush flora that wouldn't grow in Oklahoma or West Texas, was my hunger, extreme thirst and severely dry mouth. We'd driven hours, at least, but the sun had yet to set.

Or maybe it had yet to set again.

After the shifters, the succubi and the sirens were marched out of sight, a team of men opened the door to Rommily's pen. She sat at the back of her cell with her eyes closed, slowly shaking her head in denial of whatever horrific vision was playing behind her eyelids. When they told her to come out of the pen, she didn't respond. She probably couldn't even hear them.

One of the men in bite suits reached into the pen and grabbed Rommily's ankle with his bare hand. Her eyelids flew open to reveal featureless white orbs—the signature trait of an oracle in the grip of a premonition.

"Crushed by the weight of your own hubris," Rommily said, each word running into the next as they fell from her mouth. "Broken rib. Punctured lung. Massive internal bleeding."

Startled, the guard let go of Rommily and turned to his coworkers—the first lapse of judgment I'd seen from any of them so far. "What the hell is she saying?"

"That's how you're going to die." Mirela's voice was low-pitched and eerily steady, like the undisturbed surface of a deep lake. "When is anyone's guess."

"Is she serious?" the handler demanded from coworkers, who had no answer for him.

"Just grab her, Bowman," the man in tactical gear snapped.

"Bowman…" Rommily repeated, blinking shiny white eyes at him. "Grab her…"

Bowman gritted his teeth and seized the oracle's ankle again, then hauled her roughly toward the opening of the pen. Rommily's head smacked the floor of her cell, and I flinched as her normal irises returned. Pain had driven her out of her vision.

Lala gripped the door of her cell. "Please be careful. She's not dangerous. She's just confused."

The handlers led Rommily into the building with no particular care for how roughly they handled her. Yet neither of them touched her bare flesh again.

After the oracles had gone, I was alone in our trailer, and when the handlers unlocked my metal cell, I lowered myself to the ground before they could even reach for me. I didn't fight when they each took one of my arms, and I held my head high as they marched me into the building, then down a hallway lined with steel doors. My dignity and the clothes I wore were all I had left in the world, and if being sold to the menagerie had taught me anything, it was that those would soon be taken away too.

Bowman opened a door halfway down on the left side of the hall and shoved me into a six-by-eight-foot gray brick room with a tall, narrow window at one end. There was a rolled-up blanket on the floor, next to a stainless-steel toilet/sink combo and a single roll of thin toilet paper.

Bowman cut the plastic binding from my wrists, then closed

the door at my back. A soft beep told me it had locked auto-matically. The door had a square Plexiglas window at eye height and a rectangular cutout at the very bottom that was just the right size for a food tray.

As soon as the men were gone, I rubbed my sore wrists, then drank several handfuls of water from the sink, but I made myself stop when my stomach began to churn. Recovery from dehydration must be slow and steady. Then I used the toilet, my attention trained on the window in my door, to make sure no one was watching.

Seated on the blanket, I listened to footsteps and the beeping of more locked doors as the rest of my friends were marched and stored. The sun sank slowly outside my window, labeling the directions for me, but ignorance of the exact time and my own location ate at my thoughts like an infection. I'd only been imprisoned in the menagerie for about a month before our coup, and since then, I'd lost focus on the reality of cap-tivity. I remembered pain and hunger and humiliation. But I'd forgotten about ignorance and dependence, and how they preyed on the mind rather than the body.

For hours, I sat in an impenetrable concrete cell, deprived of both food and information, and with each passing second, my anger grew until it overwhelmed my fear. The Spectacle was using ignorance as a weapon, keeping us in the dark to leave us disoriented and pliable.

At some point, immeasurable hours after I'd been locked up, a folded stack of material was slid through the opening at the bottom of the door. A food tray followed the clothing, and on it was an empty paper cup lying on its side, a boiled chicken leg, a slice of white bread and half an apple.

Before I could pick up the tray, Bowman's face appeared outside the door window. "Change clothes and slide your old ones through the slot." He disappeared without waiting to see if his instructions would be followed.

Still dressed in my grubby Metzger's uniform, I filled the paper cup with water and ate every bite of food on my tray. Then I changed clothes not because I'd been told to, but because my Metzger's polo and jeans were covered in grime from a trip I couldn't remember.

The new uniform was a set of gray scrubs, a wireless sports bra and a drab but clean pair of underwear. The message sent by the prison-like clothing came through loud and clear.

I spread my blanket out on the concrete floor and curled up with my hands beneath my head, and soon I realized that the intermittent traffic past my door was now headed in the opposite direction. My fellow captives were being removed from their cells one at a time.

None of them came back.

Despite having just awoken from sedation, I fell asleep on the floor and when I woke to the scrape of metal as my door was opened, I found a beautiful starlit night shining through the window in my cell.

I sat up to find Bowman staring down at me from the doorway. He'd changed from his puffy bite suit into tactical gear and he was holding a pair of steel handcuffs. "Orientation. Let's go."

Still weak from exhaustion, I stood. He spun me around by one arm and secured my wrists at my lower back, then led me into the hall, where one of his coworkers took possession of my other arm.

"How many cryptids did Vandekamp buy?" I asked as we walked. "Is there a big guy named Gallagher?"

They said nothing as they led me through the door at the end of the hall, then down two more passageways and into a cold, lab-like room several times the size of my cell, equipped with a sink and countertop along the back wall.

Woodrow—the gamekeeper—sat on one side of a small square table with a file open in front of him. Bowman pushed me into a folding chair opposite the gamekeeper, then stood guard on my left while the man who'd had my other arm headed for the cabinets at the back of the room. I twisted to see what he was doing, but then the gamekeeper cleared his throat to capture my attention.

"Delilah Marlow." He tapped the page in front of him with the tip of a ballpoint pen, and his focus never left my file. "Also known as Drea."

"No one knows me as Drea. What are we doing here? Did Vandekamp buy *all* of us?"

"You're twenty-five?" he said, and I nodded. "It says here that you grew up believing you were human until you were exposed at Metzger's. Which you were attending as a customer. Huh." His brows rose, but his gaze stayed glued to the file. "Is this information accurate?"

"Yes." A cabinet door squealed open behind me and I turned to find the third handler lining up a syringe and two blood-sample vials on a stainless-steel tray. "But it's incomplete."

"So I see," the gamekeeper said as I turned back to him. "They still don't know what species you are. Do you?"

"I'm human."

Woodrow's gaze finally met mine. "You might as well tell us the truth. We have literally dozens of witnesses who've seen you transform into a monster. We have internet photos and video."

"And I have a blood test performed by the state of Oklahoma that says I'm human. It's in my camper, in the front pocket of a black backpack on the floor at the end of the couch."

He glanced at his wristwatch. His foot began to bounce beneath the table. "We'll run our own tests. Shaw?" Woodrow glanced over my shoulder, and the third handler's boots clomped toward us. "Let's get going."

Shaw set the stainless-steel tray on the table. Bowman cuffed my left wrist to the chair beneath me, then tilted my chin up so that I had to look at him, and at the butt of the rifle he held inches from my nose. "If you even *look* like you're going to try anything, you'll wake up two days from now naked and concussed in a hole in the ground. Do you understand?"

Clearly my reputation preceded me.

Bowman stepped back, but remained within blunt trauma range.

"Make a fist," Shaw said, and when I complied, he tied a rubber strap around my right arm, above my elbow. He didn't smile or chat as he cleaned the puncture site, but he hit my vein on the first try, so I made no objection to the two vials he filled, then labeled with my name and a number I couldn't quite read.

"What happened to the cryptids Vandekamp didn't buy?" I hadn't seen Raul and Renata, or Nalah, the *ifrit*. Or Zyanya's toddler kittens. Or Gallagher.

But they were pointedly ignoring my questions.

"So…what do we do with her?" Bowman said as Shaw untied the rubber strap and took the full vials to a mini fridge beneath the cabinets at the back of the room.

"Store her in the dormitory with the others," Woodrow said, as Shaw's boots clomped across the floor toward us again. "But keep a special eye on her until her test results come back. The boss says she's seditious."

Shaw returned to the table carrying a square gray box made

of thick, textured plastic, like an expensive tool kit. It was about the length of my hand. He set the box on the table in front of Woodrow, who unlatched it and flipped it open. Inside, nestled on a bed of laser-cut black foam, was a polished steel ring just a few inches in diameter, about the thickness of my smallest finger.

"Basic settings only, for now," Woodrow said. "We'll adjust when we have more information."

Chills crawled over my skin as the gamekeeper pulled a thin but rugged-looking device from his pocket. It vaguely resembled the cell phone I'd had until the state of Oklahoma had stripped my right to own property. Woodrow tilted the device's screen toward himself, then scrolled and tapped his way through a series of options I couldn't see. A red light flashed on the front of the steel ring, then it flashed three more times in rapid succession, as if confirming whatever settings he'd programmed.

My heart thumped so hard I could actually hear it.

"Okay." Woodrow set the remote on the table, but the screen had already gone dark. "Let's get it done."

Shaw lifted the steel ring from its formfitting padding, and I frowned when I got a better look at it. The blinking red light had come from a tiny LED bulb that sat flush with the surface of the steel. The ring was designed to swing open on a set of tiny interior hinges, which wouldn't be accessible once the device was closed around...

Around what? The circumference looked about right for my upper arm, or my...

My neck.

Terror pooled in my stomach, like fuel set ablaze. That ring was a collar.

I instinctively tried to scoot my chair away from the shiny, high-tech device, but Bowman's heavy hand landed on my shoulder. Vandekamp's collar was much lighter, sleeker and cleaner than the thick iron rings Metzger had fitted around resistant centaurs and satyrs, but even diamond-encrusted collars are for pets.

Woodrow picked up the control device and used it to point at the collar Shaw still held. "I'm going to explain this to you once. That is an electronic restraint collar, which can be controlled by any of the remotes carried by the Spectacle's staff. Those tiny spines will slide through the back of your neck and into your vertebrae, where they can deliver specialized electric signals with the press of a button."

Shaw tilted the collar to show me that the inner curve of one half of the collar held a vertical line of three very thin needles.

I stared at the steel ring, trying to control panic as it clawed at my throat. "It's a shock collar?"

"It's much more than that." Woodrow clipped the remote back onto his belt and met my gaze for what he obviously considered the most important part of my orientation briefing. "This collar can deliver a painful shock or temporarily paralyze the beast wearing it from the neck down. The settings prevent cryptids from using their monstrous abilities until those settings are changed, which only happens during scheduled engagements. Which means the sirens can't sing, the succubi can't seduce, the shifters can't shift and the beasts can't lift a hand in aggression. Until we want them to. So consider this fair warning."

"The collar's receptors also receive signals from every single door in the compound," Shaw added. "Restricting you to any room or wing we choose."

I could only stare, stunned. I'd never seen or heard of anything like it. "How can that possibly work?"

Shaw's eyes lit up. "Vandekamp designed it himself. Receptors in the spines respond instantly to the spike in adrenaline and in species-specific hormones that—"

"Shaw," Woodrow growled, and the handler's mouth snapped shut.

But I'd heard enough to understand.

Woodrow stood. "Get on with it."

"Okay, now, hold still." Shaw came toward me with the collar, and panic lit a fire in my lungs.

"No." I stood, and the folding chair scraped the floor then fell over, hanging from the cuff attached to my left wrist.

I can't wear a collar.

"Sit down," Woodrow demanded, while Bowman aimed his tranquilizer rifle at my leg. "That's the only warning you'll get."

"Please don't do this." I backed away from them both, dragging the chair, though I had nowhere to go. "I'll be reasonable if you will. There has to be another—"

Woodrow glanced at Bowman. "Do it. And don't forget to write a report and log the spent dart."

I turned to Bowman just as he fired. Pain bit into my left thigh. The tiny vial emptied its load into my leg before I could pull it out with my free hand.

As I backed farther away from them, my focus flitting warily from face to face, the edges of the room began to darken. The scrape of the metal chair against the floor sounded suddenly distant. My central vision began to blur. "Stay back."

My legs felt weak half a second before they folded beneath me, and I didn't even feel my knees slam into the tile. The ceiling spun around me as I fell onto my back. The chair clattered to the floor, and Woodrow's weathered face leaned over me.

"Gallagher's going to kill you…" I warned, but my words sounded stretched and distorted.

"Do it now, before the bitch wakes up again," Woodrow said, as the world faded to black around me. "Looks like she's going to have to learn everything the hard w—"

"Culminating in a narrow Senate victory, Congress has passed the Cryptid Containment Act, which will allow cryptids to be housed and studied in both public and private labs, for the purpose of scientific advancement."

—from the February 4, 1990, edition of the *Boston Herald*

DELILAH

"Wake up, Delilah."

The surface beneath me felt hard and rough, but neither cool nor warm. Light glared through my closed eyelids, and something snug was wrapped around my neck.

My eyes flew open, but the world remained hazy. The three women bending over me had blurry faces, and their grayish clothing was shapeless and unfamiliar.

"She's waking up," one of the blurry forms said, and I recognized Lenore's voice even without the mental tug of her siren's lure. I exhaled slowly. I was among friends.

"What happened?" Blinking to clear my vision, I pushed myself upright on a rough concrete floor and reached for my neck, but someone grabbed my hand.

"No, don't touch it!" Lala cried.

The faces were finally starting to come into focus.

Lenore. Lala. And Zyanya, the cheetah shifter. A few feet away, Mirela sat next to Rommily, who was curled up asleep on the floor with one thin arm tucked beneath her head. In addition to those stupid gray scrubs, they all wore—

My hands flew to my neck, and my fingers brushed smooth, warm steel that had taken on the temperature of my skin. I felt along the curve of the high-tech collar until I got to the hidden hinge at one side, distinguishable only by a tiny crack where the two sections were joined. "How can they—"

"Don't!" Lenore cried as I slid my finger beneath the front of the collar. Excruciating pain shot through my entire body, lighting every nerve ending on fire. My jaw spasmed, trapping a terrified cry of pain inside, and the jolt didn't end until someone knocked my hand away from the collar.

"What the hell was that?" I demanded when my jaw finally unclenched, as painful aftershocks coursed through me, far outlasting the initial pain. I leaned back against the concrete wall to keep from falling over. I felt like a human lightning rod.

"You can touch the collar, but if you pull on it or put your finger under it…that happens." Lala's gaze was full of sympathy. "We've all tried it. They *really* don't want us taking these things off."

"As if we could," Zyanya snapped. "The damn joints locked the second they snapped it closed, so this shock treatment's overkill. These things aren't coming off until someone cuts them off."

"They're not afraid we're going to take the collars off," I said, as my gaze roamed the large concrete room, where we sat among at least two dozen other women of various humanoid and hybrid species, each of whom wore the same uniform and collar. "They don't want you to pull on the collar because the needles will damage your spine."

"Like they care," Lala said.

"They care about the money Vandekamp has invested in us. Just like Metzger did. If you give yourself nerve damage, you're worth less to them. Which gives them less incentive to keep you alive."

"On the bright side," Mahsa said, and I turned to find the leopard shifter curled up in a nearby corner. "I haven't seen anyone beaten yet."

"Give it time," Zarah said, as she and Trista padded toward us on bare feet. "Only paying customers get to cause damage."

"What does that mean?" Mahsa crawled closer, and we formed a protective ring of former menagerie captives.

"Exactly what that gamekeeper said. This isn't a circus, ladies," Trista explained, pushing long pale hair over her shoulder. "The rumors about the Savage Spectacle seem to be true. They rent cryptids to their customers with no bars and cages to stand between them."

I'd heard no rumors. But then, I hadn't spent my entire life in captivity, piecing together an understanding of the outside world through stories traded with new prisoners.

"We wondered how they did that." Zarah ran one finger over the outside of her collar. "Now we know."

Mahsa blinked wide leopard eyes. "Rent us for what?"

"Don't ask questions you don't want the answers to." Finola's voice was full of bitter resentment. Like Lenore's, it now held none of the calming effect she'd once used to help her friends through the transition from captives to masters of their own fate in the liberated menagerie. The collar had robbed her of her purpose in a way no cage ever could have.

"Why is your shirt inside out?" Lala asked.

I followed her focus to the shallow V-shaped neckline of my scrubs top, where the back side of the seam showed. My jaw clenched. They'd stripped me while I was unconscious, then put my clothes back on inside out. Was that intentional, so I'd know...

Know what?

"They were looking for your tell," a soft voice said from my left, and I turned to see a young dryad sitting against the wall, braiding a long length of hair, among which grew thin woody vines blooming with small white flowers. "To figure out what you are."

She held one hand out to us, palm down, and I saw that her veins appeared bright green beneath her skin, rather than the normal blue or blue green. Her feet looked much the same. If she were ever allowed back into the woods—the forest nymph's natural habitat—she would be able to bury her feet in the dirt and draw sustenance from the earth's nutrients, like a plant.

But I could tell from her pale skin and the dark circles beneath her eyes that nothing more yielding than concrete had been beneath her feet in a long, long time.

"They couldn't have done anything more than examine you unless they paid the rental fee. There are cameras everywhere. No one gets away with anything here—neither the jailed nor the jailers." She returned to her woody braid. "I'm Magnolia, by the way."

Without waiting for us to return the introduction, she stood and wandered across the room toward a small cluster of captives gathered against the opposite wall.

My focus followed her, taking in the large, mostly empty room. "Where are we?" The walls held a series of tall, narrow windows. I couldn't tell which direction the sun was coming from, but the weak daylight felt like early morning. Equidistant apart on the ceiling were two dark security camera domes, like the kind used at any department store for 360-degree surveillance.

"At first I thought it was a holding cell." Lenore tucked her knees up to her chest with her arms wrapped around them. "But there's a bathroom through there." She nodded toward an open doorway on the opposite wall. "And I think those mats and blankets are to be slept on."

I followed her gaze to the left, where three stacks of blue vinyl-covered gymnastics mats were lined up against the interior wall, with folded blankets neatly piled on top.

"You're right. This is a dormitory." My focus skipped from face to frightened face. "Ladies, I think we're home."

Lenore slumped against the wall. "Well, it's bigger than a cage. And at least we're together."

I nodded because I didn't want to poison her optimism, but I felt none of it. Vandekamp hadn't rescued us from the misery of a new menagerie; he'd delivered us into a whole new brand of captivity. A fresh hell.

"So, has anyone tested the collars, beyond the one-finger booby trap?" I asked.

"Yeah." Zyanya tapped the concrete floor with one long, thick claw—a remnant of the feline form that, along with her eyes and incisors, remained even when she took on human form. "I tried to shift earlier, but the second I *thought* about taking on fur, my whole body froze from my chin down. I couldn't move at all." She trailed the point of one nail over the front of her collar. "How does this thing work?"

"I think it recognizes increased levels of adrenaline and feline hormones. Basically, it senses what you're going to do before you can do it, and it sends electric impulses into your spine, temporarily paralyzing you." I turned to Lenore. "What about you? Have you tried to sing?"

"No, but I tried to inject a suggestion into my tone of voice earlier. It was an accident. I was trying to help calm Rommily, and I didn't realize what I'd done until I was flat on my back, immobilized."

"It doesn't prevent visions," Lala said with a shrug. "I guess those aren't much of a threat."

That, or Vandekamp hadn't been able to isolate the proper physiological signals.

"Speaking of guards, where are they?" There was no one in the large room but us and our fellow captives, yet the door wasn't made of steel or iron, and it didn't meet the standards typically required by facilities licensed to house cryptids.

"Who knows?" Mirela said as she stroked Rommily's hair. "I'm starting to think they're not needed here. These damn collars won't let us leave the room, except to go to the bathroom. And there's one of those sensors in the bathroom doorway too, in case they need to stop us from emptying our bladders, for some reason."

"It's all about control." My hand strayed to the collar, trying to ease the persistent feeling of constriction, and only Zyanya's quick grab for my wrist saved me from another brutal shock. "This place is cleaner and nicer than the menagerie, because the upscale clientele pays for exotic and beautiful, not skinny and dirty." The thought of exactly what that clientele would expect for its money made my stomach churn. "But the truth is that Vandekamp has a measure of control over us that Metzger could never have dreamed of. We won't have any hope of getting out of here until we figure out how this system works."

"Maybe they can answer those questions for us." Mirela stared across the room at the other female cryptids.

"Maybe." I studied our new roommates. Most were shifters or anthropomorphs, like sirens and oracles, but several were species I'd never seen in person. I counted three nymphs, who had feathers, leaves and vines in place of normal human hair. A young echidna had the upper body of a human woman and the lower body and fangs—and likely the venom—of a very large snake. They watched us warily from several small cliques, however none, other than Magnolia, seemed willing to breach the gap and make an introduction. "But until we get to know them, it's probably better that we don't ask."

"Why?" Lala said.

"Because they might be willing to sell us out for extra food or privileges," Zyanya explained, and it broke my heart to know she spoke from experience. "Or for time spent with their children."

"Children!" Mirela turned to her in sudden horror. "Zyanya, what happened to your kids? Did Vandekamp buy them?"

She shook her head slowly, and an old ache reawakened deep in my chest. I'd known the cheetah shifter for weeks in captivity before I'd found out she had children. The only way Zyanya knew of to deal with being isolated from them and unable to protect them was to keep the pain of separation to herself and to hoard her memories.

"He didn't buy any of the kids," Lala said.

I exhaled slowly. The coup I'd incited had cost Zyanya her family. There had to be a way to get the kids back. I had to *find* a way.

"Do you have any idea where—" A sudden thud turned us all toward the exit, where the door was now propped open by a gray-clad figure lying on the floor, sprawled into the hall from the shoulders up.

"Rommily!" Mirela was up in an instant, dark wavy hair trailing behind her. Lala and I raced after her.

The ambient buzz of soft conversation died as the other captives turned to watch, and just as Mirela grabbed Rommily by the ankles, the poor, fractured oracle began to convulse.

"Somebody help!" Mirela shouted as she pulled her middle sister through the doorway and back into the dormitory. But when she knelt next to Rommily's head, the older oracle suddenly stiffened. Her eyes went wide and her jaw clenched so hard her teeth ground together.

"Pull them back!" I shouted at Lala, as she stared at her sisters, horrified and confused. "They're too close to the sensor."

I tugged Mirela back by one arm while Lala pulled Rommily by her ankles, and as soon as they were more than a foot away from the door, the convulsing stopped. Mirela blinked up at me in confusion, and I suddenly wished I'd pushed her into the hall instead. Surely the convulsing would have stopped once she was away from the doorway, whether she was inside or out. The sensors were based on proximity, and they didn't care which direction the signal came from. Right?

"Are you okay?" Lala asked her sisters, and her voice drew me out of my thoughts.

"Yeah." Mirela sat up and leaned over her middle sister, who only looked up at us, blinking tears from her eyes. "Rommily, what hurts?"

Heavy footsteps clomped toward us from the hallway, then two armed handlers stepped into the room. The first held his remote at the ready, the screen facing away from me. "Back up," he warned, one finger poised to cause more pain.

When Lala carefully pulled Rommily back, Mirela and I followed her.

"What happened?" the second handler demanded, glancing at the screen on his own remote. "Our system indicates that Oracle 02—known as Rommily—tried to breach the doorway."

"She wasn't trying to breach." Mirela stood, putting herself between the handlers and her younger sisters. "She just got confused."

The second handler pointed to the doorway, where I noticed that a pinpoint of red light glowed from the apex of the arch. "Do not pass. It's pretty damn simple."

"She's...disoriented." I joined Mirela, trying to decide how best to explain about Rommily, to protect her. "Traumatized.

She doesn't always understand what she's told. Or what she sees. It's not her fault, and it can't be fixed. So I suggest you get ready to make some exceptions on Rommily's behalf."

The second handler stepped closer, as if his presence could possibly intimidate me more than the collar around my neck already had. "Is that a threat?"

I crossed my arms over my chest. "Most definitely."

Neither of them seemed to know how to respond to that.

"Just keep an eye on her," the first one said at last, glancing from me to Mirela, to Rommily, then back to me.

Evidently I'd just become an honorary oracle. Which was fitting, considering that I'd just predicted an early death for anyone who messed with Rommily.

Or with me.

DELILAH

Breakfast was delivered by two of our fellow captives—a *selkie* and a dryad, whose hair looked like a curtain of woody vines and whose fingers and toes branched like delicate tree limbs. They pushed a steel cart into the room and passed out trays from two different stacks—one for the shape-shifters, who were largely carnivorous—and one for the rest of us.

The food was bland but nutritionally sound, a definite improvement over the menagerie, but what I found truly noteworthy was the fact that captives were allowed to perform work duties with minimal supervision, because their collars wouldn't allow them to go anywhere they weren't supposed to be, or do anything they weren't supposed to do.

If I earned a work detail that let me roam the property, I might be able to observe Vandekamp's security systems and procedures in search of a weakness that could be exploited.

After breakfast, two handlers in tactical gear came in to call six more women out for work duty. Lala and Mahsa were among those chosen, but they weren't told what their chores would be or when they'd be back.

Sometime later, the squeal of hinges drew my attention to the door as it opened, and the familiar, waiflike figure who stood in the hall drew a gasp from me. I stood, and Mirela joined me, but we both kept our distance from the *ifrit*—a fire *djinni*—in spite of the drugged haze lingering in her eyes. "I didn't even know they'd bought Nalah," Mirela whispered.

"Me neither." I'd secretly been afraid she'd been euthanized. After all, we'd had to keep her sedated since we took over the menagerie, and we weren't even trying to hold her prisoner.

Nalah looked tired and disoriented, standing there in the doorway, but she wasn't trying to melt the walls and her gray scrubs weren't even smoldering. Either because the sedatives we'd given her hadn't worn off yet or because Vandekamp's collar had succeeded where we'd failed.

"Go on." The handler behind her gave her a small push, and as the *ifrit* stumbled into the dormitory, long strands of tangled hair fell over her face, reflecting light in every conceivable shade of red, yellow and orange. Her hair resembled the flames the fire *djinn* lived and breathed, and could kindle out of the air with little more than an angry thought.

From the hall, the handler aimed his remote at her, then clicked something on its screen. A red light flashed in the front of her collar, and the sensor over the door flashed at the same time.

Nalah was now restricted to this room just like the rest of us.

She wobbled on her feet, and I saw no awareness or recognition in her expression. She appeared to be in a total drug fog.

"Come help me with her."

Mirela grabbed my arm. "As soon as the drugs wear off, she's going to roast you." Nalah blamed me for Adira's death.

"Not if her collar works." If Vandekamp's tyrannical tech made Nalah easier to deal with, I was more than willing to take the good with the very, very bad. "She needs help, Mirela."

"Fine." The oracle let go of my arm, still staring warily at the *ifrit*. "I'll get her some water and a mat to lie down on. You get...her."

While Mirela pulled one of the gymnastics mats from the pile stacked against the wall, I approached the teenage *djinni* cautiously. "Nalah?"

Her gaze snapped up, fiery copper eyes focused on me with a familiar, burning hatred. But a second later, they glazed over again. That was all the malice she had the strength for, at least until the drugs were out of her system.

"Do you want to lie down? Mirela's getting you some water." I reached for her arm, but the *djinni* stumbled backward to get away from me, putting her dangerously close to the doorway sensor. "You need to move away from the door. It'll—"

"Nalah?"

I turned to find a woman about my age staring at the *ifrit* through wide ice-blue eyes. Waist-length silvery hair hung down her back and the fall of light made it shimmer like water flowing in sunlight—easily the most identifiable feature of a *marid*, a water *djinni*. And she didn't look friendly.

"I'm Delilah Marlow." I stepped back, so I could keep both *djinn* in sight. "What's your name?"

"Simra."

"Do you know Nalah?" My understanding was that the young *ifrit* and her royal *marid* companion had been captured by Metzger's shortly after they'd sneaked into the United States and had no friends here.

"Everyone south of the border knows her." Simra's cold gaze narrowed on Nalah. "Where is Princess Adira?" she demanded.

Tears filled Nalah's copper eyes.

"Um…Adira was shot when we took over the menagerie," I whispered, afraid that my explanation would upset Nalah. "She didn't make it."

"You failed her." Simra glared at Nalah with feverish spite. "You should have taken the bullet for her. That was your obligation!" She let out a high-pitched war cry and lunged at the *ifrit.* I threw myself between them, but before she could crash into me, the *marid* collapsed in the grip of a seizure.

Her collar worked faster than I could, and it was a hell of a lot more effective.

Mirela led the sobbing *ifrit* to the sleeping mat she'd prepared while I knelt next to Simra with no idea how I could help her. Fortunately, her convulsions only lasted a few seconds, but she'd hit her head on the floor when she fell, and even after she stopped shaking, her eyes looked unfocused.

"Simra?" I swept glittering, silvery hair back from her forehead and searched her pale blue eyes for any sign of awareness. "Are you okay?"

She nodded, then rolled onto her side and covered her face with her hands. "I knew that would happen. Still, I had to try." She pushed herself upright and smoothed long hair back from her pale face, composing herself.

"Try what? To hurt Nalah?"

Simra's icy gaze focused on me. "To avenge the princess."

"Did you know Adira?"

"I saw her in a parade once," she replied, her expression softening with the memory. "When she was a girl. Nalah sat at her feet, and I was mad with envy. So many of us wanted to be the princess's companion, but the *ifrit* royalty sent her Nalah as a gift, when the betrothal of their prince to our princess was announced. As a cross-cultural gesture." Her gaze hardened again and she clasped her pale hands in her lap. "But Nalah let our princess die."

"She's just a kid. And she was Adira's companion, not her bodyguard," I pointed out.

"She has disgraced herself by outliving the princess she served." Simra sat up, her spine as stiff as the line of her jaw. "If I could restore her honor by taking her life, I would."

The casual brutality of her declaration sent a chill crawling over me, and for the first time, I was grateful that Sultan Bruhier, Adira's grieving father, had denied us entry into his kingdom. *Djinni* culture sounded ruthless, and the injustice of it would have driven me—and the *furiae* within me—insane.

"Delilah?" a low-pitched voice called, and I looked up to find Bowman standing in the dormitory doorway holding a clipboard.

I stood, my heart thumping in anticipation. "Yes?"

"Come with me." He pressed a button on his remote, and the red light above the door flashed, but if there was any response from my collar, I couldn't feel it.

"Where?"

Bowman only watched me. Waiting.

I gave Simra my hand, and she let me pull her to her feet. "Do you know what this is about?"

She shrugged. "It's a little early to be your first engagement, but you never know. Are you an oracle?"

"I'm human."

"They'll never believe that." The skeptical tone of her voice said she didn't believe it either.

At the door, Bowman bound my hands at my back with padded restraints, which told me that the staff wasn't sure they could control me with a collar until they knew my species. And that the clientele didn't want to see visible signs of abuse on their high-priced exotic chattel—except whatever marks they might inflict themselves.

"What's this about?" I asked as I followed Bowman into the hall, taking note of the fact that he'd come for me alone. But armed.

He pressed a button on his remote as we approached an exit on the opposite side of the building from where we'd come in the night before, but his lips remained sealed as he pushed the door open.

"You don't know, do you? You're just an errand boy, right?" I asked, as I stepped out onto a sidewalk that felt rough and cool against my bare feet.

Bowman marched me past a row of nondescript single-story buildings, each built of gray or beige brick punctuated at regular intervals by windows too narrow for a human to pass through, even if the glass were broken. We were clearly on the operational side of the grounds, which obviously wasn't meant to be seen by Vandekamp's clientele.

At the end of the row of ugly buildings, we took a right, then approached a beautiful iron gate in an intricately patterned stone wall. Bowman pressed an icon on his remote to allow me through the gate, and a red sensor blinked between two stones near the ground, embedded right into the mortar.

When we walked through the gate, concrete gave way to smooth stone pavers beneath my feet and I caught my breath as I took in the stunning series of gardens and buildings that made up the Savage Spectacle's grounds.

At first, I could only stare, wide-eyed, at the botanical zoo spread out around me, cut from various shrubs dotting the broad, neat lawn. The cryptid topiary was astonishing and incredibly intricate, yet the details conformed more to fantasy than to true anatomy.

To my left, two box-tree centaurs appeared frozen in

midtrot, alternate legs gracefully curled beneath them as they ran, long human hair trailing behind them, and their poses were so dynamic I almost expected their hooves to hit the ground when reality's stopped clock resumed ticking. On my right, a shrubbery manticore brandished its eight-foot-long stinger-tipped scorpion tail against a griffin with a twelve-foot wingspan, swooping in from overhead by the grace of the strong, bare trunk holding it up like a doll on a stand.

As Bowman led me across the courtyard, down winding stone paths and past iron arches leading to other areas of the grounds, I gawked at a small herd of shrubbery satyrs playing flutes in a semicircle, as if the artist had drawn inspiration from Renaissance-period stereotypes rather than actually going to see a satyr.

Past a gazebo surrounded by playful-looking elves that could have frolicked right off the front of a cookie box, I found a beautiful stone fountain spilling water from three tiers. Poised above it, as if they were about to dive into two feet of water, were two mermaids and a *selkie* emerging from her seal skin, all trimmed from massive bushes planted on three sides of the fountain. As with the griffin, they were held up by the pruned-bare center trunks. Unlike the griffin, however, those figures bore little resemblance to reality.

A *selkie* would shed her seal skin as she emerged from the water, not as she dived into it, and mermaids…well… In reality, their upper halves didn't resemble human lingerie models anywhere near as closely as the topiary might lead one to believe.

Disgusted, I turned away from the elaborately inaccurate portrayals and focused on the back of the building we seemed headed for: a stately three-story structure with a massive back porch set up for fine dining outdoors.

Through small gaps in a tall wall of shrubbery, I caught

glimpses of an empty parking lot set back from the building and an unattended valet stand.

Bowman marched me around the elaborate back porch, then used his remote to allow me entry through a small side door up a narrow set of steps. The door opened into a back hall, where Bowman's boots echoed against the hardwood. My bare feet were silent on the cold floor.

We passed through a tall rear foyer tiled in marble and paneled with dark wood, where abstract sculptures stood on marble pedestals. I stared at the display of wealth and opulence, awed for a second, until I realized that Willem Vandekamp financed the luxury—and no doubt his technological breakthroughs in cryptid containment—with the exploitation of helpless, suffering captives.

"This way." Bowman marched down a left-hand hallway without me, assuming I'd follow, and for a second, the uncharacteristic carelessness of that action gave me hope. Then a low-powered jolt came from my collar to spur me on, and I understood. He was demonstrating how little effort it took to keep a captive in line with the press of a single button.

At the end of the hall, Bowman tweaked another setting to allow me through another doorway into a richly adorned office suite.

A young, attractive assistant glanced up from her computer screen, her fingers paused over the keyboard. When she saw me, she frowned, then pressed a button on the telephone next to her keyboard. "Mr. Vandekamp, that cryptid is here."

"Send her in," came the reply.

Bowman opened the inner office door and escorted me inside.

Willem Vandekamp sat at his desk, but standing to his left was a petite woman in her midthirties, wearing a white blouse and a knee-length pencil skirt. She wore low heels and perfect makeup, and stood with her arms crossed over her chest. Her nose crinkled as she studied me, and I wondered if she was more offended by my appearance or my smell. I hadn't showered in at least two days, nor had I brushed my teeth.

Two chairs stood in front of the massive, ornate desk, but I was not offered one, so I stood in the middle of the room, staring back at Vandekamp while he stared at me. Bowman stood at my side, at attention, ready to disable me with his remote, should I suddenly appear threatening.

Finally, the woman exhaled with a frown. "I see the problem."

"I have your blood test results." Vandekamp lifted one edge of a sheet of paper from his desk, and he seemed both annoyed and fascinated with whatever was printed on it.

I shrugged without even a glance at the paper. "I tried to tell your handlers."

"We ran the test twice and found no trace of any nonhuman enzyme or hormone," he continued, as if I hadn't spoken. On my right, Bowman suddenly seemed to stand even stiffer with the news, though I couldn't tell that he'd actually moved. "The sheriff of your hometown said the state of Oklahoma got the same result, which they assumed to be a lab error. But even if my lab made mistakes—and it does not—two labs independently making the same error, twice each, is beyond the realm of both possibility and coincidence. Yet I've personally seen you take on characteristics no human could possibly possess. How can that be?"

I shrugged, and the padded cuffs dragged the back of my shirt. I wasn't sure how I'd been chosen as a *furiae*, or what force had chosen me, but I saw no reason to share what I did know with a man who intended to rent me out by the hour.

"Can you control it?" The woman's brown-eyed gaze stayed

glued to me, as if my every inhalation might reveal some clue. "Or are you at the mercy of your beast?"

"I am at the mercy of nothing." That one wasn't so much a lie as a personal goal.

"Show us your inner monster," she ordered, and Bowman tensed in anticipation. When I only stared back at her, she pulled a familiar remote control from her pocket and aimed it at me as she tapped something on the screen. I braced myself for searing pain in every nerve ending, but nothing happened.

She glanced at her remote in irritation. "Willem?"

"We can't program the prompt command until we know what she is," he explained.

"Why not?"

I laughed, amused to realize I understood what she did not. "Because that's done by stimulating hormonal and neurological reactions through the needles penetrating my spine. Which you can't do until you know what reactions to stimulate." And they might never know how if I denied them that information by refusing to release my inner *furiae*.

Or if the *furiae* turned out not to be triggered by anything they could stimulate.

The woman's gaze hardened, but Vandekamp looked suddenly intrigued. "How do you know that?"

His files were obviously incomplete, and I had no intention of filling in the blanks—until I looked down at him, sitting behind his desk, and a sudden moment of déjà vu reminded me where I'd seen him before.

"Willem Vandekamp." I turned the syllables over in my head. "You're *Dr.* Willem Vandekamp. I took your seminar at Colorado State." During my senior year as a cryptobiology major. He hadn't had the scar then, but... "You did a six-week lecture series on hormonal impulses in cryptid hybrids, and you had this theory that cryptids could be hormonally neutered."

A wave of nausea washed over me along with the obvious conclusion. "I guess that's more than a theory now, huh?"

The woman's eyes widened as she turned to him. "You taught her? *In class?*" Something in her voice—in the casual anger with which she addressed him—told me she was not an employee. Not *just* an employee anyway.

"You went to college." Vandekamp stood and walked around his desk to sit on the front edge of it, eyeing me more closely, and suddenly I realized that though he was now addressing me, he hadn't so much as greeted his own employee. "That's not in your files."

I shrugged. "Your university bio didn't mention your 'private collection.'" For obvious reasons. Even if the Spectacle wasn't actually breaking any laws—and I found that hard to believe—its clientele would expect the kind of total anonymity that can't come from a service advertised to the general public.

"You were my student. Fascinating!" Yet Vandekamp looked more like he wanted to dissect my brain than discuss my senior thesis.

"And you were a very good teacher. I may not understand how you're doing what you're doing, but I understand why it works. And in my case, why it won't."

"This one isn't like the others," the woman—his wife?—said, and the sharp edge in her voice could have cut glass.

"I'm like them in every way that matters," I insisted.

"Yet you look human. Like a surrogate." She spoke through clenched teeth. "What if she's a surrogate, Willem? What if the government missed one? What if this is what they look like, all grown-up?"

Vandekamp twisted to pick up a file from his desk blotter. He flipped open the folder and scanned the first page. "She's only twenty-five. Too young to be a surrogate."

"Yes, and the test results say she's human, but we know

that's not true. If she's a surrogate, you could wake up one morning to find that you've stabbed me in some kind of psychotic trance. Doesn't it say in that file that she made a man electrocute himself?"

My brow rose. "You believe that part, but not my birthday? I—"

She pressed her thumb against her remote screen, and pain shot through my throat. I cried out, and bent at the waist as I strained my shoulders trying to reach for my neck. But my voice carried no sound and my hands were still cuffed at my back.

The pain faded quickly, but my voice did not return.

"Cryptids don't have birthdays," the woman snapped, as I tried in vain to speak. My mouth opened. My lips and tongue moved. But my vocal cords did not vibrate. My brain was sending the signal to speak, but my body wasn't receiving the order.

It was being intercepted by the collar.

In the menagerie, the handlers had sometimes muzzled cryptids, but that could only stop them from biting and speaking. Muzzles can't prevent you from making sound. From hearing your own voice, as a reassurance that you do, in fact, still exist, even if only as property to be bought, sold or rented out.

But Vandekamp had found a way to *turn off* my voice, and the resulting claustrophobic terror felt as if the room was folding in on me. As if I were screaming into the void of some shrinking reality that no longer had enough space for me. As if soon they would cease to see me too, and start walking through me.

"So what do you suggest we do with her, Tabitha?" Vandekamp circled his desk again to sit behind it. "Sell her? Have her euthanized?"

My silent objection became a fruitless scream of rage. I strained the muscles in my throat, trying to be heard, until my eyes felt like they'd pop from my skull. But neither of them even looked at me.

I turned to Bowman to find him staring straight ahead, impervious to my frustration and fury.

"That seems a bit extreme," the woman—Tabitha—said. "We're going to have to inspect her. All monsters have telltale features. We just have to find hers."

She turned to me, and again I tried to shout. To tell her that I'd already been inspected. I knew my desperate effort was pointless, but I couldn't stop.

"Take off your clothes," she ordered.

My profanity-laden refusal didn't make so much as a squeak.

She pressed another icon on her remote, and pain exploded all over my body. I fell to my knees on the carpet, hunched over, my arms straining against my restraints. Screaming in silent agony.

What I'd felt when I'd slid my finger beneath my collar was a flash in the pan compared to the fire blazing through every nerve in my body.

"Tabitha," Vandekamp said. "She can't undress. She's handcuffed."

His wife finally released the button.

I slumped over my knees, breathing deeply as the pain slowly receded. I felt tender all over, but I couldn't tell if that was a residual effect of the electric current or simply the knowledge that if I didn't cooperate, she would press that button again.

"And anyway, she was inspected during the intake process. She has no cryptid features. Which is part of the problem."

"I don't understand," she complained. "Even the most

benign-looking monsters have an identifiable trait hidden somewhere. How could she have nothing?"

Finally, I made myself sit up and look at the Vandekamps, and the effort that took without the use of my hands was terrifying.

"What are we going to do with her?" Tabitha demanded as she smoothed a strand of brown hair back toward the simple twist it had escaped from. "No one's going to pay to see that." She waved one hand at me in disgust. "You're going to have to figure out what she is. Make her talk." She shrugged, and her cold gaze chased the last reverberating bolts of fire from my body. "Or I could do it."

"I'll figure something out." He stood and kissed her on the forehead. "Why don't you go tell the seamstresses what you want for the new costumes?"

She hesitated, then nodded reluctantly. "I do have a few ideas…"

As the door closed behind her, he sat on the front of his desk again. "Wait outside," he said, and I thought he was talking to me until Bowman turned sharply and headed into the outer office, closing the door at his back. Vandekamp looked down at me, where I still knelt on his rug. "You were the one responsible for the takeover of Metzger's Menagerie?"

I nodded. The truth was more complicated, but without my voice, I couldn't explain about the team effort.

"I have some questions for you, and I suggest you answer them while you still can." He pressed an icon on his remote, and when I felt no pain, I realized he'd given me back my voice.

Vandekamp twisted and lifted another folder from his blotter, then flipped it open. "According to the menagerie's records, there are two cryptids missing. A werewolf called Claudio and a young *marid* named Adira. Where are they?"

I cleared my throat and was relieved by the sound that met my ears. "Adira died during the coup. She was shot by the Lot Supervisor. Christopher Ruyle." We'd sent her body to the sultan so he could bury her.

Vandekamp glanced at the report again. "This Ruyle is also missing."

"He's dead. And for the record, he's the only employee who died in the takeover."

"And the werewolf?"

I held his gaze. And my silence.

He lifted the remote, drawing my attention to it. "You already know what this can do."

I exhaled. I didn't want to betray Claudio, but chances are that they'd never catch him anyway. "He left the menagerie last month."

"Why would he leave? A werewolf cannot pass for human."

"But he can live in the woods as long as he likes." He was looking for Genevieve, the youngest of his children, who had been sold right before the coup. But I wouldn't tell Vandekamp that no matter how much pain he put me through.

"How did you know about the coup?"

Surprise tugged up on Vandekamp's left brow. "You haven't figured out your mistake yet?"

I'd spent my time alone in that concrete cell going over every decision I'd made as the de facto manager of the liberated menagerie, trying to figure out how I'd failed the very people I'd been trying to save. I'd come up with a thousand small mistakes, but nothing I could pinpoint as our downfall.

"I found out from the Metzgers." Vandekamp watched carefully for my reaction, but I had none to give him, except confusion.

"The Metzgers don't know." Raul and Renata had flaw-lessly covered our tracks with the former owner's family.

"The Metzgers found out from old man Rudolph himself."

"But Rudolph Metzger is…" I let my words fade into silence short of a confession.

"Dead," Vandekamp finished for me. "Which is the inevitable result of dismembering a man and mailing a piece of him to each of his remaining relatives."

"We didn't—"

He shook his head, still watching me closely. "No, that didn't seem like something you would do, after all the trouble you went through to hide the takeover."

Sultan Bruhier. Adira's father got his final revenge on us by exposing the coup that had cost his daughter her life. But the sultan couldn't have shipped pieces of Rudolph Metzger all over the country if I hadn't given him the old man in the first place.

Vandekamp's viewing of my reaction seemed part entertainment, part clinical observation. So I swallowed my guilt to deny him the pleasure.

"What did you do with Gallagher?" I demanded, and his fleeting frown made my stomach flip. He didn't recognize the name.

Gallagher wasn't at the Spectacle. He'd been sold to someone else or sent to a cryptid prison or—worst-case scenario—given to a research lab.

A cold new fear overtook me. No matter where he was, he would fight to get to me.

I stared at the floor, struggling to control my horror at that thought. Or at least hide it from Vandekamp.

"Until we know what you are, you're a financial liability," he said, and I forced myself to focus on his words. "You can enlighten me, or I can let my lovely wife pull the information out of you. But I don't think that's what you want."

No use denying that. Tabitha Vandekamp was scary in a

way no thick-fisted roustabout had ever been. But she couldn't change the facts.

"I've told you." I shrugged, mentally tamping down the fear that he might recognize my half-truth. "Run the test again. The results will be the same, and no amount of torture will change that. I'm human."

Vandekamp crossed his arms over his shiny blue button-down shirt. "I've *seen* you turn into a monster, Delilah."

"The two are not mutually exclusive." I shrugged and held his gaze. "You and I have that in common."

WILLEM

Willem Vandekamp watched the office door close behind his latest purchase, and for a moment, he sat lost in his thoughts. After more than twenty years in the cryptobiology field, he'd long been convinced that nothing could surprise him.

Until Delilah.

A cryptid who went to college.

A cryptid who'd taken *his seminar.*

She understood too much, but the real problem Delilah represented wasn't how much she knew about him, but how little he knew about her.

Delilah would make the investors nervous. She would terrify his friends in Washington.

Speaking of whom…

Willem glanced at his watch, an obsolete device in the age of cell phones and handheld tablets, but one that gave him comfort in its simplicity. He was two minutes late for the conference call, but had no intention of actually picking up the phone for another three. Punctuality might give those congressional blowhards the mistaken impression that his time was less important than theirs.

What if Tabitha was right? Willem leaned back in his chair and linked his hands behind his head, still staring at the door. What if Delilah was a surrogate? No one had seen a single one of those sadistic little bastards since the government rounded them up nearly thirty years ago. They'd be thirty-five years old now—a full decade older than Delilah—but who knew whether they'd age like humans? Hell, if they were some kind of *fae*, their glamour could make them look like anything or anyone.

But Delilah wasn't *fae*. According to her file, the sheriff who'd originally arrested her had kept her in iron cuffs with no effect.

Willem's desk phone rang. His direct line. He noted the DC area code on the display and smiled. Then he let it ring two more times before he answered.

"Hello?"

"Vandekamp." Senator Aaron sounded distinctly displeased. "We had an appointment, unless I'm mistaken?"

"I apologize." Willem spun in his chair to look out the window at the topiary garden. "It's been a bit chaotic here, and I'm running on about three hours of sleep."

"Does that mean the rumors are true?" the second voice demanded in an eager baritone.

"If the rumors say that I have retaken Metzger's Menagerie from the creatures who escaped their cages and killed the owner, then yes."

"How could this have happened?"

"It couldn't have, if my restraint system were federally subsidized and put into production," Willem pointed out, without bothering to filter sharp criticism from his tone.

"If your restraint system were more than a prototype, that might be a possibility," Senator Aaron said. "Until then—"

"It's ready." Willem stood and paced the length of his office, his pulse roaring in his ears. "Come see for yourself. My technology is going to change the world, Senator. You can be on the forefront of the new wave or you can be crushed by the tide. Your choice."

He dropped his phone into its cradle and took a deep breath. Then he pressed the intercom button and spoke without waiting for a greeting from his secretary. "I want a full recording from Delilah's collar. I need to see every hormonal fluctuation on a timeline alongside video footage from her dorm. Every twelve hours."

As the only creature at the Savage Spectacle that Willem could neither identify nor control, Delilah Marlow was the one thing standing between him and a government contract that would *revolutionize* humanity's control over the beasts it shared the planet with.

She could not be allowed to derail two decades of progress.

DELILAH

A couple of hours after the sun set, Woodrow, the game-keeper, stepped into the dormitory to conclude our first-day orientation with an announcement that lights-out would be in half an hour. He told us to clean our teeth with the brushes we'd been issued and use the toilets, then warned us—again—that failure to follow orders would result in serious consequences.

The long-term Spectacle captives began filing into the bathroom in two lines, clearly accustomed to the routine. Lala and Mahsa were the first from our group to join them, and I stepped into line after them. "How was your work assignment?" I asked, as we shuffled forward after the others. "What were you doing?"

"Vacuuming some big room," Lala said.

"Scrubbing the kitchens," Mahsa added.

"Multiple kitchens?"

"Yeah." The leopard shifter shrugged. "Two of them, in two different buildings. There may be more, though." Her eyes widened. "Did you see the bushes?"

"The topiaries? Ridiculous, aren't they?"

"Yes," Lala said. "But they're beautiful. Especially the nymph with roses for hair."

We shuffled forward again, and the women who'd been first in line began to exit the bathroom. "So, did you see any way out? The property seems to be walled in, but I assume there's a gate up front? And maybe one in the back, for deliveries?" We'd all been unconscious when we'd arrived, but I couldn't imagine them driving tarp-covered cattle cars past the massive front building and the valet stand.

"I—" The oracle flinched, and her hand flew to the collar at her neck.

"Lala? What's wrong?"

Simra turned around, a couple of places in front of us and frowned at me as if I'd just asked a colossally stupid question. "She's not allowed to talk about certain things." But I didn't understand until she tapped the shiny steel collar around her own neck.

Holy shit.

Vandekamp's collar was preventing her from speaking specifically about gates and exits? How was that possible, short of paralyzing the vocal cords entirely? There was *no way* any electronic device could tell what someone intended to say before the words even formed.

Or was there? If the collars could anticipate a shifter's intention to shift based on the anticipatory hormones, maybe the speech block worked similarly. Maybe the collar's receptors simply detected the presence of whatever nervous hormone people produce when they're about to break a rule. Or maybe it sensed spikes in blood pressure, like a lie detector. Maybe the collar simply read the physiological signs of our intent.

Stunned by Simra's revelation, I shared a horrified glance with Mahsa and Lala as the line shuffled forward. Why was I allowed to ask questions about things others weren't allowed to discuss?

The most likely answer seemed to be that since I hadn't known the question was forbidden, my body didn't react with any signs of anxiety that could trigger my collar. Would that change, now that I knew?

Disturbed by the policing of my very voice, I shifted my thoughts from the fact that we weren't allowed to talk about something to *what* we weren't allowed to talk about.

Exits, locks...

Vandekamp was censoring information that might help plan an escape.

When I got to the front of the line for the toilet stalls, Finola leaned forward to whisper from behind me. "Is that hand sanitizer?"

I followed the siren's gaze to a line of four liquid dispensers on the wall. The sign hanging above them notified us that they were to be utilized every time we used the restroom, though I couldn't imagine that more than a few of the captives could read. "Looks like."

We shuffled forward as one of the stalls emptied, and Zyanya spoke up from behind the siren. "Why do they care whether we brush our teeth and wash our hands?"

"Presumably it cuts down on communicable illness in such tight quarters," Lenore said.

"Yes, but I suspect that's a secondary concern." I stepped forward again, and found myself second in line. "Our value and appeal both decline if we're sick or dirty."

When we'd all flushed, sanitized and brushed, Lala and I helped several of the other captives arrange the gymnastics mats on the floor and distribute blankets. There were no pillows or pajamas, and the mats were worn and thin, but the accommodations were both cleaner and more comfortable than anything we'd had in our carnival cages.

The menagerie refugees and I claimed spots on the left side of the room, in our own little cluster, and seconds after we'd all chosen a mat, the lights overhead were extinguished, in both the big room and the bathroom. We were left with only the light shining in from the series of tall, narrow windows, through which I could see several security light poles.

An instant later, every collar in the room briefly flashed red, and I wondered what new restriction had just been placed on us.

For several minutes, I lay on my side, thinking about collars and tranquilizer rifles and blood tests and topiary cryptids locked in their poses. After having survived the menagerie, I'd thought I knew what to expect from imprisonment. I understood how to deal with chains and cages and hunger, but this shiny, antiseptic captivity felt like the glittery wrapping on a box full of horrors, just waiting to be unwrapped.

In the near dark, one of the forms to my right sat up on her gym mat, and I recognized Zyanya's silhouette even shrouded as it was by baggy scrubs. She turned to me, waving one hand to get my attention, and I sat up to see what was wrong. Her mouth opened, but nothing came out.

Her hands flew to her throat, and even in the thick shadows, I saw the fear and desperation in every motion. Zyanya was terrified.

I scooted off my mat and reached for her, but when I tried to ask what was wrong, there was no response from my vocal cords. I remembered the flash of red from every collar in the room.

Vandekamp had silenced us—all of us—evidently for the entire night.

Anger raged like a storm inside me. Having lost my voice earlier made this instance no easier to bear.

With the press of a single button, Vandekamp ripped from all of us a right I'd considered not just inalienable, but literally impossible to steal without a scalpel and the courage to face the bloody reality and cruelty of a sadistic and permanent mutilation.

He'd made the process so neat and easy that it required no thought or effort, and his conscience probably never had to justify the reasoning behind such a barbaric practice.

Zyanya's hands began to shake. Her mouth opened, forming silent words too fast for me to read on her lips. I seized her hand, and with it, her attention. I pointed at my own collar with my free hand, then covered my mouth, trying to explain that she hadn't permanently lost the ability to speak. That we were all suffering the same temporary loss.

The shifter's forehead furrowed, fury dancing in her luminous cat eyes, and I knew she understood. And she was pissed.

Her rage called to the beast inside me, which uncoiled like a snake ready to strike. My vision sharpened until I could see Zyanya perfectly well in the dark and my hands ached for something to grab. For some damage to wreak.

But like hers, my anger was impotent, for the moment, without a target to strike.

I mimed lying down on my mat, silently encouraging both Zyanya and the *furiae* to try to get some sleep. Because there was nothing else for us to do, mired in silent darkness.

Zyanya lay down with obvious reluctance and feline grace. Her cat eyes glowed at me from two feet away, reflecting what little light shone into our room.

When I finally fell asleep, her eyes followed me into my mute nightmares.

★ ★ ★

With dawn came the return of both overhead lights and our ability to speak. I'd never in my life been more desperate to be heard, simply because for the past eight hours, I couldn't be.

I cornered Simra at one of the bathroom sinks while she brushed her teeth. "Why didn't you warn us that we would be muted at lights-out?"

She frowned at me in the mirror, mint-scented foam dripping down her pale chin. Then she spit into the sink and turned to me. "I didn't realize you needed a warning. Was it different in your last collection?"

"We're not from a collection. But that's not the point." I traced my collar with one finger. "Vandekamp invented this technology, and as far as I know, no one else has anything like it."

"We didn't have it here either, until a couple of winters ago." Magnolia spoke up from the next sink. "But Simra hasn't been here long enough to know that. Few have. They used to keep us in concrete cells in another building. Then one day, they put these collars on a few of us and put us in a separate room, with cameras on the ceiling. And they left the door unlocked."

Vandekamp had been testing his technology on a small sample of the captives, obviously.

Magnolia shrugged. "After a while, they put collars on everyone, and that's when the nightly engagements began. Before that, we were on display at events, but there was no... touching."

Chills slid down my spine, forming a cold puddle in the bottom of my stomach.

"This isn't what it's like everywhere else, ladies," I told them softly. "At the menagerie, they could put us in cages and they could put us on display and they could deny us food or clothing, but they couldn't control our words. They couldn't control our *thoughts*."

"The collars don't do that," Simra insisted as she rinsed her toothbrush. "I'm still free up here." She tapped her temple with the index finger of her free hand.

"Really? If you were to think about pulling all the water out of these faucets and those toilets—" a basic skill among *marids* "—I mean, if you were to *really* consider doing it, what would happen?"

She dropped her toothbrush into the holder on the shelf above the sink. "I'd be frozen in place. Or I might be shocked."

"Exactly. These collars not only prevent you from doing what comes naturally, they prevent you from even *thinking* about it. Vandekamp is eroding your will."

"Eroding?" She let water fill her cupped palms, but then just stared at it, frowning.

"With every thought he denies us, he robs us of a little bit of what makes us who we are. Like how massive canyons can be carved from small streams over time." A concept *marids* were intimately familiar with. "Vandekamp is the stream, and you are the rock, and by the time he's done with you, he'll have carved a hunk right out of your soul."

Simra's sad, but not truly surprised expression opened a fresh crack in my already splintered heart. She stepped back from the sink so another woman could have a turn, and I followed her toward the doorway.

"Simra, how long have you been here?"

"They don't give us calendars."

Fair enough. I knew exactly how difficult it was to keep track of time when every day was just a cruel repeat of the day before.

"How many fall seasons have you been at the Spectacle?"

"This is my second. I came north to look for Adira after

she was stolen from her groom before they could wed by terrorists trying to prevent an alliance between the *marid* and *ifrit* kingdoms."

I blinked, stunned by the story Sultan Bruhier had evidently told his people. Was he trying to avoid conflict with the *ifrits*?

Either way, it was not my place to deny her the bliss of ignorance.

"I was going to help bring her home," Simra continued. "To prove my worth as a companion."

"So you've been here about a year?"

Simra nodded.

"I grew up free too."

"And you really think it's better to live in a rolling cage and eat scraps than to be here, in a room with showers and toilets and decent food to eat? Woodrow says we're lucky. We're not in cages. We're not being starved. We're not being dragged from town to town in the back of a stifling, germ-filled trailer. Or being injected with toxic chemicals in lab tests."

And that was the true danger in the propaganda the Spectacle was feeding its captives—the idea that they weren't being abused or exploited just because they weren't being starved or experimented on.

Chains and cages were only one way to crush a person's soul.

"So what *is* happening to you?" I asked as I followed her into the dorm room. "What does Vandekamp do with his collection?"

"Whatever the client wants. It's different for everyone. For every engagement."

She tried to turn away from me, but I ducked into her path again. "What is it for you?"

"I can't tell you that." Her hand went to her collar and her mouth closed. Her jaw tensed. Then she stepped around me and practically ran to the other ride of the room.

"What was that about?" Lenore's question floated on a fresh, minty breath as she stopped at my side.

"Vandekamp has his captives convinced that they're lucky because they're not lab rats or circus exhibits, yet they're not allowed to talk about what goes on in these 'engagements.'"

"They aren't?"

"Not all of it anyway. The collars won't let them. And I see no more logical reason for that than for the fact that we can't talk at night. Vandekamp's just trying to exert as much control over us as he can. It's like he gets off on it."

"Delilah."

I dragged my focus away from Simra and turned to meet Lenore's concerned gaze. "What?"

"You can't help people who don't want to be helped."

But the *furiae* inside me disagreed.

"It's not that they don't want to be helped. It's that they truly think this is the best life has to offer." If I couldn't help them, why the hell had fate saddled me with the vengeful beast already stirring restlessly inside me? "They just need to see someone stand up to these remote-wielding bastards. Once they know it's possible, they'll fight for themselves. For each other. Humanity doesn't have the market cornered on courage and justice. That's not *human* nature. It's just nature."

GALLAGHER

Gallagher glanced around the police station in disgust. The floor was grimy, but he'd certainly seen worse. The handcuffed detainees on the bench next to him were ill-mannered and angry, but no more so than the handlers and grunts he'd spent the past year working alongside in the menagerie. It wasn't the people or the building that offended him.

It was the process.

Redcaps—the *fear dearg*—had never needed handcuffs or records or rooms made of bars. If a man sacrificed his honor, he forfeited his life. Even children understood that. Guilt was never in question, because the *fear dearg* could not lie.

Humans, though, could build entire kingdoms on a foundation of lies. They spun tall tales for their children, used fibs to avoid their parents and fed falsehoods to their lovers like chocolate and wine.

Human men would move heaven and earth for profit or pleasure or even base cruelty, but they wouldn't lift a finger for honor.

The police were no exception. The worthless pieces of

tin pinned to their chests weren't badges of honor, they were badges of authority, and in the human world, authority was little better than a high tower built on a small footing.

It was bound to crumble eventually.

Gallagher had understood the moment he'd woken up in a police van with Alyrose, Abraxas and Kevin that Vandekamp's men had mistaken him for human. He'd spent twelve hours sitting in a holding cell, waiting to be processed with half a dozen other prisoners who lacked the nerve to meet his gaze.

He had let the police take their pictures and restrain him with handcuffs that would hardly close around his wrists. He'd even exchanged his clothes for an orange uniform that rode high above his ankles and gaped at his stomach when he lifted his arms, because the police would speak more freely around him than would anyone at Vandekamp's specialized cryptid prison.

But the end of the charade was near.

The police had taken his hat, and the *fear dearg* could not be separated from their traditional red caps for long. The hat would return to Gallagher, no matter how many locks and boxes and doors separated it from its owner. The *fear dearg*'s cap was a part of him, like his limbs and his organs, yet though Gallagher could survive the loss of a foot or a spleen, he could not survive the loss of his traditional cap.

And he would not have to, because nothing made by man could destroy it.

His head felt oddly bare, exposed as it was to the world. He could feel the pull of his cap like a magnet drawn to metal, and when that pull became too strong, he would have to call for its return, or die.

Gallagher waited while all the other men handcuffed to a bench in the waiting area were removed one at a time, and he knew that he would be last. Every gaze that fell on him slid away an instant later. Every cop who picked up his file put it down again with a frown. Subconsciously, the police feared him.

While he waited, sweat began to build on his skin. A cramp flared deep in his gut, and in less than an hour, it became a raging headache, of the battle-ax-to-the-brain variety. By the time the pain reached his chest, he was alone on the bench, and he could no longer clearly remember why he was there at all.

Gallagher called for his cap, a silent tug on an invisible thread.

The cap appeared on his head, and out of habit, he used glamour to suggest to everyone around him that they were actually seeing a red baseball hat. Glamour was the reason so few *fae* had been caught after the reaping, but it couldn't disguise the sudden appearance of a cap on a prisoner handcuffed to a bench.

"Hey!" The cop behind the desk frowned at Gallagher, then stood. "Where'd you get that hat? I logged it with your personal items hours ago."

Gallagher merely blinked.

"Perez, did you give that back to him?" the cop behind the desk demanded of the officer who'd taken the hat in the first place.

"No. What the hell?" Perez reached for the hat.

Gallagher gave his wrists a good tug, and wood creaked. The arm of the bench broke, and his cuffed hands slid free.

"What the...?" Perez backpedaled, drawing his gun, and Gallagher snapped the cop's right wrist. Perez howled in pain. His gun clattered to the floor. The redcap stood over him, pondering his next move as the pain in his head slowly receded.

He'd vowed never to take a life that didn't deserve to be

taken, but short of catching a man in a dishonorable act, he could never be sure when that was the case. Because humans lied.

"Don't move!"

Gallagher turned to find another cop aiming a pistol at him. Behind that man, two more pulled their guns. The redcap towered over all three. "I don't want to hurt anyone." He held his cuffed hands out in front of his chest. "So I suggest you put down your weapons."

"He's not human," Perez said from the floor, where he cradled his broken wrist.

The first cop's trigger finger twitched, and Gallagher dived to the left. The bullet thunked into the wall at his back.

Gallagher lifted the bench he'd been sitting on to shield his head and torso. Three bullets thunked into the wood. He grunted as he heaved the heavy bench at them, and all three of the cops went down like pins in the path of a bowling ball.

He turned, heading for the double glass doors beyond a half-height swinging gate into the lobby, but pain stabbed into his massive left thigh. Gallagher pulled a familiar dart from his leg. A second hit his arm, and a third lodged in his back.

The massive redcap made it three steps toward the gate, then fell face-first onto a cheap desk.

The wood splintered beneath him, and the last thing Gallagher heard before he passed out on the ruined desk was the small-town sheriff's order.

"Call that Vandekamp fella back and tell him he missed one."

DELILAH

The day passed in a blur of sleeping mats, food trays and community showers. In the morning, handlers came in to select several ladies to perform chores. In the afternoon, more handlers showed up to escort those who'd been requested for "engagements," including Simra, two of the long-term resident shifters and Finola, the younger of our beloved sirens.

They missed dinner, then lights-out, and while I waited for them to return, I could only stare up at the ceiling, listening to the soft breathing all around me, trying not to imagine what Finola's "engagement" might be like.

Finally, hours after lights-out, the dormitory door opened and three slight female silhouettes plodded inside, each carrying a familiar bundle of folded clothing. They headed straight for the bathroom, and when the automatic light came on, I saw that their skin seemed to sparkle.

Finola was shaking all over.

I stood and picked my way through the maze of sleeping mats into the bathroom, where I froze in revulsion.

All three ladies were covered from head to toe in glittery

gold body paint and little else. It took several seconds of horrified staring for me to distinguish the straps of a skimpy bikini disguised by the paint on Finola's back, but the smeared handprints all over her were more than obvious. And they came in several different sizes.

The moment Finola saw me in the mirror, she burst into tears, and for the first time in my life, I had no idea how to help. I couldn't ask her what had happened, because I couldn't speak. I tried to hug her, but she dodged my touch and gestured at the messy body paint.

"Just take a shower and go to sleep," Simra whispered to her, which was when I realized they hadn't been muted yet. "That's all you can do."

Finola moved toward the open bank of showers, where Simra and the shifter were peeling off their sticky bikinis and stuffing them into the laundry chute on one wall. While they stood beneath the flow of water and began scrubbing at the body paint and pulling hairpins from their elaborate, curly updos, Finola tried in vain to untie the straps of her bikini top while tears left faint trails down her sparkly gold cheeks.

I gently brushed her trembling fingers away from the knot. She dropped her arms and swiped at her face with both palms. "Thank you," she whispered.

Tears blurred my vision as I worked at the tacky gold straps. I couldn't ask what had happened. I couldn't ask if she was okay. I couldn't reassure her that it was all over now, and that she could still get several hours' sleep before dawn. I couldn't even get her some water from the fountain or one of the sinks, because I didn't have anything to put it in.

When I finally got the strap untied, Finola shrugged out of her top and shed the bikini bottom, then joined the other half-clean women in the shower, as they pumped handful after handful of soap and shampoo onto their palms from the dispensers bolted to the shower walls.

They needed loofahs or washcloths, but we were given neither.

While Finola showered, I searched for something with which to write, since I had no access to my voice. Soap from the dispenser provided little contrast on the floor, and hand sanitizer was utterly useless. But as I scanned our tiled environment, I noticed the strap of a bikini top caught on the edge of the laundry chute. I seized the material, but most of the paint coating it was more sticky than wet, so I had to dampen it under the faucet in one of the bathroom sinks.

By the time Finola came out of the shower, I'd written two questions in paint on the floor for her to see.

Are you okay?
What happened?

Simra's eyes widened when she saw the writing on the floor. "Huh. I never thought to try that. But she's not allowed to tell you what happened."

More frustrated than surprised by that revelation, I groaned, yet no sound came out.

Wait… If I could get around my collar's restrictions by writing, why couldn't she?

I held the damp bikini up to Finola and mimed writing with my index finger. But fresh tears welled in the siren's bright green eyes. "Delilah, I can't read."

Which meant she couldn't write either, and that was true for the vast majority of the menagerie's captives. It was probably also true among the Spectacle's prisoners. Except for Simra, who'd grown up in freedom south of the border.

I held the bikini out to the *marid*, silently asking for her help, but she only frowned. "I don't know what happened to her. I wasn't with her tonight. But she'll be fine." Simra glanced at Finola with a look that was part sympathy and part demand for the siren to buck up. "There's no other choice."

Finola insisted that she was okay and confirmed that her collar wouldn't allow her to talk about her engagement, then she helped me wash the gold paint off the floor with trembling hands.

Only after I'd tucked her into bed with both her blanket and my own draped over her to help her stop shivering, did I realize that there was a deeper significance to our inability to communicate—one that Rommily would have understood well. With our collars preventing me from speech entirely and her from revealing the details of her engagement, Finola had no outlet. She was alone with the trauma, cut off from her friends and honorary family by a brutal wall of silence.

And she would be, as long as she wore that collar.

Vandekamp's information embargo was far crueler to those who lacked basic education, however, the writing workaround gave me hope. I'd found a weak link in his electronic chain, and it couldn't be the only one.

The rest of my night was mostly sleepless, as my thoughts raced with the possibilities. What else had Vandekamp missed? How else had he underestimated us? How big of a blind spot had pride in his own technology given him?

When the sun came up hours later, I finally noticed an empty sleep mat and realized that only one of the two shifters who'd left with Finola and Simra had made it back to the dormitory.

Dear Barbara,

Our blessings continue to grow. Willem has been awarded a full scholarship to Colorado State to study cryptobiology. This Saturday, he will graduate as valedictorian of his high school class. We hope you'll be able to make it to the ceremony. It's been a while since we've seen you, and we would love to surround him with as much family as possible on this joyous occasion...

—from a 1992 letter by Judith Vandekamp to her estranged sister

DELILAH

I spent most of the next two days in front of one of the tall, narrow windows, staring out at fresh air I hadn't had a whiff of since my trip to Vandekamp's office on my first full day at the Spectacle.

Since we'd arrived, most of my friends had been assigned chore duties and several had been requested for engagements, but Rommily and I had remained stuck in the dorm. I recognized the brutal boredom and frustration from my weeks in a menagerie cage, but my captivity at the Spectacle came with all new problems.

I couldn't study many of the security procedures from the confines of the dormitory. Beyond that, an odd kind of survivor's guilt had turned every moment of my friends' mysterious engagements into a new kind of torture for me.

Each time one of them came back in the middle of the night, covered in bruises, cuts or bite marks, I felt as guilty for being spared the same abuse as I was frustrated by my inability to help them.

When lunch came on my third day at the Spectacle, Lala

brought over a tray for each of us and sat next to me by the window. The food was healthy but bland—a boiled egg, a slice of tasteless white bread, a handful of raw broccoli and half a boiled sweet potato—and I ate though I had no appetite, because I knew better than to let my body weaken along with my spirits.

I'd forced down most of my sweet potato, a tasteless trove of vitamins A and C, when motion from outside caught my eye. I looked up to see a windowless delivery truck emerging from the woods at the back of the compound on the very narrow gravel road our cattle cars had probably traveled. The truck bore the Spectacle's logo on the side, but had no other distinguishing characteristics.

The driver backed toward the dormitory, then he and another handler got out of the cab and headed for the rear of the truck. They were joined by Woodrow, who held a tranquilizer rifle, and Bowman, who used a key to unlock and unchain the cargo doors. With the other three handlers armed and ready, he opened the back of the truck and stepped to the side, as if he expected something within to explode all over him.

"What's going on?" Lala peered through the glass over my shoulder, and I realized that our fellow captives had gathered around the other narrow windows.

"I think we're getting new company."

When no angry cryptid burst from the back of the truck, Bowman said something I couldn't hear to his fellow handlers. The driver and passenger climbed into the cargo area. A couple of seconds later, a large pair of boots slid haltingly out of the truck, followed by a pair of thick male legs clothed in dirty, ripped orange scrubs.

The kind a human prisoner wears.

"No." My protest carried little volume, but Lala heard me. "What?"

I stood, and my lunch tray clattered to the floor, spilling chunks of egg and broccoli.

Outside, the orange pants were followed by a large orange shirt, which gathered beneath the new prisoner's broad torso as he was pushed out of the truck by the two men inside and pulled out by Woodrow and Bowman, who each had one of his legs. I knew who we were seeing long before familiar arms fell, thick fingers grazing the dirt. Before I saw the strong profile, strangely altered by an uncovered head.

"Gallagher," Lala whispered, and his name echoed in murmurs from across the room as the other former menagerie inmates came to the same realization. "What is he wearing?"

"It's a jail uniform." The conclusion brought with it an odd sense of relief. "They must have thought he was human." Because back at Metzger's, he'd broken the Spectacle employee's neck, rather than ripping his head off.

All four strong handlers struggled beneath Gallagher's limp weight, and his head sagged below his shoulders. His hair fell back from his face, revealing closed eyes, as well as several bruises and gashes.

I blinked back tears, my face and hands pressed to the glass, and when my eyes opened again Gallagher was wearing his traditional faded red cap, unglamoured, because he was unconscious.

That's how they figured it out.

As they turned to carry Gallagher into the building, I caught a better look at the side of his face. His left eye was purple and swollen. There was a deep gash in his chin, and both of his lips were split open and still dripping blood.

But Gallagher's hands bore no bruises or cuts that I could see. They'd beaten him while he was unconscious—I could think of no other reason he would fail to fight back.

The *furiae* stirred within me. My veins surged with fire,

lapping at the bounds of my temper like waves crashing over a levee wall. I spun to look up at one of the cameras. "Hey! Where are you taking him?"

The entire room went still around me. The murmur of conversation died and all heads turned my way. But I got no response from anyone on the other side of the camera feed. So I ran for the door.

"Delilah, no!" Mirela grabbed for my arm, and when she missed, Mahsa stepped into my path, leopard eyes wide with concern for my sanity.

I dodged her and kept going until I saw the red light flicker over the door and felt the first warning twinge of pain from my collar. I skidded to a stop on bare feet, then inched backward until the light stopped flickering and the pain disappeared. I was two feet from the door—the programmed limit of the sensor's range.

"Zyanya!" I called, and she stepped forward from the crowd that had gathered to watch what they seemed to think was my total mental collapse. "I'm going to open the door, and I need you to push me into the hall."

"But—"

"I have a theory." I stared right into her golden cheetah eyes. "I think it'll stop hurting once I'm exactly this far away from the door, on the other side. Which means if I'm willing to take the pain, I should be able to get out. And I'm willing."

Zyanya frowned. "What if you're wrong?"

"Then at least we'll know for sure."

Mirela took my arm. "Delilah, there's no one on the other side to pull you clear if you don't get far enough away on one push. The electrocution might just continue." She turned to the shifter before I could argue. "Zyanya, don't do this."

Zyanya hesitated, then nodded. "Sorry, Delilah. I'm not going to help you hurt yourself."

As frustrated as I was, I couldn't blame her. I'd have said the same thing if our positions were reversed.

"Fine," I said, and everyone looked relieved—until I lunged forward and kicked the door open, without bothering to turn the knob. Agony shot through my neck and down my spine, then blazed into all four of my limbs. Pain pooled in my fingers and toes and exploded behind my eyelids. The top of my head felt like it was about to blow open.

Mirela pulled me backward, and the relief was immediate.

The door was open. Mission accomplished.

"Thanks," I whispered as I struggled to catch my breath. Then I shouted into the hallway. "Hey! Where are you taking Gallagher? He needs to go to the infirmary, not intake!" Surely there was an infirmary.

I got no response, but the shuffle of feet as my roommates moved away from me said they fully expected me to draw a swift, harsh reaction from our captors.

"Okay, fine!" I shouted, staring up at the camera. "I get it. You're scared of him. So let me take care of him. Please!"

Again, I got no answer, and the desperate ring of my appeal cost me some of my confidence; they would hear that as clearly as I'd heard it. Time for a new tactic.

I took a deep breath and prepared to make a sacrifice. "Tell Vandekamp I'll give him what he wants!"

For a second, nothing happened. Then static crackled from a hidden speaker. "Step away from the door. You will not be warned again."

It wasn't the response I'd hoped for, but it was proof that a response could be provoked.

"And if I—"

Mirela pulled me away from the door. "We know what will happen if you don't. And if we're wrong about that, then it'll be something worse."

Before I could argue with her, a door squealed open from somewhere down the hall. Footsteps thumped toward us, and when Bowman and another handler appeared, I assumed they'd come to close the door.

Instead, Bowman pointed his remote at me and pressed a button. The red light over the door blinked, and though I couldn't see my own collar, I knew its light had blinked, as well.

"Step into the hall," he ordered.

I practically launched myself through the doorway, and I made no objection to the padded restraints he closed a little too tight. The handlers led me down the hall and out of the building without a word, and when we headed through the iron gate into the cryptid-themed topiary—now strung with soft white lights for some kind of event—I knew Vandekamp had gotten my message.

Minutes later, I stood in front of the boss in his inner office. The handlers closed the door on their way out, but did not uncuff me.

Vandekamp folded his hands on top of his desk blotter, and though he had to look up at me from his seat, I clearly held the position of least power, standing in front of two expensive guest chairs I wasn't allowed to use. "I hear you have a request."

"Yes." And I was honestly a little surprised that he was going to entertain it, considering the precedent that could set for captives who might want to bargain in the future. "Gallagher's hurt, and I want to help him."

"Tell me about Gallagher." The scar bisecting his lower lip stretched with each word.

"What about him?" I didn't want to give him anything he could use against either of us, but he had me over a barrel, and he knew it.

Vandekamp shrugged and stood. "We know he's *fear dearg*," he said, and my surprise must have shown. "He's the first I've seen in person, but I've studied the species." Yet he obviously hadn't recognized Gallagher's species initially. "But I want to know what he is to *you*."

"He's a friend."

Vandekamp's pale blue eyes narrowed as he rounded his desk. "That feels like an incomplete answer."

"He's a very good friend."

He watched me, clearly waiting for more, and when no more came, he crossed his arms over a neatly pressed dark blue button-down shirt. "You want to help your 'friend.' I want to know what you are. What's your species, Delilah?"

The answer was my only bargaining chip. "You're asking the wrong question. The tests aren't flawed. I truly am human. But I'm not *only* human."

Vandekamp leaned back against his desk. "Not possible. Even hybrids' blood tests have recognizable animal or cryptid hormones."

"I'm not a hybrid. I'm fully human. Plus."

"Plus what?"

"Plus an ideal. An abstraction."

His eyes narrowed. "Stop speaking in riddles, or I will silence you for a week."

"It isn't a riddle. I don't fully understand this myself." I shrugged, and my restraints caught on the back of my shirt. "But based on the legend and what I've pieced together from personal experience, I am an embodiment of wrathful justice. The concept of vengeance given physical form."

I left out the fact that Gallagher was the primary source of that information, because I didn't want Vandekamp torturing him for more details about me.

"Legend?" Vandekamp scowled. "I'm asking you for scientific facts, not bedtime stories, and if you can't provide them—"

"No one can. But if you listen, you might learn something, *Dr.* Vandekamp." I held my breath, expecting him to point his remote and make my existence dissolve into excruciating pain. "Please."

"You have one minute."

"Okay. The way it was explained to me is this. Sometimes, when mankind gets too big for its collective britches, the world—the pooled power of all existence—literally gives life to certain inalienable abstract truths, to remind us that mankind is not its own final authority. Powerful, uncompromisable concepts, like honesty and love and loss and pain and joy. Ideas that transcend human laws and authority, and that apply to every living creature."

"You're saying the universe brings these concepts to life?" He still sounded skeptical, but fascinated.

"Not the cosmos. But yes, the universe, in the sense of the collective of everything. Existence itself comes together to provide what the world is missing. It endows a select few people—regardless of species—with the essence of one of those truths. Some of them have names and have attained the status of legend over the millennia. Some of them do not and have not.

"I have been endowed with the essence of justice. Specifically, I'm supposed to right wrongs where society's laws and norms have failed. I am a *furiae.*"

"A *furiae*?" Comprehension raised Vandekamp's eyebrows. "Like from Greek mythology?"

"Yes. Though the concept actually predates Greek culture. As my test results indicate, biologically, I'm human. Becoming a *furiae* hasn't changed that. But I am driven by a force I can't always control to right injustice wherever I see it."

"So, when you feel that someone has been...wronged, you what? Sprout claws and punish people?"

I could practically hear the gears grinding in Vandekamp's head as his frustration gave way to consideration. He'd achieved financial and technological success—however barbaric—not by whining about conditions that didn't suit him, but by twisting those conditions until they did suit him. And I could tell from the bright new gleam in his pale blue eyes that he was already trying to figure out how to twist the honorable nature of my gift to benefit his abominable business model.

"Sort of. But I can't control what form that punishment takes." At least not that I knew of. "And even if you could figure out how to electrocute me every time the *furiae* tries to show herself, I'm not sure that would prevent anything. Hurting me won't necessarily hurt her. Or stop her."

The *furiae* wouldn't care how much pain I was in, as long as she met her goal.

Vandekamp's brows rose. "You're saying there's no way I can stop this *furiae* from acting on any injustice she sees?"

"That's my theory, yes." Although cuffing my hands behind my back was a good start. Not that I would tell him that. Or the fact that I couldn't avenge myself.

"So, if I were to send you to Gallagher, you'd be compelled to avenge what was done to him?"

"*If* you were to send me to Gallagher?" Anger flared in my chest. "That was the deal."

"We came to no deal." Vandekamp stood, and I had to look up at him. "We each stated a desire, and you obliged mine, but I made no promise to return the favor."

"You better hope you don't need anything from me in the future." I spoke through gritted teeth.

"Whatever I want from you, I will take." His declaration

carried no emotion; it was a simple statement of fact. "I *own* you."

"But I'm human." *No* sentient being ought to be property, but because of my species, I truly wasn't, legally.

"Several hundred people have seen you become a monster. No one's going to believe a blood test over their own eyes. I'm not entirely sure I do." Before I could object, he pressed a button on his telephone dock.

"Yes, Mr. Vandekamp?" the secretary in the outer office replied.

"Send the handlers back in."

"You will regret this," I said as the door opened, but my voice held none of the *furiae*'s rich depth.

"I assure you I won't." Vandekamp looked past me to Bowman and the other handler, whose presence I could feel behind me. "Take her back."

One of them grabbed my arm.

"Wait!"

Bowman pulled me out of the room, and when I refused to walk, he and the other handler each lifted me by one arm and hauled me out of the main building, then through the topiary and the iron gate. In the housing building, they removed my cuffs, then threw me into my dormitory, where I landed with a bruising thud on one hip.

Bowman adjusted the settings on my collar to keep me in the room, then he slammed the door.

"What happened?" Mirela demanded as soon as they were gone. "Did you see Gallagher?"

"No. Vandekamp can't be trusted, no matter what he promises." I glanced around at the crowd of former Metzger's captives and the long-term residents alike, most of whom seemed to think I was stating the obvious. "Don't make any deals with him."

If I hadn't been desperate, I never would have tried.

I would not make that mistake again.

WILLEM

The lanterns hanging from gazebos and trellises left spots in Willem Vandekamp's vision as he crossed the topiary garden, and the string quartet was already giving him a headache. But he had to admit it, Tabitha knew how to throw a party.

She wore strapless white silk tonight, and in it, she looked every bit as fresh and young as she had the day they'd met, even with the snowy, feathered mask hiding the top half of her face.

"What do you think of the new painter?" she whispered, as Willem slid his arm around the gathered waist of her gown. "I think she's worth every cent."

"Which ones are hers?" He glanced around the Savage Spectacle's monthly masquerade, noting a familiar mask here and a distinctive chin there as he took inventory of the regulars among the incognito guests.

"The leopard. And the Egyptian goddess. And the snake... girl."

"She's an echidna." His gaze snagged on the cryptid in question. In human form, her most prominent tells were her diminutive fangs and her eyes—coppery, with vertically oriented oval pupils. But thanks to Tabitha's latest hire, the echidna now sported hand-painted scales down her spine and the backs of both of her legs in a luminous python-like gold. Which didn't resemble her natural coloring in the least.

As usual, Tabitha was more concerned with the aesthetics of her projects than the accuracy of them. And as usual, she'd made the right call.

"Gorgeous." Willem pulled her close to murmur against the back of her jaw, just beneath her ear. "The governor and her guest seem to agree."

The governor, a small woman in red sequins, was recognizable in spite of her nondescript black mask by her petite stature and her ubiquitous French twist. And—for those who knew her—by the covetous way she ran one hand down the echidna's back when the cryptid turned to offer a tray of hors d'oeuvres to another guest.

The governor's companion also wore a mask, but she would have had to wear much more than that to pass as the First Gentleman of the state.

"How long before we can engage the rest of the new additions?" Tabitha asked. "It's time they earned their keep."

"Any that don't need costumes can be used immediately. Just like her." He nodded at the leopard shifter as she carried a fresh tray of champagne from the outdoor bar set up on the fringes of the party. "Except for Delilah."

"But I thought—" Tabitha swallowed the rest of her sentence as a pair of guests approached the host couple.

The man wore a laser-cut mask inlaid with jade and copper in a harlequin diamond design. "Beautiful evening," he said, smoothing down the front of an elegantly cut dark gray suit jacket, buttoned over a tie that matched his mask.

"It's even more beautiful now." Willem offered his hand to

the man's wife, a curvy woman in jade satin with a neckline that plunged nearly to her navel.

She smiled beneath a simple black feathered mask and gave him her hand.

"How are you enjoying the party?" Tabitha asked, as the man's gaze trailed down her dress, then finally wandered back up.

"It's splendid, as always," the man said.

"Really lovely," his wife agreed.

"I'm so glad." Tabitha smiled and ran one hand up her husband's arm. "Will you be booking an extended engagement this evening?"

"We will, and we've made our selection. Dear?" The husband turned to his wife.

"That one," the woman said, pointing with one finger at a young naiad as she emerged, naked and dripping, from the fountain at the center of the garden. "We'll take her. For the rest of the evening."

"Wonderful choice." Tabitha let go of her husband's arm and took a step back. "Come this way, and I'll get that set up for you."

Willem watched his wife as she escorted the couple toward one of the event coordinators standing on the edge of the party, electronic tablets in hand. She returned minutes later, as the coordinator led the customers toward the main building, tapping on her tablet and chatting with them as they left the party, to make sure they understood the options and limitations their private event would include.

"That was the candy couple?"

Willem chucked. "Their corporation owns the companies that produce nearly every candy bar you've ever eaten."

"Well, they better not be paying in chocolate coins." Tabitha returned a nod from a guest in a maroon suit and a *Phantom of the Opera*–style mask studded with matching red rhinestones, then she snuggled closer to her husband. "Tell me again who the man in the silver suit is?" Tabitha's gaze settled on the man in question, standing off from the rest of the guests. "The one in the silver-and-black gladiator mask?"

"Senator Aaron," Willem whispered. "Chairman of the Cryptid Regulation Committee. I've been inviting him for months, but this is the first time he's come."

"A senator. So this is about influence, not money, right?"

Willem gave his wife a private frown, but Tabitha only shrugged her bare, shapely shoulders.

"You said most politicians can't afford our services," she reminded him.

"Yes, but that's a generalization, and a crass frame of mind." *Though accurate, in this instance.* A strong champion in the senate would enable Willem's containment collars to move beyond the current small-scale beta-testing phase. "If you think like that, it'll inevitably show in your bearing," he scolded gently. "So just be your usual charming self, and I'm sure he'll be eating out of our hands."

"I think he's more interested in a different set of hands." She nodded subtly at the masked senator as he accepted a flute of champagne from a slim cryptid who had been meticulously painted with leopard rosettes across her exposed breasts, limbs, and the sides of her torso, leaving her navel undisguised. Her bikini bottom had been decorated to match the rest of her, but she wore significantly more paint than material. "I assume any services he requests are on the house?"

Willem nodded. "For tonight, at least. Let's give him a taste of the possibilities and hope he develops an appetite."

A man with a secret is useful, Willem's father used to say. *But a powerful man with a secret is indispensable.*

DELILAH

"Mirela," I said as the oracle stepped into the line behind me. We'd stacked the sleeping mats and folded the blankets, which put us near the back of the bathroom queue. "Were you awake when they got back?" I nodded toward Lenore and Mahsa, who were several spots ahead of us in line.

"Yeah. You?"

I nodded. "Who could sleep?" We shuffled forward a couple of feet, and I rubbed my temples, as if that would actually fend off my day-old headache.

"Did they say anything?" Mirela whispered, staring at the siren's back.

"No, but I haven't asked." It killed me to see our friends taken out of the dorm night after night, knowing they were headed for humiliation and abuse, and that there was nothing I could do to stop it. "I assume they're bound by the same gag order that crippled Finola and the others."

Mahsa turned to us with a small, cryptic smile, showing off her feline incisors. "We are," she said. I should have realized she'd hear us—shifters have great ears no matter what form they take. "And that's a real shame, considering how much trouble I had brushing blood and tiny chunks of human flesh from my teeth when we got back."

My eyes widened. "You bit someone?"

The shifter shrugged. "I can't answer that. But what I can tell you is that—hypothetically—if one of these collars is set to let a shifter shift, it might not be able to stop that shifter from biting."

"Mahsa, you're brilliant!" I seized her hand and gave it a tight squeeze. Hypotheticals were a very clever work-around for Vandekamp's standard gag order!

She shrugged, but her face practically glowed with pride.

"But why would they let you shift in the first place?" Mirela asked.

"It's usually more of a requirement than an allowance." Simra spoke up from behind us. She was the last in line. "Some of the clients just want to look. Some want to touch. Others want to see ladies with nonhuman parts dressed up in six-inch heels, holding trays of fancy food. Some like to see shifters shift. Whatever the client wants, he makes us do."

"He can *make* shifters shift?" Horror surged through me like ice in my veins, chilling me from the inside.

Simra shrugged. "He can make anyone do anything."

My mind spun with the horrific implications. Was she saying that he would simply shock those who refused to perform? Or that Vandekamp's collars could trigger the release of hormones that led to the performance he wanted to see?

That was it. Understanding slid into place in my head with an ominous, nearly audible *click*.

That's why he'd been so desperate to find out what I was—so he could make me transform.

Vandekamp had figured out how to effectively disarm cryptids of their distinguishing traits and abilities, while retaining the ability to draw out those same traits and abilities on demand. On display. For money.

He had created push-and-play functionality in his living captives, with a built-in punishment for failure to perform.

"I thought you weren't allowed to talk about that," Mirela said.

Simra shrugged. "I'm not allowed to talk about *my* engagements."

Because I was still reeling from her previous revelation, it took me a second to realize she'd just revealed another gap in Vandekamp's security system. A *big* one. "Thank you!" I seized the *marid*'s hand and squeezed it.

Simra looked puzzled. "Why does that make you so happy?"

I hadn't even realized I was smiling. "Because Vandekamp denies us information and communication to isolate us, even from each other. To keep us weak, scared and dependent. Every single thing we learn that he doesn't want us to know is a victory. It's a crack driven through the chains keeping us here. And you only have to break one link to destroy a chain."

Simra frowned, her fingers grazing the front of her collar. "Is that what you're doing? Trying to break the chains?"

I had to think about that. I hadn't been consciously planning an escape. Where would we go, even if we could break free?

"That's what she does," Zyanya said softly, passing by us on her way from the bathroom. "That's all she knows how to do."

"I'm just keeping my eyes and ears open," I insisted. I had no concrete plans—no real ideas—and I didn't want to get anyone's hopes up.

The *marid*'s eyes sparkled even more than usual. "Yeah. Me too."

Mirela frowned at Simra as she stepped into the bathroom just ahead of us. "You've been here almost a year, and you're just now figuring out you can speak in generalizations?"

"It never occurred to me to try, before. I mean, talking typically hurts, so…" The *marid* shrugged.

"So you all just stopped trying," I finished for her.

Simra nodded. "Yeah, I guess so."

"But none of that answers my question," Mirela said. "Why would Vandekamp let—or make—Mahsa shift if he knew that would also allow her to bite?"

"He didn't know." I shuffled forward in the line again, and the closer we got to the bathroom, the better we could hear water running in the sink. "His long-term captives quit trying to fight back, so he had no true gauge of the limits of his technology. It's trial and error." Because Vandekamp wasn't just trying to exert control over us. He was still testing his technology. He had to be, if it had been implemented so recently. "Now that he knows about the weakness, he'll fix it." I tuned back to Mahsa. "Were you punished for biting?"

Mahsa flinched and stiffened for a moment, and I realized that trying to answer had triggered pain from her collar. Then her eyes brightened with a new idea. She twisted and lifted her scrub top to show me a fresh, oblong bruise slanting across her rib cage.

"That's from a baton," Simra said. "But if that's all they did, there must not have been any complaint from the customer."

"No complaint?" Mirela echoed as I finally stepped into the bathroom. "But she took a bite out of him."

Simra shrugged. "Some of the customers like that. They seem to think the scar makes them look tough."

"Sick fuckers," Lenore said, as she stepped up to one of the available sinks.

"Yeah, and that's the one thing the Spectacle won't give them. We're not allowed to hurt them, no matter what they want."

"It's probably a legal liability," I explained, as more of

Vandekamp's business model began to fall into place in my head. "They may think they want pain—and some of them truly may—but most will change their minds when the reality sinks in. Others will go home to husbands and wives who have objections. A single lawsuit could put the Savage Spectacle out of business." And cripple any future endeavors.

"We should be so lucky." Light shone brightly on Mahsa's pale brown skin as she stepped up to the sink beside Lenore. "I bet—" But the shifter's words were cut off by a piercing scream from the other side of a row of toilet stalls.

"Rommily!" Mirela took off toward the showers. Lala and I raced after her to find Rommily still screaming in front of the communal shower block, where water already poured from one of the heads. Her eyes were wide with panic. A handler loomed over her, pointing into the shower with one hand, holding a handful of her shirt in the other. According to the embroidery over his heart, his name was Sutton.

"It's been five days!" he shouted. "If you're not willing to meet the minimum hygiene standard, I'll meet it for you."

"Wait! She just needs—" Mirela reached for her sister, but the guard turned to block her, his forehead furrowed, eyes narrowed, and too late, I realized he'd mistaken her gesture as an act of aggression. He let go of Rommily, then shoved the butt of his rifle at Mirela's head.

A spray of blood burst from her nose and she fell backward, clutching her face with both hands.

Eyes full of tears, Lala pulled Mirela across the floor, away from their middle sister and the guard. She grabbed a handful of brown paper towels from a dispenser on the wall and held them to her older sister's nose.

Sutton turned back to Rommily and tried to pull her shirt over her head without losing control of his tranquilizer rifle. When the material ripped, her screaming intensified. But then he grabbed her exposed shoulder, and the oracle fell eerily still and quiet. Her eyes glazed over with a white film so thick that her irises and pupils were hardly visible beneath.

"Sepsis." Rommily's voice sounded strangely hollow and detached. As if it belonged to someone else. "Our staff didn't find the bedsore until it was too late. What a tragic way for a young man to die."

The handler blinked at her, and though he couldn't possibly have realized he was hearing what a doctor would someday say to his loved ones, her words triggered an instinctive, violent fear in him. "Shut the fuck up and get in the shower." He pulled at the tear he'd already started in her shirt and ripped the material wide-open.

Rommily's eyes cleared and she screamed again, a terrified shrieking that bounced back at us all from the tiled walls.

Sutton flinched, then punched her in the side of the head. Rommily slammed into the shower wall with a thud. Her mouth snapped shut as she slid down the tile to sit in a puddle on the floor, still half-clothed, her gaze out of focus.

But as her cry died, a fiery howl of fury kindled inside me. My vision sharpened until I could see light bouncing off individual drops of water rolling down the shower wall. My hair rose from my shoulders and slowly writhed around my head. My nails hardened and lengthened into the needle-thin claws of a creature no lab test had ever been able to identify.

I crossed the white tile floor silently, aware only of the wrathful need pulsing through me. As Sutton reached for Rommily, cursing the spray of water from the tap, my hands were pulled toward his head, my claws eager to sink into his temples. But then he turned, and my hand landed on the side of his neck instead.

My claws found no flesh, but his skin burned beneath mine.

Sutton froze. His arms fell limp at his sides, then began to tremble. His teeth chattered.

Pick on someone your own size, the *furiae* within me mumbled, as I obliged her vengeful demands. *Someone* exactly *your size...*

When the fire inside me began to abate, I removed my hand from the handler's neck. My claws were gone. My hair had settled over my shoulders.

Someone gasped behind me. Where I'd touched Sutton's bare flesh, there now appeared a red imprint in the shape of my hand, with a pinpoint of red at the tip of each finger, where my claws had rested but had not broken through.

As I stared, Sutton curled his right hand into a fist and launched it at his own nose.

I flinched and stepped back, but the handler threw another punch at himself, then another and another, without complaint or any sign of hesitation. He grunted with the violence of each blow. His nose crunched and spurted blood. His cheek split open and showed gory strands of muscle.

The crowd at my back inched closer. I could feel their bewilderment, but it was the murmured buzz of relief—a quiet celebration of justice—that sent a peaceful thread of contentment through me as I watched the *furiae*'s handiwork.

In seconds, Sutton's face was ruined. Bone showed through in several places, and his eyes were both swelling shut. His lips were split and he'd chipped several of his own teeth with his elaborate wedding band. Yet the punching did not stop.

"What's happening?" Simra whispered from behind me, but I was too fascinated by the bloody spectacle to answer her.

"Delilah made him pay. That's what she—" Zyanya's answer ended in an agonized scream, but before I could turn, fire shot through my neck and down my spine. Agony raced down my arms and legs with a clinical precision that could only have come from the cruel shock collar.

A chorus of screams rose in echo of my pain, as behind me, my dormmates were each crippled by an electric current of their own.

My legs folded and I collapsed, immobilized on my left side on the cold floor as fire shot through me over and over. The others lay spread out around me on the tile, several frozen in the threshold, unable to vocalize more than a whimper of pain. Terrified and in agony, I rolled my eyes to look through the doorway and saw that everyone still in the dorm had collapsed as well, and several were seizing from the force of the electricity being pumped through them.

My lungs burned with every rapid breath I sucked in. My heart raced and my vision swam.

The dormitory door opened with a familiar squeal, and a dozen handlers burst into the room. One of them clicked something on his remote, and the pain ended. I exhaled, blissfully numb for a second. But when I tried to sit up, my body would not respond to the order from my brain. The paralysis had not ended. We all lay frozen and helpless on the floor.

And through it all, I heard the repetitive thunk of flesh on flesh as Sutton continued to punch his own ruined face.

"What the *fuck*?" Woodrow demanded, pushing his way into the bathroom while his men aimed tranquilizer rifles at the cryptids they considered most dangerous, just in case.

Three of the guns were aimed at me.

Woodrow stepped over several prone forms, and on the edge of my vision, he grabbed Sutton's arm, to end the self-inflicted violence. "Sutton! Stop it!" The gamekeeper had to hold back the handler's bloody fist with both hands, visibly struggling to control him. "Cuffs!" he shouted to his other men, and two of them lowered the rifles they were aiming at me and helped cuff their coworker to protect him from himself.

Neither of them even glanced at Rommily, who lay in the shower, immobilized, with water pouring over her torn clothing. Or at Mirela, whose ruined nose was still dribbling blood on the tile floor.

"What's that on his neck?" one of the men asked.

Woodrow pulled down the collar of Sutton's shirt and studied the fresh red mark. "It's a handprint. Right where she touched him." The gamekeeper turned to me, and I realized he'd seen the whole thing. Either the camera in the dormitory could see into the bathroom, or there was one hidden in the bathroom, as well. "Cuff her and throw her in a cell. Keep her paralyzed until the door's locked."

Two of the handlers rolled me onto my stomach, and though I couldn't move, one pressed his knee into my back. My lungs could not expand beneath his weight. Panic made my head spin, and pinpoints of light floated across my vision. When the weight was finally lifted, I gasped for air, but the sound was eerily hollow without the use of my vocal cords.

Woodrow turned to the man who'd cuffed Sutton. "Take him to the infirmary, but don't take the cuffs off. I'll radio the boss." Then he marched out of the room.

The handlers who'd cuffed me picked me up by my arms and carried me through the dormitory and into the hall. Still frozen on the floor, my friends could only watch, mute, as I was hauled away.

I'd been in the small concrete cell for no more than an hour when the lock clicked. I looked up from where I sat on the floor as Woodrow opened the door, but he stayed in the hall, out of my reach, even though I was still cuffed. "Are you going to behave, or do we need to paralyze you again?" He held up his remote for emphasis.

"As long as you don't try to beat up any defenseless women, we should be just fine."

"Get up."

I stood, which wasn't easy with my hands bound at my back. Woodrow took my arm in a tight grip. "How are Rommily and Mirela?" I asked as he marched me out of the building and through the iron gate for my third trip to the boss's office in my first week at the Savage Spectacle.

Woodrow remained silent all the way across the grounds and into the main building.

Both Vandekamp and his wife were waiting for me in his office. They stood as soon as the door opened.

"What did you do to Sutton?" Vandekamp demanded before the gamekeeper could even close the door.

I shrugged. "You can't stop justice with a collar. I warned you."

"Justice?" Tabitha Vandekamp demanded. "He knocked out four of his own teeth and exposed his skull in three places. They had to sedate him to keep him from killing himself in the ambulance."

I tried to look unaffected by the gory details, but now that the whole thing had passed, knowing that I was the conduit for such violence made me uncomfortable, even though Sutton deserved what he'd gotten.

"How long will he be like that?" Vandekamp demanded.

"I don't know." I was as interested as they were in finding out how long their man would suffer self-destructive urges. But they would probably never tell me.

"How long will the handprint last?" his wife asked.

"I don't know. That's never happened before."

Vandekamp's gaze narrowed on me. "Then why did it happen now?"

Another shrug. "I can only assume I'm growing into my potential."

"Willem." His name sounded like a weapon, the way his wife wielded it, and I realized she was continuing some conversation I hadn't heard the start of.

"She's not a surrogate, Tabitha," he insisted. "Surrogates didn't leave marks on anyone."

No, they'd brainwashed thousands of parents into killing their own children. At least, as near as anyone had been able to piece the whole thing together.

"Whatever she is, she can't perform on demand and you can't control her. What's to stop her from making the handlers kill one another, then us?" Tabitha demanded.

"Ma'am, that wouldn't—" Woodrow began, but she cut him off.

"You don't know anything about her. That's the problem." She turned to her husband again. "She's dangerous. Put a bullet in her head."

"They're right." I had to fight past the lump of terror in my throat to be heard. "I couldn't turn someone into a murderer even if I wanted to. That's not how justice works. The *furiae* rights wrongs. She doesn't make new ones."

Mrs. Vandekamp's jaw clenched. "Take her back to isolation," she ordered Woodrow.

"No," Vandekamp said, before the gamekeeper could do more than grab my arm. "Take her to the dorm. She'll be serving tonight."

"Serving?" I glanced from face to face, but no one even acknowledged that I'd spoken.

Woodrow frowned. "Sir, are you sure that's a good—"

The look Vandekamp gave him could have withered an oak tree. "They're expecting her in costuming and makeup at three, with the others." His gaze narrowed on me. "Many of our beasts aren't safe to touch, and we're prepared to deal with that possibility for you. Until further notice, I'm instructing my men to treat any problem from you as an emergency. At the first sign of trouble, you will be paralyzed, then handled with gloves and a snare—a cable loop on an aluminum pole, like dogcatchers use. Should that become necessary, you can forget about ever speaking to Gallagher again."

As I was hauled into the outer office, Mrs. Vandekamp turned a fiercely angry look on her husband. "Willem—"

"We paid good money for her. I'm not going to euthanize her until I *know* she can't be used."

"Then sell her. Get your money back."

"You know exactly why we can't sell—"

And as Woodrow closed the door behind me, I realized I too knew why the Vandekamps couldn't sell me. Or likely any of the other captives they'd ever taken.

The Savage Spectacle's business model wasn't entirely legal. If he sold me, I'd be free of the limits of my collar and might tell my next owner exactly what was going on in the well-kept open secret that was the Spectacle. Old man Metzger had obviously been willing to keep private dealings private, in exchange for the rental fee he charged for his off-season acts, but most others would not be. Vandekamp's world could come crumbling down around him.

The obvious conclusion settled over me with a fresh jolt of fear.

None of us were ever going to leave the Savage Spectacle.

DELILAH

Woodrow adjusted my collar to lock me in the dormitory, then pushed the door closed in my face.

The long-term residents of the Spectacle stared at me as I crossed the room to sit on the floor by one of the windows. I couldn't make out much of what they were whispering, but the distance they kept from me was telling. However fascinated they might have been by my ability and the vengeful form it had taken, I had caused them all a lot of pain.

I would have avoided me too.

Mirela and Rommily weren't in the dorm. Nalah sat against one wall, shooting rage-filled looks my way. Zyanya and Mahsa were busy comforting Lala, and I decided to give them some distance.

Lunch came shortly after I arrived, and as soon as I sat with my tray of raw spinach, bread and a chicken thigh, Simra settled onto the floor next to me.

"Zyanya said you're a *furiae*. What does that mean, exactly?" she asked, pushing strands of fine, silvery hair back from her pale face.

"Basically, I'm possessed by the spirit of vengeance."

"Possessed?"

"That's what it feels like." I bit a chunk from my chicken thigh, then began stripping the meat from the bone.

"But you really are human?"

"I really, really am. Not that it matters." Not that it *should* matter. Deciding who should be free and who should be locked up based on chromosomal features made no more sense than basing that decision on eye color.

Simra plucked a leaf of spinach from her tray and stared at the tiny green veins on the back side. "What did you do to that guard?"

I arranged my chicken and spinach on my slice of bread and folded it over to form half a sandwich. "I just made Sutton want to do to himself what he'd done to Mirela and Rommily. I like to think of it as poetic justice." Though I had little control over what form that justice took.

Simra seemed to think about that while I took a bite of my makeshift sandwich. But I had little appetite.

As I pushed my tray away, the dormitory door opened, and one of the handlers shoved Magnolia inside. She stumbled and fell to her knees, and her face was shielded by a curtain of her fallen-leaf-colored hair, threaded through with thin woody vines. The handler aimed his remote at her, and both the sensor over the door and the one in her collar blinked red.

Magnolia didn't even look up.

I frowned, studying the dryad. She looked different from when they'd taken her the afternoon before, but I couldn't...

Her hair. She'd had several beautiful whitish blooms blossoming in her hair.

Now those blossoms were gone.

One of the other ladies knelt next to her and laid a hand on Magnolia's shoulder, but the nymph turned on her, teeth gnashing. Mossy-green eyes flashed beneath the tiny woody tendrils growing in place of her eyelashes.

"Oh…" Simra breathed, and I turned to her with a questioning look. "They got rid of it."

"It?"

"The baby."

"She was pregnant?" I whispered, horrified. "Vandekamp ended it?"

"His wife. She won't let the 'monsters' breed."

The only thing I could imagine worse than being forced to end the pregnancy was how Magnolia might have gotten pregnant in the first place.

The handlers called my name a couple of hours after lunch, and along with two of the long-term captives, they also called Zyanya and Lenore. That choice was not random. Vandekamp had selected women he knew I would want to protect.

The shifter and the siren were living threats, intended to keep me in line.

The five of us were marched down a series of hallways into a bright, cold room equipped with six salon-style chairs, several racks of skimpy clothing, an entire arsenal of makeup and three women in khaki pants, collared shirts and pink aprons bearing the Savage Spectacle's silver logo.

The ambient scents were a confusion of perfume, hair spray, lotion and various cosmetic pastes, glosses and powders. And glue.

We were each seated in one of the chairs, but were neither handcuffed nor shackled. Instead, our collars were programmed to paralyze us for the duration of the makeup session. Which took hours.

The "artists" moved us into whatever position their work required, posing us like dolls as they drew on our faces. As they curled, pinned and sprayed our hair. There were no mirrors in the room, because it didn't matter what we thought of their efforts, so while I could see some of what was being done to my fellow captives, I couldn't really tell what was being done to me. Except for the heavy false eyelashes. Those were impossible to miss.

The artists chatted as they worked, asking for opinions and offering suggestions as they discussed their families and social lives. It took most of my concentration to keep tears at bay as I listened to them discuss the very things I'd lost, while I sat there locked out of my own body, one step away from being rented out by the hour.

When my makeup was finished, the artist fitted me with a black lace masquerade mask, which fastened beneath the mass of dark curls she'd created. The mask was small enough to display the ridiculous lashes and whatever else she'd done to my face. I felt as if I were wearing several pounds of primer, foundation, glitter and whatever art had been drawn onto my temples and cheeks.

The other two artists finished with their living palettes early and moved on to the two remaining captives while my extensive makeover was completed. When they were finished, the makeup artists headed out for a coffee break, leaving us immobilized in our chairs, staring at a blank wall.

For a long time, we sat there like corpses, imprisoned in our own minds, and I wouldn't have known the handlers were still stationed against the wall behind us if I hadn't heard them breathing.

I couldn't ask the other captives if the wait was normal. I couldn't even turn to look at them. I could do nothing more than swallow the saliva gathering at the back of my throat, and try not to let the itch inside my left ear drive me out of my mind.

Finally, the hair and makeup ladies returned, smelling of coffee, and they solved the mystery of how we were supposed to get dressed without messing up their work.

We weren't.

The handlers pulled us to our feet, and we could only stand there, immobilized, while the makeup artists stripped us down to bare skin, then stood back to assess the as yet unpainted portions of their canvases.

My face flamed. The indignity was a familiar one, but no less infuriating than it had ever been, and the knowledge that an audience of handlers stood behind me made my flesh crawl.

After they'd taken stock, the artists rubbed thick, glittering lotions and oils into our skin, then dressed us in skimpy costumes that didn't have to go over our heads or slide over our sparkling limbs.

Zyanya's costume was a cheetah-print bikini top with a micro skirt, slit up both sides, all the way to the waistband. Lenore got a skimpy, asymmetrical gold dress that wrapped over one shoulder and draped—barely—over her breasts before falling to midthigh. Her artist tied a matching sash at her waist, then helped her into a pair of gold gladiator sandals that laced up to the top of her calves.

The others were both in variations of generically sexy scraps of cloth draped over strategic parts of their flesh, and everyone but me was decked out in bright colors and extravagant fabrics.

But just like in the menagerie, I wore all black. I was also the only one in a masquerade mask, presumably to help disguise the fact that I had no telltale cryptid features to highlight.

Like Zyanya, I was given no shoes.

Once we were dressed and touched up, our handlers readjusted the settings on our collars and marched us through the topiary zoo into a large kitchen at the back of the main building, where a chef and his staff were putting the finishing touches on hundreds of bite-size appetizers.

The scent of food I would probably never taste made my mouth water.

Bottles of champagne stood chilling in a wall-sized glass refrigerator, along with bottles of white wine. Bottles of red were lined up on a countertop behind several rows of champagne flutes and stemmed wineglasses waiting to be filled.

A man in a formal server's uniform, complete with a silver vest and bow tie, took us aside for an "engagement briefing." The tag pinned to his vest read Event Coordinator.

"This bachelor party is as simple as it gets." The coordinator avoided eye contact as he spoke. "The groom is Michael Hayes, who has some curiosities he'd like satisfied, but the client is James Lansing. His is the credit card on file, so he's your boss for the night."

The coordinator glanced at his clipboard. "Lenore…" His gaze finally landed on the siren, whom he clearly recognized. She'd already been "engaged" for two events since we'd been sold to the Spectacle, and rumor among the captives said that putting her onstage added several thousand dollars to the bill. "Lenore, you're the entertainment." He pulled a familiar remote from his pocket and pressed a button which pulled up a series of options on a screen I only got a glance at. "I've set your collar to allow *minor* influence in your voice. Make them feel good. Lower their inhibitions and help them enjoy themselves. Encourage them to spend. But if you try anything malicious, you'll spend the night in the infirmary."

Thoughts chased each other through my head in a dizzying funnel of possibility as I tried to take in everything I was seeing and hearing at once.

If they could truly limit Lenore to "minor" vocal influence, why would they need to warn her not to take things too far?

And if we were to be allowed in and out of the kitchen, would we have access to knives, meat mallets and other potential weapons? Would having weapons even matter, if we could be paralyzed with the press of a button?

Even if I could disable a guard and take his remote, at best I'd have seconds to figure out how to work it. And if I somehow managed to escape not just the room, but the building, then the grounds, I'd be abandoning everyone I cared about in the entire world. I'd have no other choice.

Would escape be worth an on-the-run existence that would only last for however long it took them to track my collar? Which I had no idea how to remove.

Would my friends be punished for my escape?

The coordinator glanced at his clipboard again, and the movement refocused my attention. "Mr. Lansing has requested the 'hypnotist' package, so about halfway through the evening, Lenore will pick a couple of volunteers from the party and bring them up onstage. The crowd will shout out things they want to see their friends do, and she will make it happen." He turned directly to her for the next part. "Just whisper in their ears and do your thing. Most of the requests are stupid, and they've put down a huge security deposit, so it doesn't really matter what they mess up. As for the rest of you…"

The coordinator turned to those of us who wouldn't be singing, and I got the impression that the instructions were specifically aimed at Zyanya and me, because the others had presumably done this many times. "You'll be carrying trays of champagne and hors d'oeuvres. No one expects you to be good at it, and we have professional servers who'll make sure everyone's fed and liquored up. All you really have to do is balance your tray and look exotic. Stay in the center of things. Make sure all your freaky features are visible. They're going to want to see claws and teeth. They'll want to touch feathers and scales. Let them. There will be security all over the place, and if the customers try to get more than they've paid for, the handlers will take care of it."

More than they've paid for. My skin crawled at the thought.

The coordinator gave us a quick lecture on the Savage Spectacle's serving procedures and showed us how to balance a semifull tray with one hand. Then he made us practice with trays of water-filled plastic stemmed glasses. I sloshed three times in a span of five minutes—even in my normal human life, I'd never waited tables—which got me demoted to hors d'oeuvres, along with Zyanya, because those were harder to spill.

While we practiced, the professional servers came in and out of a set of swinging doors on the left every few minutes as they set things up in the next room.

An identical set of doors on the opposite side of the kitchen presumably led to another room on our right, but nothing was going on in there.

About an hour after our engagement briefing, the coordinator disappeared into the party room and the quiet buzz of activity in the kitchen became a tense bustle. Music poured from the other side of the swinging doors. I glanced at the huge clock high on one wall and saw that it was five minutes until 9:00 p.m. The party was about to start.

A minute later, the swinging door opened again, and this time a man in dark slacks and a green button-down shirt followed the coordinator into the kitchen. His gaze slid over thousands of dollars' worth of top-shelf alcohol and gourmet appetizers as if they were everyday fare, and I realized that he was not a Spectacle employee.

"Mr. Lansing, these are the cryptids we've prepared for your party. We have Belinda, an echidna, and a female werewolf named Clarisse." The coordinator gestured to the first women in our row.

"Echidna? Isn't that a snake woman?" Lansing lifted Belinda's chin as he studied the painted scales trailing down both sides of her face. "Where's her tail?"

"She doesn't have one in this form."

"But she'll shift later?"

The coordinator nodded. "If that's what you'd like."

Lansing grunted. "The freakier the better. What are these two?"

"Zyanya is a cheetah shifter. Notice her eyes and her teeth." The coordinator grabbed her chin and tilted her head up. "She's a gorgeous specimen."

Lansing's gaze lingered on Zyanya long enough to make me nervous.

"And her?" The client stopped in front of me. "Is this the siren?"

"No, Lenore is our siren, and she's ready to lend a unique aura to your party." The pair of men moved past me.

"I look forward to hearing her," Lansing said. "Are we ready to go?"

"Yes. Let's go show your guests in." The coordinator escorted Lansing out of the kitchen.

Minutes later, voices rang out from behind the swinging doors. The guests had arrived, and they sounded as excited as I was horrified.

The coordinator stepped back into the kitchen and glanced at each of us in turn, evidently looking for flaws in the presentation. "Everybody ready?"

No one answered.

"You four each take a tray, and Lenore, you'll follow them into the room, then head for the stage. They're all set up for you." When no one moved, he waved his arm impatiently. "Let's go!"

We picked up our loaded trays and the coordinator pushed open one of the swinging doors and held it back with his body.

"Gentlemen, welcome to the Savage Spectacle!" he called out as we entered the room. "Where your most exotic desire is our pleasure to provide!"

I wanted nothing more than to crawl back into my menagerie cage and cry, and the truth of that thought killed something fragile deep inside me.

ROMMILY

The oracle sat on the floor of a bright, cold room, with her spine pressed into the corner. She didn't like this room full of cold tile and steel cots. She didn't like white coats and rubber gloves.

She didn't like men with guns, or the collar around her neck, which sent pain throughout her body, like being shocked with a cattle prod from the inside.

"It's definitely broken," the man in the white coat said, as he pressed on the sides of Mirela's swollen nose. Mirela flinched, and tears filled her eyes, but she made no complaint. "You're not going to be able to use her for a couple of weeks, at least."

"Wonderful." The woman in pressed pink pants touched something on her tablet, and the light it reflected on her face changed. "Less than a week off the truck, and she's out of commission."

Rommily traced the grout between the white tiles with her finger, wishing it were dirt. Wishing it were grass, wet with dew, shining in the sunlight. She missed the sunlight.

She missed the wind and the smell of fresh hay and wandering barefoot through the sawdust.

She missed Eryx, with his silent strength and comfort.

"They're both oracles? What's wrong with that one, Dr. Hill?" the woman in pink said, and when Rommily looked up, she found herself pinned to the corner where she sat by the woman's cold gaze.

"Physically, nothing that I can see," the doctor in the white coat said. "Not that I can get close enough to examine her."

"She doesn't like to be touched." Mirela's voice sounded oddly nasal as she pressed a tissue to her bloody nose. As if she'd been crying.

"Well, that's too bad. This is not a hands-off facility." The woman in pink clacked closer in heels that reminded Rommily of carnival clowns on stilts. Her thin nose wrinkled. "Why does she smell?"

"She won't shower," the doctor said. "That's evidently what caused this mess."

Rommily tugged on the loose thread hanging from the hem of her torn shirt. She didn't like these clothes. These drab pants that were all one color. If gray could be called a color.

"Is she dangerous?" the woman asked.

"No." The doctor swiveled on his stool to face Rommily. "But there's something wrong with her. If she were human, I'd call her a head case."

"And since she's not human, what would you call her?"

The doctor shrugged. "Useless."

"Fury reaps its own reward." Rommily's words ran together like watercolors as she closed her eyes. An image formed, and she gasped. Her eyes flew open again, but the image was still there. Still every bit as real as the cold tile room and the pink-clad woman staring down at her.

"What did she say?" the woman demanded, as the doctor walked his stool closer. "And what the hell is wrong with her eyes?"

"She's having a vision," Mirela said. "Just leave her alone, and it'll be over in a minute."

The woman in pink knelt in front of Rommily in her clown heels, clutching her tablet to her chest. "Well, she's certainly useless as long as she smells like that. Let's get her up and hose her down, if we have to." The lady in pink stood. "Help me with her?"

The stool groaned as the doctor stood and rolled it back. "I'll take her right arm. You take her left."

"I wouldn't do that…" Mirela said from the padded table, but they weren't listening.

The woman in pink grabbed Rommily's left hand while the doctor took her right arm. Rommily sucked in a sharp breath as they pulled her to her feet. "Scalpel born. Belly full of blood."

"What the hell did she say?" The lady in pink tried to let go of Rommily, but the oracle had her hand in a grip of steel.

She laughed, as if her white-blind eyes saw straight into the woman's soul. "Fate's bastard is coming for you."

DELILAH

The coordinator waved us out of the kitchen. Only the habit of putting one foot in front of the other kept me from freezing in shock when I saw the room. Though really, calling it a room was like calling a cave a crack in the wall.

The space could easily have held several times the fifty guests invited to Michael Hayes's bachelor party.

The windowless walls were lined with panels of gathered black drapery, which gave the room a formal look and dampened the echo most spaces that size would have suffered. The floor was white marble with black veins, shining in the light from several elaborate chandeliers hanging from the ornately coffered ceiling.

The huge room swallowed my footsteps and amplified my fear, making me feel insignificant in a way that being locked in a small cage never could have.

The guests were college-age men in business-casual dress, most of whom had already found the alcoholic beverage of their choice. Their chatter died as we entered the room, and I could feel every gaze on me. The attention felt simultaneously familiar and completely foreign, because though I'd been on display at Metzger's, a menagerie patron's motivation to plop down his credit card was almost always simple curiosity, tempered by fear. He or she wanted to see dangerous creatures—perhaps even those responsible for the reaping—removed from true threat by miracle of steel cages and iron bars.

But the patrons at the Savage Spectacle didn't just look curious, they looked *hungry*. Greedy. These men—most of them near my age—didn't believe we represented any threat, and it had never occurred to them, probably in their entire lives, that they might not have the right to do whatever they wanted in any given moment.

I could practically smell their anticipation in the air.

The coordinator whispered for us to spread out and carry our trays around the room, and the ladies in front of me did just that. Crowds formed around them instantly. Hands reached for flutes of champagne and handfuls of hair in equal numbers. Someone pulled Belinda's lip down to inspect her sharp fangs, while a man in a red button-down shirt ran his hand down the length of Zyanya's arm, then lifted her free hand so he could examine her claws.

Lenore's flat-soled sandals whispered on the floor behind me as she headed for the stage, where red velvet curtains had been drawn back to reveal an orchestral quartet formally dressed in blue-and-silver tuxes, except for the female violinist, who wore a blue sequined gown. The siren climbed the steps on one side of the stage and conferred softly with the violinist. After several whispered questions and a couple of nods, Lenore took up her position behind the microphone, and when the music began, she sang.

I realized immediately that despite her instructions, her melody and its push were intended not for the paying audience, but for those of us forced to endure wandering hands and intrusive gazes. Her voice felt like a gentle wave of calm floating over me, blunting the sharp edge of my temper and relaxing the fist clenched at my side.

I was disgusted by what I was being forced to endure, but it would not kill me. And I wouldn't have to kill anyone either.

If any of the employees were able to think beyond their own suddenly eased tensions and realize she was projecting the wrong atmosphere, she might get into trouble. But I was beyond grateful for her efforts.

As my tension eased, I glanced across the room and was surprised to see two familiar, large forms standing near the opposite wall. Eryx and...

"Gallagher!" I breathed, and though he couldn't possibly have heard me, his gaze met mine, and his gray eyes brightened.

Mine filled with tears. Gallagher was a liberator. A protector. A man of uncompromising character who held others to the same high standard. The sight of him in a collar bruised me all the way to my soul. The collar looked so incredibly out of place that at first I didn't notice he was wearing little else.

Nothing, in fact, but his unglamoured traditional red cap and a gray loincloth trimmed with a matching red cord.

He bore the indignity like a soldier. As if near nudity were a bruise or a gash, or some other battle scar earned at the hands of an enemy, but humiliation for him warmed my cheeks. I'd never seen Gallagher subjugated.

Even after seeing him hauled from the back of a van, I hadn't really thought it was possible.

Yet as sad as I was to see him in captivity, I was elated to see him alive.

I worked my way slowly across the room, pausing to let men ogle me and take food from my tray, but I dodged reaching hands without hearing a word said to me. I couldn't see anything but Gallagher.

His bruises were mostly healed, and the cuts on his face had been treated with narrow butterfly bandages. His dark hair had been cut short, which looked strange to me, but his eyes were the same. Steely-gray windows into a soul like none other I'd ever met.

When he saw me heading toward him, the tension in his shoulders seemed to ease. I waited until the last bite from my tray had been taken and the guests wandered toward one of the more obviously "freaky" cryptids. Then I tucked the tray beneath my arm and headed straight for Gallagher.

"Delilah." His voice rumbled through me, though it held little volume. "Are you okay?"

I nodded. Even if I hadn't been okay, I would have told him I was. "You?" I took in every bruise and cut. Every line of a dire expression I knew well.

"No man here could hold his own among the fearsome *fear dearg* I battled in my youth."

I couldn't resist a small smile. "So you're humoring their authority in order to stay close to me?"

His jaw clenched, and the muscles in his neck strained against the steel collar. "Something like that."

"It was the hat, wasn't it?"

He nodded. "My human guise was never meant to last."

"I know." But there was something in the slight curve of his mouth. In the glint of light shining in his gray eyes. "You got caught on purpose."

His upper lip twitched. "Why on earth would I do that?" But he hadn't denied it. Because *fear dearg* cannot lie.

"Why *would* you do that?"

Gallagher shrugged broad, strong shoulders. "Sometimes

it is easier to break out of a fortress than to break into one," he whispered.

On his left, the minotaur snorted.

Before I could ask him what he'd seen of the Spectacle and its security procedures so far, one of the handlers stationed behind Eryx and Gallagher—the only two male cryptids in the room—frowned at me. "Go refill your tray."

I nodded, but before I turned back to the bacchanalia, I gave Gallagher a pleading look. "Please don't cause trouble," I whispered. "No matter what you see, I'm more okay than I will be if you interfere. Okay?"

"No."

"Gallagher, I can take care of myself," I hissed. "In here, I *have* to."

"Move along," the handler ordered.

I turned to Eryx. "Keep him in check, okay?"

The bull nodded, giving me his mute promise to try. They'd dressed him in nothing but a loincloth, similar in style to what he'd worn in the menagerie, which gave me a clear view of his massively muscled human chest and arms, beneath the fur that began on his shoulders and grew over his bovine head, up to the base of two enormous, curved horns. I saw no new cuts or bruises, and no sign that he'd been denied food or water. The only real change in him was the massive steel collar around his thick neck.

I couldn't understand why the women had been given beautiful costumes but the men had not, until Willem Vandekamp walked through the grand entrance, then made his way toward the stage, shaking guests' hands as he went.

Onstage, he eschewed the microphone and congratulated the groom in a voice that carried the width of the room on its own. He thanked the guests for coming and the host for choosing the Savage Spectacle as the venue. Then he signaled to someone at the back of the room, and the crowd parted as Eryx and Gallagher were marched forward to stand in front of the stage.

"You may have noticed these two beasts standing at the back of the room all evening," Vandekamp began. "I've brought them in to give you an early glimpse, on the house, of our newest competitors. Our minotaur and redcap will be making their debuts in the ring later this week, and I promise you, it will be an event like no other."

"What's a redcap?" someone shouted from the crowd, words slurred together.

Vandekamp smiled. "Watch this." He knelt on the stage and plucked Gallagher's hat from his head, then tossed it into the crowd. It hit the floor, and though everyone stared, no one reached for it.

"Galla—"

Gallagher called his cap before Vandekamp could order him to perform, and a collective gasp echoed across the room. No one actually saw the hat disappear from the floor, and no one actually saw it reappear on his head. Somehow, it happened in midblink. For everyone. All at once.

The audience burst into applause and excited chatter. And like a true showman, Vandekamp dismounted the stage without offering any further information, keeping them curious for Gallagher's event in "the ring."

He shook more hands on his way out of the room, then disappeared through the massive double doors without even a glance my way.

Gallagher and Eryx remained on display in front of the stage.

For the next hour, I avoided invasive questions and wandering hands, eager to escape into the kitchen every time my tray was emptied. Lenore sang and the rest of us served, and the patrons quickly got drunk on top-shelf alcohol and their own egos.

"What are you?" a man asked, plucking a tiny caprese skewer from my tray.

"I'm a Gemini," I said, as he stuffed the bite into his mouth. "That makes us totally incompatible."

The man next to him laughed into a fragrant glass of expensive whiskey.

As I left to refill my tray, the event coordinator brought Lansing and the groom onto the stage and announced the start of the hypnotist game.

At first, the "tricks" were simple and stupid, but the guests were all drunk and privileged, so the game devolved quickly. Lansing made Lenore compel his friends to tell their most humiliating secrets and when one of them admitted onstage to having slept with the bride, the host told Lenore to make him strip to nothing and take one of the servers' trays. He spent the next half hour serving his friends in the nude, with a cloth napkin draped over the erection Lenore had made sure he wouldn't be able to get rid of.

I was leaving the kitchen with another tray, reluctant to rejoin a group of men evidently determined to prove that money doesn't equal class, when something clattered to the floor across the room, accompanied by a familiar low-pitched feline growl.

Eryx took three thundering steps into the fray, eager to protect a friend, and his handlers grabbed him. I waved him back, to keep him out of trouble, then pushed my way through the crowd toward Zyanya.

I found her surrounded by half a dozen drunk partiers. Her tray was on the floor, bits of fancy cheese, crackers and tapenade scattered across the marble.

"I'm just saying, we paid to see her. We should get to see all of her." The groom reached for the tie of Zyanya's cheetah-print bikini top and tried to pull it loose. Again.

Zyanya turned to put her back out of his reach, and then it became a game. Each time she turned, there was another set of hands eager to tug on the straps. A man in gray slacks finally succeeded, and Zyanya clutched her loose top to her chest with both hands.

"Let her go." I put one arm around the shifter's shoulders and turned to the nearest handler, who was leaning against one black-draped wall, sipping from a bottle of water. "Aren't you supposed to step in here?"

The handler slowly screwed the lid on his water, then pushed away from the wall and sauntered toward us. He towered over most of the partygoers. "What's the problem?"

"I paid to see her, so I want to see her." The guest of honor pouted like a child as he flicked the untied bikini strap from beneath my protective grip. Before I could point out that *he* hadn't paid for anything, the handler shot me a censoring glance.

"That's not part of your package." He crossed thick arms over his chest, and I was almost as relieved to hear that as I was horrified that such a package existed.

"This should cover it." James Lansing pulled a clip of bills from his pocket as he pushed his way into the huddle, and though I only got a glance, they all appeared to be hundreds. "But for that much, I want a private show. Just me and the groom and your pretty little pussycat."

"That can certainly be arranged," the handler said.

Lansing tossed him the entire clip. "Take one for your trouble."

The handler thanked him and peeled a bill from the stack, then shoved it into his pocket. "Follow me."

"Wait!" I tightened my grip around Zyanya's shoulders.

The handler grabbed her arm and pulled her away from me. "Customers get anything they want at the Spectacle—as long as they're willing to pay."

"Hey," Lansing said as the handler pulled back a section of the black drape to reveal a door in the rear wall. "I want her too." He nodded at me, then pulled a credit card from his wallet.

A cold wash of fear froze me in place. The handler shoved Zyanya into the room he'd just opened, then marched toward me. "No." My voice was hardly a whisper, but it wouldn't have mattered if I'd screamed. The handler dragged me toward the small room as if I weighed nothing. "*No*. I won't do this." I closed my eyes and dragged my feet, to no effect.

Over the handler's shoulder, I saw Gallagher clench both fists. Eryx's bovine nostrils widened when he huffed, and he pawed the marble floor with his right hoof. His promise to keep Gallagher in check seemed to have been forgotten.

"Let her go!" Gallagher bellowed.

The entire room went still. Every head swiveled toward him, and several people gasped. He looked *swollen* with rage, every muscle in his body standing out beneath his skin, his neck bulging against the confines of the steel collar.

"Gallagher, don't!" I cried.

One of the handlers stepped in front of him and ordered him back. Gallagher reached out and snapped the man's neck with one hand.

The body fell to the floor. The crowd gasped. A current of fear ran through them, raising the hair on my arms. Stroking the sleeping *furiae* inside me like petting a purring cat.

But Gallagher fell to his knees. He roared, his face contorted with the agony coursing through him.

Three more handlers ran toward him, each wielding a remote control, and he fell onto the floor, convulsing in pain.

"The bigger they are…" My handler laughed. His grip on my arm tightened, and he pulled me toward Zyanya and that empty room.

"It'll be okay," she whispered from the doorway.

But it wouldn't. She didn't deserve this. Gallagher didn't deserve to be electrocuted for trying to protect me.

Rage surged inside me. I felt my hair lift from my scalp, fighting the pins that held it in place. My nail beds began to itch and burn as my nails hardened, growing into thin points.

Behind me, someone gasped, and when I opened my eyes, my vision had sharpened so dramatically that I could see individual folds in the fabric draping the wall all the way across the large room.

The handler dropped my arm and stepped back.

"What the fuck?" Lansing demanded, staring at my eyes. "What is she?" But he didn't back away. In fact, the entire crowd of inebriated, privileged young men was closing in on me, as if wealth and entitlement exempted them from a healthy fear of death.

The handler pressed an icon on his remote, then frowned at the screen when the collar failed to inhibit my transformation.

Rage coursing through me, I reached for Lansing.

The handler cursed and grabbed my arm. The moment his skin touched mine, he froze. The *furiae* wanted Lansing, but she would accept the man who'd been willing to give Zyanya to him. Who'd accepted payment for her humiliation and degradation.

"Take her indignity upon yourself." The words fell from my lips, though I hadn't felt them form. They were simply there, channeling justice with every syllable.

The handler dropped my arm.

"What are you doing, man?" the groom demanded. "Don't let her go! That damn collar's not working!"

Other handlers rushed toward us from both sides of the room, but they had to push their way through a crowd that didn't yet feel threatened enough to disperse.

The handler who'd taken Lansing's money pulled his shirt over his head and dropped it on the floor. He unbuckled his utility belt and let it fall, Taser and all, then pulled his boots off, one by one. By the time the fastest of his coworkers got close enough to see what was going on, he was standing in front of the mesmerized crowd in a stained pair of white underpants and a single ripped athletic sock.

"Murphy!" the approaching handler shouted at his nearly naked coworker. "What the hell are you doing, man?"

"He touched her." Lansing pointed at me as he backed farther away from us. "She said something, then he just started stripping!"

Murphy bent to pull his remaining sock off, and the soft pooch of an aging belly folded over the band of his underwear.

"Man, put your clothes back on." Another handler stepped forward, aiming his remote at me, but he didn't press any of the buttons. I wasn't an immediate threat, now that my hair had fallen and my nails had receded, and if he paralyzed me, he wouldn't get any answers. "What did you do to him?" he demanded, as two more handlers pushed back the still-gathering crowd.

Onstage, Lenore had stopped singing, and the string quartet stood behind her, trying to see over the crowd.

"I gave him a dose of his own medicine."

Murphy hooked both thumbs beneath the waistband of his underwear, and the crowd groaned in unison as he pushed the stained material to the floor. He stepped out of the pile of shed clothing and dropped onto his knees.

"Murphy, get up," one of the handlers said, while another spoke softly into a handheld radio, calling for backup.

Murphy didn't get up. He just stood there on his knees, exposed in front of the crowd, while one of the other handlers pulled Zyanya toward the edge of the room, where the other cryptid servers had already been gathered.

And suddenly, the groom burst into laughter. "Is he just going to stay there like that?" He pointed at Murphy, and his amusement seemed to spread through the crowd, now that I no longer seemed dangerous.

The partygoers snickered, and Murphy's cheeks flushed. He knew what was happening. He knew what he was doing and what they were saying, but he was helpless to make it stop. He was living out the degradation he'd tried to heap upon Zyanya.

"Get up," one of the handlers said, as the double doors at the front of the room flew open and more handlers poured in, tranquilizer rifles aimed and ready.

"He can't," I told them, as Murphy shuffled toward the door on his knees, tears trailing down his scarlet face, loose flesh wobbling. "I don't think he ever will again."

"What the *hell* did you do?" Vandekamp paced back and forth in front of his desk, and the drastic change in his demeanor made me nervous. I'd never seen him angry.

"I didn't do anything," I insisted, wishing I could pull the stupid mask from my face, but I'd been handcuffed again, still in my costume. "Seriously. Murphy grabbed my arm and it just happened. I was merely a conduit for justice." My head swiveled as I watched Vandekamp pace past me, while a man stationed to the right of the desk kept his gun aimed at my chest.

"I told you what would happen if you didn't behave."

"I'm not in control of the *furiae*." Not always. "I tried to tell you that."

Vandekamp turned to the pair of handlers stationed by the door. "Where are the others she was serving with?"

"We're holding them down the hall, sir, waiting for your decision."

"Isolate each of them. No lights. No windows. No sleep mat. No communication with anyone. No food or water for forty-eight hours."

"But I couldn't help it!" I insisted. "Punishing them won't teach me a lesson, because I didn't do it on purpose!"

Vandekamp didn't even seem to hear me.

"What about her?" one of the handlers asked, and though I couldn't see him, I could hear hatred and fear in every word he spoke.

"Send her back to the dorm. Shut her down if she comes within three feet of any employee."

Shut her down. As if I were a machine that could simply be turned off when it wasn't needed.

"Sir, are you sure? She's the problem. Shouldn't she be punished too?"

But the handler clearly didn't understand—the whole time I sat in a well-lit room surrounded by friends and fed three meals a day, I'd be able to think about nothing but the suffering I'd brought upon Zyanya, Lenore, Belinda and Clarisse.

"That is her punishment."

"In an unprecedented event, nearly two dozen cryptids of multiple species have escaped from the Massachusetts state preserve. Residents are advised to stay inside and lock their doors."

—from the *Boston Gazette*, September 1996

DELILAH

I refused food for the next thirty-six hours.

Lala tried to convince me that what was happening to the others wasn't my fault. But she was wrong.

Mirela and Finola told me that making myself suffer wouldn't help those being punished for what I'd done. They were right, but that didn't change anything. I couldn't stop their suffering, but I could make sure they didn't suffer alone.

After lunch on the second day after the bachelor party, the dormitory door opened and Bowman called my name. He wore thick leather gloves and the collar of his shirt was folded up, leaving none of his neck exposed.

"What?" I didn't bother to stand. My insides had become one vicious cramp with the kind of hunger I remembered from my first few days in the menagerie, before Gallagher had started sneaking me extra food.

I hadn't seen Gallagher since the bachelor party. None of the others who'd been taken out for engagements had seen him either.

"Delilah, you've been engaged," Bowman said. "Let's go."

I stood, and the room spun around me. My legs felt shaky. "By myself?" In the week and a half we'd been at the Spectacle, I hadn't seen anyone leave for an engagement alone.

"Come on."

My first few steps were unsteady.

He adjusted the settings on my collar, then escorted me down the hall toward the makeup room. "I guess you shouldn't have given your lunch away, huh?"

Of course they'd been watching.

Bowman held the makeup-room door open for me, revealing that three women and two men were already reclined in five of the six available chairs. "We have a late addition to the roster," he said, gesturing for me to sit in the empty chair.

"We'll get to her when we're done here," one of the makeup artists said, without looking up from the man whose face she was painting. With his sculpted features exaggerated by subtle, miraculously masculine makeup, I hardly recognized Drusus, the incubus our menagerie had picked up about a month before we were recaptured.

After at least two hours in the reclining chair, I was rubbed in body glitter and dressed in the same outfit I'd worn to the bachelor party, only this time I was given a pair of sandals with three-inch heels.

The handlers marched us through the topiary, then through a second iron gate I'd never noticed before, toward the back of the stone garden wall along a winding sidewalk.

Beyond that gate was a vast section of the Savage Spectacle I'd never seen before, completely surrounded by a tall iron fence and hidden by a thick grove of tall trees. The sidewalk wound through the grove, lit by light posts at regular intervals, and we emerged from the thicket in front of two imposing brick structures both almost absent of windows. The one on the right sat just a few hundred feet from the iron fence at the back of the property. The other was huge and octagonal, and it was surrounded by a parking lot of its own. Which implied that it also had its own entrance and driveway, though I could see neither from our vantage point.

Our handlers marched us toward a service entrance at the rear of the octagonal building, and as we approached, the familiar shape of the building finally sank in.

This is the ring.

We stepped into a large, cold room with white tile on both the floor and the walls. Three large drains in the floor formed a broad triangle, and two industrial hoses were wrapped around large hooks above faucets set into the wall.

The white tile room was made to clean up messes. Big messes.

My throat tightened so suddenly and severely I could hardly breathe but the others marched straight ahead, as if they'd seen it all before.

Our handlers led us down a wide concrete hallway lit by hanging fluorescent fixtures, then into a kitchen virtually identical to the one in the main building. The same chef I'd seen the night of the bachelor party was hard at work again with an even larger staff.

A new event coordinator greeted us in the kitchen. Her name tag read Olive Burnette, and her smile looked frozen in place. She gave Drusus and the others each an assignment number, then dismissed them, and as their handlers led them out of the kitchen—oddly, none of them carried trays—the coordinator turned to me.

"Okay, I'm only going to say this once, so listen closely. You'll be serving one of our wealthiest guests in one of our luxury boxes." She tucked a strand of her blond bob behind one ear. "Keep his glass full and food within reach. The box seats are pretty well stocked with everything customers could want, but if you run low on anything, just press the red button on the wall, and someone will come see what you need." She glanced over my shoulder at Bowman. "Obviously you'll be monitored by a handler at all times."

The coordinator straightened her fitted silver suit jacket, then marched out of the kitchen. Bowman shoved me into the hall after her.

A service elevator took us up four floors and opened into an empty, curving hallway, which obviously ran around the perimeter of the arena. Burnette led me past several open doors, where I could see into private viewing boxes, each of which held either a professional server or an engaged cryptid waiting to serve guests who hadn't yet arrived.

Finally, she stopped to open a closed door, then waved me into a box where three tiers of plush theater-style seats faced a wall shielded from view by a red curtain.

Bowman followed me inside and Burnette quickly closed the door behind him, clearly glad to be relieved of my company.

"Delilah."

Startled, I turned to find Woodrow, the gamekeeper, standing on the other side of the box, his black tactical gear blending in with a sidewall painted a very dark gray. Like Bowman, he wore leather gloves and had turned up his collar, to expose as little of his skin as possible.

"If you're any trouble tonight, the boss will put a bullet in your head. But first, he'll make you watch your boyfriend die."

"Boyfriend?" But then I understood. "Gallagher and I aren't together. Not like that."

"Bullshit," Bowman said from my left. "He snapped a man's neck trying to get to you, and after they dragged you out, he pulled Hilliard's head clean off. He would have killed everyone else in the room to get to you, if not for his collar."

I started to argue, but then I recognized the futility. They obviously couldn't conceive of a motivation that didn't involve either money or sex.

The gamekeeper grabbed my chin in his gloved hand and made me look at him. "Are you as protective of Gallagher as he is of you?"

I didn't have to answer. He saw it in my eyes. But there was a bigger problem at hand. "I didn't do anything to Murphy. *He* touched *me*. I can't prevent what happens to people who touch the *furiae* voluntarily."

"So we've heard. If you feel this *furiae* surfacing, gesture to one of us, and we'll take care of it." His hand settled onto the tranquilizer pistol holstered at his waist, in case I had any doubt about what he meant. "Tonight's guest knows he can't touch you. He's just here to watch the fight. The only way this can go wrong is if you make it go wrong, and if that happens, you can kiss your boyfriend goodbye. But not literally, of course. Do you understand?"

I nodded, then swallowed the sick-tasting lump at the back of my throat.

"Good." Woodrow pointed to the back wall of the box, where a countertop was equipped with a bar sink and a small refrigerator. An assortment of stemmed glasses hung upside down from a rack over the sink. "There's white wine and champagne chilling in the fridge. Red wine and liquor are on the counter. Soda and beer are on tap. The basic snacks are in that cabinet, and someone will come by with food soon."

"I'm not a bartender."

"Anything more complicated than beer or wine will come in from the bar down the hall. Just tell us what you need, and we'll radio it in."

"So, I just give this guy drinks and food, and Gallagher gets to live?"

"What happens in the ring is up to him. But if you behave, *we* won't kill him. That's the deal."

Gallagher was scheduled to fight.

Fighting for someone else's entertainment is barbaric, even when humans get paid to do it. But being *forced* to fight? That was an especially cruel assignment for a redcap, a warrior sworn to fight for something real. Something important.

I wasn't sure Gallagher would participate at all. He would never willingly smudge his honor, no matter how much pain the collar could put him through. But if they could somehow make him fight, surely it would be a short bout. I'd never met anyone, human or cryptid, who could take Gallagher in a fair fight.

Would the fight be fair? Would they handicap him, for entertainment's sake?

The door opened before I could ask any of my questions—not that Woodrow would have answered them—and Olive Burnette escorted a portly man in his early sixties down to the center of the first row, her arm looped through his. Her smile no longer looked frozen in place. When he slid a one-hundred-dollar bill into the pocket of her suit jacket, I understood why.

"Mr. Arroway, this is Delilah. She'll be taking care of you tonight. Now, did the hostess go over the restrictions with you? Delilah isn't safe to touch."

"What is she?" Mr. Arroway twisted in his chair to look at me, and his neck cracked audibly.

"She's very rare and very special. If you need anything, just let her know. The event will be starting in about ten minutes. Have you placed your bets?"

"I've got six figures riding on the first two bouts." Mr. Arroway resettled into his chair and pulled a folded piece of paper from his jacket pocket. "But I don't know anything about the challenger in round three. Is he new?"

"Yes, and we don't think you'll be disappointed!"

Olive gave me a private wink on her way out of the box, and I clenched my jaw. The new beast in round three was obviously Gallagher.

Before the door could fall closed behind her, a waitress in slacks and a silver vest pushed the door open again with one elbow, then set a tray of appetizers on the counter.

"Well?" Mr. Arroway twisted awkwardly in his chair and looked not at me, but at Bowman. "Is she going to bring me something to eat or not?"

Bowman glanced at me with his brows raised, and I grabbed the tray. Weakened by my hunger strike, I wobbled beneath the additional weight, and for a second I thought I was going to drop the entire tray full of tiny crackers topped with seafood paste or goat cheese and tiny scones filled with smoked turkey.

But then the room came back into focus and my legs remembered how to work stairs.

"Sir, would you like an hors d'oeuvre?" I asked, bending to put the tray within Mr. Arroway's reach, even though the indignity of being dressed up like a doll and forced to work for no pay burned all the way into my soul.

Gallagher's life was worth it.

"Hell no, I don't want any of that fancy shit." Arroway pushed the tray away, and I scrambled to keep it from tipping over. "I want peanut butter crackers. And beer. Something American. But none of that light crap."

"I'll see what I can find," I said through clenched teeth. But when I stood, I found Woodrow scowling at me, pointing at the old man's nearly bald head. "Sir," I finished. Then I raced up all four steps and set the full tray on the counter.

After a panicked scan of the countertop, I opened one of

the lower cabinets and rifled through small bags of chips, pretzels and trail mix. At the back were three cellophane-wrapped packages of peanut butter cracker sandwiches. They must have been stocked just for Mr. Arroway.

I plucked all three packets from the assortment and set them on an empty tray, then filled a beer stein from the first domestic beer tap my gaze landed on, leaving room for a significant head of foam.

Mr. Arroway didn't acknowledge me as I set his snacks on the built-in tray that folded over his lap from the arm of his chair, and as I stood to return to my spot at the back of the room, the red velvet drapes along the front wall slid open with the soft hum of a small motor and the gentle swish of the fabric.

Through the wall-sized picture window, I saw that Mr. Arroway's private viewing box sat at the top of a steep, narrow arena overlooking a sand-filled oval ring several stories below us. The ring itself was encircled by a tall, thick, transparent barrier, like a hockey rink's safety shield on steroids.

The size of the enclosed space and the concentration of lights at the center gave it an intimate feel more like that of a theater than a ballpark. All the seats were good seats, but the box seats were great.

The less expensive stadium chairs were mostly filled, and as the remaining patrons found their seats, I stared out at them in fascinated horror. From the outside of the building, little of its size had been evident because much of the arena had been dug out of the ground—though we'd only gone up four floors in the elevator, we were at least six stories in the air.

I made my way slowly up the shallow risers as the house lights began to dim, and by the time I leaned against the wall at the back of Mr. Arroway's private box, someone had appeared in the center of the ring wearing a suit and carrying a wireless microphone. I couldn't make out his face, but the moment he spoke, I recognized Willem Vandekamp's voice.

"Ladies and gentlemen, welcome to the arena! As most of you know, the fights were our very first event—the original savage spectacle—and they continue to be our biggest draw. In fact, tonight we are *completely sold-out*, because making his debut in our third and final match of the evening is a creature you can't see in captivity anywhere else in the *world*."

The crowd cheered, and I took a deep breath, trying to slow my heartbeat.

"If you haven't completed your wagers yet, please do so in the next few minutes. As always, the house minimum is a total of ten thousand dollars placed in any combination over the course of the evening's three fights. For those of you joining us for the first time, the rules are simple. No restrictions. No weapons. No time-outs. And in our third match, two combatants enter the ring, but only one may leave alive. I promise you that tonight's show will be both savage and spectacular!"

Horror hit me like a stab to the gut, and I hunched against the pain. I grabbed the countertop to keep from falling.

It's a fight to the death. But Gallagher had sworn only to kill those who deserve a violent death.

If he refused to participate, he would be slaughtered in the arena.

If he won—and he would win if he fought—breaking his oath would kill him.

Regardless of the outcome, if Gallagher took the ring, he would die.

"And now…let the games begin!" Vandekamp threw his hands into the air, still holding the microphone, and the stadium erupted into applause. Mr. Arroway cheered around his mouthful of peanut butter, spewing crumbs all over his lap and the floor.

My stomach lurched toward my throat, and I had to swallow to keep from vomiting.

Vandekamp jogged out of the arena as the house lights dimmed even further, and I found myself holding my breath. A single spotlight appeared in the center of the arena, and the buzz from the audience swelled. I watched, fascinated, while two combatants were introduced. The first was an ogre in his midtwenties. He wore only a large loincloth, and in the close-up on a high-definition screen suspended above the arena, I could see that his body was scarred all over with whip marks and healed cuts and gashes. Several of those scars came from wounds that would easily have killed a human.

Yet this ogre was only the challenger.

His opponent, and the reigning champion in the "bipedal beast" category, was a giant in his late thirties, who towered over the ogre by at least three feet and outweighed him by a good two hundred pounds, by my best guess.

When they stood alone on the sand, facing each other, an eerie hush settled over crowd.

A high-pitched tone made my head ring, and even from Mr. Arroway's box at the top of the stadium I could see the twin flashes of red when the combatants' collars were stripped of all restrictions. Except, presumably, the one that would let them leave the ring.

The ogre and the giant ran at each other, massive lungs expanding with each breath, thick muscles bulging with every movement. They kicked up sand with each racing step, then crashed into each other near the middle of the ring, and the sound was like a clap of thunder. The impact sent a tremor through the arena, all the way up to the box where I stood.

The crowd roared its approval, hoisting overpriced bottles of beer and glasses of wine into the air, where the beverages sloshed onto patrons already drunk with anticipation, if not yet with alcohol.

Mr. Arroway leaned forward, littering the carpet with more crumbs, and shoved another cracker sandwich into his mouth, transfixed by every bloody blow, the full horror of which was captured in high definition on the screen overhead.

I made it through about ninety seconds of barbaric violence before I looked away in disgust, determined not to legitimize the savagery by granting it even one more set of eyes.

The gamekeeper wasn't watching the match either. He was watching me.

Mr. Arroway was too absorbed by the fight to require any service, but the moment the house lights went down so they could drag the poor unconscious ogre out of the ring, he twisted in his seat to demand another beer and a bowl of butter-pecan ice cream.

Once again, the staff had anticipated his oddly specific request—I found an unopened pint waiting in the small freezer, as well as a bowl, scoop and spoon in the cabinet.

The second match pitted a manticore—a huge red lion with the tail of a giant scorpion—against a hydra—a snakelike dragon with multiple heads. This particular specimen only had two heads, which was the most common genetic variation, despite the fact that the topiary version in Vandekamp's garden was of the rare seven-headed variety.

Though I watched as little of the fight as possible, I could tell every time blood was spilled based on the roar of the crowd, including Mr. Arroway's inarticulate, full-mouthed grunts of pleasure.

Before the third and final round of the evening, I poured another beer for my client, but my thoughts were on the ring. I'd assumed Gallagher would face someone near his own size and strength and number of limbs, but what if I was wrong?

Redcaps were truly fearsome warriors, but they weren't fire-proof, and they only had one head.

As I served the full stein, a spotlight appeared in the center of the ring again, where Willem Vandekamp had reappeared to introduce the final fight.

"As most of you have already read in your programs, to-night we are excited to bring something extraordinary to our finale—a creature brand-new to the Savage Spectacle's stables—and we're thrilled to be able to tell you that he is the only member of his species currently in captivity in the *entire world*. But we're so confident in his ability to take down our reigning champion that rather than make him work his way up through the lesser fights, we're going to start him at the top. Tonight he will either spill blood and emerge a cham-pion or leave the ring in a box.

"Ladies and gentlemen, tonight I present to you one of the least-studied varieties of *fae*, the only redcap confirmed to exist not just in captivity, but anywhere on the planet. Please put your hands together for our challenger…Gallagher!"

DELILAH

A second spotlight appeared in the ring, and Gallagher stood in the middle of it, bound in enormous chains and staring at the ground. He wore only tattered black pants and his traditional red cap, his feet and enormously muscled chest and arms bared to the crowd.

For one long moment, I couldn't breathe. I couldn't feel or hear a thing. I couldn't drag my focus from his form standing on the sand, until I realized the screen overhead offered a much closer look.

"No..." I murmured, and Woodrow stepped closer with his remote control in hand, anticipating whatever fit he thought I was about to throw. "Please don't make him do this," I whispered. "You don't know what this will do to him. You don't know anything about him."

The gamekeeper shrugged. "We know that *fear dearg* need to spill blood like they need to breathe air. They have to kill to survive. Look how tense he is. He's like an addict staring at a needle." Woodrow took my chin in his gloved hand and made me look at Gallagher's image on the huge screen. "He needs this. He won't be able to resist the blood."

"He won't do it," I said when he released my chin. "He won't kill an innocent creature for your amusement."

Woodrow chuckled. "We're pretty sure he will." He reached to his left and twisted the adjustable knob by the door. The lights in Mr. Arroway's box brightened dramatically, and I squinted, disoriented by the unexpected glare.

Woodrow grabbed my arm in his gloved grip and hauled me down all three tiers while I blinked, still stunned. I tripped over my stupidly tall left heel, and he pulled me upright, then pushed me up against the glass. As my eyes adjusted, I realized that the rest of the stadium had gone nearly dark. Ours was the only bright spot in the arena, except spotlights on the sand.

Gallagher looked up from the ring, his attention drawn by the sudden light. He could see me perfectly well from the ring, and when his jaw clenched, I knew he'd gotten the message.

I hadn't been engaged to bring beer and ice cream to a customer. I'd been hauled from my dormitory to make sure Gallagher would perform as instructed.

"What the hell is he?" Mr. Arroway demanded, but before I could push myself back from the glass, Woodrow's other gloved hand landed on my left arm, holding me in place. "He just looks like a big man. Argos will tear him apart."

Argos?

"Why are the lights up?"

Even if I could have turned to answer Mr. Arroway, I couldn't look away from Gallagher. Across the distance, he was watching me. Waiting for some sign. And he wasn't the only one.

Most of the spectators had turned to stare up into our lit box, obviously as puzzled as the man who'd rented it.

I pressed my palms against the glass, and on the large screen suspended over the arena, Gallagher nodded, returning my mute greeting.

"What's the holdup?" Arroway demanded, and though I could hear Bowman explaining something to him softly, I couldn't make out the words. Not that it mattered. Gallagher had vowed not to take an innocent life. But he'd also sworn to protect me, which he couldn't do from the grave.

He couldn't keep both vows, but neither could he willingly break one of them.

And I couldn't watch him die.

Vandekamp marched from the sand, still lauding the reigning champion, and the moment he was clear of danger, though his voice still boomed from the speakers, another spotlight highlighted a huge gate on one end of the oval ring. "Ladies and gentlemen, I give you your champion…Argos!"

The gate slid open, and leather creaked behind me, as Mr. Arroway leaned forward in his seat.

A strange shadow slid into the spotlight on the sand—an ever-shifting silhouette I did not recognize. Then the creature stepped into the light, and I gasped. Argos was a Cerberean hound, colloquially known as a hellhound: a huge multiheaded dog with the tail of a snake, the claws of a lion and a mane of small but venomous snakes around each snarling canine head.

This particular hound had five heads. Every last one of them growled as it walked through the gate on thick, muscular legs, and two of the dog's muzzles actually dripped with foamy saliva.

If my guess was right, Argos had been denied food long enough to make him angry, but not long enough to weaken him.

As the gate slid closed behind the hound, Gallagher spread his arms and bent his knees, adopting an easy fighting stance, yet I could tell from his balance and from the set of his jaw that he was prepared to defend himself, but not to attack. Because he'd given his word.

"Damn it, Gallagher," I whispered.

Woodrow leaned closer. "What was that?"

"He won't do it." My breath puffed against the glass. "The hound will kill him, and you'll be out a very rare and valuable cryptid. And your audience will be very disappointed."

"If he can't kill Argos, how valuable can he be?"

"He can kill the hound. But he won't." I sucked in a deep breath, then said the only thing I could think of that might save Gallagher's life, miserably aware that in the process, I'd be giving them more information to use against both of us. "He took an oath, and he can't break it."

Woodrow spun me around to face him, and my heart pounded. I could no longer see Gallagher or tell how close he was to the snarling, snapping hellhound. "What oath?"

"Gallagher is *honora militem*. His tribe took an oath of honor centuries ago. He can only kill those who've earned a violent end. Or in defense of me."

"So, what, the killer hellhound doesn't deserve a violent end?" The gamekeeper scowled. "He's killed eleven opponents in a row."

"A hellhound is a natural predator. Would you say a tiger deserves a violent end just for living its life?" I demanded. But when Woodrow's scowl only deepened, I exhaled and came at the issue from another angle. "You and Vandekamp put Argos in a kill-or-be-killed situation. If anyone in this scenario deserves a violent end, it's the two of you. Gallagher knows that."

Woodrow's jaw clenched. But I saw no fear. "You better hope you're wrong, or your boyfriend's about to die a very brutal, public death."

"Her boyfriend?" More leather creaked, then footsteps shuffled behind us as Arroway approached the glass.

I didn't bother explaining again that Gallagher and I were not romantically involved.

I glanced at the screen again, hoping to see Gallagher, but instead found a close-up of three of Argos's five heads. The one in the center wore a collar just like mine.

When I turned back to the ring, Gallagher's collar flashed red briefly, but brightly enough for me to see even from across the stadium. His restrictions had just been removed. Which meant the hound was unrestricted, as well.

Argos growled as he approached Gallagher, and terror raced through me like a jolt from a cattle prod. My champion wasn't paying any attention to the threat. He was still looking at me.

"Is he just going to stand there?" Arroway demanded, clutching his beer inches from the glass, on my left.

And suddenly I understood how to help Gallagher. "You want a show?" I whispered to Woodrow. He nodded, and I sucked in a deep breath. "Then hit me."

"Why?" the gamekeeper demanded, suspicion evident in his narrow-eyed gaze.

"Because if he thinks I'll pay for his failure, he'll fight to protect me. But he has to see it."

Woodrow glanced over my shoulder at Arroway. "Sir, step back please."

Shoes shuffled against carpet as the guest moved out of the way.

The gamekeeper looked down into the ring, and I followed his gaze to see Gallagher still watching me.

I never saw the blow coming.

Pain exploded in my cheek and light flashed behind my eyes. I stumbled backward two steps, then caught myself against the glass, and for a second, as the pain radiated with a stunning intensity, I forgot that I'd gotten what I'd asked for.

Until it worked.

Gallagher's bellow of outrage echoed across the stadium. I blinked and looked into the ring again, one hand over my throbbing, already-swelling cheek. He stared up at me with his fists clenched, his massive arms bulging. His dark eyes caught the spotlight as the camera found him, and the unspent violence charging his expression drew a gasp from the audience.

But he was still looking at me. Not at Argos.

"Damn it, Gallagher," I mumbled, as the hound flexed its claws, digging into the sand. Its muzzles snarled and growled, while the hiss of its snake manes formed a disturbing cacophony.

"His skull must be as thick as the rest of him." Bowman's voice startled me from inches away, and before I could turn, he grabbed a handful of my hair and jerked my head back. I gasped, but the cold point of a knife at my throat froze me midbreath.

Bowman pushed me closer to the glass, and the tip of the blade bit into my flesh. A warm drop of blood rolled down my neck.

On the screen, Gallagher's face became a mask of rage. His eyes narrowed and his lips curled into a snarl. Savage rage shone in his eyes like reflected points of light, and I realized we were witnessing the death of his internal struggle.

He'd just decided that protecting me trumped his other, older oath—a vow his people had been making and keeping for centuries.

Argos snarled from three muzzles at once, then barreled across the sand toward his opponent. Snakes squirmed and hissed around his heads, protecting all five vulnerable throats. His thick serpent's tail whipped back and forth behind him, creating a strangely effective counterbalance to the chaotic sway of his heavier front end.

Gallagher dropped onto his knees and rolled to his left.

Argos's closest muzzle snapped at the redcap's arm and several of the snake heads seemed to graze his skin, but my champion rose into a capable crouch again with no visible effort. If he was bleeding, I couldn't see it.

Bowman's grip relaxed a little as he watched the show, and the blade slid down my skin a fraction of an inch. I breathed easier as the personal threat decreased, but my heart pounded painfully while I watched Gallagher fight, his traditional cap clinging steadily to his head no matter which way he ducked or dodged.

The hound was huge—easily six feet long, without counting his massive snake tail—and he was fast. But Gallagher was faster. Nimbler. He moved with more ease and grace than any human his size could have. Of course, there were few humans his size. The only reason he'd avoided standing out in a crowd at the menagerie was the glamour that made him appear smaller.

"Argos can't catch him," Woodrow muttered from my right. "That's a show in itself."

"The hell it is," Mr. Arroway blustered, still standing in front of the glass several feet to my left. "I didn't pay to see this redcap fella run away all night. I want to see *blood*."

The rising grumble from the rest of the stadium seemed to support his sentiment.

"He must not be taking the threat to his girlfriend very seriously." Woodrow frowned at Bowman, and my heart leapt into my throat.

"That's not it," I insisted. Then I froze when the knife bit into my skin again.

"If he doesn't draw blood soon. I will," Bowman promised. "That'll motivate him."

"Wait," Woodrow said. "Let her talk."

Bowman loosened his grip again, and I exhaled shakily.

"Just give him some time," I said. "He's having trouble getting a grip." It was easy to see why Argos was the reigning champ—Gallagher couldn't get close enough to grab the hound, thanks to heads that could see and snap in every direction at once.

The redcap ducked and rolled again, and when he stood, he stole another glance at our lit box. His scowl deepened on-screen, and I recognized the resurgence of his determination.

Argos ran at him again, drool flying, snake manes hissing and snapping. Instead of rolling out of the way, Gallagher lunged to the side and took a two-handed grip on the nearest head's mane. He came up with several small snakes in each hand, and with a simple twist of his wrist, he broke them all in half.

The hound whimpered and backed away, seven dead snakes hanging from its far left head, which was rendered suddenly vulnerable by the loss.

The dog regrouped and ran at Gallagher again. This time the redcap feinted right, and in a repeat of the same move, he snapped the spines of nine more thin snakes. The video close-up showed half a dozen double-puncture wounds on his bare arms—the price he'd paid for the minor victory.

The crowd cheered, and Mr. Arroway took a drink of his beer, apparently mollified.

Argos stumbled over one of his own feet. Several of his heads wagged back and forth, as if they were trying to shake off exhaustion. Or disorientation. Gallagher could have dealt a death blow right then, but he only backed away from the hound. The crowd booed, but where they saw weakness, I saw nobility.

Vandekamp and his staff could make Gallagher kill another creature forced into battle, but they couldn't make him press an advantage. Instead, he waited until Argos turned and relocated his opponent. The wounded heads looked stunned, but the three in the middle were back in the game.

The hound ran at him again, snarling, snapping and hissing, and when Argos got close, Gallagher lunged to the left. But instead of rolling out of the way, he grabbed the nearest disabled head and pulled himself onto the dog's back. The outermost heads were too injured to arch back for him, and the middle one was out of range. Gallagher grabbed another double bouquet of snakes and twisted them fiercely. When they hung limp, he wrapped both hands around Argos's central head—the one wearing the collar—and snapped the dog's thick neck.

The center head fell limp, and the crowd roared its approval. Argos stumbled, then fell onto his left side. Gallagher's leg was pinned beneath the beast's weight, but he pulled himself free, and the crowd cheered again in anticipation of the death blow.

Gallagher stood over the dying body of the celebrated Cerberean hound, but there was no victory in his expression as the remaining heads snapped weakly at his shins. There was no joy and no relief. Gallagher's eyes held nothing but grief for the life he was about to take.

He bent over Argos and efficiently, mercifully snapped the two remaining necks. Putting the poor, spasming beast out of his misery.

The crowd leapt to its collective feet, stomping as it cheered. The arena had a new victor. A new monster to ogle and bet on. But I knew what they did not. He could have given them a much bloodier show. He could have literally ripped the hound limb from limb, leaving pieces of him spread across the sand.

Instead, he gave Argos as merciful and dignified a death as he could.

Gallagher had not performed for their amusement. He was not their champion—he was mine.

WILLEM

Stadium fixtures lit the indoor arena like sunlight, glittering on sequined dresses and diamond rings as the crowd mingled. On the sand, the body of the Cerberean hound lay just as it had fallen in the final bout, broken necks ringed by manes of limp snakes. Canine jaws gaping, tongues sprawled onto the ground, dusted with sand.

Willem Vandekamp stood inside the challenger's gate at one end of the oval ring, hidden by deep shadows as he assessed what he could see of the crowd. The after-party was always well attended, but tonight, almost everyone had stayed. Patrons spilled into the hallways lining the perimeter of the arena and down onto the sand itself, eager for a close look at the felled beast.

But neither the number of guests nor the size of their respective bank balances could put Willem at ease as he watched them mingle, accepting glasses of wine and bite-size appetizers from waiters in silver vests and matching bow ties. Willem was looking for a specific face in the crowd.

Light footsteps tapped on the concrete behind him, in a

rhythm he knew well. "How does it look?" Tabitha appeared at his side in a floor-length gray satin gown, her shoulders bare but for a layer of appliquéd chiffon.

"Gallagher was a hit. But it doesn't look like Bruce Aaron stayed for the party."

"Are you sure he came at all?"

Willem nodded. "I comped him a box. Olive said he brought Senator Wilson and Senator Pickering and his wife. They're both on the committee. This could be very good or very bad."

"But the fight went well?"

"It was a *flawless* demonstration of the technology."

When he couldn't put off his entrance off any longer, Willem took his wife's hand and stepped into the ring. The first cluster of guests who noticed them began to clap, and everyone else turned to look. Within seconds, the entire arena had burst into applause.

Willem nodded, graciously accepting approval he knew he deserved. Yet still he scanned the crowd.

"I hate the sand," Tabitha whispered as she subtly clutched his arm for balance in her heels. "Can we let them come to us?"

"Of course." Willem led his wife a few steps farther into the ring, then stopped as the first cluster of guests approached.

"Great show tonight!" A man in a shiny blue button-down raised a glass of red wine, and his friends followed through with an informal toast. "That last one—the red hat?"

"Redcap," the woman to his left corrected as her elaborate cascade of curls caught the light.

"Yes, the redcap. He was something. You said he's *fae*?"

Willem nodded. "*Fear dearg* specifically. They're a race of warriors required to dip their caps in the blood of their victims to survive."

"How perfectly savage!" The woman with the curls smiled, her blue eyes alight with excitement. "He's a killing machine!"

"Yes, he is." Tabitha Vandekamp gestured to the corpse of the massive hound, where it lay on the sand fifty feet away. "You can see the result for yourselves." At her invitation, they moved toward the body, breathlessly recapping the hound's demise as the next group of guests came forward.

Willem settled into his postfight routine, answering questions about the competitors and accepting praise from enthusiastic fans of the event as they ate and drank. In the stands, a crowd had formed around Olive Burnette, who was taking ticket requests for future bouts on her tablet, increasing the Spectacle's cash flow with every order she took. But Willem didn't begin to truly enjoy himself until he spotted a familiar pair of gentlemen standing with a woman in her fifties on the opposite side of the ring, studying the hound's corpse from a respectable distance.

"Excuse me, please." Willem slid his arm from Tabitha's tight grip and abandoned both his wife and a cluster of patrons as he walked purposefully across the sand.

"Senator Wilson." He offered his hand to each of them in turn. "Senator Pickering. Mrs. Pickering. I'm Dr. Willem Vandekamp. My event coordinator tells me you were both guests of Senator Aaron's tonight. Is he still here?"

"No, he left during the first round," Pickering said, as Wilson took a sip from a glass of red wine. "But we enjoyed the exhibition."

Willem swallowed his frustration and forced his jaw to unlock. "I'm glad to hear that."

"*Enjoyed* may be overstating it a bit," Senator Wilson said. "But I was quite entertained, especially by that last match. We both expected the hound to bite several chunks out of the fellow in the hat, but he hardly got a taste at all."

"Yes. Gallagher is formidable." He followed the senator's gaze to the broken body of the hound. "We hope to get several months out of him, at least."

"And what will you do with him afterward?" Pickering asked. "I assume you'd be willing to donate the remains of such a rare find?"

"Of course. We have a standing agreement with a research facility in Atlanta, and they have permission to report all their findings to the government."

"Who was the creature in the lit window?" Pickering used his wineglass to point to the box where Willem had arranged for Delilah to be displayed. "From across the stadium, she looked like a normal woman wearing a costume."

"And a collar," his wife added.

"I assure you she is anything but normal. She's a *furiae*. We acquired her at the same time as Gallagher, and she seems to be the only thing that motivates him."

"They're a couple?" Mrs. Pickering asked, as she plucked a bacon-wrapped scallop from the tray of a passing waitress. "Some cryptids form couples, right? Like the ones that can pass for human?"

"Some do," her husband said. "But scientists believe most of them to be incapable of complex emotions, hon. They're driven by procreative instinct and base needs, much like any household pet or zoo animal. Very few of them mate for life."

"Yet he was willing to kill for her." Mrs. Pickering shrugged. "Sounds pretty romantic to me."

"They're simplistic creatures, dear," her husband insisted.

Willem knew better. But he never made a point that would cost him money.

Wilson turned to Willem with a frown. "Regardless, what you're really saying is that you need this *furiae* because your collar can't control him?"

"It can, and it does." Willem's posture relaxed and his speech quickened with the opportunity to discuss his technological innovation. "At the first sign of aggression from him—a surge of either testosterone, adrenaline or a species-specific hormone we haven't yet assigned a name to—the collar paralyzes him completely. Our difficulty lies not in preventing violence from him outside the ring, but in eliciting it for the sake of the fight."

Pickering gave him a puzzled look over the rim of his glass. "Didn't you say he needs to kill to survive?"

"Yes. But he doesn't like to perform. So tonight we used Delilah—the *furiae*—as both a reward and a threat. To motivate him. But make no mistake. The collar can neutralize *any* cryptid. Under any circumstance. I'm so confident in my technology that I routinely take the sand with them, to introduce them, with nothing standing between me and the beasts but my collars."

"We noticed that." Wilson nodded. But his eye was drawn back up to that same box seat. "What exactly is a *furiae*? Another species of *fae*?"

"No." Willem considered his phrasing, well aware that an outright lie could come back to haunt him, if he were granted an audience on Capitol Hill. "She's a beast driven by revenge. Under normal circumstances, she looks so ordinary as to be nearly useless here at the Spectacle. But when she gets mad, she turns into a monster. Unfortunately, as with Gallagher, we can easily neutralize her, but we can't make her perform on command."

"That's a shame." Pickering drained the last of his wine. "I hope you didn't pay much for her."

"I think a revenge cryptid sounds quite useful." His wife transferred her weight onto the ball of her left foot and pulled her right heel from the sand. "I'd unleash her the next time one of the ladies from my garden club gets bitchy."

Her husband and his colleague laughed, but Willem was struck silent with a sudden epiphany. "I'm afraid you'll have to excuse me. Please enjoy the rest of your evening, and let me know if you'd like to see another show. On the house, of course." With that, he headed straight for the champion's entrance.

His wife watched him go from the other side of the ring.

DELILAH

"Where are we going?" I demanded.

Woodrow and Bowman still wore gloves as they half led, half dragged me down a wide concrete hallway deep in the bowels of the stadium. The floor was rough but warm against my bare feet, the way a basement is always warm in the winter, because of the insulation of the earth.

Based on the noise echoing above and around us from the massive after-party going on in the stands, my guess was that we were somewhere far beneath the top-tier box from which I'd been forced to inspire Gallagher's victory.

"Shouldn't I be headed back to the dormitory?"

"Not tonight," Bowman said, and I glanced at Woodrow just in time to catch the censuring look he shot his subordinate.

"Why not?" Would Lala and Mirela spend the entire night worrying about me in silence?

Should they be worried?

We turned to the left into a hallway lined with steel doors nearly twice as wide and a third again as tall as I was. Trolls, ogres and giants hunched over to peek through the windows in about half the doors, but the other rooms appeared to be empty. They also appeared to be much taller and wider than the holding cells I'd spent my first few hours at the Spectacle in.

This was where they kept the poor creatures forced to fight in the ring. The "bipedal beasts," anyway.

A third of the way down the hall, something slammed into a door as we passed it. I jumped, then flinched again when Oki, the *adlet* from Metzger's, rammed the glass again. How many of the other menagerie beasts had been forced to—

"Eryx!" I had to swallow a sob when I saw the gentle minotaur watching me through one of the windows. "Has he already fought?"

Neither of the handlers answered, but a gash had scabbed over on Eryx's forehead, beneath his left horn, and there was a chip missing from the tip of his right. I couldn't see how much other damage had been done to him in the ring, but he was alive and upright.

"Rommily's okay!" I shouted as they dragged me past. "Everyone's looking after her!"

"The minotaur and the oracle?" Bowman snorted, and I realized I'd accidentally given them something to use against two of my friends.

When we reached the fourth room on the right, Bowman opened the door and pushed me inside.

Woodrow aimed his remote at me to program the door restriction. "Take a shower," he said. "Someone will come by with food and a change of clothes." He closed the door, and I got no further explanation for my isolation.

At the back of the cell was a doorway to a bathroom, where the facilities were sufficiently large and sturdy enough for any creature that could have required the twelve-foot-tall space. A toothbrush and a roll of toothpaste sat on the edge of the stainless-steel sink basin. At the end of the bathroom, the floor slanted toward a drain beneath a basic showerhead.

A soap dispenser was built into the wall, but unlike the facilities in my dormitory, there was no shampoo. And there were no towels. Evidently the beasts were expected to air dry.

Nausea made my stomach churn as I looked around the cell. *Why am I here?* Was this the arena's equivalent of the private rooms hidden by draperies in the main building? Had one of the guests requested time alone with me?

Surely Vandekamp wouldn't take such a risk. Unless he'd figured out that I couldn't avenge myself. But how would he...?

A bitter lump formed at the back of my throat. I'd told them about Gallagher's oath. There would be no reason for him to swear to protect me, if I could protect myself.

But if this was some kind of big spender, after-the-fight service for a wealthy patron, why had they told me wash off all the makeup? Why had they put me in a concrete room in the basement? Was the cell part of the experience for some sick fight fanatic?

Maybe I was reading too much into the cell. Maybe the handlers were just too lazy to walk me all the way across the grounds to the dorm.

I stripped off the skimpy costume, then turned on the shower and stood beneath the stream of water. It wasn't hot, but it wasn't cold either, so I counted my blessings.

It took five handfuls of scentless hand soap to wash off all the body glitter and scrub my face clean, and another three to wash all the stiffening and holding products from my hair.

While I was rinsing my head for the third time, the cell door squealed open from the other room. I assumed someone had come with food and clothing—and hopefully a towel—

until that eerie feeling that I was not alone didn't fade when the door closed again.

I stood frozen under the lukewarm shower, my heart pounding almost hard enough to hear.

When no one spoke, I turned off the water and stood dripping on the floor, desperately wishing for a towel. Or some clothes. Or a weapon. I stood as still as I could, listening. And finally I heard a single deep exhalation, as if the breather had run out of patience.

"Who's there?" I demanded, in as strong a voice as I could muster. "This room is already occupied." As if there were any chance in hell that they'd accidentally put someone else in the cell with me.

"Delilah?"

Gallagher's voice was such a relief that I burst into tears. I rushed out of the bathroom, so eager to verify what my ears had told me that I forgot for a second that I was naked and dripping wet.

He stood in the middle of the floor, still dressed only in his cap and the tattered pants he'd fought in, now extra tattered from Argo's claws. Sand clung to his feet, and his arms were covered with welted snake bites. In his left hand, he clutched a bundle of clean clothing.

I froze the minute his gaze landed on me. His eyes widened when he took in my vulnerable state, then his focus snapped back up to my face with the same professionalism he'd always displayed as my handler in the menagerie. Only now there was no professional detachment. He no longer had to pretend he didn't care about me. That he hadn't pledged his entire existence to serving at my side and protecting me with his own life.

Gallagher dropped the clean pants he was holding and shook out the shirt, then held it out to me. "Here. Put this on."

I tugged it over my head without argument. As soon as the huge garment settled around my bare thighs, he pulled me into a hug.

"They wouldn't let me see you after the party," he said into the wet hair on the top of my head. "They wouldn't even tell me if you were still alive, after what you did to that guard."

"I'm fine," I assured him. "They said you killed two men."

"The slaughter would have been much greater, if not for the tranquilizers."

I took a step back and looked up at him. "I asked you not to make trouble."

"I swore to rip apart anyone who lays a hostile hand on you—to litter the ground with the corpses of our enemies—and my word is my honor, Delilah."

"I know."

"I cannot watch them humiliate and abuse you. You can't ask me to. You accepted me as your sword and your shield and that's—"

"For life. I know. And I wouldn't have it any other way. But we have to come to some kind of compromise. If you do that again, they'll kill you."

"I'm not going to break my vow just because it's become inconvenient." His scowl was heavy with censure. "That's not how this works."

"Your death is more than an inconvenience, Gallagher." But it wasn't something he feared. Every redcap hopes to die in battle, so I'd have to put a different spin on the issue. "You can't protect me from the grave."

"You're suggesting I stand by and watch them hurt you?" His body trembled with stifled rage at just the thought.

"No. Nor am I suggesting that you break your vow. I'm just asking you to defer your vengeance until we can use it wisely. To help get us all out of here. Why die for a small victory—

one or two unworthy lives—when you can fight for greater honor on a much bigger scale?" I could tell from how dark and eager his focus became that I'd hit the right note.

"During our escape?"

"That's what I'm hoping. They aren't prepared for cryptids who understand their technology. If I can get ahold of one of their remotes, or find wherever the doors are programmed, or something like that, I think we'll have a shot."

"But none of that will matter if they kill you. I can't let that happen."

"I'm not asking you to. If they try to kill me, do what you have to do. But anything short of that, I need you to prevent using your head, rather than your fists. Or add it to the list of deferred grievances."

His thick, dark brows furrowed.

"Promise me, Gallagher."

"You know I can't—"

"Then promise you'll try."

"Fine," he growled. "You have my word that if you are in nonlethal danger, I will *try* to prevent you from getting hurt using means not fatal to our captors."

"Thank you." I glanced around the concrete cell, relieved to have his promise. "Is this your room?"

"If such a place can be called a room. Though I've certainly lived under worse conditions."

What bothered me wasn't the bare concrete cell, but the collar, which evidently worked just fine on him, in spite of the *fae*'s tendency to short-circuit electronic gadgets.

"As glad as I am to see you… Why am I here, Gallagher?"

He took a step back and glanced at the floor, but I could hear the answer in what he wasn't saying.

"I'm a reward, aren't I? Because you won." As far as they

knew, if they didn't reward him for his cooperation, he might have less incentive to fight for me.

"Like most humans, they seem incapable of understanding the true nature of our relationship." Redcaps considered the lifelong bond between a champion and the one he served to be the most sacred of unions, held even above marriages. Suggesting that he and I were sexually involved was an insult to the entire concept of a *fear dearg* champion.

"Screw 'em." I scrounged up a smile, and he must have heard it in my voice, because he looked up again. "I'm glad for the time with you, no matter what they think we're going to do with it. Are you okay?" I took his hand and pulled his arm out straight.

Gallagher didn't flinch, though the motion must have hurt. His arms were both swollen from a multitude of snake bites. "I'm fine. They gave me an injection of antivenom. I told them I didn't need it, but they don't listen."

"Well, you probably did need it."

Gallagher shrugged. "I'm not human. The bites would be gone in the morning either way." His focus dropped to my throat, and he reached out to brush one finger over the nick from Bowman's knife. "I'll kill him."

I didn't bother to argue. Bowman had sealed his fate the moment he'd threatened me. "I know. Eventually," I reminded him.

"Let me shower, then we'll talk." He stepped past me into the bathroom, and I sat on his sleep mat facing the other direction to give him as much privacy as possible in a suite with no doors.

Gallagher emerged from the shower minutes later smelling like soap from the wall dispenser. Beads of water still rolled down his chest and his scrub pants clung to his legs with the moisture. His arms already looked better, either because of the antivenom or because he was *fae*.

His cap still sat on his head, but it didn't even look damp. My gaze lingered there, and I realized that he no longer bothered glamouring it to make it look like a baseball cap. Or maybe he couldn't, because of the collar. "Why didn't you didn't take the hound's blood?"

"Because I didn't deserve it. Argos wasn't my enemy. I killed him to keep you safe, and I'm sure I'll have to do that again, but I won't accept any personal benefit from it unless I have no choice."

I couldn't drag my gaze from his face, and again I was both confused and fascinated by the disparities that seemed to define him. He was biologically driven to shed blood and required to practically bathe in it in order to survive. Yet he took no personal pleasure in the act, even when his body felt physically satiated by it.

His restraint and self-discipline were boundless, yet if I were in imminent danger, he would tear through everything standing between us until I was safe. Or he was dead.

"When will you fight again?"

"From what I've heard, there are two events a week, but no one competes in both of them, because if we don't have time to properly heal, the fights will be too short. Eryx fought a couple of days ago. He and I both currently stand as champions."

"Why did Vandekamp shave your head?" I asked as he sat on the other end of the mat, leaning against the wall.

"They did that while I was unconscious. I think they were looking for identifying marks. I woke up bald and in chains. But the collar was a surprise." The cautious way he ran one finger over the smooth steel told me that he'd already been shocked by it more than once.

"So it's effective on you?"

"Infuriatingly so. The moment I even think about raising a fist, this contraption shoots some kind of electric signal throughout my body, paralyzing me."

I frowned. "It doesn't just cause pain? The collar paralyzes you every time?"

Gallagher nodded. "Ever since I killed two handlers at that party."

"Because pain didn't stop you."

"Of course not. I ripped the head from the man who pushed the button and soaked my cap in his blood." Because that sadistic bastard had established himself as Gallagher's willing foe. "Would they truly have hurt you if I hadn't killed the hound?" His gaze pinned me, and I resisted the urge to look away. He deserved the truth.

"Once they realized that was the right button to push, yes. This place is built to maximize profit. They'll do whatever they have to do."

"And you told them about that button?" His disapproval made me ache deep inside.

"I had to. They would have let Argos kill you if you hadn't fought back."

Gallagher took my hand and squeezed it. "We're going to get out of here, Delilah. They will make a mistake, and I will be ready. Even if I have to paint the entire world with their blood, I *will* set you free."

I was more worried about the blood he would lose than what he would spill.

Some time later, when Gallagher and I had settled into a comfortable and comforting silence, his cell door opened on squealing hinges. Two unfamiliar handlers stood in the hall. One aimed a tranquilizer rifle at Gallagher while the other set two food trays on the floor and slid them inside.

"Hey, could I get some clothes?" I plucked at the huge borrowed shirt for emphasis.

The handler slammed the door without even acknowledging me.

"Bastards."

My tray held my typical dinner, but Gallagher had been given an entire baked chicken, half a loaf of white bread, a quart of milk, a wedge of cheese and two tablets that could only be vitamins.

"Do they always feed you like that?" I asked as he stood to bring the trays closer.

"They have to feed the fighters well to keep them in fighting shape." He sat on the mat again and handed me my tray. "Would you like some cheese?"

I laughed out loud, amused by his manners, considering the barbaric circumstances. "Sure. Thanks."

He broke off a hunk of his cheese for me and insisted that I have some of his milk, as well.

When we'd eaten and slid our trays under the door into the hall, I asked Gallagher about everything he'd seen and experienced since he got to the Spectacle, hoping he'd seen more of the security precautions than I had. I'd just started telling him about everything I'd seen and learned when the lights went out. But our collars didn't flash. Our speech was not restricted.

When I realized that the sudden darkness meant I would not be removed from Gallagher's room anytime soon, I curled up with him on his sleep mat—we had little choice but to share—and told him everything I'd seen and heard since we were separated at Metzger's.

At some point after I stopped talking, he fell asleep, and though his presence at my back was the only comfort I'd found so far at the Savage Spectacle, it wasn't enough to truly relax me. My thoughts were a storm of escape plans and revenge plots, and with so much to work out, I didn't think I'd ever get to sleep.

But I was wrong about that, as I'd been about so much else.

PART TWO

OUBLIÉ

DELILAH

I woke up with sunlight shining in my eyes from a window high on the wall, and I knew immediately that something was wrong. Gallagher was gone, and though I'd fallen asleep in his shirt, I'd awoken fully dressed in gray uniform scrubs that fit.

Stranger still, I was alone in a concrete room, smaller in scale than the bipedal beast cells, yet more spacious than the holding cell where I'd waited to be processed and issued a collar.

At that thought, my hand flew to my throat. The collar was still there. It was the only thing I'd gone to sleep with that remained with me in the morning. *What the hell?*

When I stood, my feet sank deeper than they should have into the padding beneath me. I looked down to see that the sleeping mat I'd woken up on was actually a stack of three. A pillow in a clean white case lay on the floor next to the mat, as if I'd lost it in my sleep.

An eerie unease slithered up my spine.

Why was I given a pillow? Why was I in a private cell? Why couldn't I remember any of that happening?

And why was I so tired after a full night's sleep?

The food. Obviously I'd been drugged. Probably sedated. But why? What could possibly be accomplished through drugging me that couldn't be accomplished with the collar? Or by threatening someone I cared about?

Had Gallagher been drugged too? I closed my eyes and thought back to the night before. I'd eaten some of his food, but he hadn't taken any of mine. Were the drugs in *his* food? Were they to prevent him from fighting my removal from his cell?

I opened my eyes and spun to study the rest of the room, but my vision seemed to move slower than my body. The room spun around me with a strange sluggishness, and my stomach lurched. I sank onto my knees and took several long, steady breaths while I waited for the feeling to pass.

I'd definitely been drugged.

When I was sure I could stand without vomiting, I opened my eyes again and slowly pushed myself to my feet. The back corner of my cell held a prison-style stainless-steel toilet/sink combination. A toothbrush with a plastic bristle cover and a tube of toothpaste sat on the edge of the small sink, along with an inverted plastic cup.

I grabbed the toothbrush and opened its cover. The bristles were dry and in good shape, but obviously used. The toothpaste tube was half-empty and rolled up from the end, just the way I'd taught Gallagher when he and I had shared a camper back at the menagerie.

I set the toothbrush down and picked up the pillow. It smelled like an unfamiliar shampoo. The scent triggered another wave of nausea.

What had they drugged me with? How long before it wore off?

What the *hell* was going on?

Light footsteps echoed from the hall. I crossed the cell to peer out the window in my door, through which I saw a narrow, unfamiliar hallway. I could only count three doors along the opposite wall, so there were presumably at least two more on my own side. But if those rooms were occupied, I could hear nothing of my neighbors.

An unfamiliar guard appeared at the end of the hall, carrying a plastic-wrapped tray of food. He stopped in front of my door and seemed surprised to see me through the window.

"You're awake." He opened my door and held the tray out to me with gloved hands. I accepted it without thinking, the way people will automatically catch a ball lobbed at them.

"Where am I?" I peered over his shoulder for a better look at the hallway. "What am I doing here?"

The handler frowned. "Is that a philosophical question, or did you hit your head on something?"

A handler with a sense of humor. I was not amused. "What did you bastards put in my food?"

He exhaled slowly, as if he were fighting for patience, which was worthy of alarm all on its own. None of the guards at the Spectacle had ever demonstrated patience with a cryptid, that I'd seen. "There's nothing wrong with your food, Delilah."

Delilah.

The problem wasn't that he knew my name, even though I'd never seen him before. The problem was the way he'd said it. As if we knew each other personally.

As if I should have known his name too.

I glanced up from my tray without really seeing the contents, and my gaze settled on the name embroidered on the left side of his uniform shirt. *Pagano.* Italian. That wasn't much help, but I took a shot. "Tony?"

"Michael." His frown deepened. "Why do you suddenly care about my name?"

Okay, so I wasn't supposed to know his first name. But "suddenly" seemed to imply that we'd dealt with each other before. Yet even after mentally sorting through all the faces I'd seen at the Spectacle, I had no memory of ever having seen Michael Pagano.

"Eat your breakfast and get some rest. I'll be back for you later." He closed the door before I could ask anything else.

"Back for me?" I shouted. I didn't dare get too close to the door, in case proximity to the sensor triggered my collar. "Why will you come back for me?"

When his footsteps faded, I sank onto my triple-layer sleep mat with my breakfast tray, and for the first time, I truly noticed the contents. Beneath a layer of transparent cling wrap, I found half an apple, a slice of whole wheat toast—the kind with seeds and oats in it—as well as a sausage patty, a hard-boiled egg and a small carton of two percent milk lying on its side. Also on the tray was a single large pill, similar to the one on Gallagher's tray the night before.

I'd been given a multivitamin and a very healthy breakfast.

Why? If they were planning to make me fight in the arena, they'd be sorely disappointed in my performance unless whoever they put on the sand with me had done something to piss off the *furiae*.

I pulled back the plastic film and stared at my food. The sausage smelled delicious for about a second. Then another wave of nausea obliterated my appetite and made me suspect the entire meal. Was this food drugged, as well?

However, when the nausea passed, both hunger and logic won out. If Vandekamp wanted to drug me, he could do it just as easily with an injection as with food, if I refused to eat. So I ate everything on the tray, except for the apple core and the vitamin—the most suspicious part of the meal. Then I drank the milk.

I flattened the empty milk carton and slid the tray through the slot at the bottom of my door into the hallway. Then I turned to look up at the window, determined to figure out where I was. The sill was at least a foot above my head, but the triple stack of sleep mats gave me a good boost.

The glass was so thick that the world beyond looked distorted. My view was nothing but trees, and since I couldn't see the sun, I couldn't tell which direction I was facing.

I spent the next few hours alternately willing the door to open and going over everything I could remember from the night before, searching for some memory of being removed from Gallagher's cell. Of being dressed and taken to another room. Of falling asleep with an actual pillow. But the memories were not there. I must have been unconscious when I was moved.

Just when I thought I'd lose my mind from the solitude and the unanswered questions, Pagano opened the door with my empty breakfast tray in one hand and scowled at me. "You didn't take your vitamin."

"I don't believe it's just a vitamin."

"Let's not do this today. You can't leave the room until you take the vitamin." He set the tray on the ground and slid it into my cell. "Take it, and I'll give you an extra lap around the building. It's nice out today."

I picked up the vitamin because I was intrigued not just by the concept of an extra lap around the building—how many came before the "extra" one?—but because he seemed to think I knew what he was talking about. My morning made no sense, and I wouldn't get any answers sitting alone in a cell.

So I ran water in the cup and swallowed the huge pill, then opened my mouth to show that it was gone.

"Good. Come on." Pagano aimed his remote control at my collar and clicked an icon on the screen, then waved me into the hall with one gloved hand. He'd come prepared to avoid contact with my skin, but that was the only thing he seemed to have in common with the other handlers. He wasn't aggressive or easily provoked. His tone was condescending, but not entirely without respect—he spoke to me like he might to a human child, rather than to a dangerous creature.

I stepped out of the cell, and Pagano took my left arm, but he didn't cuff me. On our way down the hall, I glanced into the other rooms and found them all empty. The door at the end of the hall opened into an empty foyer, which led us out of a building I didn't recognize and into what was indeed a beautiful day, if unseasonably cool for September.

The lawn and the sidewalk surrounding the building were unfamiliar. To one side was the patch of woods I'd seen from my window. Opposite that, the sidewalk led away from the building and through an arched gate in the stone wall, beyond which presumably stood the topiary garden.

"Where are we going?" I asked as Pagano led me around the first corner of the building.

"I thought we'd go counterclockwise today." He shrugged. "I get bored too."

Instead of answering my question, his reply had led to several new ones, but I swallowed them. He seemed to think I should remember things I didn't remember, which meant he was ignorant of my ignorance. I'd never fared well from tipping my hand to the enemy, so I decided to trust my instinct. I would figure this out on my own.

My handler's semicordial familiarity with me. The change in my diet and living quarters. Clothes I hadn't put on.

I felt as if I'd woken up in the middle of a day I didn't remember starting.

With that realization, my hand flew to my face. There was no mirror in my room, and there'd been so many discrepancies in my memory that I'd completely forgotten about the bruise from Woodrow's punch. Which had been easy, because it no longer hurt.

As we completed our third lap around the isolated, nondescript building, my fingers found my cheekbone. There was no tenderness. The scab that had formed over the nick on my throat was gone.

That wouldn't be possible overnight without the liberal application of some sort of healing aid, like phoenix tears. But phoenix tears wouldn't explain the discrepancies in my memory.

The conclusion was obvious, if inexplicable. I hadn't been punched and cut the night before. I wasn't just missing the memory of dressing and leaving Gallagher's room last night.

I was missing several *days*.

Pagano seemed confused by my sudden silence as he walked me back to my cell, but not entirely disappointed by it. About an hour after he left—though I could never be sure of the time—he came back with my lunch tray, which held a ham sandwich with lettuce and tomato, steamed broccoli, half a peach and a school-lunch-sized carton of orange juice. I could hardly enjoy the best meal I'd eaten since Vandekamp shot me with a tranquilizer dart because of the questions swirling around in my head.

What had changed during the days I was missing? Why was I missing them at all?

Around midafternoon, Pagano came back to escort me to an engagement he seemed to think I was expecting. I wound up in the prep room with five other captives, including Zy-anya. She was already paralyzed in her chair when I got there, but I saw nothing unusual in her gaze. She seemed pleased but not surprised to see me.

Nothing the makeup artists said or did gave me any clue about my missing days.

Once I was painted, dressed and rubbed with body glitter, the other captives and I were marched through the topiary and the rear iron gate toward the arena, where we were led to individual box seats. Just like the previous evening.

Which wasn't actually the previous evening at all.

The fact that it was arena night again confirmed my suspicion that I was missing a significant amount of time. Gallagher had told me that fights were only held twice a week, to give the combatants a chance to heal and rest. That put my missing time at three or four days, at least.

My head spun with the realization. How could I have lost so much time? How could no one else know about it?

Pagano was waiting in my box—the same one I'd served Mr. Arroway in—along with Bowman, who didn't seem surprised by my presence, or by the fact that my face had healed. Which told me that I hadn't actually *gone* missing during my missing days. I just couldn't remember them.

Half an hour before the fight was scheduled to begin, Olive Burnette escorted a party of six into my box. Four men and two women, all dressed to kill.

The larger party kept me busy serving food and refilling drinks for most of the first two matches, in which a new troll and the manticore I'd seen before successfully and gorily defended their titles.

During the break before the final fight, conversation buzzed in my box while my customers discussed the reigning champion. I listened closely, because as of the last fight I remembered, Gallagher and Eryx had both been champions. If either was no longer a reigning champion, then he was dead.

My chest tightened at the thought, and for a second I had trouble drawing a deep breath. Could Gallagher be dead?

Could my reaction to losing him be what had led to my loss of memory? Had I blocked the entire event? Or had I been so much trouble as a result that Vandekamp had me medicated? Was the memory loss an unforeseen side effect?

That could explain why no one else seemed to know about my missing time.

I shook those thoughts from my head and focused on pouring drinks and offering bite-size delicacies, because I couldn't believe it. Gallagher couldn't be dead.

Soon the house lights dimmed, and Vandekamp appeared alone on the sand in his spotlight. With his usual booming voice and composed showmanship, he introduced the challenger: Belua, a behemoth, which looked like a cross between a wild boar and a black rhino. The twelve-foot-long, two-ton beast pawed the ground and paced back and forth, snorting aggressively. The only thing keeping her from charging Vandekamp was the huge steel collar around her neck.

When he announced that Belua's opponent, one of the reigning champions, was the rare and prized *fear dearg*, my relief was so consuming that I almost dropped a tray full of stemmed glasses of red wine.

"So what is a *fear dearg* anyway?" a woman on the front row asked.

"I don't know, but he's undefeated," the man next to her said, and no one pointed out that winning a couple of fights—how many could there have been in a few days?—doesn't really count as being undefeated.

I held my breath as I stared down at the sand, waiting to see Gallagher. To verify for myself that he was okay.

Lights dimmed all over the stadium, except for three spotlights in the ring. The gate at the other side of the arena slid open. And finally Gallagher stepped onto the sand, into the empty spotlight a third of the way into the oval ring. Then he turned to look up at me. As if he knew exactly where I'd be.

The lights in my box brightened, throwing a square of illumination on the stadium seats just below. Gallagher's gaze found me, and the image of him on the overhead screen zoomed in for a close-up. The audience turned to follow his gaze.

I gasped, surprised to find myself the center of attention again, and in my peripheral vision, all six of my customers turned as if they'd just then noticed I was there.

"Why are the lights on?" one of the men demanded.

"So he can see her," Pagano answered.

"It's her!" the woman next to him half whispered, her focus suddenly fixed on my face, though she'd hardly looked at me all evening. "So it's true? He fights for her?"

"It's true. Nothing else seems to motivate him," Bowman said as if I weren't standing right there, listening. "Not even his own safety."

"That's so beautiful!" one of the women said, but the man to her left scoffed.

"It's a gimmick, Cherie. They don't feel things the way we do. They've just been trained for this act, to draw in new customers. Like teaching a monkey to dance."

My face flushed red-hot, but I only bit my tongue and clutched the tray, trying to pretend I couldn't hear them.

"What is she?" a man in the second row asked. But I fixed my gaze on the screen, where a close-up of Gallagher showed details I couldn't see from the private box.

His wounds had completely healed, and somehow they'd multiplied. His torso and arms were covered in thick, irregular scars, which had already begun to fade from fresh pink to an older shade of white.

That couldn't be right. I stepped closer to the glass.

Gallagher's hair had grown out beneath his cap, not just to stubble, but to a full inch and a half of hair, where there'd been only scruff the last time I'd seen him.

That could *not* have been just days ago.

My tray clattered to the floor. Glass shattered and wine splashed the wall and pooled on the wood floor.

How much time had I missed?

"Damn it!" the nearest lady cursed, using a napkin to brush drops of pinot noir from her shoes. "What the hell is wrong with her?"

"What's the date?" I demanded, stepping over the tray and the broken glass.

On-screen, Gallagher frowned. He could tell I was upset.

Bowman and Pagano rushed toward me from the rear of the box, but they froze when I grabbed the lady's arm. So did she. Bowman aimed his remote at me, while Pagano pulled his stun gun from his belt. "Let her go, Delilah," Pagano said.

"What day is it?" I demanded.

The woman began to hyperventilate. "I…I don't…"

I grabbed the phone sitting on the arm of her chair and pressed a button to wake it up. The date slid across her lock screen, and my eyes widened.

Two months. Two *fucking* months.

I hadn't lost days. I'd lost eight full weeks of my life.

"In a landslide decision, the US House of Representatives has declined to pass the so-called cryptid labor law, which would have allowed ownership of several specific species of cryptids by private citizens. Insiders cite concern for public safety as the reason the bill did not pass."

—from the September 27, 1997, edition of the *Toledo Tribune*

DELILAH

Pagano pulled me away from the woman—Cherie?—and cuffed my hands at my back while Bowman radioed the event coordinator and asked for a server to fill in.

But instead of removing me from the box, Pagano took me closer to the glass, his gloved hand on my arm, careful to keep himself positioned between me and the guests I was no longer serving. He seemed to think that if they removed me from the box, Gallagher would refuse to fight.

He also seemed to think I posed no real threat to the customers. How much had they figured out about me during my missing time? Did they know I couldn't hurt the customers unless the *furiae* saw them get away with committing an injustice?

I hardly saw the match, not because I couldn't bear to watch—which was true—but because I couldn't make sense of my loss. Where had the time gone? How was it taken? *Why* was it taken?

How many times had Gallagher been in the ring? How many creatures had he been forced to kill? Had I seen it all?

Why couldn't I remember?

On the sand, the behemoth gored Gallagher's arm, and blood arced across the sand. He pivoted and regrouped as the two-ton beast slowed to a thundering stop, then turned to charge again. But the only part that sank in through my shock was that Gallagher was alive.

Which meant that his death could not have caused my memory loss.

Minutes later, he stood on the sand over the body of the felled beast, and in the roar everyone else assumed to be a proclamation of his victory, I heard a bellow of anguish. Unlike with Argos, he hadn't been able to kill such a huge creature without spilling its blood, and this time I knew that would not be the end. It couldn't be.

His cap was too pale. Too dry. He might not make it until the next match if he didn't use the blood he'd spilled, even if his victim hadn't deserved death.

The spectators watched, mystified, as he knelt beside the body of the beast and took off his cap. For a moment, he appeared to be praying. Then he carefully, almost reverently, set his cap in the pool of blood still pouring from the massive tear in the behemoth's stomach, inches from its spilled intestines.

The camera zoomed in for a close-up on-screen, and audience members who'd already risen to join the after-party, buzzing with excitement over what they'd seen, sat back down to watch.

At first, nothing seemed to happen, except for the return of its original bright red color to Gallagher's hat. But then the pool of blood began to shrink, even as the last of it poured from the poor animal's jagged flesh.

The audience stared at the high-definition screen, transfixed, in near silence. When the large puddle was gone, individual drops of blood began to roll toward Gallagher's cap from where they'd landed in the initial splatter.

With a spectacular disregard for the laws of physics, blood rolled out of the behemoth one drop at a time, crossing the sand like a line of fat red ants until there was no more to be found. Until both the corpse and the sand were dry and colorless. Until the hat had taken it all.

Gallagher picked up his cap, and the audience gasped. He stood, then placed the hat on his head with deliberate, precise movements which could only be part of a ceremony they would never understand or truly appreciate.

Though he'd been forced to kill, the behemoth's death had not been in vain. His blood would keep Gallagher alive.

Gallagher, in turn, would keep me alive.

His room was empty when I arrived, just like the night before.

No, just like that night eight weeks before.

Again, I was told to shower, but given no clothes or towel. Did I see Gallagher after every fight? Did Vandekamp still misunderstand the nature of our relationship?

As I rinsed the last of the products from my hair, the cell door squealed open, and I went still. What if this wasn't his cell? There were no personal effects, other than a generic toothbrush. They could have given me to anyone. They could have been doing it for eight weeks straight, if they'd figured out that the *furiae* could not come to my defense.

My heart pounded in terror. I would have only my own abilities to count on, if someone else walked through that door.

"Gallagher?" I called, forcing confidence and volume into my voice, though I felt neither.

"Delilah?" he said, and his voice brought tears to my eyes. Evidently this had not become routine, because he sounded not just relieved, but stunned. "I'm going to set a shirt on the floor for you, okay?"

"Thank you." As water poured over my face and hair, his hand appeared around the bathroom wall holding a familiar folded bundle of cloth. He set it down, and his arm disappeared, but not before I saw that it was wrapped in bloodstained gauze.

I finished rinsing and turned off the faucet, then squeezed water from my hair and brushed as much of it down my body toward the drain as I could. When I was as dry as I could get without a towel, I pulled his clean shirt over my head and stepped out of the bathroom.

Gallagher's gaze studied every inch of my exposed skin, and while that would have made me uncomfortable coming from anyone else, he was just doing his job. Searching for wounds or bruises. For any sign that he'd failed to protect me.

But he didn't reach out to hug me. In fact, he stayed several steps away, and he looked more worried than my bruise-free skin should have made him.

"I'm fine. Really. But you…" I frowned. He'd already showered, probably so that the infirmary could treat his wounds. Which were plentiful. If the behemoth hadn't been slow, she could easily have killed him.

"I will heal," he said as my gaze fell toward the bulge of a bandage puffing beneath his pants, at his calf. "I always do."

"How many fights have there been?" I reached for him, and he looked surprised, but he let me trace a thick scar curling around his forearm toward his wrist.

"Fifteen. They gave me a break after that one, remember?" he said with a glance at the scar. "It required tears of the phoenix, and even then took a week to heal."

"What did this?" I couldn't look away from the scar. That injury might have meant amputation for any human.

Gallagher looked puzzled. "You don't remember?"

My eyes watered again, and his scars blurred. His injuries and my memory loss were each terrifying on their own, but taken together, with absolutely no context, they were overwhelming. "There've been so many. And all because of me."

"No." He folded his arms over a broad chest marred by dozens of new marks. He was born into a warrior race, but this was not how he was meant to fight. This was not *why* he was meant to fight. "Because of Vandekamp," he insisted. "This is not your fault, Delilah. I put myself here."

"For me." I didn't know what else to say.

I couldn't absorb it all. I couldn't think.

"Your hair." I said the first thing that popped into my mind as I sat down and wiped unspilled tears from my eyes. "It grew back." Too late, I realized that I shouldn't have been surprised by that.

Gallagher lifted his cap from his head and ran one hand over his dark hair. "Yes. I suppose you haven't seen it up close in a while."

I tried to hide my surprise. "How long has it been?"

"I'm not sure. A couple of months?"

My eyes widened, and he noticed. "Since your first fight?"

"No. Since the night of my second. You don't remember?" He studied my face, and his concern set off alarms deep inside me. "What's going on, Delilah?"

"Nothing. I'm fine."

"Why are you lying to me?" His voice held no accusation, but guilt flooded me anyway. He had to tell me the truth, and he deserved the same from me. But if he found out someone had taken my memory, he wouldn't stop fighting until he knew what had happened to me and who had done it. Until the guilty party was dead.

Or until *he* was dead.

I couldn't let that happen, but short of a lie, I had no good answer. "I…"

"You don't remember the last time we were in the same room?" There was something strange in his voice. Some odd mixture of disparate emotions. Concern and…relief? Or was I imagining that? "What happened, Delilah? How much time are you missing?"

I blinked up at him, surprised by a conclusion I probably should have expected. He knew me better than anyone in the world, since my mother had died, and redcaps were experts at interpreting things left unsaid. They had to be.

Still… "How did you know?"

He almost answered. I saw the impulse in his eyes. In the automatic opening of his mouth, as if he were about to speak. Then he thought better of it.

Though the *fae* couldn't tell an outright lie, their methods of avoiding the truth ranged from simple omission of key details to the intentionally misleading delivery of information. The conscious decision not to tell me whatever he'd been about to say meant something. Something important.

"What aren't you telling me, Gallagher?"

"What aren't *you* telling *me*?" he demanded. "You don't remember the night of my second fight. You don't know what happened to my arm. You're surprised by the length of my hair. What's the last thing you remember?"

"Falling asleep in your room the night of your first fight. You were newly bald, and they'd just used me to make you kill Argos, the hellhound."

"That's it?" His brows furrowed low over gray eyes. "There's nothing else?"

"Nothing until I woke up this morning in a private cell. My new guard seems to know me. And evidently serving in the arena is my regular gig."

"You've been at every one of my fights," Gallagher confirmed. "But they haven't let me speak to you in weeks."

"Why not?"

"I don't know. I heard from Eryx that you'd been removed from the dormitory, but he didn't know why."

"How did he find out?"

Gallagher's frown deepened. "Delilah, you see him all the time. He's a favorite at parties. He's a favorite at everything."

"You don't do parties?"

He nodded. "They won't let me, if you're serving. But they know better than to expect me to fight unless you're there. To prove that you're okay."

"I'm so sorry—"

The cell door opened to reveal one handler carrying two food trays and another aiming his tranquilizer rifle at Gallagher. The man with the trays set them on the floor and slid them inside.

"Hey, can I get some clothes?" I stood to show them how badly Gallagher's shirt fit me, but neither handler said a word. "Please. I'm just asking for a little dignity."

The first handler closed the door, and their footsteps faded down the hall.

"Bastards."

Gallagher chuckled. "You call them that every time."

"How many times have we done this?"

"This?" he said as I handed him a tray loaded with a full rack of pork ribs without sauce, a baked potato with none of the fixings, a scoop of canned green beans and two pint cartons of milk. "We've only done this twice."

"Twice before tonight, or including tonight?"

"Before tonight."

I sank onto his sleep mat next to him with my tray.

"At least they're feeding you better," he said with a glance at my bowl of potato-and-ham soup, a whole wheat roll and two small plums.

"Yes, and I have no idea why. What am I missing, Gallagher?"

"I don't know." But he didn't look at me when he said it. He was telling me the truth, but not the whole truth.

"What do you know?" I tucked my legs beneath me and set the tray on the mat.

"Nothing relevant to your memory loss, as far as I know. You have my word, and my word is my honor."

"Then why won't you tell me?"

"My reasons are personal. You saw me in undignified circumstances." He looked up, and his gray-eyed gaze pleaded with me, even before his words did. "Please let that be enough, Delilah."

"Of course." If I could erase the memory of every undignified circumstance he'd seen me in, I would. I took a bite of soup and thought while I chewed. "What could have taken my memory? An *encantado*?"

"No." He hadn't touched his food. "They can alter how you experience reality, which can create a false memory, but they can't leave your memory blank. It might be simpler than that, Delilah. Vandekamp has highly trained medical personnel, both doctors and cryptid vets."

My pulse swooshed harder. "What are you saying?"

"Large doses of electric shock can damage a person's memory. This could all be because of your collar, if they use it too often. Like a side effect."

"Are you missing any memories?" I dipped my bread in soup, then took another bite. I was hungry in spite of the circumstances. "Is anyone else, that you know of?"

"No." Finally he pulled one rib from the rack.

"Then it doesn't make much sense that I would be," I said,

as he tore a chunk of meat from the bone with his teeth. Unless they'd shocked me over and over, during my missing weeks. "It could be the drugs."

He dropped the rib onto his tray again, almost untouched, and his voice rumbled with anger. "Someone drugged you?"

"I think so. I woke up sluggish and disoriented this morning, and there are several different pharmaceutical sources of memory loss. Vandekamp could have given me anything."

"But why?"

I shrugged. "Memory loss could be an unintended side effect. Or maybe there's something he doesn't want me to remember." I tore a hunk from my roll, and again it occurred to me that my food could be poisoned. "So what have I forgotten?"

"That I know of?" Gallagher ripped one rib from his rack. "Thirteen of my fights. At least as many trips to the infirmary. And the occasional noncombat event where people wearing expensive clothes want to see the reigning arena champion, for the additional cost of five thousand dollars a night."

"It costs them five grand just to look at you?"

Instead of answering, Gallagher took renewed interest in his dinner.

"They don't just look, do they?"

He took his time chewing and swallowing, and when I hadn't moved on by the time he'd finished his bite, he sighed. "Willem Vandekamp has amassed a large list of very wealthy and very depraved clients."

I knew that much even without eight weeks' worth of memories. "When we're free, we will burn this place to the ground."

Gallagher's smile was the slow coalescence of every violent, indignant, vengeful impulse we shared. "Flames are a particularly poetic form of destruction."

"So is blood." I lifted my milk carton and held it toward him. "To fire and blood."

He tapped my carton with his own. "To vengeance and death. May they all get what they deserve."

I drained my milk carton. Then I crushed it.

"How long did I stay that night?" I asked a while later, as I slid our empty trays into the hall. "The night you killed Argos. Did they leave me here until morning?"

"No. They came for you in the middle of the night," he said as I sank onto the mat next to him and tucked my feet beneath me. "And they didn't let you keep my shirt."

My dinner threatened to come back up. They'd made me march naked through the grounds. And they would do it again.

When the lights went out, instead of curling up on Gallagher's sleep mat, we sat side by side in the dark while he told me about all the beasts he'd been forced to kill, including the two whose blood had kept him alive.

In the middle of the night, footsteps echoed from the hall, and my heart lurched into my throat. Gallagher's light came on. I stood, and he stood with me. My hands hovered at the hem of the borrowed shirt, but I wasn't going to take it off voluntarily.

The door opened, and Bowman tossed a set of scrubs and underwear at me. "Change quickly."

I headed into the bathroom to get dressed, trying not to look too grateful.

"I hope to see you sooner than eight weeks from now," Gallagher said, when I emerged, fully dressed.

"Me too." I stepped closer to whisper the rest. "Promise me that if I don't remember this, you'll tell me everything we've talked about tonight."

"You have my word." Gallagher pulled me into a hug, and

I gasped at the sudden aching pain in my breasts. "What's wrong?" He stepped back to study my eyes, searching for the source of my pain.

"Nothing," I mumbled. But my eyes fell closed as the sudden, surreal truth coalesced from the bits and pieces of information I had.

Nausea. Exhaustion. Sore breasts. Though I still had no idea how my memory had been taken, I understood exactly why.

I hadn't been drugged. I was pregnant.

DELILAH

Alone in my cell again, I used the restroom and brushed my teeth, but I didn't taste the toothpaste or feel the bristles.

Pregnant.

The enormity of that idea was so overwhelming that at first, I couldn't think past it. A lifetime ago, I'd thought I might want kids someday. Back when I'd had a normal life and inalienable rights. When the best thing about my boyfriend's compulsive stability was what a great dad he'd be.

But now?

I didn't have a boyfriend. I hadn't had sex since the day I was sold into the menagerie.

Except obviously I was wrong about that.

Tears filled my eyes, so I closed them. I clenched my jaw to keep from screaming as images flickered behind my eyelids.

Hands reaching for Zyanya's straps. The private room hidden by drapes. The party host handing his credit card to the guard.

Was that how it had happened? Was I rented for a night? An hour?

Did I fight?

My stomach heaved, and I lurched for the toilet. My dinner came back up and I flushed it away, but the nausea remained.

I lay down on the floor and pressed my burning face to the cool concrete, and I couldn't stop thinking about it.

Who was he? Was it just once, or was I missing multiple memories of abuse?

Somehow, not knowing made it worse.

Could it be a guard? It would have to be one the *furiae* had never seen abuse anyone, or touching me would have had serious consequences for him. But the Spectacle had plenty of guards who didn't actively mistreat their charges.

Magnolia said the handlers couldn't touch us without paying the rental fee. Had one paid for me? Had I seen him today?

Did I walk right past him without knowing what he'd done to me?

My skin crawled with the possibility.

Someone had touched me. Someone had been *inside* me, in some brutal moment I'd had no control over. I couldn't remember it, yet I couldn't stop picturing it, and suddenly my body itself seemed to be my biggest adversary.

My brain was withholding the truth. My womb was harboring an uninvited stranger. And the *furiae*...

She who could avenge any wrong had put me in the path of danger, then refused to defend me. Or to avenge me.

Or even tell me whose face had been stricken from my memory.

Maybe he was a stranger I'd never see again. But he could be someone I saw every day. Someone I talked to and worked with. Someone who had absolute power over my living conditions and my meals and my body.

And maybe over my mind.

There must be a reason I couldn't remember.

I forced myself off the floor and curled up on my stack of

sleep mats, where I stared at the concrete wall inches from my face.

Obviously, the fact that I was pregnant meant that whoever he was, he'd taken no precautions. What if I'd caught something?

A fresh wave of nausea rolled over me with that thought. I needed to see a doctor.

Maybe the doctor could tell me about the…fetus. Was it human? Could it be born a *furiae*?

Questions tumbled through my head too fast for me to focus on, but ultimately, none of the answers about what would happen to a child born in captivity—even if it were human—mattered.

They wouldn't let me have a baby.

When Tabitha Vandekamp found out, she would do to me what she'd done to Magnolia. I would have no more say in the fate of my unborn child than I'd had in its conception.

She must not know yet, or that would already have happened.

How far along was I? If I'd lost another month's memories, Tabitha Vandekamp could have ended the pregnancy, and I might never even have known about it.

Could that still happen? Could I wake up tomorrow missing another two months and never remember that I was pregnant?

Does the baby have to do with my missing memories? Why bother to erase the conception, if they didn't know about the pregnancy? Why bother at all? They didn't do that for Magnolia.

After trying to untangle a knot of possibilities that led nowhere, I felt like I somehow knew even less than I'd started with.

What I *did* know was that to buy time to think it through, I'd have to hide my pregnancy for as long as possible.

I could not go see a doctor, even to test for communicable diseases.

Disgusted, terrified and exhausted beyond measure, I closed my eyes. Then noticed that though it must have been well past midnight, the light was still on. How was I supposed to sleep with—

Footsteps echoed down the hall, then stopped on the other side of my door.

"Who's there?" I called.

A tray slid through the slot at the bottom of the door. It held half a red apple and about an ounce of cubed cheddar.

"Hey!" I crossed the small space to stand as close to the door as I dared. "Who's out there?"

But the window only showed an empty hallway, and I could already hear footsteps receding toward the door at the end. As I knelt to pick up the tray, the overhead light dimmed to a level that would be comfortable to sleep in, yet still let me see the food in front of me.

I sank onto the stack of thin mattresses with the tray in my lap, and at first I could only stare at the food. Apple and cheese. A perfectly healthy snack, which was an extravagance in a facility that labeled itself "savage." I'd never been given a snack by the Spectacle staff—not that I could remember anyway. Neither had anyone else, that I knew of. So why…?

Because I'd lost my dinner.

The answer hit me with the emotional force of a sledgehammer swung right at my soul. A private cell. Exercise and sunlight. Vitamins. Late-night snacks.

Someone knew about the baby. Someone with the authority to give me healthy privileges and protect both me and my unborn child from Tabitha Vandekamp and her infanticidal tendencies.

I could think of only one person who fit that bill, and who could have arranged to make me forget eight weeks of my life.

Willem Vandekamp knew about the baby.

And wanted it to live.

Untitled Document

"Scientists at Colorado State announce that they have isolated the specific hormone that initiates the change in form of *canis lupus lycanus*, otherwise known as the common werewolf."

—from the June 2, 1998, edition of the *New York Times*

DELILAH

When Pagano brought my breakfast, he had to open the door, because my milk carton wouldn't fit under it.

"I need to talk to Vandekamp." I had to know how I got pregnant. I had to look into his eyes while I demanded information, so I could see the truth and hopefully rule him out as a suspect.

I needed to know why he'd locked me away from everyone else and put me on a prenatal health food diet, and what all of that meant for the fate of the baby I shouldn't even be carrying.

I needed to shove my thumbs into his eye sockets and listen to him scream.

"That's not a request you get to make." Pagano pushed my breakfast into my room, then picked up the snack tray I'd slid into the hall untouched in the middle of the night. He frowned at the browning apple as he started to close the door to my cell.

"Wait. Please. Just tell him I want to talk."

"Not gonna happen."

"If you don't let me talk to him, I won't eat a bite of this."

Pagano shrugged. "Do what you've got to do." But the

tight line of his jaw said something else entirely. If he'd been instructed to make sure I took my vitamin, he was probably also supposed to make sure I ate.

I picked up the tray he'd slid into my room and held it over the toilet, tilting it so that the blueberries would have tumbled from their compartment, if not for the plastic wrap. "How much trouble are you going to be in if I flush this?"

He gave me an exasperated sigh. "Yes, you'll get me in trouble. But you'll also lose your work privileges."

I retracted my breakfast tray, surprised by the news. "Why didn't I have work privileges yesterday?"

Pagano frowned. "Yesterday you had an engagement." At the arena, of course.

"So, if I play nice, I get to work this afternoon? Outside my cell? Where I'll see other people?"

My handler's frown deepened. "What's wrong with you?" His gaze narrowed on me. "Should I call the infirmary?"

"I'm fine." I sank onto my stack of mats with my tray. "Close the door on your way out."

He frowned at me for several more seconds, then left.

When his footsteps receded down the hall, I peeled the plastic wrap from my breakfast tray. The scents of the sausage and egg-white omelet sent me lurching for the toilet, but heaving for several minutes produced nothing more than the water I'd drunk an hour earlier.

Only the fact that I'd never been pregnant—and hadn't known it was a possibility—could have led me to mistake morning sickness for a side effect of sedation.

When the nausea finally passed, I sat on the floor by the toilet for several more minutes, staring at my breakfast as if it had betrayed me. Then I scooped the omelet into the toilet and flushed it out of my life. I ate the fruit and the biscuit, then washed the vitamin down with my carton of milk. Then I brushed my teeth, ran my hands through my hair and sat on my stacked sleep mats and stared at the door, waiting for it to open.

With no way to measure time, I couldn't be sure how much of it passed before Pagano finally came back, but the interval felt like eternity. I was up and ready to go before he got my door open.

Pagano walked me from my own isolated building to the dormitory kitchen, where two men in plain white aprons were cooking, while a staff of four filled trays according to the specifications listed on the charts hanging above a prep table.

Mahsa and Simra were among the women loading carts with prepared trays. They both smiled and nodded, unsurprised to see me in what was evidently our normal routine. But when I headed for the empty cart next to theirs, Pagano grabbed my arm and redirected me with a frown. He hadn't yet figured out that I was missing memories, but he couldn't be far off the conclusion.

To my utter shock, Mahsa and Simra each left pushing a cart full of trays *unattended*. I couldn't understand that until I heard a handler warn them at the kitchen doorway that they had exactly fifteen minutes to complete their rounds and return the carts, before they would be paralyzed on the spot and collected by their handlers. That knowledge, along with the fact that their collars kept them from leaving the building or passing through any unauthorized doorway seemed to satisfy the staff that this was a perfectly safe arrangement.

Evidently the collars *were* equipped with locators, as I'd suspected.

The cart my handler led me to was being loaded with trays of gooey lasagna, aromatic garlic bread and a fresh spinach-and-cherry-tomato salad drizzled with balsamic vinaigrette. Unless Vandekamp was hiding another two dozen pregnant women, my best guess was that I would be delivering lunch trays to the guards, rather than to my fellow captives.

Pagano escorted me around the building, where I delivered the first few lunches to guards assigned to monitor the dormitories. They were all men. Every time I handed one of them a tray, I held my breath and looked right into his eyes, both hoping for and dreading the possibility of finding some private kind of recognition in them. Some cruel knowledge.

Would I be able to tell, if I were looking at the father of my child? Did I truly want to know, if there was nothing I could do about it?

After the dormitory, Pagano led me to the main building, where he knocked on a door labeled Security, and I gave a tray apiece to two men watching a huge bank of wall-mounted monitors. I tried not to be too obvious as I glanced at a tall shelf stacked with boxes identical to the one my collar had come in.

Were those extras, waiting to be programmed for new arrivals?

Was the security room also ground central for collar programming?

Pagano pulled me from the room before I'd learned anything useful, and I followed him back through the topiary and another iron gate, then into an unfamiliar building he called "the stable."

Inside, I found a small foyer joining two hallways.

"Are you good from here?" my handler asked, as he pointed his remote at me and pressed a button. I blinked at him in confusion. "You remember where you're going?" he clarified, and I noticed that Olive Burnett, the arena event coordinator, was hovering in the doorway, waiting to claim his full attention. He rolled his eyes at me in exasperation. "There are only two hallways, Delilah."

"Yeah." I glanced from Pagano to Burnette, then back. Evidently this was our regular arrangement. "I got it."

I couldn't leave the building, but I would get no better chance to snoop on my own.

I turned down the left-hand hallway and knocked on the first door, encouraged by the fact that I wasn't paralyzed or driven to my knees with pain by the proximity sensor in my collar.

"Yeah?" a guard said as he opened the door. His gaze brightened when it fell on my cart. "Great. We're starving."

I gave him two trays while I stared over his shoulder at a room lined with sterile white-tiled horse stalls, each occupied by a centaur or satyr. The centaurs each had room for only a couple of steps forward or backward, and they couldn't turn around at all in the cramped space.

My heart ached for them.

I recognized three of the centaurs and four of the satyrs from Metzger's, but they did not smile when they saw me. Their glazed gazes held nothing but fear, and just the sight of their misery made the *furiae* stir deep inside me.

But before my inner beast could get me in trouble, the handler closed the door in my face.

I distributed trays to three more rooms, then I knocked on the last door in the left-hand hallway. "Come in," a woman's voice called.

I opened the door to see a female handler holding an electric rotary file—it looked like an electric toothbrush, with a rough metal cylinder in place of the bristle head. Strapped to the table in front of her was an adolescent feline shifter I'd never seen before. That I could remember. Her eyes were closed, and her breathing was deep enough to indicate sedation, rather than true sleep.

"Just set the trays over there." The handler hardly glanced

at me as she pulled the poor girl's mouth open and began filing the points of her sharp canines.

I had to force myself to look away.

The back of the room—just like the four before it—was lined with built-in cages, each of which contained a single young shifter. I counted three boys and two girls. The last pen on the left stood open, waiting for the girl on the table to return.

I set two trays on the desk the handler had pointed at, and as I was heading back into the hall, my gaze caught on a familiar set of golden wolf eyes and long, tangled blond hair in one of the pens. "Genni!" I whispered, glad that the handler couldn't hear me over the grinding sound of her electric file.

But Genevieve heard me just fine; a werewolf's hearing is much better than any human's.

"What are you doing here?" I threaded my fingers through the mesh front of her cage, amazed that the guard had so much confidence in my collar that she hadn't even glanced up from her work. How long had I been serving her lunch?

"Where else would I be?" Genni whispered in her distinctive French accent, and I realized I shouldn't be surprised to see her.

Right before our coup, she'd been sold to the All American Menagerie. Gallagher and I had tried to buy her back as soon as we took over, but All American had already sold her because they couldn't make her perform and she'd been too feral to breed.

Her father, Claudio, had been devastated. He'd left the menagerie to look for her.

Genni looked thin, yet much healthier than she'd ever been in the menagerie. But she and the other young shifters were pale, as if they rarely saw the sun.

"Did you bring me *quelque chose*?" Genni asked, her gaze wandering to the trays I'd delivered.

"Um…sure. Just a sec." I glanced at the handler, to make sure she was still busy, then I snatched the garlic bread from both trays and slid it through the tray slot of Geni's cage, into her eager hands. "Eat fast."

Yet as soon as I'd given her the food, I felt guilty. Five other pairs of wide eyes watched our interaction, and I couldn't tell whether they were more hungry for food or for kindness. But I had nothing else to give.

"*Merci*. Have you figured out *les colliers* yet?" Genni whispered around a mouth full of bread. "How to…" she hesitated while she searched for the word "…turn them off?"

My eyes widened. I'd been trying to turn the collars off? All of them? Was that possible? Had I figured it out?

Could Vandekamp have erased my memory to take that knowledge from me?

"Hey! You know better, Delilah," a voice called out from behind me. Startled, I whirled around to see a second guard standing in the doorway. "Get moving."

I turned to give Genni an apologetic look, but she had her back to me, no doubt trying to eat the rest of her bread before the guard saw.

As I pushed my cart toward the next hallway, the guard glanced at his lunch tray in disgust.

"What? No garlic bread today?"

DELILAH

"What's going on?" I demanded as Pagano opened my door early one evening, several days after I'd awoken in the private cell.

He adjusted my collar's settings with the press of a button and waved me into the hall. "You've been engaged."

"But I delivered lunches today."

"You're filling in for one of the other females."

"Who?" My pulse spiked with worry as he led me down the hall toward the exit. "What happened to her?" Had someone else been injured? Been robbed of an unborn child? Or had I lost another friend?

Pagano's refusal to answer as he marched me down the hall left a bitter silence my brain filled with every horrible possibility for what had happened. For where we were going. For what might happen to my baby if this engagement went wrong.

Or if it went right.

The baby was never far from my thoughts. Every wave of nausea, bite of food and moment of inexplicable fatigue reminded me that I was pregnant. Each occasional beat of joy that pulsed through me with that thought immediately triggered an answering wave of guilt and anger. I couldn't be happy about the life growing inside me without agonizing over how it got there. Without feeling like I was betraying the past version of myself who'd suffered through the conception.

A hundred times a day, a bitter carousel of unanswered questions turned around and around my head, forever seeking answers that couldn't be caught. I knew only two things for sure.

First: I wanted the baby, no matter how I got it. No matter who its father was.

And second: I would not get to keep it, even if I got to birth it.

"Is this another one of those boring political parties?" I asked Pagano, desperate to reroute my thoughts. I'd served at two of them in the past few days, and though *boring* could reasonably be called a synonym for *safe*, it also made the time drag terribly.

Pagano gave me a strange look as he held the exterior door open. As if he hadn't expected me to notice that Vandekamp had addressed several of his guests as congressmen and two as governors.

His hand tightened on my arm as my bare feet hit the cool sidewalk. We walked the rest of the way to the prep room in silence, but this time only two of the chairs were occupied, one by Simra, the other by Zyanya.

Pagano led me to an unoccupied chair, where the third makeup artist stood ready to work on me, and when I was seated, he aimed his remote at my collar and took away my ability to move. And speak.

By then I'd been paralyzed countless times, but as always, my sudden helplessness hit me like a knife driven straight through my gut. I'd spent days at a time locked up in a menagerie cage, yet I'd never felt as vulnerable there as I did in the Spectacle's makeup chair, unable to either defend or express myself.

When we were all dressed and ready, the handlers led us out of the prep room, and I got a look at my fellow captives. The *marid*'s costume consisted only of strategically draped swaths of a filmy, sparkly blue material, so that she appeared to be wearing a flowing sheet of water. Her glittering silver hair had been pulled back from her face, where her huge blue eyes were magnified by expertly applied makeup.

Zyanya had been rubbed with body glitter so that she seemed to glow everywhere except the small patches of skin covered by her cheetah-print bikini. Her hair was pulled back and tied into a tight bun so it couldn't fall and obscure her cat eyes, and bright red lipstick made a stark contrast to her sharp feline incisors.

As we were escorted into the kitchen, where a dozen silver trays were already loaded and ready to serve, the event coordinator announced to the handlers, "The hunt starts in about ten minutes. The spectators are placing their final bets now."

The hunt? Dread twisted my stomach, triggering a resurgence of nausea."You go out in two minutes," the event coordinator said to us, as Pagano left me in line with my fellow servers.

"I hate the hunts," Simra whispered.

Zyanya nodded. "One of these days they're going to take me out of the kitchen and set me loose in the woods, and I'll come back with an arrow sticking out of my chest. Or not at all."

"That won't happen." But I was speaking from a platform of ignorance. I had no idea who Vandekamp used as prey for his hunts. I'd just found out there *were* hunts.

"Of course it will happen." Simra shrugged bare, sparkly shoulders. "When she's no longer young or pretty enough to serve food, they will hunt her. If she goes feral before that, they will hunt her. If they run out of prey, they will hunt her. That's how this works. Everyone dies eventually, during a private engagement, on the sand or in the hunts."

I could only stare at the *marid*, too horrified to argue.

Could I truly bring a child into this world? Would it be more merciful to let Tabitha Vandekamp end the whole thing, before the poor kid had a chance to truly suffer?

The event coordinator—Glen Fischer, according to his name tag—told us to pick up our trays.

I followed Simra through another door into the back of a large, dark room. The walls and floor were covered with black carpet, which dampened sound and seemed to absorb light. I started to step forward, but Zyanya grabbed my arm. When my eyes finally adjusted, I realized she'd stopped me from tumbling down a series of broad steps that formed stadium-style tiers the entire length of the room.

Instead of individual seats, each tier held a long, cloth-draped table with chairs lined up on one side, facing the sunken front of the large room, where a grid of huge television screens was mounted high on the wall. The seats were filled almost to capacity with an audience that was ninety percent male.

In front of the screens, low enough that his head wouldn't block anyone's view, a man wearing all black sat in front of a bank of computer monitors and what looked like high-tech editing equipment.

Though the overhead screens were blank, the tech was already busy adjusting settings on the displays in front of him, most of which showed various shots of the woods, filmed in the flat green glow of night-vision cameras.

Pagano stepped up to my side from his position with the other handlers against the back wall, when he noticed my confusion. "Those are live," he explained with a nod at the technician's monitors. "When the hunt begins, he'll throw those feeds up onto the big screens, so everyone can see."

He stepped back, and I followed Simra down the unoccupied side of the topmost table while Zyanya took the second tier. They distributed glasses of red and white wine while I offered a selection of heavy hors d'oeuvres. The meatball sliders and pork-belly wontons were big favorites, and it took most of my self-control not to vomit all over the tray at the scent of the meat.

Since when did morning sickness stretch into the evening?

The men all ogled, and several reached out to touch Simra. Either they'd been warned not to touch me, or my lack of cryptid features failed to fascinate them, either of which was fine with me. All I cared about was not falling down the tiered floor or throwing up my balanced lunch all over the guests.

The women looked at us with interest, yet only one reached up to run her finger over Zyanya's lower lip, boldly pulling it down to expose her canines. But when the lights dimmed and the television monitors at the front of the room lit up, Fischer waved us toward one wall, so we couldn't block anyone's view.

"Ladies and gentlemen, welcome to the Savage Spectacle's weekly hunt," he called out from the front of the room. "At this time, all wagers should already have been placed. If you've misplaced your receipt, please see the lovely lady at the back of the room."

I turned to find Olive Burnette, the other event coordinator, standing near the rear exit with her hands folded in front of her silver pencil skirt.

"Tonight's hunters reserved their spots several months ago, as we advise, because the wait is generally pretty long, but a spot in early December has opened up unexpectedly. If you're interested in claiming that spot, again, please see Ms. Burnette at the back of the room."

Two of the men and one woman stood, and all three made quick but polite strides toward Burnette.

"In case anyone is new to the event, let me go over the rules. There will be two hunters per round, competing to track down one prey. The level of difficulty increases with each round, as does the strength of the weapons issued to our hunters. Round-one hunters will be using Tasers. Round-two hunters will each use a longbow. Round-three hunters will be given hunting rifles. All hunters must use the weapons issued here at the Savage Spectacle. No personal weapons are allowed. All hunters must also use the safety equipment provided here at the Savage Spectacle, including Kevlar helmets fitted with night-vision cameras, safety goggles and Kevlar vests. Hunters in rounds two and three must be certified with their respective weapons either through the courses taught here at the Spectacle or through a qualifying third-party instructor.

"Each hunter will enter the hunting ground from a separate location, equidistant from the prey's starting point. For the safety of the general public, the hunting grounds are fully enclosed and impossible for the prey to escape, thanks to our proprietary containment collars. To keep the event both fair and challenging, only the first hunter to track down his prey is allowed to fire, and he's allowed one shot only. In rounds two and three, if that shot proves fatal, the hunter receives the top honor given here at the Spectacle, and everyone who bet on him will go home happy, drunk and with a wallet full of cash. And as an added incentive, if both the round-two and round-three prey are killed in accordance with the rules of the game, Mr. Vandekamp will issue a full refund to both champions!"

A cheer went up all across the room, but it was clear from Fischer's chuckle that such an event was rare.

"Okay, is everybody ready?"

The crowd cheered again. I clenched my teeth.

"Ladies and gentlemen, this is our technical guru, Charles Wheeler." Fischer gestured to the man seated in front of the bank of equipment. "Charles is in charge of the cameras, their feeds and the screens you see before you, and he's promised to give you the best show he can. Are you ready, Charles?"

"Always," Charles answered, to another round of cheers.

"And is our first pair of hunters ready?"

"Yes, they are. Up in round one, we have Henry Brewer and Jensen Miles. Mr. Brewer, please wave your hand in front of your helmet cam, so we can find you."

A hand appeared in front of one of the screens. "I'm here. Locked and loaded." He held his Taser up in front of the camera, and several of the audience members laughed.

At Charles's instruction, Mr. Miles also waved for the camera. Then the event coordinator began counting backward from ten. The audience chanted along with the countdown. Their gleeful, sadistic anticipation made my stomach churn.

When they got to the number five, one final television screen lit up, treating the entire room to a view, in shades of night-vision green, of the intended target, crouched on the ground in human form.

I sucked in a horrified breath.

A terrified squeak leaked from Zyanya's throat before she slapped one hand over her mouth, clutching her empty tray to her chest with the other.

"Who is it?" Simra whispered from my right.

When the audience shouted "One!" Charles pressed a button on his keyboard with a dramatic flourish. On-screen, the crouched form stiffened, then howled in pain as a red light flashed from his collar. Then he took off running.

"Ladies and gentlemen, tonight's target is a male cheetah

shifter, approximately twenty-five years old, who goes by the name of Payat."

"He's her brother," I whispered to Simra, as Zyanya trembled in silence against the wall.

On-screen, both hunters took off at a run, crashing through the woods with limbs scratching their faces and snagging on their clothes. The screens on the front wall showed each of their perspectives, and as soon as the camera that had showed Payat lost track of him, the image on that screen switched to his point of view. They'd strapped a camera onto him too, and had presumably attached it so that it wouldn't be dropped if he shifted into cheetah form. Which would be a serious risk for him, because of the time it would take.

Several other screens showed different views of the woods from some high vantage point. The cameras were probably strapped to the upper branches of trees.

"They're armed with Tasers," I reminded Zyanya in a whisper. "He'll survive." Physically. But being hunted through the woods in front of a live studio audience was a trauma and humiliation he might never truly recover from.

Zyanya nodded, but her gaze stayed glued to the screens. After twenty minutes of watching two amateur hunters thrash their way through dense forest, Olive Burnette motioned for us to follow her from the room. I had to practically drag Zyanya away.

We reloaded our trays in the kitchen, then headed back into the viewing room, where one glance at the screens on the front wall made me catch my breath. One of the hunters was squatting, staring right at a thin, hunched figure in the brush.

"I've got him," the hunter whispered into his microphone. "If I can just...get...close enough."

The audience had gone silent, as had the event coordinators and the handlers. The only person in the room who wasn't frozen in fascination was Charles, who was quietly monitoring the screens in front of him, to make sure that his audience had the best possible view.

"Ladies and gentlemen, Mr. Miles has the target in his sight. If you placed money on him this evening, it looks like you made a very wise decision."

"If I could just…get a little…closer," Mr. Miles said, clearly oblivious to Fischer's narration. On-screen, he lunged through the brush. We heard a soft thunk, then a grunt and the buzz of electricity. The shadowy hunched form in front of him fell into the greenish underbrush with a thump and the crackle of dead leaves. "Got him!" Miles shouted, and Zyanya's sob was swallowed by cheers from the audience.

"Ladies and gentlemen, it looks like we have a—"

"There he is!" Mr. Brewer whispered from his feed, on the far left.

The coordinator spun toward the wall of screens at his back, and the hand holding the microphone fell to his side in surprise. Square in the middle of Brewer's view was a thin, hunched figure, similar in silhouette to the form his competitor had just dropped with a stun gun, and was now carefully approaching across a bed of underbrush.

My focus volleyed from feed to feed, and the general movement of heads from the crowd in front of me appeared to be doing the same thing.

"Charles, are you seeing this?" Fischer seemed to have forgotten that the rest of us could hear him. "Did we release two captives onto the hunting grounds?"

Charles shook his head, but I couldn't hear what he said.

"Can you patch me through?"

"Of course," Charles said. "Which one do you want to talk to?"

A confused buzz of voices rose from the crowd in front of

us and Zyanya grabbed my arm so tightly in her free hand that I almost dropped my full tray.

"Give me Brewer," Fischer said. Then he turned to face the room full of spectators. "Ladies and gentlemen, there seems to be some confusion in the field. Give us just a moment to sort it out." His smile blossomed wide enough for me to see from across the room, even in the near dark. "And please consider this extra excitement to be on the house!"

The audience chuckled, but their gazes stayed glued to the screens. As did mine. And when the coordinator waved a handler forward and spoke to him privately, I knew exactly what he was saying.

Go get Vandekamp.

"You're hooked in," Charles said, and the coordinator turned back to the screen on the far left.

"Mr. Brewer, are you certain you've spotted your target?"

The image on Brewer's screen jumped as he did, startled by a voice he obviously hadn't expected to hear from inside his helmet. "Yes. He's just feet away," the hunter whispered. "Can you see him?"

"We see something," Fischer said, and the tension in his voice was quite clear. "But we aren't sure what, exactly. Please approach with caution."

"Will do." Brewer stepped almost silently out of his hiding place, and at the bottom of his screen, his hands extended in front of him, holding his stun gun.

On the other screen, Miles slowly approached his downed target, twigs cracking with every step he took.

Brewer fired his stun gun with an audible jolt of electricity. The form in front of him jumped with the impact, then shook as electricity passed through him. An instant later, he hit the ground with hardly a sound. He'd landed in a patch of bare dirt.

"He's down!" Brewer bounded forward and his hand rose toward the screen. Something clicked, and a flashlight shone from his helmet onto the form at his feet. "I've got him! I won!"

And he had. Payat lay on the ground, unconscious. Still in human form.

"What the hell...?" Again, the coordinator forgot he was holding his microphone, and this time Brewer heard him, as well. "Then what did the other guy catch?"

As one, we turned to Miles's screen as he finally switched on his own flashlight. The beam skirted the underbrush, then settled on a fur-covered form lying on its side, its ribs rising and falling with each labored breath. "What the hell is that?" Miles demanded, as the audience gasped. "That's not a cheetah."

"No, it isn't." The coordinator turned to Charles. "It's a werewolf. Patch me through to him."

"You've got Miles," Charles said with the click of a few buttons.

"Mr. Miles, slowly back away from the creature, and stand very still. We're sending help your way immediately."

"What the hell's going on?" Instead of backing away, Miles leaned forward for a closer look. "What the—"

The creature lunged at him in a blur of sharp-toothed muzzle and glowing eyes.

Miles shouted and stumbled back. The werewolf's muzzle clamped closed around his left forearm. Miles screamed and swung his stun gun like a hammer. The wolf let him go and backed away, growling.

Blood soaked through Miles's sleeve, a darker shade of green on the infrared cameras. He fired the last load from his stun gun, and the werewolf collapsed on the ground, trembling as the second dose of electricity coursed through him.

"We appear to have had a breach." Fischer had clearly seen what I'd already noticed—the fur-covered form on the ground in Miles's feed wasn't wearing a collar. And while the coordinator clearly thought one of the Savage Spectacle's captives had somehow gotten out of his collar and escaped his cell, I knew better.

I recognized the form on the screen in front of me, even though it was painted several shades of night-vision green. I knew that fur, and I knew that muzzle, and I knew the single eye blinking sluggishly up at the camera.

Vandekamp hadn't lost one of his werewolves; he'd gained one.

Claudio had come to claim his daughter.

For Immediate Release: January 18, 2002
AFCR contact: Rebecca Foster

WASHINGTON, DC—The American Foundation for Cryptid Research has awarded $9.9 million in research grants to three projects, each of which hopes to unlock genetic secrets of a specific cryptid species. This award marks the Foundation's largest grants to date, the majority of which will go to a project at Colorado State University, seeking to map the genome of several species of shifter hybrids...

DELILAH

Claudio was tranquilized on a live camera feed, in spite of the very active interest of Mr. Miles, who seemed unconcerned with his own injury and thrilled by the unexpected excitement. While handlers fitted the wolf with a muzzle and a paramedic bandaged Miles's arm, Willem Vandekamp came into the viewing room and whispered something to Olive Burnette, who left with her orders. Then Vandekamp marched to the front of the room and took the microphone from Fischer.

Over the mic, he effusively congratulated Mr. Brewer on his quick and virtually effortless mastery of a vicious cheetah shifter and apologized for the "technical difficulties." To make it up to such a valued customer, Vandekamp offered him a makeup hunt, on the house.

That must have been quite a generous financial offer, because Brewer, who'd been vocally disappointed in the reaction to his victory, suddenly seemed quite satisfied with his hunting experience.

The screens went blank while they reset the game field for

the second round, and the handlers gave us a signal to start refilling drinks and plates.

After a fifteen-minute intermission, the house lights went down again, and this time Vandekamp ran the show himself. He announced that the second-round hunters would be chasing a feral adolescent werewolf named Genevieve who would as soon tear their throats out as look at them. Which was why the hunters had been outfitted with bite-proof sleeves and collars, and why they'd be hunting this vicious creature not with stun guns, but with the lethal longbow.

For one long, terrifying moment, I couldn't breathe.

That's why Genni was in the stables, rather than the dormitory. The very night her father had broken into the Spectacle to save her, Vandekamp had scheduled her to die.

"Oh, shit," Zyanya whispered from my right.

"What?" Simra's gaze roamed the screens, looking for the source of our distress.

"We know her," I said softly. "She's only thirteen years old."

"I've seen her hunted twice, both times in the first round," Simra said. "She's very hard to catch, because she can fit into very small spaces, and she doesn't go down easy."

I swallowed a bitter taste at the back of my mouth. "How often do they die in this round?"

"About half the time," Simra said, and my hand clenched around the edge of my tray.

"Hunters, are you ready?" Vandekamp asked.

My attention narrowed on his face, then slid to the wall of screens behind him.

"Ready." A gloved hand appeared on one of the right-hand screens, and about half

the audience cheered.

"Good to go!" A second hand, also gloved, appeared on

one of the left-hand screens, and the other half of the audience cheered.

"Mr. Wheeler, is the prey ready?" Vandekamp stepped to one side of the room, while Charles Wheeler pressed a series of buttons on the keyboard in front of him. The center overhead screen changed to show a small, slim humanoid shape, too dark to reveal much detail. But I would have recognized Genevieve's silhouette anywhere.

Charles punched a few more buttons then twisted a small dial, and the image lightened to reveal Genni in full detail, painted in a monochromatic scheme of green.

As Payat had, she wore nothing but her collar and a small video camera mounted on a headband.

Vandekamp lifted his hands, then dropped them with a flourish. "Let the hunt begin!"

Charles's hand hovered over his keyboard for a single dramatic second. Then he punched the space bar with one finger, and a gate slid open on-screen. For a five count, Genni pressed herself against the bars at her back, and in the greenish view, I could see her focus shift back and forth as she assessed her surroundings. She knew where she was; I could see that in her calm assessment. She was afraid, but not panicked, because she'd been through it all before. But she probably had no idea that this time the hunters were wielding arrows, rather than stun guns.

"Let's get her moving, Mr. Wheeler," Vandekamp said from his position against the right-hand wall, and Charles pressed another series of buttons.

A second later, the front of Genni's collar blinked bright red, and she jumped, startled by an obvious jolt of pain. Then she ran.

I watched, my heart pounding as she nimbly ducked below branches, dodged vines and leapt over roots I wouldn't have been able to see with my human eyes. At times she was little more than a green-tinged blur, moving virtually silently through the underbrush, effortlessly avoiding twigs and dead leaves which would make noise and give away her position.

I'd never seen a shifter let loose in her natural environment before, and where Payat had been terrified and timid, Genni was breathtaking.

She's done this before. And not just in her two previous hunts. Like Payat, Genevieve had grown up in a cage, with no experience in the wild. At some point after All American sold her, Genni must have logged serious hours in the woods.

The odds were actually in her favor, and that fact left me both happy and terrified for her. If she survived this round, next time they'd put her up against hunting rifles, and even if she recovered from being shot once, she couldn't recover over and over.

The ending would ultimately be the same for everyone sentenced to the hunt: they may survive the round, but they could not survive the game itself.

Still, for nearly an hour, Genni evaded not just capture, but detection, and when one of the men chasing her finally got a glimpse, he lost it a second later.

From her viewpoint camera, the audience could see that she had climbed a tree, but the hunter was completely unaware until she leapt from one branch to the next, and the limb she landed on held her slight weight but creaked beneath the burden.

I gasped when the hunter looked up, and Genevieve appeared in the center of his viewpoint screen.

The woman I was serving a meatball slider to shoved me out of her field of vision. I tripped over the edge of the tier and would have crashed into other guests if Simra hadn't grabbed my arm with her spare hand.

We rushed toward the side of the room and turned back to the screens just in time to see an arrow fly.

Genni leapt for another branch. The arrow hit her thigh in midair with a barely perceptible thunk.

The audience burst into applause. Genevieve crashed to the ground, already growling, and when the hunter approached, she swiped at him with fingers tipped with canine claws, even in human form.

"Mr. Perry, hold your fire," Charles said into his microphone, when the hunter on-screen pulled a second arrow from his quiver. "You've already taken your shot." He pressed another button, and the red light on Genni's collar flashed. She froze in the hunter's viewpoint screen, immobilized, and the hunter lowered his weapon.

"I won?"

"Yes, sir, you are tonight's round-two victor." Vandekamp took center stage again, then he covered his mic and gave Charles instructions to set up for round three. But Charles was already tapping away at his keyboard and speaking softly into his microphone. "Unfortunately, Mr. Perry, it looks like your quarry will survive."

Simra, Zyanya and I were the only ones in the room who didn't boo.

ROMMILY

The oracle sat on the end of the exam table, her hands cuffed in her lap, her bare feet dangling over the pull-out step. The paper beneath her made a loud crinkling sound when she moved, so she sat as still as she could.

"Hey, Oakland, did she say anything to you?" the man in the white coat whispered from the other side of the room.

Rommily heard him, but she was much more interested in the lines of grout running through the tile floor.

"No, but she told Perkins he'd be trampled by a 'mad pageant,'" the man in the black uniform answered. "Whatever the hell that means."

The tiles were several different sizes, and the grout between them appeared to follow no pattern. It was like a maze with no center, and Rommily couldn't seem to find her way out...

Sharp footsteps clicked into the room, and a pair of shiny white shoes with very tall heels stepped into the tile maze.

Rommily blinked, then looked up to see the woman with tightly twisted hair staring at her. Scowling.

"Mrs. Vandekamp." The man in the white coat stepped forward, but Rommily's handler stayed on the edge of the room.

"So?" the woman said. "What's the prognosis? Is there any damage?"

"Nothing physical. We had to sedate her to do an exam and run X-rays, but there're no healed fractures. No significant scarring. Her anatomy is virtually identical to that of a human, except in the ocular region, and—"

"Then what's wrong with her?"

The man in the coat shrugged. "The problem seems to be psychological."

"Are you suggesting we call in a therapist? For an *animal*?"

Rommily's gaze fell to the floor again, watching the woman's pointed left heel stab into an intersection of the grout maze.

"That's your call, ma'am. All I'm saying is that oracles are so similar to us that they don't actually fall within my training as a cryptoveterinarian. According to Rommily's record, her entire family passed for human until she was around four years old, and—"

"So did the surrogates, Doctor," the woman snapped. "Looking human doesn't make her human. What I need to know is whether or not she can be fixed in a manner cost-effective enough to be practical."

"Probably not." The man in the coat cleared his throat. "But she might be worth keeping around if you want to maintain her sisters' mental health and profitability. Considering the psychological fragility of oracles, in general…"

The woman groaned, and her right heel stepped into the middle of a small rectangular tile. "Send her back to the dorm," she called over her shoulder on her way out of the room. But Rommily hardly registered her fate. Now that the intruding shoes were gone, she was feverishly tracing the grout lines. Searching for a way out.

"Come on." Oakland pulled Rommily down from the table by one arm, careful only to touch her sleeve, even though he wore gloves.

The oracle dragged her feet, staring at the floor.

"Rommily," the handler snapped. He gasped when she looked up at him through eyes clouded with a white film.

"Crushed by a child in the night…" she mumbled.

"What?" Chill bumps rose over Oakland's arms. But the oracle wasn't finished.

"The cock will crow at midnight, and the bull will rule the maze."

DELILAH

I spent the next day in isolation, in my concrete cell. Except for Pagano, who brought breakfast and lunch, I saw no one, and when I asked why I'd been given neither exercise nor a shift of delivering lunch trays, my handler replied only with silence.

When my cell door creaked open at dusk, I stood, expecting to find Pagano carrying my dinner tray. Instead, I came face-to-face with Willem Vandekamp. Pagano stood just behind him, in the hallway.

"You've been requested for another private engagement," Vandekamp said.

Blood rushed to my head, and the small room seemed to swim around me.

Private engagement. Me, alone with a guest. I had no exotic features and no marketable cryptid abilities, so there was no reason for a client to want to see me alone, up close and personal, that I could think of. Except for one.

"No." I held Vandekamp's gaze, searching for some change in the way he looked at me. Some sign of cruel or intimate knowledge. If he knew I was pregnant, he must know how it happened. "I need to talk to you privately."

"We're not negotiating. You're going, and you'll do what's expected, or Gallagher's collar will malfunction for a full thirty seconds during his next match." Which would be plenty of time for any opponent to do serious damage. Vandekamp had me, and he knew it. "I don't know why you bother arguing. We both know you like it." He gave me an infuriatingly casual shrug. "And even if you don't, you won't remember it."

A bolt of surprise shot up my spine. "Why not?"

He gave me a strange look, then turned to Pagano without answering. "Get her ready. The van is fueled and ready."

I blinked, trying to make sense of what I'd just heard. I was leaving the Spectacle, and Vandekamp was going to have my memory of an engagement erased. Had he done that before? Was he responsible for the entire two-month gap? Was that intentional, or had something gone wrong with what was evidently a standard practice?

"Erasing the memory of something doesn't mean it never happened," I said, as the questions compounded in my head.

Vandekamp laughed. "That's exactly what you said last time." As he turned to leave, he put one hand on Pagano's shoulder. "Bring her to me as soon as you get back. I'll be waiting."

"Where are they sending me?" I asked the moment Vandekamp's footsteps faded.

"I don't know where you're going," Pagano said as he programmed my collar to let me out of the room. "They always preprogram the address into the van's GPS."

Was I supposed to know that, or was that detail among those they evidently repeatedly stole from me?

"You have to know something," I insisted as I stepped into the hall. But if he did, he kept it to himself.

In a bathroom at the end of the hall, my handler instructed me to shower, then change into the clean scrubs waiting folded up on the floor. Pagano didn't turn away, but he didn't look particularly interested in seeing me naked either, so I mentally crossed him off the paternity-possibility list. And though I had no memories to support that conclusion, it felt right.

The makeup room was empty when we arrived, except for the one artist evidently waiting for me. As I settled into the chair she'd set up, I noticed that the makeup laid out on her tray didn't include body glitter, sparkly fake eyelashes or little pots of paint and small brushes. She had only collected things I might have put on my own face when I'd been a normal woman with a normal apartment, a normal job and a normal boyfriend. Forever ago.

She worked quickly and quietly, and when she was finished, instead of dressing me in my typical skimpy, lacy black costume, she brought out a surprisingly modest gray-and-white housekeeper's uniform and a pair of black flat-soled shoes.

As I pulled the dress over my head and tugged it into place, I wondered how soon my pregnancy would start to show. Surely the lady in charge of dressing me would be the first to notice. Did Vandekamp have a plan for that? Would he keep me totally isolated once the baby became obvious?

When I was dressed, the makeup artist wrapped a simple black scarf around my neck to conceal my collar, and the implications of that one detail nearly paralyzed me with morbid curiosity.

When I was ready, Pagano walked me to the parking lot behind the dormitory, where an unmarked black van sat waiting. The sight of it made my stomach twist and my palms sweat. I stopped walking. My comfortable black work shoes seemed to be glued to the sidewalk.

"Come on, Delilah." Pagano tugged on my arm with one gloved hand.

"I can't." I couldn't let Vandekamp rig Gallagher's next fight, but… "I can't do this."

"You always say that. Don't make me use the remote."

I forced my feet to move, because he wouldn't just be shocking me; he'd also be shocking the baby.

Pagano cuffed my hands to the armrests and my ankles to the base of a seat in the middle row of the van, then he closed the sliding side door and got into the driver's seat.

"How many times have we done this now?" I asked as we pulled out of the parking lot onto a long gravel drive cut through the woods behind the dorm.

He took a left-hand turn onto a narrow two-lane road and drove west, toward the setting sun. "I haven't been keeping count."

For several miles, I stared out the windshield at the sunset, trying to figure out how to get more information out of him without exposing my own ignorance. "So, what's going to happen?" I was pretty sure I understood the basics, but was the maid's uniform to suit some kind of specific fetish, or was it standard? "I mean, is this just like the other engagements, or…?"

"I don't go in with you." He met my gaze in the rearview mirror. "I don't know any more than you do, Delilah."

"How is that possible? They take my memory before I even…come out?"

Pagano accelerated to the speed limit, then engaged the cruise control. "No, they do that back at the infirmary, but they take pretty much everything from the moment you leave your cell until they're done messing around in your head."

The very thought raised chill bumps all over me.

"So I'm not going to remember any of this?"

"Nope."

Yet even knowing that, he hadn't gotten mean or grabby. Maybe he was scared to touch me. Or maybe he wasn't a bad guy—for an armed man holding me against my will. Was that why he'd been assigned to me? Had Vandekamp realized he'd need someone the *furiae* had no reason to punish?

"How do they do it? How do they take the memory?"

Pagano glanced at me in the mirror. "I'm not supposed to…"

I clutched the arm of my chair as we accelerated onto the highway. "If they're going to make me forget anyway, why does it matter if you tell me?"

"Because there are rules. If I break them, I lose my job."

I squinted as the glare from the setting sun caught my eye. "Who's going to tell, if I can't remember?"

He scowled at me in the mirror. "Delilah…"

"Fine." I thought in silence for a few more miles, while the sun slipped below the horizon, then I took another shot. "If they don't mess around in my head until we get back to the Spectacle, then I must know what happened immediately after an engagement, right? When I get back in the van?"

"Yes." Pagano accelerated to pass a slow moving truck. "But you never talk about it when you come out, and I never ask. But I can tell you that you always ask these same questions. You're nervous every time you go in."

"And when I come out?" I sucked in a deep breath, then let it out. "How do I look? Am I crying?" Am I hurt?

"Delilah, you don't want to do this. Just get it over with and let them take the memory. You're always better after that."

Horror washed over me, and suddenly the van seemed to be closing in around me. "So, you send me in and let them take whatever they want, then you drive me back and let

Vandekamp steal the memory? Why? To keep me functional? If you cut out the rot, the fruit stays fresh longer?"

His gaze met mine in the mirror again, and it wasn't unsympathetic, but his voice carried thick threads of warning. "This is the way it works."

"I'm going to be sick." They hadn't gotten all the rot. I could feel it growing inside me, and if I didn't get rid of it, it would infect the baby. And maybe the *furiae*.

"No, you're not." Oncoming headlights painted the inside of the van with bright light. "Take a deep breath."

My stomach heaved. Bile burned in the back of my throat. "Stop the car. I'm going to vomit."

"Just take a deep breath and lean back. You'll be fine. You always are."

Maybe. But only because afterward they would open me up and scrape out all the parts that weren't good anymore.

Why would Vandekamp erase the memory, but leave me with the living, growing proof of what had happened? Did the father know? Did he want the child? Was he paying the Spectacle to keep the baby healthy? Surely Vandekamp wouldn't protect my pregnancy unless he could somehow profit from it.

Unless the baby was his…

After a nearly silent hour-and-a-half-long drive, according to the dashboard clock, we drove into a neighborhood full of large houses seated back from the road on sprawling lawns. Pagano turned the van onto a long brick driveway, then drove past the huge lawn, an elaborate circular drive and a massive house strategically lit by garden and floodlights. He parked behind the house, next to a black sedan.

Pagano uncuffed me, and my heart thumped harder as we climbed the back porch steps. A man in a black suit opened the door and ushered us into a huge kitchen that smelled like sugar cookies but looked as if it had never been used.

Paralyzing pressure built around my lungs as I eyed the man, trying to determine what kind of person he was based on the look in his eyes and the set of his jaw, but I couldn't catch his gaze.

Pagano turned me toward the door we'd just come through and pointed at the top of the frame, where I found a device clipped to the wood, steadily blinking red. "If you go more than two hundred feet from this sensor or my remote control you'll be paralyzed and in a great deal of pain."

Before I could respond, a woman in understated but expensive clothes stepped into the room, followed by a second woman in her fifties wearing the very same housekeeper's uniform I wore. Minus the scarf.

My confusion mounted. I'd assumed I'd been engaged by the man of the house, and that his wife would not be home.

"This is the temp girl?" The well-dressed woman's gaze swept over me, lingering nowhere but my eyes, where she seemed to be looking for something specific.

"Yes, ma'am," Pagano said, and still the woman's gaze held mine.

"I'm going out. You are to dust all the second-floor bedrooms." With that, the woman marched out the back door and down the steps, followed by the man in the suit, who was evidently her driver.

Confused, I glanced at Pagano, but he only shrugged and headed out the door after them to wait in the van. Leaving me alone in the house with the real housekeeper.

"Here."

I turned to find her holding out a dust rag and a spray bottle of furniture polish. When I took them, she pulled a vacuum cleaner from a closet in a dark hallway off the kitchen, then disappeared into another room. A moment later, the vacuum cleaner turned on, and the sound echoed throughout the house.

Alone, I stared around the cavernous kitchen, as bewildered as I'd been terrified moments before. Then I ventured toward the front of the house and found a curving staircase leading up from the lavish entry. Was I actually supposed to dust? Who spends an obscene amount of money to hire a cryptid that doesn't even look like a cryptid to dust the upstairs bedrooms?

With the vacuum cleaner masking the sound of my footsteps, I climbed the stairs to a landing in the middle of a hallway branching to either side. To the left were three closed doors and on my right I counted four.

Exactly how many rooms would I be dusting?

In the first bedroom on the left, I sprayed the dust rag with the cleaner and began wiping down the furniture, careful not to turn my back to the door. There had to be more to the engagement than dusting, and if the vacuum cleaner would cover my steps, it would cover someone else's too.

The dresser, both nightstands, all three bookshelves and the sleigh bed frames were all spotless and free of dust. But I dusted them anyway. Then, when no one came looking for me, I went through the drawers.

Hers held a well-worn paperback novel, a bottle of lotion, a pair of fingernail clippers and a hospital ID badge identifying her as Dr. Sarah Aaron, trauma surgeon.

His held a handful of change, a comb, a wad of receipts and a wallet, confirming my terrifying suspicion that the man of the house was still home. His Virginia state driver's license identified him as Bruce Aaron. Age forty-two. Organ donor.

I used some of Sarah's lotion—an expensive, silky formula I couldn't have afforded in my life before captivity and an unparalleled indulgence under my current circumstances—then put everything back the way I'd found it and headed into the hall. I had one hand on the doorknob to the next room when something thunked from within it. A cry of pain followed, too high-pitched to be drowned out by the low hum of the vacuum.

I pushed the door open, assuming someone had fallen. Inside, I found a child's bedroom full of toys and small furniture. A large man in a white button-down shirt stood with his fist raised over his head. At his feet sat a little boy clutching his side in pain. Finger-shaped bruises ringed the child's arm.

The *furiae* perked up like a cat catching a whiff of food. She stretched inside me, and my fingertips began to tingle as my nails reacted to her touch. She blinked, and my vision sharpened as she took control of it.

The man turned, his face a mask of fury. "Who the fuck are you?" His fist fell to his side but remained clenched. He stomped toward me, each step aggressive and pronounced, like a bull about to charge.

The *furiae* blinked at him through my eyes and smiled at him with my mouth. She was practically daring him to touch her, and he didn't see it. He didn't know...

The father grabbed my arm and hauled me into the hall. His grip hurt, but the *furiae* felt only righteous anger. The man slammed his son's door and grabbed my other arm, lifting me onto my toes. He looked down into my eyes, and I could see that he expected to find fear. That he craved it.

What he found instead were the empty, black-veined orbs my eyes became when the *furiae* took control of them.

The man choked on a startled gasp and let me go. He backed away, but the living anger coiled up inside me wanted much more from him than fear. Much more than remorse.

I grabbed his arm. My needlelike nails sank through his skin, and the man's mouth fell open as he stared at me. As my rage poured into him. He seemed to be screaming, yet he made no sound.

All you need is a little discipline. The words floated through my head, and I couldn't tell whether they were his or the *furiae*'s. *You'll thank me when you're older.*

When the rage abated, I let him go. He blinked once, then gripped the frame of an open door across the hall and slammed his head into it. Wood creaked beneath the force of the blow. The man stood upright, and a trickle of blood ran from the gash in his forehead down his nose, then dripped onto his shirt.

He smashed his head into the wood again. And again. And again.

The *furiae* purred inside me, then curled up to watch the show as my vision returned to normal and my hair settled around my shoulders.

The father pounded his head against the door frame over and over and over. Blood poured from the ever-widening gash and smeared on the dark wood. When the frame became too slippery to grip, he stood up straight, and a flash of bone peeked through his torn flesh. Then he turned and gripped the other side of the door frame and continued slamming his head into the wood.

"Dad?" a soft voice called from the boy's room.

Shit.

I opened the door and peeked inside, careful to shield the child's view of the hall with my body. He stared up at me from the floor, still clutching his side, and my gaze traveled over the cobblestone pattern of bruises climbing his arms and legs, in varying shades of old and new.

"Stay here," I said. "Your mother will be back for you very soon. Do you understand? Don't go into the hall."

The boy nodded. I forced a smile for him, then I turned on the television set up on his dresser and closed the door. I turned my back on the man still beating himself against the door frame and walked down the stairs as calmly as I could, clutching the railing. Trying not to panic.

When Vandekamp found out what I'd done, he'd kill me. Or he'd hurt Gallagher. Or he'd kill me after he made me watch him hurt Gallagher.

Downstairs, I raced for the back door, trying to figure out how to tell Pagano that I'd messed up. That we needed to go. That someone needed to go see about the poor boy crying in his bedroom. Then call an ambulance.

I skidded to a stop in the kitchen when I saw the boy's mother standing in front of her island, gripping the edge of the dark granite countertop.

"Is it done?" She looked so tense. So hopeful. "Is he...?"

And suddenly I understood.

I hadn't been sent for the pleasure of some sick man with a cryptid fetish.

His wife had engaged me to save her son—and maybe herself—from an abusive husband, in some manner that wouldn't involve a messy divorce or the splitting of assets. And though my inner beast had curled up to enjoy the sleep of the righteous, I felt used in a way I'd never thought possible.

Vandekamp had found a way to manipulate and profit from justice.

"Your husband needs immediate medical attention," I told the woman staring at me from across her kitchen island. "And likely a long-term care facility."

She frowned. "No. My son. Is he...?"

And that's when I realized that the hardest part for her wasn't hiring someone to hurt her husband. It was having to leave her son alone with him, to be sure the *furiae* saw what she needed to see.

The hardest part for me was knowing that if my child were

born into captivity, it would never see such a miraculous end to its suffering.

"Your son is fine. You should go to him. He doesn't understand what happened."

"Yes. Thank you." Tears filled the woman's eyes. She grabbed my hand, squeezing my fingers in mute gratitude, and I was suddenly terrified that she'd know I'd used her lotion. Then she turned and raced out of the room, headed for the stairs.

Her driver opened the back door for Pagano, who came in and pressed a button on his remote. The light over the rear door flashed, and he waved me forward. "Someone will be by shortly to collect the rest of the sensors," he said to the driver. "Please thank your boss for his business and let us know if he requires any further services."

He. Pagano had no idea who'd hired me or why.

The driver locked the door behind us.

"That was fast," Pagano said as he cuffed me to my seat in the van. His gaze scanned what he could see of my face and limbs, then settled on the hand-shaped bruises on my arms. "Do you want to tell me about it?"

"No." I stared at the house through the windshield as he circled the van, then slid into the driver's seat, and I wondered what the woman inside was doing. How long would it take the ambulance to arrive? Would she call one, or would she just let him beat himself to death?

"Who lives in that house?" Who are Bruce and Sarah Aaron, that she could afford Vandekamp's services. Surely surgeons don't make *that* much money.

Pagano shook his head. "I can't tell you that."

"They're going to make me forget anyway. What does it matter?"

"Delilah..."

I glanced at the number on the bricked mailbox as he pulled the van out of the long driveway and onto the deserted street. "Please. Who am I going to tell?"

He sighed and met my gaze in the rearview mirror. "That was the home of Senator Bruce Aaron, chairman of some kind of committee up in Washington. Evidently a very powerful man. He attended a couple of events a few weeks ago and must have taken a liking to you then."

A senator. Some kind of political bigwig. And Vandekamp had accepted money to let me put him out of business.

"Well, he won't be a repeat customer."

DELILAH

"How did it go?" Vandekamp demanded the second Pagano closed the door, leaving me alone with the boss in his office, handcuffed, but otherwise unrestrained.

"How many times have you erased my memory?"

He sat on the edge of his desk and picked up his remote control, but surely the implied threat was empty. If he silenced me, I couldn't answer his questions, and he couldn't shock me without hurting the baby he obviously wanted to protect.

I shrugged. "You answer my question, and I'll answer yours."

"No, you answer my question, or I'll lock you in a room with no window for the next month and make sure your boyfriend suffers in the ring." He gave me a moment to let that sink in, and I could only clench my fists at my back.

"Is he dead?" Vandekamp pressed.

"Who? Bruce Aaron?" I asked, and his brows rose. I shrugged. "He left his ID lying around. Why would you want a United States senator to kill himself?"

"So, he is dead?"

Another shrug. "When I left, he was beating his own head against a door frame. Whether or not his wife chooses to call an ambulance is up to her."

His cold smile was the most genuine emotional reaction I'd seen from the owner of the Savage Spectacle. No doubt he only let me see it because I wouldn't remember it.

"Why erase my memory? Who am I going to tell? The next client? A party guest?"

Vandekamp circled his desk and made a note on a sticky pad.

"Are all my private engagements like this? Just...vengeance?" Nothing that could get me pregnant?

He continued scribbling.

"Do I always come here afterward? Are we always alone?" Was I looking at the father of my unborn child?

"Are you going to make me silence you?"

"Is that what you like? Women who can't say no?"

He finally looked up, his gaze narrowed. "Do not assume I share my clientele's fetishes."

Was that a yes or a no? Was he saying one of his clients had done this to me?

My eyes watered. I swallowed compulsively, trying to hold back words that would show him how desperate I was for information. But the pressure was too much. The opportunity was too rare. "What don't I remember?"

Vandekamp put his pen down and looked up at me, as if he suddenly found my questions fascinating.

"Tell me what I'm missing," I demanded through clenched teeth. "Do you have any idea what it's like not to know what you've done? What's been done to you?"

"You're saying ignorance isn't bliss?" That odd smile was back, and I realized he was studying my pain, like a scientist conducting research. Yet enjoying it like a psychopath. He came around the desk again and looked down at me from inches away. "You're upset because you can't remember all the time we've spent together? All these private meetings?" He ran one hand boldly down my arm, and there wasn't even a hint of fear in his gaze. He knew I couldn't hurt him unless I saw him hurt someone else.

He wasn't afraid of me.

"You know, most people think cryptids raised free are harder to control than the rest, but I think it's just a matter of pressing the right button. And you have *so* many buttons."

I closed my eyes as he trailed one finger up the side of my neck and over my chin. "Just tell me."

"Ask me nicely."

I exhaled slowly and opened my eyes. "Tell me *please*, Dr. Vandekamp."

He laughed and took a step back. "No."

Deep in the bowels of the infirmary, Pagano took me down a hall I'd never noticed before, which shouldn't have been possible. I'd been in the infirmary half a dozen times to deliver lunch trays, that I could remember, and my duties had taken me all over the building.

Halls don't just suddenly appear. But they can be made to disappear. Or rather, to go unnoticed. Which meant that Vandekamp had cryptids in his collection that I'd never met, or even seen. Cryptids with very interesting abilities.

Or maybe I had met them, but couldn't remember.

My handler opened a door near the end of the strange hallway and led me into a small, unoccupied room, where a single barber-style chair was bolted to the floor. Laid out on a counter that ran along one wall was a set of gray scrubs.

"Change clothes and put the costume and shoes on the counter."

Pagano watched while I changed, but again I saw no real interest in his assessing gaze. When I was dressed in gray scrubs, the tile floor cold against my newly bare feet, he gestured at the chair in the center of the room.

I sat, and he pressed a button on his remote.

The realization that I couldn't move brought with it that familiar sense of panic, but when I cleared my throat, trying to dislodge a psychological lump, I realized he hadn't turned off my voice. There had to be a reason for that.

"How does this work?" I asked as, on the edge of my vision, he took up a position next to the door. "How do they take my memory?"

"I don't understand the process," the handler admitted. "But I can tell you it won't hurt."

"Yes, it will." Would I wake up in my cell again, missing nine and a half weeks, instead of eight? Would I have to rediscover my own pregnancy? Reimagine the horror of the conception?

"But you're always happier afterward," Pagano insisted, and his confidence caught me by surprise. Did he seriously think having someone mess with my head was in my best interest?

People have to be able to remember trauma in order to deal with it.

"They're going to keep taking until there's nothing left of me, and not being able to remember the loss doesn't mean I won't feel it."

To his credit, he didn't try to argue.

"How long will I last?" My voice carried almost no volume. "How long do most of us last here, before Vandekamp decides that watching us die is worth more than making us work?"

Pagano cleared his throat. "We've never had one like you before. This..." His broad-armed gesture seemed to indicate the entire room. "This isn't the norm."

"How long, Michael?"

Maybe it was my use of his first name that made him answer, or maybe he had a rare moment of true compassion. Or maybe he just knew I'd forget it all in a few minutes anyway. "Weeks, for those who go straight to the hunt or the arena. Gallagher and Eryx have both had a great run, but eventually the boss will find something that can kill them. Or he'll pit them against each other."

I closed my eyes, and tears rolled down my cheeks. "How long for those of us in the dorms?"

"A year. Two at the most, for the ones that don't get much personal interest. But the client favorites…they have it hard."

Two years.

Even if I managed to carry the baby to term, I would never see it grow up.

I might never see it at all.

Someone knocked on the door, and Pagano opened it, but I couldn't see who he'd let in until one of the few female handlers led a child into my field of vision. The girl was small, with wide yellowish eyes and long dark hair, and she couldn't have been more than ten or eleven years old.

I recognized both her and her guard from my lunch route, but I had no idea what her species was.

"Okay, Sandrine, do your thing," the female handler said, and as the child approached me, both guards stepped out of my vision to continue a conversation they'd evidently struck up on some previous occasion.

Sandrine stood on my right and looked down into my eyes. "Hello, Delilah," she whispered, and though her lips moved, her voice seemed to come from within my own head.

"Do I know you?"

"No." Again her mouth formed the word, but the sound seemed to belong only to me. "And you never will." Her hands came toward my face, and even as panic dumped adrenaline into my bloodstream, I realized that something was wrong with her fingers. Something subtle, but real. They were too… smooth.

Sandrine had no fingerprints. Her palms had no lines, as if the everyday motion of her hands left no imprint upon her skin.

She laid one hand across my forehead, and her touch was impossibly light. Her eyes closed. "Tell me about the house," she said, and I understood why Pagano hadn't taken my voice. "Just enough to help me find it."

"Wait!" I whispered, and her yellow eyes opened in surprise. "Sandrine, don't do this. I need this memory. Please."

"There are rules…" The words bounced around my head as if they'd been born there.

"I won't tell anyone." My voice was as soft as I could make it. "I'll pretend I don't remember. I swear."

"I can't…"

"Please. I'll owe you. I'll…" But I had nothing with which to pay her. The only thing I even had easy access to was… "Do you like cookies?"

Her eyes widened, and I knew I'd said the right thing. A child growing up in captivity probably saw very little luxury. "Chocolate?" Her voice bounced around my head with excitement.

"Yes. I'll bring you a cookie next time I see you. A big chocolate one. All for you. That'll be our secret, just like this is."

Pagano and the female guard were still talking, just outside my field of vision, and I realized that they couldn't hear her at all, and even if they heard me, they were paying no attention. They expected me to talk to Sandrine. That was part of the process.

"Okay. Our secret." The child's lips turned up in a hesitant smile, and I was heartbroken to realize she might treasure the secret as much as she would the cookie. "Close your eyes."

Her hand slid over my forehead again, and I obeyed. "You can't remember anything after you left your cell, until you step into your cell again. You can't remember me being here. Touching you. You can't remember this room."

I panicked for a moment, until I realized she wasn't taking my memory; she was giving me instructions on how to fake it.

"Thank you," I whispered.

When she removed her hand from my face, I opened my eyes. She started to step away from me, signaling the end of her job. "Sandrine," I whispered and she frowned. "I can't remember the past two months. Did you take those memories too?"

She shook her head. "That wasn't me," her lips said, though I heard the words from that other, internal source.

"Are you sure? Could you have been made to forget what you did?"

That time her wide eyes hinted at deep sadness. "I can't forget *anything*."

The next day, I was both relieved and disappointed when Pagano came to get me for lunch duty. Relieved, because I didn't have lunch duty on fight days, which meant that Gallagher would not be forced into the arena that night. Disappointed because that meant I wouldn't get to see him.

In the kitchen, I chatted with Mirela as we loaded trays, and my preoccupation with the fact that she had less than two years to live if we couldn't break out of the Spectacle almost made me miss what she was saying.

"...and Lala saw her yesterday during the dinner shift in the infirmary. She may have a limp, but she's going to be fine."

Genevieve. She was talking about Genni. However, news

that the werewolf pup would recover was bittersweet at best, because she'd be hunted again as soon as she could run. "None of us are going to be fine, Mirela. Not if we don't get out of here."

"I know. We're watching, and making lists, like you asked."

"Like I...?"

Mirela's hand paused as she lifted a cookie from the tray. They were freshly baked, but came from premade dough, which put them squarely in the middle of the food-quality spectrum, which stretched from the gourmet bites served at events to the tasteless but nutritionally sound fare doled out to the captives. "You asked us to watch the handlers and make mental lists of who works when, and where, remember? There are three that rotate shifts in the security room, two at a time, so that it's never empty, even when one goes to the bathroom. But you can tell when there's only one there, because the control room door stands open but the nearest bathroom door is closed."

I'd asked my friends to gather intel?

"Good. That's good work. Thanks."

"I don't see how it'll help, if we can't get through the door. And even if we could, we don't know how to disable the system."

The whole system? Of course. Why bother with one or two collars, when we could take them all out at once? Or at least remove their restrictions. "I'm working on that." Though for all I knew, I'd already figured it out once.

I glanced at the chart hanging on the wall over the tray she was filling. "You're going to the stables. Could you make sure Genni knows her father is here? That might improve her spirits as she recuperates."

Mirela's eyes widened. "Claudio is here? How? When?"

"Zyanya didn't tell you?"

The oracle shook her head. "She just said Payat survived."

Naturally her brother would have been her priority. "Claudio breached the hunting grounds and was brought in during the first round the other night. I don't know how he figured out Genni is here, but he got himself caught to get her out. Or at least to be near her."

"Okay. I'll tell her." Mirela slid her last tray onto the cart and headed for the door. While the guard on duty reminded her that she'd be shocked and paralyzed if she wasn't back in half an hour, I slipped an extra cookie onto my own cart, beneath one of the trays.

The infirmary was the last building on my route, and as Pagano led me through the front door, my gaze homed in on the "unnoticeable" hallway. It was suddenly perfectly noticeable, probably because I knew what to look for, since my memory of it hadn't been erased. But my route didn't take me in that direction.

The third room on my list was Sandrine's. In the hall, I took a tray from the cart, but as I was giving it to the handler, I tripped over my own feet and made sure her lunch hit her square in the chest.

The handler gasped and stood frozen with her arms out at her sides. Beef stroganoff, Italian dressing and bits of lettuce clung to her uniform.

"You bitch!" She pulled back one hand to slap me, but Pagano rushed in to grab her wrist.

"Don't touch her! It's not safe for the guards." He held up his gloved hands for emphasis, while the woman glared at me. "Come on." He slid one arm around her waist, and I remembered their conversation in the "forget things" room the night before. "I'll help you clean up." Pagano was a player.

The female handler nodded, still angry, and he pressed a

button on his remote, restricting me to Sandrine's room until he got back. "Be good, Delilah," he said as he escorted the other handler from the room.

The second the door closed behind them, I retrieved the cookie I'd hidden beneath a tray and headed for the pen where Sandrine was kept locked up with one other girl a couple of years older. "Sandrine. Thanks again," I whispered as I handed it to her through the bars. "Eat quickly."

She devoured a third of the treat in one bite.

The girl next to her watched with quiet, passive envy, blinking yellowish eyes similar to Sandrine's. She too had smooth palms and fingertips.

"What's your name?" I asked the girl.

"Laure." The word seemed to echo from within my head, as if I'd spoken it myself, with my ears plugged.

"Laure, have you ever..." I mimed touching my own forehead. "Have you ever made me forget something?"

She nodded.

"Did you make me forget a long period of time? Like, several weeks?"

Laure nodded again, and relief washed over me as I gripped the bars between us. Answers were seconds away.

"Do you know what you made me forget?"

She shook her head. "I used a starting point and an ending point, but I didn't see what fell between."

"So, you can't tell me what I'm missing?" I asked, and she shook her head again. "Can you...put it back?"

Sandrine laughed, a timid tinkling sound in my head. "We don't take memories. We..." she mimed digging with an invisible shovel "...bury them."

My hands tightened around the bars. "Can you dig them back up?" *Please, please let that be possible...*

"No," Laure said. "But you might be able to uncover them yourself."

"How?"

"You have to find the right tool." Again, she mimed shoveling. "A sight. A sound. Sometimes reexperiencing an element of the memory can help you dig up what's buried."

I swallowed a groan. The only things I knew for sure had been buried were private engagements—yet last night's hadn't triggered any memory—and the conception of my child.

"Okay. Thanks." Footsteps from the hallway made my pulse trip faster, and I turned back to the girls, speaking in an urgent whisper. "Laure, who asked you to take my memories? Was it the boss? Vandekamp?"

She shook her head and gave me a very strange look. "You did. And you brought me a chocolate chip cookie."

DELILAH

You did.

Laure's words played through my head while I finished my shift in the infirmary, handing out trays to handlers without seeing them. Paying no attention to where Pagano led me.

I'd had my own memory erased, and I'd paid Laure for the service with a cookie.

Then, in trying to uncover that fact, I'd subconsciously replayed my own actions by bribing Laure's friend Sandrine with the very same reward. Which told me that Laure was right. The information was still in here. How else could I have been so sure that Sandrine would be willing to bargain for a cookie?

Yet the biggest of my questions had gone unanswered. Why would I ask Laure to bury my memories?

It *had* to be related to my pregnancy. But what was the point of shielding myself from a traumatic conception, when the pregnancy itself remained as evidence that something had happened?

"Delilah." Pagano's voice startled me back into awareness,

and I realized I'd stopped pushing the cart. "One more tray. Let's go."

I checked the list hanging from the cart and saw an unfamiliar name, next to a room I didn't recognize.

Dr. Hill. Lab.

Frowning, I looked up at Pagano. "Where's the lab?"

"In the basement. But it's only open as needed. I don't think you've been down there." He led me into the elevator, then pressed the L button. Which I'd never noticed. Was the basement lab, like the secret hallway, hidden from casual observation?

The elevator descended, and when the doors opened, a wave of nausea washed over me. Pagano stepped out into a tiled foyer in front of a long glass wall, beyond which was a room furnished more like an infirmary wing than a research lab.

My handler was wrong. I'd been there before.

I didn't recognize the row of padded exam tables or the countertop stretching across the opposite wall. I didn't recognize the trays of sterile equipment or the curtains hanging from tracks mounted on the ceiling, separating one table from the next. But I recognized the astringent scent and the cold air. The echo of Pagano's boots on the tile made my stomach churn.

"Delilah. Come on," he said, and when I didn't move, he pulled the cart into the foyer, then hauled me out of the elevator by one arm.

"Finally!" An unfamiliar man looked up from the form he'd been scribbling on and pulled one of the frameless glass doors open. "You're late," he said as I pushed the lunch cart into the lab. I was supposed to hand him the last tray. But I couldn't move.

Why had I been in there before? Had I buried the memory

for a reason, or was my time in the basement lab just collateral damage from my two-month system wipe?

"Delilah. Wake up," Pagano said, and I lifted the tray without feeling its weight. Without smelling the food.

The man in the lab coat rolled his eyes and snatched his lunch from me.

"Sorry, Dr. Hill. She's been acting pretty weird lately."

I studied the doctor's face, but it didn't set off any mental or psychological alarms. He was not the source of my discomfort in the lab.

"Delilah?" The voice was soft and it cracked on the last syllable of my name, but I would have recognized it anywhere.

I turned to find Lenore staring at me from one of the padded tables, holding back the curtain between us with one arm. The siren's eyes were glazed, and her voice carried more pain than I could fathom, but no compulsion whatsoever.

"Lenore!" I jogged across the floor toward her, and when the doctor tried to grab me, Pagano blocked his reach.

"It's not safe to touch her with bare hands."

"What happened?" I pushed back the curtain to see that Lenore was covered by a white hospital sheet. "Are you okay?" If she was sick, why wasn't she upstairs on the main infirmary floor?

"Get her out of here," Dr. Hill said, but I hardly heard him.

"They took it." Lenore's words were slurred; she'd been sedated. "I don't know whether I wanted it, but now that it's gone…" Tears slid down her cheeks and left wet spots on the paper-covered pillow beneath her head.

They took it. Magnolia's face flashed behind my eyes, but it was Simra's voice I heard, explaining what happened to captives who got pregnant.

"Oh, Lenore." I brushed hair back from her face and blinked

away tears of my own. This basement lab, only open as needed, was where Tabitha sent them to have the problem removed.

So, why had I been there, if not to end my pregnancy?

To confirm it with a test or an exam?

"Don't tell Kevin." The siren eyes fluttered closed as she spoke. She'd passed out, which meant I didn't have to remind her that her husband had been arrested along with Alyrose and Abraxas for helping us take over the menagerie. Kevin was in prison.

His wife was in hell.

"You did this to her?" I turned on the doctor and felt my hair begin to stand up at the roots. "You operated on her without her consent?"

"Consent?" He crunched into a carrot stick from his tray. "She's not a patient, she's a cryptid. If you ask me, you should all be fixed when you're brought in. That'd be cheaper in the long run."

"*Fixed?*" The *furiae* roared within me, her outrage echoing through every cell in my body.

Lenore would be avenged.

"Delilah." Pagano had one hand on his stun gun, but he hadn't pulled it yet. His other hand held the remote control. With one click, he could immobilize me, but he was waiting. Giving me a chance to rein it in.

"It's okay," I lied. My voice sounded strangely full and my vision was so sharp I could see individual threads in the weave of his uniform. "Let's go before I lose control of it."

Pagano didn't holster his remote, but his stance lost a little of its tension.

"Control of what?" the doctor said around his carrot. "What's her deal?"

I headed toward Pagano, and his gaze was glued to my eyes, which were no doubt absent irises and threaded with black veins. As I drew even with Dr. Hill on my way to the door, I sucked in a deep breath. Then I leapt at him.

"No!" Pagano pressed the button on his remote, paralyzing me even as pain shot through my entire body. But I was already airborne. Momentum drove me into the doctor, throwing us both to the ground.

The doctor's elbow cracked against the floor, and he howled in pain.

"Don't touch her!" Pagano cried, but Hill shoved my limp, pain-racked form onto the floor. His hand brushed my arm, and my pulse surged as rage poured out of me and into him. As fire raced through my veins from my collar, scorching every inch of me.

The doctor froze. Then he pushed himself upright, while I lay panting on the ground at his feet.

Both my paralysis and the sadistic electric current ended.

"Dr. Hill?" Pagano seemed to have forgotten me as he watched the doctor, well aware of the brutal inevitability of whatever was about to happen.

The doctor picked up a scalpel from a tray of tools on the counter.

I pushed myself up and scooted back until my spine hit the cabinets, trying to ignore the pain still echoing in my every nerve ending. From there, I had an unobstructed view of the doctor as he lifted his shirt and sliced his own belly open, just below the pooch middle age had given him.

"Oh, fuck…" The guard pocketed his stun gun and pulled the radio from his belt. Static burst through the silence of the lab. "This is Pagano. I need backup down in the infirmary basement lab. Delilah freaked out again, and Doc Hill just opened himself up with his own scalpel."

"Shit! I mean, roger that," the voice over the radio said. "We're sending everyone we've got."

But it was far too late for Dr. Hill. I watched, stunned, while he sliced into his belly again, deepening the original wound. Then he dropped the bloody scalpel on the tile and reached into his gut with his right hand. The doctor who'd operated on Lenore without her consent then began to pull his own intestines from his body, one bloody, lumpy length at a time.

Pagano retched, and the acrid, sweet stench of vomit filled the room.

Deep inside me, the gleeful *furiae* curled up to watch her gruesome handiwork play out. Gallagher too would have gloried in the spilled blood of an enemy, if he'd been there to see it. But I turned away.

Lenore was avenged, but I still needed answers. "Michael."

His boots shuffled away from me, and from the doctor crying as he slowly disemboweled himself onto the floor. "Holy *fuck*, Delilah, what did you do?"

"Vengeance is never pretty. He made his own choice, but Lenore didn't get one." She hadn't chosen to get pregnant, and she hadn't chosen to get unpregnant. "This is what I do. If you can't handle it, request a transfer."

"Fuck!" Pagano wiped sweat from his forehead with the back of one arm, still clutching the radio.

I stood slowly, holding my hands out to show him that I was no threat. Anymore. "Take me to Vandekamp."

"Hell no, I'm not taking you anywhere!"

"Look at me, Michael." I struggled to control my voice. To keep from shouting. "Don't I look normal again? It's over." Though the sickening wet sliding sounds to my left said otherwise. "And you're wearing gloves. I'm not going to hurt you. But I need to see Vandekamp."

"You're not going to see anything but the inside of a hole in the ground!"

His backup would arrive any second. Out of time and options, I sucked in a deep breath and spat out the truth. "Michael, I'm pregnant."

"What?" The hand clutching his radio fell to his side.

"I'm pregnant. But instead of strapping me to that bastard's table, someone's been making sure I'm isolated from everyone else, and that I get good food, vitamins and exercise. I need to know why. I need to know what's happening to me."

Pagano's unfocused gaze fell to the floor. "I just thought... You're an exception. A problem. They said that was why they isolated you. And I don't know what they feed the others, so..." He shrugged, and his gaze found mine again. "I never put the pieces together."

"Vandekamp has all the pieces. Take me to him, before—" The hum of the elevator cut me off, as it was called back to the first floor. "Please. We can take the stairs."

"I can't—"

I glanced at the elevator doors, and each beat of my heart felt like the tick of a clock counting down. "If you don't, I'll tell everyone who steps out of that elevator that I'm pregnant. You know damn well that if your boss wanted anyone else to know, he wouldn't have isolated me."

Pagano aimed his remote control, obviously ready to electronically silence me.

"The next time I can talk, I'll tell Vandekamp it's your baby." The threat flew from my mouth like one long word. "He'll fire you long before the paternity results come in."

The handler hesitated, obviously trying to think that through in a hurry.

I glanced pointedly at the stairwell. "If you want to keep your job, get me out of here. Now."

Behind him, the elevator rumbled as it descended toward us, and he drew in a panicked breath. "Fine. Come on." He pushed through the glass door and headed for the stairwell to the left of the elevator, and I raced after him. The door closed behind us just as the elevator slid open, and for a moment, we stood frozen, listening as several sets of heavy boots clomped into the foyer we'd just vacated. Voices shouted for space and supplies as handlers and medics descended upon Dr. Hill.

"Turn around," Pagano ordered in a whisper, pulling a set of padded cuffs from his belt. He restrained me, then led me quickly up the stairs and out of the building through a rear exit.

"Do you know who the father is?" Pagano asked as he escorted me swiftly through the topiary garden, where the sun reflecting from the fountain nearly blinded me. There was a strange quality to his voice. As if his question wasn't really a question.

"Do *you*?" I asked.

Instead of answering, he marched me straight through the main building to Vandekamp's office, where the secretary tersely informed us that we didn't have an appointment.

"Is he with someone?" Pagano demanded. She shook her head. "Then he'll want to see us."

As we marched past her desk, she pressed a button and warned her boss. His office door opened before Pagano could knock.

"Why isn't she in an observation cell, writhing in a great deal of pain?" Vandekamp demanded. "Because those are the orders I sent your backup in with."

Pagano lowered his voice. "She's threatening to spill sensitive information."

The secretary leaned forward for a better view and, presumably, better hearing.

"What sensitive information?" Vandekamp demanded, still blocking his office doorway.

"I think I should let her speak for herself."

"Bullshit." But the boss finally stepped back and waved us into his office. He slammed the door behind us, then marched straight to his desk and picked up a remote control, which he aimed at my neck. "Explain yourself."

"Explain *yourself*," I spat, before I could rethink my approach. "Why am I still pregnant, when Lenore and Magnolia are not?"

For one long moment Vandekamp's expression registered no change. Then he frowned and his lips moved silently, repeating the question, trying to make sense of it. "*Still* pregnant?"

"You didn't know?" I studied him, trying to find truth in features trained for showmanship. For politics.

In the end, I decided to believe him not because of the authentic ring to his anger and disbelief, but because I could see no reason for him to lie. I was no threat to him. He could make sure I never spoke another word to anyone in my life as easily as he could have me killed and fed to the arena beasts.

"You really didn't know." I believed him. But I didn't understand it.

"I still don't know. Has this been verified?" he demanded, looking over my shoulder to my handler.

Pagano shrugged. "I haven't seen anything official, but someone's ordered vitamins and exercise for her, and what's evidently a specialized menu—"

Vandekamp's face flushed. "Someone *what*?" he roared.

My handler shrugged. "I thought it was you."

His flush deepened and his jaw clenched. "Why would you follow ridiculous orders like that without question?"

"Sir, handlers who question orders don't last long here," Pagano said, and again I was impressed with his nerve.

Vandekamp scowled. "Wait in the outer office."

"Sir, she just made Doc Hill slice open his own stomach and pull his guts out one handful at a time."

"I'm well aware of the threat she represents." Vandekamp pulled one of his guest chairs into the center of the floor space, then backed away from it. "Sit," he ordered.

When I sat, my cuffed wrists pressing into the leather cushion at my back, he aimed his remote at me and selected an option from the screen.

I lost all feeling from the neck down, as well as the ability to move. Panic sped my pulse and oddly, I felt like I was drowning. As if a sudden pressure was keeping my lungs from expanding.

"There. She's harmless. And if you'd acted quickly enough, Dr. Hill wouldn't require sedation and restraints in the ambulance, to keep him from making balloon animals out of his own intestines."

Pagano flinched.

"Out," Vandekamp ordered, and my handler backed out of my line of sight. A second later, the door clicked closed behind him.

Vandekamp sat on the edge of his massive wooden desk and watched me concentrate on breathing, to counter my body's insistence that it couldn't do that very thing.

"If you hyperventilate, you're as good as dead," he said at last. "After what you did to the doctor, I won't be able to get anyone to treat you."

He was right.

I closed my eyes and willed myself to forget about how hard breathing seemed, now that I couldn't feel my lungs expand. My body would do what needed to be done, if I just let it.

That got easier when Vandekamp started talking. "How far along are you?"

"I was hoping you could tell me that. I can't—" I nearly bit my tongue off trying to stop that thought from flying out.

I couldn't tell him that I'd paid Laure to erase my memory;

I wasn't going to let a child pay for what I'd done. But it wouldn't take him long to figure out why I didn't have the answers to his questions, especially once I started asking questions of my own.

"I don't know how this happened. Okay? Last week I woke up in a private cell with no memory of the previous eight weeks. I don't know how I got pregnant or why other pregnancies have been terminated, but mine has been protected."

Vandekamp's gaze narrowed on me. "That doesn't make any sense."

I tried to shrug, but my body was unresponsive. "Maybe you've messed with my memory one too many times." I wasn't supposed to remember how that had happened, but I should remember that it *had* happened.

His mouth opened, then closed, and I recognized caution in his hesitation. He was trying to sort out what I should and shouldn't remember of our interactions, considering all my trips to the secret room.

"And you really don't remember…the father?" There was a careful quality to the phrase. Just because he hadn't known I was pregnant didn't mean he couldn't be responsible.

A sick feeling swelled inside me. "Did you do this to me?" My head felt light with the sudden rush of my pulse, though I couldn't feel my heart pound. "Is this your baby?"

"No." He held my gaze without flinching. But he'd lied to me before.

"I don't believe you."

"I don't care what you believe, and I don't care who the father is," he said, as if pregnancy among his captives was so common as to be unworthy of notice. "What I care about is finding out who authorized the change in your menu and your exercise breaks."

That, I believed. The fact that he was more concerned about

insubordination than about the baby told me that it truly wasn't his. And since Vandekamp obviously wasn't being paid by a client to keep me pregnant, surely finding out who had ordered my new living conditions would tell me who the father was.

"Who else knows about this?" he demanded.

"Just Pagano, as far as I know. And he only found out minutes ago. Do any of the guards have the authority to arrange this without needing you to sign off on it?"

"Woodrow. But he wouldn't do that."

"Unless he's the father."

Vandekamp shook his head. "He had a vasectomy a decade ago."

"Is he the one who removed me from the dorm?"

"No, that was Tabitha. She said you were a threat to—" He bit off the end of his thought and exhaled slowly. Then his eyes closed.

Tabitha. But that made no sense. She was the one who wouldn't let "monsters" breed.

Vandekamp twisted on the edge of his desk to pick up his phone. "Tell my wife I need to see her. Now," he barked into the mouthpiece. Then he slammed the phone back into its cradle.

"Whose—" I cleared my throat and started over, trying to inject strength into my words, though I was no longer sure I actually wanted the answer. "Whose baby am I carrying?"

"That doesn't matter."

"The hell it doesn't. Did you rent me out?"

Instead of answering, he circled his desk to sit in his chair again and began typing on his keyboard.

"You can't just—"

Hinges squealed behind me. "Willem?" The door swung shut with a thud and a click, and I desperately wished I could turn and see Tabitha Vandekamp's face.

Her husband stood and gestured toward a guest chair against the wall, but she only stepped into my field of vision and crossed her arms over her tailored gray suit jacket. "I'd rather stand. What's going on?" Her gaze skipped from her husband to me, where it lingered with a weight I didn't understand. As if she were silently asking me for something.

"Tabitha, why did you change Delilah's diet?"

"Because she's human." She glanced at her husband again, then her gaze slid back to me, and I felt like I was missing some vital piece of information. Again. "We discussed this." She turned back to him, and I could no longer tell which of us she was truly talking to. "You're the one who convinced me she's not a surrogate. If she's human, we don't have the authority to hold her here, but she's obviously too dangerous to simply let go. So I did what I could for her. A private room. Good food. Fresh air. Exercise."

Vandekamp crossed his arms over his chest, mirroring her defensive posture. But on him, the pose looked like skepticism. "Why didn't you tell me?"

Tabitha shrugged. "You've had your hands full drafting the bill, so I just took care of it."

The bill?

"So, there's no other—"

"Why am I still pregnant?" I demanded, tired of watching while he doled out enough rope for her hang herself with.

Tabitha swiveled to face me, her eyes wide with shock and…betrayal? "We had an agreement," she spat.

"We *what*?"

Vandekamp sank onto the edge of his desk and crossed his arms over his chest. "Tabitha, what did you do?"

"I turned a thorn in the Spectacle's paw into an opportunity. Just like you did." Tabitha turned back to me, expectantly, as

Vandekamp stood. "You told him about the pregnancy, but not our agreement?"

"I don't remember making any agreement. Last week, I woke up missing two months' worth of memories."

"You're missing…?" She turned a fiery gaze on her husband, hands on her narrow hips. "I told you there would be long-term damage. She's not a cryptid, Willem. You can't just go plucking things from her brain and expect her mind to remain intact!"

"There's no way the girls accidentally took two entire months from her memory." Vandekamp sank onto the edge of his desk again. "That's not how it works. Someone did this intentionally."

"Well, I had nothing to do with it," his wife insisted. "Her memory loss doesn't benefit me if she doesn't remember our agreement."

The truth was that I couldn't see how my memory loss benefited me either. Had I meant to erase the recollection of whatever deal I'd made with her, or was that another unintended casualty of my mass memory wipe?

"What did you agree to?" I demanded.

"To let the pregnancy continue, of course." Tabitha frowned at her husband. "Is she paralyzed?" She dug a remote from her pocket and pressed a button over his objections. Feeling returned to my chest and stomach, then spread with a tingling sensation to my limbs, and I exhaled in relief. "You can't do that. We don't know what kind of effect that has on the baby."

"Why do you care?" In my mind, I saw the young nymph Magnolia fall to her knees in the dorm, weak from both her unwanted medical procedure and her brutal loss. "Why protect my baby, when you have all the others terminated?"

"Because the others weren't *babies*. They were foals or colts or puppies. Animals that may as well have been born in a barn.

You're different, Delilah." She pulled the extra guest chair closer and sat in it, putting herself at eye level with me, as if we were going to have a deep, reaffirming girl chat. "You're human. We've had that verified with test after test. We've had you examined."

I'd been examined?

"At first, I couldn't figure out how that was possible. Then the oracle told me that you were going to have a baby, and I realized that you were given to us, just like the *furiae* was given to you."

"She wasn't given," Vandekamp insisted. "I caught her myself. She and all the others were payment for the service I provided the Metzgers."

His wife frowned at him, then turned back to me. "My point is that this is fate. How else can you explain Willem stumbling across a monster who's one hundred percent human. For all we know, there isn't another like you in the entire world. And then you got pregnant, just like the oracle said you would, and it all started to make sense."

"What oracle?" I asked. "Mirela? Lala?"

"No, the middle one. The one who doesn't talk much."

"Rommily." *Shit.* I closed my eyes and took a couple of deep breaths. "What did she say, exactly? And I mean *exactly.*"

"I don't remember the specific words, but she said something about fury. I thought she was talking about anger until Willem told me about your calling."

"What else?" Vandekamp said from his perch on the edge of his desk.

"She said fate's bastard. That's your baby, obviously, since you're not married."

No, fate's bastard was me, not my unborn child. Rommily had called me that before. It meant "orphan." But I could see her confusion. "What else did she say?"

"Something about a knife. No, a scalpel. And a belly full of blood."

I groaned, and when Vandekamp's gaze met mine, I knew he'd come to the same conclusion.

Tabitha was oblivious. "I assume that means you'll need a cesarean. Which is no big deal, from what I've read…" Her words faded into nothing when she noticed that her husband and I were both staring at her. "What?"

"Rommily is broken, for lack of a better term," I explained. "Death is just about the only thing she can predict."

Tabitha smoothed her knee-length gray pencil skirt with one hand. "What does that mean?"

"Dr. Hill just sliced open his own stomach with a scalpel after making physical contact with Delilah," Vandekamp told her. "Rommily wasn't predicting Delilah's pregnancy. She was predicting Dr. Hill's death by self-evisceration."

Tabitha blinked. Then she blinked again. "No." She shook her head, and a strand of hair fell from her neat French twist. "That's a coincidence." She smoothed her hair back and sat straighter, and I could practically see her pushing a mental reset button. "What matters is that you're here and you're pregnant and that is very fortunate for you. If you'd gotten pregnant anywhere else, your baby would be born in chains, even if it turns out to be human, because no one else understands what you really are. But we understand." She turned to her husband, evidently expecting some sign of affirmation, but he seemed at a loss for words.

"Meaning what? You're going to save my baby? How? Throw it into foster care?" As horrified as I was by the thought, wasn't that better than what I could offer the poor child?

But Tabitha only stared at me, and the look in her eyes made my skin crawl. "You really don't remember, do you?"

"Remember what?" Vandekamp asked.

I did *not* remember. But suddenly I understood. "You're infertile."

Tabitha flinched.

"You can't have a baby of your own, so you're going to take mine."

"Assuming it's human," she admitted. "That was the deal. I agreed to safeguard your pregnancy—I gave you vitamins and exercise, and I took you off the menu for full-contact engagements."

The fact that there was such a roster and the fact that I'd been on it horrified me in equal parts. How often had I been scheduled? How many possibilities were there for my child's paternity?

"...and you agreed to keep the pregnancy hidden until we know the baby's species. If it's human, Willem and I will raise it."

"*Tabitha.*" Vandekamp looked dumbfounded and livid.

I shook my head. "I would never agree to that." Unless she'd given me no choice. What *wouldn't* I have agreed to, to keep my baby alive?

But neither of them were looking at me anymore.

"You promised me a baby ten years ago," she said. "But it's obvious that this project is your baby, and I need more than that."

He stood and pulled her to her feet. "Tabitha, this project—the bill, the collars, all of it—is for us. For the baby we'll have someday."

"Then you better work fast, because someday's coming in seven months."

My teeth refused to unclench, so I spoke through them. "You can't have my baby."

She shrugged out of her husband's grip and turned on me.

"You should be grateful. I'm giving your baby a chance at a real life. He'll have real parents who can give him everything. Who can shower him with love and opportunity. Even if we were to let you keep him, what would you have to offer the poor child? Chains? Scraps of clothing and food?" She turned back to her husband. "If the baby is human, we're keeping it. You made me a promise, and you're damn well going to come through, or I will bring all of this crumbling *right down on your head*." Her spread arms seemed to indicate the Savage Spectacle, and everything within it.

He exhaled slowly, and I heard resignation in the sound. "When will we know if it's human?"

"Amniocentesis is risky before the twelfth week, and if the ultrasound is right, she's just now eight weeks along."

"She's had an ultrasound?"

"At six weeks," Tabitha said, and my head spun. No wonder the basement lab had felt so familiar, even though I had no conscious memory of it. "Everything looked fine, but you can't tell much that early."

"Okay," he said. "Just promise me you won't get your hopes up until we know for sure."

Her smile made me want to vomit. "I promise to try."

It doesn't matter. Let them think what they want, if that keeps the baby alive. I wouldn't be at the Spectacle long enough to give birth.

"Who else knows about this?" he asked.

"Just me and Dr. Grantham," Tabitha said. "And Delilah."

Dr. Grantham. Not Dr. Hill, of the sliced open belly.

Vandekamp frowned. "Now Michael Pagano knows, as well. Tabitha, if Grantham finds out what Delilah did to Hill, he'll refuse to treat her."

"Well then, we won't tell—"

"Whose is it?" I sounded just as stunned as I felt. "Who's the father?"

They looked at me. Then they turned back to each other, and the look that passed between them chilled me all the way to my bone marrow.

"You rented me out." I hadn't truly believed it until that moment. Despite the evidence occupying my womb, deep down, I'd been convinced that if it had happened, I'd remember on some level. "How many times?"

"Call Dr. Grantham and let's get another checkup," Vandekamp said, and I realized he wasn't going to answer.

"How many possibilities are there?" I demanded, unable to stop my eyes from watering. When no one spoke, I stood. "At least give me a number. What does it matter to you?"

"Sit," Vandekamp ordered, aiming his remote at me. But Tabitha put her hand over the screen.

"I'm not taking any chances with this baby," she insisted. "Let's just try to keep her calm."

"This isn't going to work, Tabitha," Vandekamp said, as if I couldn't hear them. "We can't control her without the collar."

"We have nothing to fear from Delilah, because her *furiae* has no bone to pick with us." She was watching me, though she spoke to him, and her infuriatingly calm smile triggered a realization—she'd made sure that I'd never seen either of them personally abuse any of the captives. "Besides that, she cares about the baby." Tabitha met my gaze. "Sit down, Delilah, and I'll answer your questions."

I sat, as much to indulge her sense of security as for the promised answers.

"There was only one client," she said. "I'm not going to tell you who he was. It doesn't matter."

"Does he know about the baby?"

"Of course not. That would complicate things."

"Wait." Tension made my shoulders strain against my restraints. "If there was only one client, and he was human, how could the baby possibly be cryptid? Why do you need an amniocentesis?"

She glanced at Vandekamp, and he shrugged as he sat on the edge of his desk again. "You wanted to answer her questions."

Before he'd known about the baby—before he'd told his wife she could have it—he would have had me dragged back to my cell in excruciating pain rather than voluntarily give me information.

"There's another possibility for paternity," Tabitha finally said. "One of the clients was a voyeur. He rented a selection of cryptids and paid extra for the right to…pair them."

Her words played over and over in my head, but for a few merciful seconds, they meant nothing. Comprehension would not come.

"No," I said as the brutal understanding finally crashed over me, paralyzing me as surely as my collar ever had. "What the *hell* gives you the right to play with people's lives like that? As if locking us up and trotting us out on display wasn't bad enough, you sick fucks have to double down on horror and abuse, like you invented the concepts. You can't just rent people out like toys. You can't pair people off and make them perform for you."

I closed my eyes, but when I tried to scrub my face with my hands, pain shot through my shoulders. I'd forgotten I was cuffed.

"I didn't do that," I insisted, shaking my head firmly. "I *wouldn't* do that. Not ever."

But I had. I could see it in their faces. I'd given up that last piece of myself because if I hadn't, someone would have taken it.

That's what I'd been trying to forget when I hid my own memories. It had to be.

But buried secrets have a way of digging themselves up.

Voyeur.

A selection of cryptids.

With a cruel resurgence of horror, I realized I might be the only one at the Spectacle who didn't know.

"Who was it?" I demanded, my voice as steady as I could make it, while I stared at the floor. I wasn't ready to hear, but I had to know.

Tabitha sighed, and I could hear her disgust in that one long breath. "It was Gallagher."

For Immediate Release

Dr. Willem Vandekamp has been granted the world's
first patent for a hormonal suppression technique
designed to prevent the metamorphosis of
cryptid hybrid shifters...

**—from a 2005 press release by the United States Patent
and Trademark Office**

DELILAH

"No." My vision swam, warping Vandekamp's office furniture until I could have been looking into the mirror maze at the menagerie. "No. Gallagher would never sacrifice his honor like that, and I wouldn't either. We wouldn't... He *couldn't*. He swore to protect..."

Understanding hit me like a punch to the gut. "That's what he was doing, wasn't he? Protecting me?"

Tabitha shrugged. "My understanding is that if it hadn't been him, it would have been someone else."

Gallagher. My sworn champion and best friend, who chafed at the misconception that our relationship was based on anything as trivial and fleeting as physical attraction, might be the father of a baby neither of us ever meant to have. A child that could be human or *fear dearg* or some unprecedented combination of the two.

"I don't..." I closed my eyes, trying to block the Vandekamps out. I wanted nothing else in the world but to be alone. To process my shock and trauma away from cruel mouths and prying eyes.

"We'll know how to proceed in a month," Tabitha said in a tone that fell horrifically short of the comfort she obviously thought she was providing. Protecting my baby *in case* it was human didn't absolve her of her willingness to kill that same child if Gallagher turned out to be the father.

I opened my eyes, and all I could think about was how badly I wanted to claw their eyes out and spit on their corpses, and how little help the *furiae* would be in that endeavor.

"I want the test. Now." I hadn't even known what I was going to say until the words were out, and I didn't realize I meant them until I heard them. "The amniocentesis."

"But there's a risk for the baby," Tabitha protested.

"*Life* is a risk for this baby."

"What's the biggest risk from amniocentesis? Miscarriage?" Vandekamp asked. Tabitha nodded. "What's the risk? Give me the numbers."

"Not quite a one percent chance."

"And probably less, under ideal circumstances, which we can easily provide," he said. "I want to know now. Call Dr. Grantham and schedule the test for tomorrow." Before she could argue further, he twisted to push a button on his desk phone. "Send Pagano back in."

My guard stepped into the office behind me and closed the door.

"Pagano, are you married?" Vandekamp asked. "Have kids?"

"No, sir."

"Excellent. You are now assigned to Delilah exclusively, so we're going to need you here around the clock until further notice. My assistant will set up a room for you and see that your salary is doubled. Any objection?"

Pagano hesitated, but just for a moment. "No, sir."

"Take her back to her cell," Vandekamp ordered. "She'll

be seeing Dr. Grantham tomorrow, and you are not to tell him about Dr. Hill. Nor will you tell anyone else about the pregnancy. Do you understand?"

"Of course, sir," Pagano said from behind me. "Any change to her diet or exercise program?"

"No. Keep everything as is, and notify me personally of any change at all in her condition or health. Dismissed."

Pagano pulled me up by one arm.

"Send Gallagher to me," I said, as he escorted me out of the room. "I need to talk to him."

Vandekamp didn't reply, but I could feel his gaze following me until we turned the corner out of sight.

"You knew about Gallagher, didn't you?" I demanded as Pagano led me through the topiary. The sun still rode high in the sky, though it felt like I'd spent forever in Vandekamp's office, watching while what little life I still had was ripped apart at the seams. "That's what you didn't want to tell me?" What no one, evidently, wanted to tell me.

"I wasn't there. I just heard about it."

And he couldn't have been the only one.

A strange sound caught in my throat when I tried to swallow a sob. I stopped walking, but Pagano didn't reach for me.

"You weren't alone. That kind of engagement takes a toll on the cryptids, which is why the boss charges so much for them."

"He charges a lot because he likes money." I walked on, and Pagano matched me step by step without touching me, even though he wore gloves.

"So, Dr. Hill?"

"What about him?" I stared at the cold, rough sidewalk as we stepped onto it, headed down a curving path toward the isolated building where my cell was.

"Will he survive?"

"Rommily says he won't." I shrugged. "They don't typically give me updates on those who draw the *furiae*'s wrath, but I'm guessing it won't do them any good to stuff his guts back in and sew him shut unless they figure out how to stop him from slicing himself open again."

Pagano seemed to think about that in silence until we got to my building. "How does it work?" he asked as he pulled the door open. "I mean how do you decide who...deserves it?"

"I don't." I stood still while he programmed my collar to stop me from leaving the building. "No knife chooses its own target."

"You're saying someone else is wielding you?"

"Some*thing* else. Something bigger. Something wiser."

"So...how can I stay on the good side of this something bigger?"

I stopped to look up at him as he led me down the hall toward my cell. "If you keep working here, you can't. Eventually Vandekamp will ask you to do something horrible. If you do it, the *furiae* will come for you. If you don't, you'll lose your job."

He opened his mouth, and I could see the protest coming.

Instead of listening to how unfair a choice that was, I walked down the hall and into my cell, leaving him staring after me.

A second later, the light over the door flashed red.

I sat with my back to the window, watching the square of fading daylight shift across the floor with the sun's slow descent. Trying not to obsess over answers I didn't have. Footsteps clomped in the hall, and my cell door opened. Gallagher stepped inside, wearing only a pair of threadbare pants and his traditional red cap. Behind him, Pagano was already programming his collar to lock him in my cell.

The door closed, and Gallagher studied my face. "They said you asked for me. Why would they oblige?"

"I have something they want." That wouldn't buy me endless requests, but it would apparently get me this one, at least.

"What's wrong?" Gallagher tried to pull me into a hug, but I backed away from him. I didn't know how to be touched by him anymore.

Hurt flitted across his normally unreadable features.

"Sit down." I glanced at the stack of mats, my only furnishing, other than the toilet. "Please."

"You remember." The pain in his voice seemed to bring the earth to a grinding halt beneath us. As hard as this was for me, it was hard for him too.

"No. But I've heard."

"That's worse," he growled. "I'm so sorry. It was difficult enough the first time around, but to have to hear about it…" His brow furrowed and his fists clenched. "Who told you?"

"The Vandekamps."

"So, they know about your memory?"

I nodded. "So does Pagano."

"Did you figure out what happened? How you lost the memories?"

Another nod. I sank onto the mats with my back against the wall, but still he stood. "Gallagher, I need to know what happened that night."

"You're better off without the memory."

"That's not your choice to make." He flinched, and I exhaled slowly. "I know you were trying to protect me. I know you wouldn't have… Unless the alternative would have been worse. For me."

He nodded. "And when the time comes, everyone who played a part will die a slow and painful death for what they did to you."

"They did it to you too."

Gallagher frowned. He seemed unable to understand that he too had been a victim. "I am a warrior, even in chains."

"I know." The canvas of scars his torso had become would never let either of us forget that. "Tell me what happened. Please."

He sighed and finally sank onto the stack of mats, maintaining as much respectful space between us as he could. "I don't want you to hate me, but I'll understand if you do. However, that won't change anything for me. My oath can't be broken. Even if you loathe the very sight of me, I will protect you with my dying breath."

"I understand." But I also understood that he wasn't yet armed with all the facts. If I was carrying his child, would that complicate his oath? It would certainly complicate everything else. "Start from the beginning. Please. When did it happen?"

Gallagher took a deep breath, and his thick chest swelled. "It was my second night in the arena. Our second week here. After the fight, two guards took me back to my cell, but you weren't there. They stayed while I showered, then they gave me a clean pair of pants and said I'd been requested for a private engagement.

"I didn't even know what that meant. I had done nothing but fight since the bachelor party. But they wouldn't answer any of my questions. They just said that if I cared about you, I'd do whatever the client told me to. When I arrived, there you were, standing with two other women."

"Where?"

"I don't know. It was a small room, with thick rugs and pillows all over the floor. The lights were dim. They lined me up between a shifter I'd never seen and Drusus." The incubus from Metzger's.

"Who was the client?"

"They didn't tell me his name. He was tall, for a human, and painfully thin, and he obviously had a good deal of money. The handlers said no one had ever requested a champion before, and that Vandekamp charged him a fortune."

That was no surprise. The Spectacle's clientele could afford anything they wanted, and all they seemed to want was something no one else had ever had. Like a *fae* champion who drew his lifeblood from the gaping wounds of his victims.

"He paired the others on rugs arranged around the room, while he stood in the middle. Then he turned to us. I thought it was coincidence that he'd paired us, but finally I realized he'd overheard something at the fight. Something about you and me."

"He heard that you would only fight for me." The same thing I'd heard in the private viewing box. "We've become some kind of a Savage Spectacle legend, and Vandekamp plays it up."

Gallagher nodded. "I told him that our relationship wasn't sexual in nature. That to even imply such a thing was an insult to both of us, and could not be suffered.

"You started crying, and I wanted to rip his head from his body, but he wasn't threatening your life, so I couldn't, and I felt so…"

"Helpless?" I said, and he nodded. He didn't have easy access to that word.

"When I refused, he put you with the incubus. Drusus promised you'd like it. He was trying to comfort you, but you didn't want to like it."

Of course not. I wouldn't have wanted him inside my head any more than I wanted him inside my body. Being forced to enjoy something I didn't want would have been another choice taken from me. Another humiliation.

"He… Drusus reached for you. He was just trying to save

you both. But you started screaming." Gallagher's voice sounded thick, as if each word had to be forced from his throat. "You were terrified, but I'd promised you I wouldn't kill anyone who wasn't threatening your life. So I did the only thing I could think of."

"You took his place," I whispered.

"It was the best I could do."

I squeezed my eyes shut and suddenly the memory was there.

Cushions and pillows. Thick rugs in shades of blue and purple, as if the room is one big bruise. Tear-streaked faces and bare bodies. Guards standing against the wall, watching with various levels of disgust and fascination.

Gallagher, naked, his face a mask of self-loathing, looking at me as if I were the source of all his pain, yet his only hope of redemption.

"Forgive me," he whispers.

Then he reaches for me—

I opened my eyes, and the images were gone. And suddenly I was terrified to close them. I'd needed to know, and now I was ready to forget again.

"You remember?" Gallagher said.

"Some of it."

His gray-eyed gaze captured mine, and the fear swimming in them was unprecedented. "Do you hate me?"

I hated everything that had happened in that room. Everything that had ever taken place at the Savage Spectacle. Everyone who'd ever worn the uniform or handed over a credit card. But Gallagher?

"No." The truth was there, sitting right on the surface of our shared trauma. "You had no choice. The crime is theirs."

But I didn't know how to look at him anymore. I didn't know how to be near him.

"Indeed. Release me from my promise and let me rend limbs from the people who would send you on such an engagement, as well as any man who would pay to see you abused in such a manner."

"Gallagher…"

His brow furrowed and his thick fists tensed with pent-up wrath. "Delilah. I cannot stand by and watch while you suffer." Outrage burned deep in his eyes. "Let me do what I was born to do."

Every muscle in his body strained against the promise he'd made me. He actually shook with rage, but beneath that was something even more visceral. Some combination of intense pain, profound affection and acute distress. And that's when I finally understood.

It wasn't just that the promise I'd demanded from him was in direct opposition to his oath to protect me. It was that with or without his oath, beyond the respect he had for my calling, he cared about me as a person. Probably in some honorable *fear dearg* manner that defied human understanding and vocabulary.

And watching me suffer—becoming a part of my suffering— was killing him.

If he knew I'd been sent on another engagement of a similar nature…

Oh, shit.

Suddenly the memory was there, disinterred by digging through my own psyche.

I'd realized that breaking his oath to me to keep a lesser promise was literally killing him. That's why I'd had my own memory wiped.

I hadn't been trying to forget what Gallagher and I were

forced to do. I'd been trying to forget the *other* engagement, because if I didn't know about it, he wouldn't know. And if he didn't know, he wouldn't have to choose between slaughtering everyone involved—and getting himself killed in the process— or dying from breaching his own oath to do that very thing.

"Soon," I promised. "Soon. We'll get our chance to escape, and you'll be free to tear the entire world in two, if that's what it takes to get us all out of here. But that time hasn't come yet." And it couldn't, at least until I knew about the baby. If it was Gallagher's, he would never have to know about that other engagement.

"The time for patience has passed. Vandekamp doesn't deserve to live, much less profit from what he's doing to you. To all of us."

"You won't have to wait much longer. You have my word. Okay?"

Gallagher nodded reluctantly. "Until then, I will sate my thirst for blood on the memory of past vengeance and the promise of more to come."

DELILAH

Pagano came for me the next morning, before my break-fast arrived. Before the sun had truly topped the horizon. He led me to the basement lab, where the elevator doors slid open to reveal Tabitha Vandekamp standing next to a doctor in a white lab coat.

The sight of her there, next to the padded table already prepared for me, struck me with a startling sense of déjà vu.

We've been here before. Together. Was that during my initial pregnancy test?

"Delilah," the doctor said by way of a greeting. "Lie down."

As I settled onto the table, he pulled a wheeled tray of instruments closer, then rolled an ultrasound machine toward the head of the table. He didn't look me in the eye or tell me what he was doing, but not because he was scared. In fact, he didn't seem nervous at all. Somehow, the Vandekamps had actually managed to keep his colleague's condition from him.

Tabitha rounded the table to stand on my other side, where she had a much better view of the machinery than I had.

"Because she's not yet in her second trimester, it's too early to safely use amniocentesis, so we're going to try chorionic villus sampling instead," Dr. Grantham said to Tabitha, without even glancing at me. "Rather than sampling the amniotic fluid, which isn't present in large amounts at this stage, we're going to take a sample of the placenta."

"Is that safe for the baby?" Tabitha asked, while I tried to swallow my rage over the fact that neither of them seemed to think I belonged in the discussion about what was about to happen to my body.

"There are risks with CVS, but they're much fewer than with amniocentesis." Dr. Grantham pulled on a pair of latex gloves, then ducked to take something from beneath the table.

Fear obliterated all logic when I saw the padded restraint, and when he took my arm, I jerked it free. "That won't be necessary, Doctor."

He looked across the table at Tabitha. "I can't paralyze her without affecting the procedure. If she won't cooperate, we'll have to sedate her again."

Again? When had I been sedated?

Tabitha leaned forward until her face appeared over mine. "Delilah. It's in your best interest to cooperate…"

But her words faded into indistinct syllables as her familiar posture and tone triggered a buried memory.

Tabitha Vandekamp wears a light blue dress, tailored to her shape. Her hair is pulled back in an artful bun, and her eyes are alight with hope. But I can hardly keep her face in focus. I can hardly make sense of her words.

My eyes close, and it's an effort to force them open again. That's the sedation. I can't fight it.

"This is fate, Dr. Grantham," she says. "What else could it be?"

She believes everything she is saying. I am so tired, but I can see that. I can hear it.

"She won't remember this, will she, Doctor?"

"No. The sedation is retroactive. But if this takes, she'll figure it out eventually."

"I'll deal with that when the time comes. These next nine months are going to fly by!"

My sudden wave of nausea had nothing to do with pregnancy. "What happened in this lab?" I demanded, staring up at her. "What did you do?" The resemblance between my present reality and the hazy memory were startling, but there was one clear difference.

There'd been no reluctance or hesitation in Tabitha's words, in my recovered memory. There'd been no doubt on her face. She hadn't been preparing herself for the chance that my baby might be human. She'd been *convinced* that would be the case.

How could she be so certain, after what she knew about Gallagher?

"Delilah, you asked for this test," Tabitha said, ignoring my question. "We're giving you what you want, but the doctor has to take basic safety precautions. Let him use the cuffs so we can get on with this."

I hardly heard her, because my mind was still mired in the hazily remembered past. In a time when Tabitha Vandekamp *knew* my baby would be human. When she'd looked forward to the next nine months.

But it takes a minimum of two or three weeks to notice pregnancy symptoms, and I definitely would not have reported any even once I'd noticed them, because Tabitha had a history of forcing abortions. So she shouldn't have known about my pregnancy until I could no longer hide the symptoms.

She *still* shouldn't know, even eight weeks in. Especially considering that the first two weeks of the nine-month pregnancy calendar are actually preimplantation of the fertilized egg. Even in most cryptids, according to my college classes. So how had she known from the very beginning? From before implantation?

She couldn't have. And she certainly couldn't have been sure that the baby was human.

Unless…

"What the hell did you do?" I sat up on the table, and Dr. Grantham backed away from me, startled. "I've been here before, but it wasn't for an ultrasound, was it?"

"You've been here twice, for your initial exam, then the ultrasound. If you hadn't lost your memory, you'd remember," Tabitha insisted calmly.

"But I wouldn't remember the very first time, would I?" I demanded, as pieces of the puzzle began to slide into place, forming a horrifying picture. "You made sure I wouldn't."

"Mrs. Vandekamp?" Dr. Grantham backed farther from the table, reaching for a preloaded syringe lying on the rolling tray to his left. "Calm her down, or I'm going to have to use this. But that's not ideal."

"Tabitha?" I demanded, boldly using her first name. "What did you do?"

She glanced back and forth between me and the doctor. "I only helped fate along. The oracle told me you'd give me a baby. I just wanted to speed things along. And make sure it was Willem's."

No.

I clutched my stomach. "This is your husband's baby?" I turned to the doctor, my hands shaking against my scrubs top. "You inseminated me? Without my permission? Without my *knowledge*?"

"I had you sedated," Tabitha admitted. "Willem wasn't ready to know, and you didn't need to know until you started having symptoms. Dr. Grantham wasn't even sure it would take."

"You didn't tell your husband. How did you even—" I bit off the end of my question. I didn't want to know how she'd gotten a donation from Vandekamp without his knowledge.

And since he didn't know, he'd had no reason to take me off that sadistic full-contact roster. "Now you don't know whose baby I'm carrying." I swung my legs over the bed and stood on the cold tile floor. "You and your husband are *both* sick. You deserve each other. But neither one of you deserves a kid, and you're sure as hell not getting mine."

I marched past them both, my focus on the glass door, beyond which Pagano stood watching the whole thing unfold, wide-eyed. Waiting for instructions.

"Grab her!" Tabitha ordered, and the doctor's shoes shuffled behind me. I didn't think he'd touch me—surely he knew what I was capable of—until pain stabbed into my right thigh.

I stumbled backward and made it four steps before the room started to look…fuzzy. "Help me catch her!" Dr. Grantham shouted as I began to wobble, and though Tabitha didn't move, someone caught me from behind. Someone braced my back with one arm and swung my legs up with the other, until I was being carried like a child.

Pagano stared down at me, frowning.

"Put her on the table," Dr. Grantham ordered, and a second later I felt cold paper beneath me.

I tried to sit up, but my body wouldn't cooperate. My limbs were too heavy.

"Help me strap her down." The doctor's voice sounded like it was being stretched, and Tabitha's face seemed to have suffered the same fate.

"No. Let me up," I insisted, but the syllables came out all

mashed together. As if I were somehow speaking without the use of my teeth.

Tabitha's oddly loose and stretchy face turned toward the end of the table. "I'll get her feet."

Something soft surrounded my wrists and ankles, but I no longer felt like struggling. My head rolled to the side, where the doctor's gut took up most of my field of vision. The weave in the sweater beneath his lab coat began to scroll strangely, as if the threads were constantly moving, stitching themselves together over and over.

While I knew that that made no sense, I found the whole thing more fascinating than truly bizarre.

Someone lifted my shirt up to my rib cage, and I gasped when something cold and wet landed on my stomach.

"What's that for?" Tabitha asked, but I had to listen carefully to understand her. Time seemed to be stretching, and taking the rest of us along for the ride.

"We use an ultrasound to guide the needle." The doctor pressed something into the goop on my stomach and began to move it back and forth in small motions that spread the goo. The machine on my right beeped, then erupted in a soft whooshing sound. "That's the baby's heartbeat."

Tabitha's hands flew to her mouth and her eyes widened. Mine filled with tears.

"Don't get too attached..." the doctor warned, his voice fading in and out, along with my vision "...won't have the results for a few days."

Tabitha nodded, staring at the screen as if it were a glass ball about to show her future.

"Delilah, I need...hold still," the doctor said.

"And I need you to go fuck yourself." I'm not sure anyone understood me, but that didn't matter. Even if all the energy hadn't been sucked from my body by the sedative, I wouldn't have moved. That would only mean hurting myself or the baby.

My plan was to hurt everyone else.

"Okay, I think we're ready."

I gasped at the pinch in my abdomen, then I let my head fall to the side again, where the threads in the doctor's shirt were still weaving their way around his soft belly toward his back.

When I blinked, tears ran down my face onto the padded table.

"I think that will do it…the heartbeat is still strong." The doctor set something on the wheeled tray, then began wiping goop from my belly. "She'll need to rest… No work, no intercourse and obviously no travel. A little fluid leakage from the site is… If there are any other symptoms…me immediately." He finished wiping my stomach, then tugged my shirt over my still-sticky skin, and I struggled to bring the world back into crisp focus. "And in a few days, we'll know whether we need to reorder those prenatal vitamins or schedule an end to this whole thing."

Dr. Grantham picked up the sample he'd pulled from my womb and as he walked away, I stared at his back and willed the *furiae* to wake up. To find a reason—any reason—to give him the self-inflicted, gory end he so richly deserved.

DELILAH

I was confined to my cell for three straight days, and by the end of the second, I'd decided that solitary confinement qualified more as torture than rest. I saw no one but Pagano, who was evidently under orders to check on me every few hours, in spite of the fact that a camera had been installed in the corner of my cell while I was doped out of my mind and being stabbed by a needle.

They wouldn't let me see or talk to Gallagher, but when I told Pagano that isolation was stressful, and that stress wasn't good for the baby, he told me that Gallagher had been given the night off from the arena, since I couldn't be there to make him perform.

It worried me to think that he might not know why I wasn't there. He might think I was dead. He might try to tear through everyone he came into contact with until someone got off a lucky head shot.

After breakfast on the fourth day, when I'd run out of songs to sing, stories to tell myself and gruesome deaths to plot for my enemies, Pagano showed up to take me for a walk around the grounds.

"Thank you," I said as we rounded the building, headed for the topiary garden. "If I had to stare at those walls for another minute, I might have lost my mind."

"In that case, I hate to tell you what your evening's going to look like."

"Let me guess. More grilled chicken, green peas and wall staring?"

He actually gave me a small smile as he clicked something on his remote to allow me through the iron gate. "How are you feeling?"

"Like a caged hamster without a wheel. Any word on those test results?"

"Not that they've told me. I'm sure you'll be the first to know."

But he was wrong. If the baby was Gallagher's, I wouldn't know until I was strapped to another table. "Michael, I need a night out."

He laughed. "So, what, Italian food and a movie?"

"I'm serious. Can you get me the dinner shift? I feel good, and I need more than a stroll around the yard. Seriously. Tell Tabitha the baby needs it."

Pagano stopped and studied my face, looking for any sign of a ruse, but there was none to find. I truly needed to see something other than the inside of my cell. The fact that a work shift would give me time to observe more of the Spectacle's security measures and potentially talk to several of my fellow captives was incidental, at that point.

"She's not going to go for it. This isolation isn't just about rest. She's enforcing a gag order. I don't think she's told her husband about your…insemination yet."

I blinked at him. "You heard?"

"Through the glass door. Tabitha's threatened to fire me if I tell a soul, and she's paying me triple overtime. She's not going to let you near anyone you could tell about her plan."

"So tell her to silence me. I don't think that'll hurt the baby, and I won't make a fuss." But Pagano looked reluctant. "Please. Just try."

"Okay," he said, as he gestured for me to head back in the direction we'd come from. "But I'm not promising anything."

Dinner came and went with no word from Pagano. Someone slid my tray beneath my door, and by the time I got close enough to the window to see through it, there was no one left in the hall.

The sun set, and the lights came on in my cell. I brushed my teeth and paced across the length of my room 467 times. Then Pagano opened my door. He was smiling.

"I couldn't get you the dinner shift, but I told Tabitha how upset you were and mentioned that your mental health could have a direct effect on the baby. So she said you could have one hour of a special duty."

"Special duty?" I stopped and ran my fingers through my damp hair. "What duty?"

"Nurse's aide. One of the shifters got hurt during the hunt last night, and since we're down one doctor…" He shrugged. "But you'll be restricted to one room, and you won't be crossing paths with any of the other staff, just in case."

"Then what good will I be?"

Another shrug. "It's mostly just to give you something to do and someone to talk to, to elevate your mood. To keep the baby happy." But I could tell with one look at him that he hadn't really been thinking about the baby.

"Thank you."

He adjusted the settings on my collar and led me down the

hall and out of the building. The air outside was unexpectedly crisp and the night was so clear that the earth seemed to be blanketed by a sheet of stars.

"Do you think I could just lie on the grass and look up at the sky for a minute? You can't see anything but treetops from my window, and it's been a while."

"Tabitha would kill me if I let you catch a cold from lying on the ground."

"But the earth holds heat much longer than the air. The ground's probably still warm."

He shook his head, so I continued down the path reluctantly, the sidewalk rough but not really cold against my bare feet.

"My favorite part about running the menagerie was closing time. For hours, there was nothing but calliope music and bright lights, and callers shouting at the customers, trying to get them to play a game or buy some food. But when the customers went home, we could turn all that off, and the world just felt so…still. So quiet. So civilized."

Pagano chuckled. "That's not a word often used to describe carnival life."

"Well, after we'd freed everyone who could safely be free, that's what it felt like. It was the first time most of them had been allowed to step out of their cages and eat real food. Put on real clothes. Spin around and around, then fall down on the grass, too dizzy to move. There's nothing more civilized than freedom."

"But they can't read. They can't add."

I shook my head. "Civilization isn't about what you know. It's about how you behave. How much respect and dignity you give to those around you. The staff here…" I let that thought fade away, because insulting my handler when he'd gone to bat for me wasn't a great way to buy future favors.

"Say it," he insisted, as the infirmary drew nearer.

I stopped walking and turned to look at him. "You guys have never been denied adequate food. Proper shelter. The right to raise your own children. To choose to have them. To choose who to have them with. You don't know what it's like to truly suffer, so it means nothing to you to perpetuate suffering in others."

"You've given this a lot of thought."

"No, I really haven't. It doesn't require much thought. Dignity and respect are the most basic of social concepts. Children understand them before they can even say the words."

Pagano rolled his eyes and started walking again, leaving me no choice but to follow. "Okay, but not all cryptids are like you. You were raised human. You *are* human."

"That's bullshit. People are different just like cryptids are different. Some are kind, and some are cruel. This isn't a one-species-fits-all world."

Pagano looked like he had something to say. Or something to ask. But we were feet from the infirmary, and someone was already waving at us from the well-lit foyer.

He opened the glass door and waved me inside, where a woman in pink scrubs and a white lab coat looked me up and down. Then took a step back. "You're sure this is safe?" she said to Pagano over my shoulder.

He nodded as he clicked something on the remote, restricting me to the infirmary. "But you won't be with her anyway. Lead the way."

Instead, the nurse gave us directions. "Third door on the right. Restrict her to the back half of the room. There's a shifter cuffed to the last bed. She can get him water and talk to him. But that's it." Then she crossed her arms over her chest and watched us follow her directions, mumbling under her breath about how unsafe it was to have me "wandering the halls."

As far as I could tell from glancing through the long viewing windows, the first two rooms were full. In each, a row of narrow, sturdy steel cots was bolted to the floor. The occupants were all cuffed to the cots and covered up to their chests by a white sheet. Most appeared to be sleeping.

A small figure in the second room caught my attention, and I stopped to stare through the window. "Genni."

Pagano followed my gaze. "They say she'll have a limp, but she's going to be fine."

"For how long?" How could a thirteen-year-old with a limp possibly survive another round of hunts? "Why do you even know that?"

He didn't answer. Yet I understood.

"You're betting on her? Or against her?"

"I don't gamble," he insisted. "But I hear the talk. Her odds are good, if she gets placed in the second round again."

"And if she's placed in the third?"

He shrugged. "No one's odds are good in the last round." He waved me forward again, and I had to leave little Genni asleep, chained to her bed.

The third room looked empty, but unlike the first two, it was divided in half by a wall and a doorway fitted with a red sensor, and I couldn't see much of the back half.

Pagano adjusted my collar to allow me through the first two doorways, but when I stepped into the rear section, I forgot he was even there.

"Claudio!" The werewolf's hands were cuffed to the side rails of an actual hospital bed and his ankles were secured with chains to something beneath the thin mattress. "What happened?"

"*J'ai survécu.*" His voice was even huskier than usual for a shifter, as if his throat were very dry. "They hit me with a Taser, not an arrow, so I will live to run for my life another day."

"Those bastards." I took a small plastic cup from the counter to my left and filled it with cold water from the sink. "The game is rigged in their favor and you can't fight back, yet they think they've somehow conquered the universe by cornering an unarmed man in a closed course."

Claudio lifted his head, and I helped hold it up so he could drink from the cup. *"Merci,"* he said, when he'd finished. "Have you seen Genni?"

"She's next door. She took an arrow to the thigh, but they say she's going to be fine. She's strong, Claudio. Just like her father." And it killed me to know that thirteen years may be all the parenting she would get.

"Have you spoken to her?"

"Not since the hunt."

While I was refilling Claudio's cup for the third time, footsteps clomped into the other half of the room, blocked from sight by the wall. A handler told whoever he'd escorted to have a seat on the bed. Steel groaned, and I heard the metallic click of cuffs being locked, accompanied by the rattle of heavy chains.

"Not that I'm not glad to see you," Claudio said, as I carried the water back to him. "But why are you here?"

I shrugged, and a drop splashed over the rim of the cup. "I have friends in high places." Wherein *friends* could only be defined as *mortal enemies*. But Claudio didn't buy that for a second, so I told him as much of the truth as I could. "I've been in isolation for four days, and my handler finally had pity on me."

"Why…?" Claudio sniffed the air in my direction. Then his

golden wolf eyes widened. "Congratulations." He frowned. "Or condolences. Which is it?"

I gaped at him. "How can you tell?" I whispered, hoping whoever was in the other room couldn't hear me and hadn't understood him.

"I can smell the hormones," he whispered, following my lead as Pagano clomped toward the bed.

I turned to find my handler scowling at the werewolf. "You can tell just from smelling her?"

Claudio nodded, his hair catching on the rough material of the pillow. "But only because I know what to look for." His voice was so low I could hardly hear him. "Is it a secret?"

I could tell from his lack of concern that he had no idea what the Spectacle's official pregnancy policy was. "Yeah, it's…complicated." I whirled to face Pagano. "He won't tell anyone." Then I turned back to Claudio, and whispered, "You won't tell anyone, will you?"

Tabitha must not have known that shifters could smell my hormones, or she wouldn't have let me come see him. Which meant that if she'd left me in the dorm with Zyanya and the other female shifters, everyone at the Spectacle would probably already know.

"I won't tell," Claudio whispered. His gaze held mine with a conflicted gravity. "Delilah, Melisande and I were forced to breed five children in captivity, and each was both a blessing and a curse."

I slid my hand into his and tried not to think about how much of my situation I couldn't explain to him.

"Each was taken from us early, and it kills me to know that they're growing up in cages all over the country. But I know that the world is a better place with them in it. And I know that they will fight for their children just like I fought for mine. Just like you will fight for yours."

My eyes watered and I sniffled. Pagano retreated to a chair by the wall, evidently satisfied that Claudio wouldn't tell anyone.

The sharp squeal of metal made me gasp. A chain rattled, and Gallagher appeared in the doorway, clutching the rail he'd ripped from the hospital bed. The cuff dangled from his wrist, where it had been freed from the broken metal bar.

Since he hadn't intended to hurt anyone—thus didn't produce the monitored hormone—his collar hadn't stopped him from tearing the bed in two.

Whichever handler had left him alone was about to be *very* fired.

Gallagher's gray-eyed gaze found mine. "You're…?" His expression cracked and fell apart, exposing a vulnerability I'd never expected to see in him. "Are you sure?"

Claudio's eyes widened, as he drew conclusions I didn't have time to explain.

I nodded. "About eight weeks. I wanted to tell you, but—"

"Gallagher, drop the bed frame." Pagano lifted his remote, and I could tell from the way he clutched it that he was considering going for his gun instead.

"Don't." I turned to my handler, arms spread to show him that I meant no harm. "He's not going to hurt anyone. Right, Gallagher?"

Gallagher's eyes closed, as if Pagano presented no threat, and when his lips moved silently, I realized he was counting backward. Trying to confirm that he was going to be a father.

"It's not an exact science," I said, my voice steady and low for Pagano's benefit. Trying to keep everyone calm. "But yes, the baby may be yours."

Gallagher's eyes opened, and swimming in them, I found a stunning confusion of emotions. Joy. Fear. Wonder. Confusion. Then that all collapsed in one horrible instant of pain. "Wait, *may* be mine? Who else's could it be?"

"There are a couple of other possibilities." My gaze dropped to the ground, but then I dragged it up again. What had happened to me was wrong, but it wasn't *my* wrong. It wasn't his wrong. It was a wrong made possible by the world we lived in. By a man who thought it acceptable to own people. By a woman willing to ruin several other lives to get what she wanted.

"Delilah, what happened?" Gallagher's voice was so deep I could hardly hear it and so gruff it must have scraped his throat raw. His grip on the bed frame tightened until his fingers were white with tension. Until the metal began to groan. "I'll kill *every last one of them*."

He'd said it. He couldn't take it back. And as tears burned twin paths down my face, I realized I didn't want him to. I wanted him to tear into everyone who'd ever made me do anything against my will. Who'd ever put me in chains, touched me without invitation, drugged me or locked me up.

"Put the bed frame down and put your hands in the air." Pagano aimed his remote at Gallagher with one hand and pulled his gun with the other. His real gun. Nervous sweat dripped down his forehead. "I don't want to hurt you, but I will if I have to."

Gallagher's fist tightened. Metal squealed in his grip. His biceps bulged with tension, his gaze trained on my handler.

Pagano raised his pistol, aiming at Gallagher's chest.

"No!" I cried.

Gallagher lifted the bed frame.

Pagano put his finger on the trigger.

I lunged between them, blocking the handler's shot, but Gallagher leaned around me. His arm rose so fast I saw only a blur of motion on the edge of my vision. Something long flew across the room, end over end.

The handler pressed a button on his remote, and Gallagher made a stunned choking sound. He fell to the floor with a heavy thud just as the broken end of the metal bed frame punctured Pagano's chest like a pencil through a sheet of paper, driving him backward until he hit the wall.

Pagano coughed up blood. Then he slid down the wall and fell over sideways, staring sightlessly at the doorway.

"No!" I sank onto my knees next to Gallagher. His legs were shaking, his heels crashing into the floor over and over; he was having a seizure. "Gallagher! What can I do?"

His eyes rolled back and his teeth clacked together.

"Get the remote!" Claudio growled, fighting his restraints in a vain attempt to get out of the bed. "It's still shocking him!"

I scrambled across the floor and pulled the remote control from Pagano's limp hand, silently apologizing for his bloody death, after the relative kindness he'd shown me. The remote had a smart screen, with half a dozen "quick touch" options. An icon at the bottom of the display read End Voltage.

I pressed it three times before I was sure the device had accepted my command.

Gallagher went still. I crawled back to him with the remote control in hand. His eyes were closed. "Gallagher." I bent low to speak into his ear. "Gallagher. Please wake up! We have to move." We weren't going to get a better chance to escape, and we had no choice.

He'd killed a handler.

If Vandekamp caught us, he would have Gallagher killed slowly, brutally in the arena. In front of a crowd. And he'd make me watch.

"Is he okay?" Claudio asked, still straining for a better view.

"I don't—"

Gallagher's eyelids twitched. Then they opened. He blinked, and his gaze focused on me. "Delilah. Are you—" He sat up with no sign of vertigo, and when he saw Pagano's corpse, he exhaled. "I got him."

"He didn't hurt me, Gallagher."

"He wasn't…?" His gaze fell to my stomach.

"No!"

Gallagher shrugged. "Pagano was keeping you locked up. That made him our enemy." And for him, it was truly that simple.

He pushed himself to his feet, then reached down to help me up. "We're leaving."

"Okay," I said, and he looked surprised that I wasn't arguing. "But we can't leave all the others."

"We won't." Gallagher turned to Claudio. "Can you walk?"

The werewolf's cuffs rattled when he shrugged. "Not quickly."

"Okay, then you'll stay here—stay safe—until we come back for you." Gallagher glanced at me. "You figure out the remote. I'll find the keys. It won't be long before the nurse comes in to check my stitches." He lifted his arm, and I saw that a long gash stretching toward his elbow had popped three stitches and begun to bleed. Which was why they'd brought him to the infirmary.

While Gallagher dug in Pagano's pockets, I went through the remote control's menus and functions, careful not to press anything that might hurt any of us. "Okay," I said, when I'd found what seemed to be the home menu. "There's an option that will remove all restrictions. I'm going to try that, but anyone else with a remote will still be able to reprogram them."

"Not for long." Gallagher unlocked his cuffs and dropped them into a trash can against one wall. Next he unlocked one of Claudio's cuffs and handed him the key, then covered the unlocked hand with the white sheet. "Stay put until we come for you, or until we give the all clear. Then you can unlock the rest of the cuffs."

Claudio nodded.

"Okay." Gallagher turned to me. "Remove my restrictions."

I aimed the remote at him, and a new line appeared on the screen, confirming that whatever command I issued would take effect on "Gallagher. Collar number 47924." I pressed the button marked Remove All Restrictions.

The remote asked me to confirm my command, and I pressed the button again.

Gallaher's collar flashed red.

"Okay, I think we're good. But maybe we should test it."

"There's no time." He turned to the cabinet against one wall and gave the locked drawer a hard pull. The lock gave and the drawer slid open. Gallagher rifled through the contents until he came up with a slim pair of scissors with long handles. "Okay, I need you to slide these between the collar and my skin, then carefully snip the metal...spine...things."

I held the scissors up to the light to examine them. "These are suture scissors. They're made to cut thread, not metal."

"They're the only set slim enough to fit. And these spines are very thin."

"But for all we know, that could kill you."

"That's why we're not trying it out on you."

"Try it on me," Claudio said.

"No!" I insisted. "Genni needs you."

"I'm doing this for Genevieve. Just promise you'll get her out of here. No matter what."

"We promise." Gallagher grabbed the scissors from me and helped Claudio sit up, which was only possible because we'd freed one of his hands. He examined the werewolf's collar. "Remove the restrictions."

"Done." I was a step ahead of them. "But that doesn't mean the collar won't shock him—or worse—the minute you try to sever the connection to his spine."

"We're willing to take that chance," Claudio insisted.

Gallagher gently slid the scissors between the back of Claudio's neck and his collar. When the werewolf reported no pain, Gallagher carefully snipped the first spine. Claudio flinched, but made no complaint, so Gallagher slid the scissors a little deeper and snipped again. "This last one's hard to reach. Any pain yet?"

"No." Claudio held his head stiff and still.

"Okay, here goes." Gallagher snipped again.

The remote in my hand beeped, and a notice popped up on the screen. "'Collar deactivated,'" I read. "Claudio. Collar 47927."

Claudio exhaled, and Gallagher actually smiled. Then he slid the collar up as far as it would go on the werewolf's neck. "I can't get this off, but that's just as well. If they see you without the collar, they'll know something's wrong. But I can get these spines out. Hold very still."

Gallagher gripped the highest of the three tiny spines with the tips of his blunt fingernails and pulled it straight out of the wolf's neck.

Claudio's eyes squeezed shut and he took a deep breath, but when he reported no pain, Gallagher removed the other two spines and dropped all three into the trash. "They can't hurt you with this thing anymore."

I snipped and removed Gallagher's spines next, then he removed mine. My neck stung when he pulled the metal free, but the euphoria I felt when they clinked into the trash more than made up for it.

Vandekamp had placed his faith, his safety and his entire career on his collars, and that had led him to drop his guard. He would have no idea what hit him.

"According to the current rate of research, it would take
approximately one hundred fifty years to map
the genome of every known species of cryptid. If this
Dr. Vandekamp has come up with another way—a faster
way—to understand and control these beasts, I think we
owe it to ourselves and our children to listen to what
he has to say."

**—from an NPR interview with Barbara Gray, president of
the Mothers Against Cryptid Violence organization,
August 8, 2012**

DELILAH

We hid Pagano's body beneath Claudio's bed. Anyone who looked would find it, but it wouldn't be visible at a glance. The towels that mopped up his blood went into the trash, which conveniently covered Gallagher's handcuffs with legitimate-looking medical waste.

The hardest part of sneaking out of the infirmary was leaving the rest of the patients behind, but we couldn't stage a full-scale escape until we'd disabled all the collars and taken out as many of the handlers as possible. As far as I could tell, none of the patients' injuries were life-threatening. Evidently, Vandekamp considered it more financially feasible to exterminate the mortally wounded than to treat the wounds.

With any luck, most would be able to walk away from the Spectacle under their own power—if and when Gallagher and I could free them.

But without a captured carnival to hide us…

"We need a plan," I whispered as I led him down a back hallway of the infirmary toward the service entrance, where

I'd often seen Eryx unloading supplies during lunch delivery. Hopefully at night, it would be empty.

"I have a plan. Kill them all."

"That's not what I mean," I said as we slipped out the back door into the night. "We need a plan for afterward. We have nowhere to go and no way to get there."

"If we wait for those things to fall into our laps, we'll die here, Delilah."

"And if we don't have a plan, we'll die out there." I pulled him to a stop in the shadows behind the building, acutely aware that the next time a handler did a security check in the infirmary, the whole compound would know we were missing. "In the menagerie, you had a plan. You were calm and smart, and you made balanced decisions. We need some of that tonight."

"In the menagerie, I spent a year strategizing and laying the groundwork. Here, we have minutes. If they find us before we can deactivate the rest of the collars, we will never leave this place alive. And do you know what they'll do when they find out about the baby?"

"They already know. That's why they put me in a private cell. That's why they're feeding me better and giving me exercise."

"They...?" He blinked at me in the dark. "What?"

"Tabitha Vandekamp had me artificially inseminated— while I was unconscious—with her husband's sperm. She's infertile, and because I'm genetically human, she's decided that fate sent me here to give them a baby."

"Why would they let you be paired with me if they want you to have their baby?"

"Vandekamp didn't know about it. She wasn't going to tell him until she knew I was pregnant, but by then, he'd already sent me on other engagements."

His scowl darkened. "Wait, other engagements? Plural?"

"Just one, other than…you. I can't remember it. Gallagher, *I'm* the one who had my memory buried, and I think I did it so you wouldn't find out about the other…event. Because I knew you'd get yourself killed trying to avenge me."

"Dying in your service would be an honor." He sounded almost wistful. "You're not supposed to choose my well-being over your own."

"None of that matters now. I had a test a few days ago, to determine the baby's species. If it's not human, she's going to kill it."

"Meaning…if it's mine?"

"Yes." I glanced at my feet on the pavement, barely visible in the dark. Then I made myself look him in the eye. "I know this is weird. I know neither of us asked for this. But…" I didn't know how to put my conflicted tangle of emotions into words.

"But it's happening."

"Yeah. It is."

"No." He shook his head firmly. "I apologize. My words were woefully inadequate for what I intended to express. What I mean is that you are the most important thing in the world to me. What you do… I've pledged my life to making sure you can do it safely. I will be by your side as long as I have air to breathe and blood to spill, and that's a stronger vow than any minister or court official has ever presided over. Whether or not the baby is mine, the baby is *yours*. I will protect him or her with the same vehemence with which I protect you. Which is why I'm getting you—both of you—out of here. Come on."

He took my arm and tried to guide me deeper into the shadows, but I pulled him back.

I'd been thrown away by every friend I'd ever had, when fate had called me into service, and I'd been so bitter about what life had taken from me that I hadn't thought to be thankful for what it had given me in return. Twice, I'd been taken in by people who shared no blood with me and owed me nothing. And twice those people—first my parents, then Gallagher—had set aside their own lives to make sure I was cared for.

"Thank you," I said when he turned to see why I hadn't moved. "My words are also 'woefully inadequate,' but I mean them sincerely."

Gallagher nodded, accepting my gratitude with the same grave formality with which he approached important events in his life. "Now, we really must go. And we're damn lucky it's Sunday."

"It is?" I'd lost track of the days in isolation, but the empty parking lots we passed as we moved from shadow to shadow supported his declaration. The Savage Spectacle was closed on Sundays, which meant it would be operating on minimum manning until nearly dawn.

We would get no better chance to make our move.

We stuck to the shadows, which Gallagher's *fear dearg* heritage let him fade into almost seamlessly, and we were nearly to the main building when we saw the first handler on patrol. He carried a flashlight and an automatic rifle, as well as the usual stun gun and remote control, and while he peered into every shadow, he only walked on the well-lit sidewalk. He didn't expect to find trouble, because he never had before.

"Stay here," Gallagher whispered, and before I could argue, he disappeared into the shadows entirely.

A second later, he reached into the light. The guard grunted as he was pulled off his feet and into the dark. His grunt of surprise became a wet gurgle, followed by the gristly sound of ripping flesh. I flinched as something thumped to the ground. An empty, bloodstained shoe tumbled onto the sidewalk.

Then Gallagher was suddenly beside me, holding the dead guard's remote control and his employee ID, which had a bar code across the bottom. "Will this be of any use?"

"With any luck, it'll open the door to the control room."

He huffed. "No door lock has ever kept me out."

"But plenty of broken door locks have set off alarms. We'll use the card."

We headed for the main building, skirting pools of light along the sidewalk to tread in darkness. Gallagher faded into it so well that at times I couldn't even tell if he was still next to me. The grass beneath my feet was dry and crisp, and sharp in places, with fall in full swing. The night was cold and clear. Every breath seemed to invigorate me, and the fact that I couldn't be paralyzed or shocked into compliance gave me more confidence in our mission than I probably should have had.

At the back of the building, I used the dead guard's ID to unlock the door, and we stepped inside, traversing the marble silently on bare feet. "Where's the control room?" Gallagher whispered.

I led the way down one dark hallway and into another, avoiding cameras as much as possible, until we stood outside the locked control room door. "You can't kill whoever's in here," I whispered, as I held up the stolen ID card. "We need him to disarm all the other collars."

"You mean I can't kill him *until* he's disarmed the other collars."

I nodded because that was as much of a compromise as I was going to get out of Gallagher. We'd taken over the menagerie with minimal blood spilled, but that wouldn't be possible at the Spectacle, in part because we weren't merely taking it over.

We were putting it out of business.

"I need you to get ahold of the guard before he can raise an alert. Ready?"

Gallagher nodded.

I held the ID badge beneath the scanner built into the wall. The door beeped softly, and there was a metallic scraping sound as the bolt slid back. I opened the door just as the guard swiveled toward us in his chair.

Gallagher rushed past me. The guard's eyes widened. He tried to stand, but Gallagher grabbed him by the neck and lifted him six inches off the floor. "Delilah, confiscate his devices."

While the guard clawed at Gallagher's hand, trying in vain to breathe, I plucked the pistol, stun gun and remote control from his belt, then pulled the communication headset from his head and turned it off.

Gallagher set the guard down, and as the man bent over, coughing and gasping I saw that his name tag read Petit.

"Petit," I said, as Gallagher pushed the door closed behind us. "If you want to live, sit down at your desk and disable the collars." No need to tell him that cooperating wouldn't actually save his life.

"How did you get in here?" he gasped, rubbing his throat.

"Disable the collars," Gallagher growled. "Now."

Petit took a step back and bumped his chair, which rolled toward the console. "Which ones?"

"All of them." I glanced at the wall full of live camera feeds, watching for any sign that Pagano's body had been discovered. "Turn them all off."

The guard glanced nervously from me to Gallagher, then back. "I can't."

"Bullshit," Gallagher growled.

"No, seriously. It doesn't work that way, for this very reason. It's a fail-safe. I can turn them off one at a time, but not all at once. And turning off more than three in a five-minute period sets off an alarm."

"We don't have time for that." Gallagher glanced around at the equipment. "I'm just going to smash it all."

"Wait," I said, when Petit made no objection. "That'll set off an alarm too, won't it?"

He shrugged. "Probably."

"Okay, we can't turn off all the collars at once, and we don't have time to do them individually." I paced the length of the small room, while Gallagher stood over Petit. "And we can't smash the system. So..." I turned and looked up at the guard. "Can you shut the system down? Just...turn it off?"

Petit shrugged, but the brief, slight dip in his brows was telling. "I don't think so."

"He's lying," I said.

Gallagher picked him up by the throat again. "Turn it off," he demanded, while Petit clawed at his hand again, feet kicking ineffectually. "And if you trigger an alarm, I will make sure that you die very slowly."

He let Petit down, and the guard sank into his chair, coughing and gasping again.

I stood over him while he worked, watching every keystroke, unsure that I'd recognize an alarm if he raised one. Gallagher watched the video monitors.

After a couple of minutes and several open windows on the screen in front of him, Petit found a software menu with a shutdown option. But he hesitated to click it.

"Do it." I laid one hand on his shoulder—a silent threat—and he flinched. Then he clicked the command.

A box popped up, demanding an administrator password.

"Damn it."

"What?" Gallagher glanced down at the screen. "Are you an administrator?" he asked.

Petit shook his head. "I'm just the night guard."

"So, what, you have to wake someone up every time there's a glitch or an update?" I demanded.

Petit's brows dipped again, and his gaze flicked to the left for a second before dropping to the ground. He was a terrible liar.

I looked to the left, searching for whatever he'd automatically glanced at.

A row of shelves full of technical manuals. Those would take forever to search. A pod-based coffee system. A folding metal chair, with a jacket draped over the seat.

Bingo. I grabbed the jacket—clearly his—and searched the pockets. They were all empty. Then I noticed the employee ID clipped to the front. I flipped it over. Written on the back in block letters was an eight-digit code comprised of four letters, two numbers and two other symbols.

"Got it." I unclipped the badge and rolled Petit out of the way, then typed the password into the box.

"Don't do this," Petit begged. "You're going to get a lot of people hurt."

"No," Gallagher growled. "We're going to get a lot of people killed."

I clicked Enter. The window disappeared, and another one popped up, asking if I was sure I wanted to shut down the system. I clicked Yes, and a third window popped up, informing me that I had just shut down the system.

Relief flooded me. "We did it." Every cryptid on the property would be able to fight back, walk through any unlocked door, and use any and all natural abilities.

The odds had been evened.

I looked up at Gallagher with a triumphant smile.

Then the remote controls I'd stolen from Pagano and Petit began to flash red. They made a single high-pitched beeping sound. Then they powered down automatically.

Petit laughed, and I realized that every remote control on the grounds would be doing the very same thing.

We hadn't merely shut down the system. We'd *announced* that we'd shut down the system.

We'd just raised the alarm ourselves.

"It's just not possible. We will never be able to trust these creatures, no matter what they're wearing. No matter how much control we think we have over them. You don't see us slapping collars on tigers and letting them play in our backyards—with our children—do you?"

—from the transcript of Senate Subcommittee Hearing into Cryptid Placement, October 19, 2013

DELILAH

"Gallagher. Smash the equipment."

"But you said—"

I held up the dead remote. "Everyone who's carrying one of these knows what we just did. If they restart the system, we're screwed. Smash it."

Gallagher grabbed the folding metal chair and slammed it into three of the wall-mounted monitors at once.

"No, those just show what's happening." He had no experience with electronics, because as *fear dearg*, every electronic device he picked up shorted-circuited. The collar had only worked on him because it was hardwired into his nervous system. "You have to smash the machines themselves." I pointed out the row of computers beneath the operating console. "There."

Gallagher jerked the first from its shelf, wires dangling, and threw it at the floor. Electronic shrapnel flew all over the room, peppering us with harmless scratches. While he smashed the others, I used a police-style baton hanging from

Petit's chair to further decimate the machines he'd already broken open.

A door squealed open behind me, and I looked up as Petit ran into the hallway.

Gallagher took off after him. I caught up with them around the corner just in time to see him break Petit's neck. One-handed.

The corpse crumpled to the floor, and I flinched.

"He was a threat," Gallagher whispered.

"Fine. But let's try to limit the bloodshed to those who've actually done harm or are threatening to. Okay?"

"They've all done harm."

"If we slaughter the entire staff, people won't just *think* we're animals that have to be caged or put down—they'll believe it. Promise me you won't kill anyone who doesn't have to die."

"Delilah…" He glanced at my stomach, and I knew what he was thinking. What he wanted to do to everyone associated with the Savage Spectacle.

"Promise me."

"Those I've already sworn to kill must die. As for the rest… are concussions okay?"

"Yes. Unconsciousness is preferred. Let them wake up later with a huge headache and the knowledge that we could have killed them, but didn't. I'm planning to use this." I held up the confiscated stun gun.

Gallagher frowned. "You'd have to be within arm's reach to use that. Let's get you something bigger." He headed down the hall toward the back door and I followed, bewildered until he stopped next to a door marked Armory.

The ID scanner next to the door still glowed a soft green, even though we'd taken out the main security system. Either Vandekamp had a backup or the door locks were on a different system than the collars.

Gallagher held the stolen employee ID beneath the wall scanner, and when the door unlocked, he pulled it open.

Inside the small room, we found rack after rack of automatic rifles, pistols, stun guns and…

He pulled an eighteen-inch baton from a bin full of others, and the cord plugged into it fell away. "Here." Gallagher handed me the baton, and my thumb found a switch on the side, near the grip. When I turned it on, the stick hummed to life.

"A stun baton. I've never seen one of these."

"They use them behind the scenes at the arena. The current runs down the outside of the stick as well as the end, so no one can take it from you. Don't hold it anywhere but the rubber grip."

I nodded. "Um…grab the rest of those, will you?"

He unplugged the other dozen or so batons and handed them to me. I clutched them in a bundle beneath one arm, and as we left the room, I had an idea.

"Can you destroy that?" I pointed at the card reader. "Without it, they may not be able to get to the rest of the weapons." The door's hinges were on the inside, so Vandekamp's men couldn't just remove them.

Gallagher gripped the scanner in both hands and wrenched it from the wall. Then he crushed it in both fists.

"Perfect. Okay, I'm going to pass these out to everyone who doesn't have a natural defense. I need you to destroy all the other computers, starting with Vandekamp's. He'll have a backup of the collar software. He probably wrote it himself. And he might have a backup security system. His office is the last one on that left-hand hallway."

Gallagher glanced down the hall, then turned back to me. "We're not splitting up."

"We don't have time not to. Don't worry, I'll stick to the shadows. And I'm armed now." I held up my activated baton for emphasis. "Meet me in the dormitory when you're done here. Okay?"

He nodded reluctantly, then headed toward the other hallway.

"And Gallagher?"

"Yes?" He turned back to me.

"The computers are the boxes containing the hardware, not the screens."

He gave me another gruff nod, then I took off out the back door.

GALLAGHER

The door at the end of the hall slammed shut as Gallagher turned the corner. But not before he saw Willem Vandekamp disappear into his office, his hand clutching the grip of a pistol. His eyes wide with fear—an emotion thus far unseen from the Spectacle's owner.

Gallagher smiled, an expression no man in his right mind would have mistaken for joy. He inhaled deeply, savoring the scent of fear on the air as he let his hunger build.

He hadn't been hunting in ages.

The redcap strode down the hall silently and kicked the door in with his bare foot. Ripped from its hinges, it flew into the room and smashed into the chairs lined up along the opposite wall. The splinter of wood was merely a taste of violence he planned to consume, but it was enough to whet his appetite.

The blood he spilled in the arena every week kept Gallagher alive, but that exploitative carnage didn't fulfill his purpose.

It didn't feed his soul.

"What the fuck?" The woman behind the desk stood, eyes wide, right hand clutching her phone. "Please. Don't hurt me."

"Run," Gallagher growled, veins swollen with rage and adrenaline. Muscles aching to rend flesh from bone.

She raced past him into the hall, tripping over her high heels.

The inner office door slammed, and metal scraped wood as Vandekamp locked himself in. "The police are on the way," he shouted from inside.

"Tell them to send the coroner instead." Gallagher sucked in a deep, invigorating breath, then kicked the next door in. The force of the blow shattered not just the door, but the chair wedged in front of it.

He shoved the tangle of wood and upholstery aside and pushed his way into the office. Vandekamp stood behind his desk, aiming the pistol at the redcap's chest. "I should have realized the first time I saw you. There was something about you. I thought it was your size, but it was more than that."

"Humans should put more faith in their instinct. And less in weapons." Gallagher took a step forward, and Vandekamp fired. The redcap dived to the ground and smacked the light switch on his way down. More wood splintered beneath him. The room descended into shadows.

The gun thundered again, and Vandekamp stood exposed in the muzzle flash.

Gallagher slid into the shadows as if he were made of them. He stepped over obstacles no human could have seen in the dark, and his feet made no sound.

Vandekamp fired again, scanning the room during the flash, wide-eyed. The redcap stood two feet away. Towering over him.

Gallagher ripped an arm from the darkness. The gun clattered to the floor. His victim screamed as blood arched into the air, splattering shadowy files and furniture. Painting the ceiling in artful splashes of dark red.

He fell upon the owner of the Savage Spectacle with a brutal enthusiasm that would have brought thunderous applause from the crowd, had it taken place in the arena. Hands flew across the room. Legs thunked onto the floor. Vandekamp's spinal column was severed with a single vicious snap, breaking his head from his body like a cork from a bottle of champagne.

When the violence was over—when his bloodlust was sated—Gallagher knelt and dropped his cap into the fragrant red puddle.

As blood rolled across the ceiling and down the walls one drop at a time, soaking into the *fear dearg*'s traditional cap with a speed that spoke of true hunger, Gallagher glanced around the room, taking note of the computer on a shelf under the desk. When the blood had been consumed, he stood, hat in hand, ready to demolish the technology that had brought pain to so many. Then something else caught his eye.

On Vandekamp's desk lay a single white envelope with *Greenlake Diagnostic and Laboratory Services* printed on the top left corner. Handwritten on the envelope were two words that somehow seemed to carry the weight of his entire world.

Marlow, Delilah.

DELILAH

I stuck close to the building for as long as I could, then raced across the well-lit garden into the deepest patch of shade I could find—the shadow cast by the minotaur topiary.

I'd made it halfway across the courtyard using that method when a door slammed somewhere across the grounds. Seconds later, I heard a stampede of boots headed my way.

I pressed myself against a bush shaped like a griffin, careful not to drop any of the batons, and let a dozen armed guards jog past me, fifty feet away. Headed for the main building.

Gallagher's smart. He can handle himself. But I couldn't help worrying. He wasn't bulletproof.

When they'd passed out of sight and earshot, I raced as fast as I could across the last half of the courtyard, then ducked through the gate into the employees-only section of the Spectacle.

The dormitory was the nearest building. The entrance was locked, but the collar sensor mounted over it was dark. The stolen employee ID opened the door, and I slipped into the dimly lit rear hall as it fell shut behind me.

I went to the women's dorm first, but before I could use my key card on the locked door, I heard footsteps approaching from the left.

"Hey!" a familiar voice shouted. I turned to find Bowman aiming his pistol at me. "I should have known you were involved in this."

I dropped my armload of unactivated batons, which clattered to the floor and rolled in all directions. "If you value your life, you'll turn around and go home. Right now."

"What, because the system's down?" He shrugged, holding a remote control with a dark screen. "They'll get it restarted in a few minutes—we've trained for glitches like this—and until then, all the doors are automatically locked."

I slid the stolen employee ID beneath the waistband of my pants as subtly as I could. "The system's not just down. It's destroyed. We smashed every computer in the control room." I couldn't resist a smile when his face paled. "Did you train for that?"

"You're lying."

"I'm offering you a chance to live. Every cryptid in this place, hybrid and beast alike, is unrestricted. If you don't want to be gored by a manticore or eaten by an ogre, you should leave. Now."

Bowman's eyes narrowed. He took several steps toward me, his gun aimed at my chest. "Drop the baton!"

Reluctantly, I dropped my weapon a foot away, and it buzzed on the ground. He hadn't told me to turn it off.

Bowman shifted to a one-handed grip on his pistol and pulled a set of metal cuffs from his waistband. "I'm going to give you these, and you're going to cuff yourself." Because he wouldn't touch me without wearing gloves.

Unfortunately, while I was sure he deserved the worst the

furiae had to give, she still slept peacefully. I hadn't actually seen Bowman hurt anyone but me.

I would have to take him down on my own.

He marched slowly closer, holding the cuffs out at arm's length. When he was close enough, I reached out as if I'd take them. Instead, I shoved his gun hand upward.

The pistol went off, and bits of Styrofoam tile drifted down from the ceiling. I dropped into a squat and grabbed the baton by the rubber grip and swung it at him.

The side of the baton hit his leg as he tried to aim. His muscles spasmed, and the gun went off again.

The bullet whizzed past my head. My ears rang, then the world went silent. I spun to find the bullet lodged in the wall behind me.

Still spasming, Bowman fell to his knees and lost contact with the baton. He blinked, then frowned, as his eyes began to regain focus. So I hit him with the baton again and electrocuted him until he passed out.

Stunned and with my head still ringing, I stood and pulled the ID card from my waistband, then held it under the scanner. The door unlocked with the soft scrape of metal, and I pulled it open to find a crowd of women staring at me.

"Delilah?" Mirela's lips moved, and I recognized my name on them, but I heard nothing. "What—"

"I can't hear you, so just listen, okay?"

An entire room full of women nodded, eyes wide and terrified.

"It's time to go. Just a sec." I ducked into the hall again and grabbed one of the unactivated batons. "Gallagher and I destroyed the collar system, which means the door sensors and remote controls don't function. So here's how this is going to work. There are a dozen more of these on the floor in the hall." I held up the weapon. "This is an electrified baton. If you don't have claws or fangs or some kind of natural defensive ability, grab one. Turn it on, but only touch this rubber handle, because the rest of it will shock you. If someone tries to grab you, hit him or her with it."

"What's the best way off the compound?" Lenore said, and I actually heard most of her question, though it seemed to be coming at me from the other end of a long tunnel.

"Through the woods," Magnolia said.

"No." Simra shook her head. "That's too slow. We need cars."

"She's right." I turned to Lenore and Zyanya. "Take them to the parking lot and find the largest vehicles. Do you remember what Abraxas showed us? How to hot-wire a car?"

Several of the former menagerie captives nodded. Most of them had been taught to drive out of necessity, because Metzger's was a *traveling* menagerie.

"Good. Pile into the vehicles and leave. Just go."

"Where?" Lala asked, as I handed her my baton.

"I don't know. I *shouldn't* know, that way if they catch me, I can't tell them. Later, when and if it's safe, we'll try to find each other. You and Mirela will be our best hope of that." Through their premonitions. Though the shifters might be able to track anyone who fled on foot. "But tonight the goal is to get out of the Spectacle. Okay?"

The crowd nodded again, though several of the women looked more scared than eager.

"Okay. Go."

"What about you?" Zyanya asked as the women pushed past me into the hall, wide-eyed gazes searching for danger in every direction.

"I have to open the rest of the doors, but then I'll be right behind you."

She pushed a poof of dark curls back from her face. "I'll help."

"No." I met her gaze. "Help them." I nodded at the rest of the women. "You know how to drive and you can pass for human. They need you. I'll be fine."

The shifter nodded reluctantly. Then she stepped into the hall and began herding the women toward the rear exit.

I freed the men and gave them the same instructions, though I had no more batons to hand out. For safety in numbers, I ran with them in the direction of the employee lot, then veered toward the "stable," where Vandekamp kept prey for the hunt. But before I could open the door, it opened on its own, and nearly two dozen shifters and nonshifting hybrids—including three centaurs and a satyr—nearly trampled me.

The last one out the door was Payat, who'd recovered from the hunt.

"Hey!" I grabbed his arm, and he whirled on me, ready to fight until he saw my face.

"Delilah!" He pulled me into a hug. "I'm so glad to see you!"

"You too. How'd you get out?"

"Gallagher unlocked us. He's looking for you."

Alive with relief, I kissed him on the cheek. "Zyanya and the others are heading for the parking lot. Can you help her get everybody out of here? And if you see Gallagher, tell him I'm heading to the infirmary."

Payat nodded and gave me another brief, tight hug. Then he took off running.

ERYX

Deep in the maze of hallways beneath the arena, the minotaur sat up, suddenly wide-awake in his windowless cell. From two doors down, the cockatrice gave another ear-piercing shriek and clawed the concrete. She'd been irritable since her narrow defeat of the *wendigo*, because she'd lost the last two inches of her tail to the cannibal in the ring, but this wasn't her usual angry ranting.

The cockatrice sounded…excited.

Across the hall, the chimera roared, and the hairs stood up on Eryx's thick forearms. He stood and looked through the window in his cell door, and at first he couldn't process what he was seeing. The chimera's goat and lion heads were pushing each other aside to claim the view through its window. They were so close to the door that breath from the lion's muzzle fogged the glass.

The minotaur's eyes narrowed as he watched. The collars should have shocked and immobilized the beast before it got within two feet of its door.

From farther down the hall came a great thud, and the

groan of heavy hinges as one of the other beasts rammed its cell door.

Eryx looked up at the sensor over his own door. It was dark, as usual, and there was only one way to test its functionality. The minotaur's massive lungs expanded as he sucked in a great breath. Then he stepped closer to the door.

The sensor remained dark. No pain came.

He took another step and slowly exhaled. The sensors were broken.

The cockatrice crowed again, and the minotaur's huge heart seemed ready to burst through his thick chest.

The time had come.

Eryx studied the door as carefully as he'd ever considered any opponent in the ring. He bent at the waist and took another deep breath. His left hoof pawed the dusty concrete floor, but he was as unaware of the motion as he was of the ancient instinct that drove it. He was lost in a memory of himself as a younger bull in a much smaller box made of rough wood planks rather than concrete.

The minotaur backed up as far as he could and pawed the ground again. Then he ran at the door with every bit of energy and strength he had.

His massive horns punctured the steel like a fork through a tin can, but the hinges held.

Eryx yanked his head free and backed up to try again. The wooden box faded from his thoughts, as did the infant minotaur who'd failed to breach it. The beast who ran at his cell door this time was more than two thousand pounds of solid muscle and sheer determination, driven straight at the only obstacle standing in the way of his freedom.

He barreled into the door and ripped it off its hinges with a groan of tearing steel. Momentum carried both the bull and the punctured door across the hall, where they rammed into the cinder-block wall beside the chimera's cell.

Eryx stood and wrenched the door from his horns. He dropped the ruined hunk of metal at his feet just as another door flew open down the hall. A young giant—no more than twelve years old, yet seven feet tall—barreled into the dim passageway and glanced around to gain his bearings. Then he charged down the broad hallway past the minotaur, the earth shaking beneath his huge bare feet with every step.

Cacophony rose from the cells all around Eryx as the other beasts rammed their doors, eager to gain freedom. He looked to the left, then the right, then finally took off behind the giant.

As the minotaur approached a corner to the left, a sharp scream rose above the low-pitched growls and grunts from the beasts enclosed in cells on both sides of the hall. The scream ended in a gurgle, and Eryx rounded the corner, he saw the young giant running up ahead, blood dripping from his thick, pale fingers. On the ground behind him lay the corpse of a black-clad handler, still leaking blood from his crushed skull.

Eryx knelt carefully and plucked the ID from the dead handler's uniform, which he'd often seen used to unlock doors. The badge read Derek Oakland. He turned the badge over to examine the bar code on the back, then he gave it an experimental swipe beneath the card reader beside the nearest cell door.

The card reader flashed green, and Eryx pulled open the door. The troll inside gave him an aggressive grunt, then barreled toward the opening. The minotaur lunged to the side, narrowly avoiding a clash with the hairy, gray-skinned biped, then watched, amused, as the troll raced down the hall and around a corner in his uneven gait.

For a moment, the minotaur only stared at the card in his

thick grip, considering. Freeing the animal hybrids and sentient predators would cause a panic. With good reason.

It would also cause one hell of a distraction...

Eryx raced down curving hallways and around sharp corners, opening doors and dodging newly freed beasts as he searched for a way out. But no exit appeared in the labyrinthine passageways.

Frustrated, Eryx turned and retraced his own steps, pushing his way past furry forms and dodging scaled and horned appendages, searching for whatever wrong turn he'd taken. Within minutes, he found himself standing again in front of his own destroyed door. Most of his neighbors were still locked in their cells, growling, roaring and howling their outrage.

The minotaur stood before the chimera's door, stolen ID badge ready.

"Eryx?"

He turned, his heart thumping madly beneath his chest at the familiar voice. Rommily stood near the end of the hall, dwarfed by the high, arched ceiling and exaggerated width of the passage. Swallowed by her own ill-fitting clothes.

Never had the bull so thoroughly hated his mute bovine tongue.

A smile broke over the oracle's face, and she ran toward him, thin arms outstretched.

Behind her a steel door flew open and crashed against the cinder-block wall. The *ammit*—a one-ton beast with the hindquarters of a hippo, the front half of a lion and the head of a crocodile—burst from her cell and barreled down the hall, cracking the concrete floor beneath her huge four-toed rear hooves. Content to trample anyone in her path.

Rommily screamed and lurched forward. Eryx raced toward them both. The *ammit* snorted as it charged toward freedom, blowing Rommily's hair forward as she ran.

At the last second, Eryx darted into an open cell, reaching out for Rommily. His thick hand wrapped around her arm and he pulled the oracle into the deserted room, shielding her with his own body as the *ammit* barreled down the hall. Past them both.

When the threat was gone, Eryx stepped back. Rommily looked up at him, dark eyes wide. Then she smiled and took his hand.

And the oracle led the mighty minotaur out of the maze through a service entrance.

DELILAH

The synchronized clomp of boots sent my pulse racing. I lurched around the corner of the dormitory building and dropped into the shadows just as an entire squad of armed handlers jogged around the corner from the building that housed cryptids destined for the hunt.

"What the hell happened?" the man in the lead demanded into his radio. "The stable was standing wide-open. Perkins nearly got trampled by three centaurs and a satyr."

"The collars are disengaged," the staticky voice over the radio shouted. "Repeat—*the collars are disengaged*. Approach with caution and shoot to kill. Lethal force *is* authorized. Don't take any chances out there, guys."

"Fuck that." One of the men stopped jogging, and the others came to a haphazard halt around him. "I didn't sign up for this."

The handler in the lead grabbed his man by the edge of his puffy protective vest. "The hell you didn't. What did you think the hazard pay was for? Now, shut up and keep your eyes open."

"Do you hear that?" Another handler turned toward the

rumble of several engines echoing across the quiet compound. "Backup's on the way. I think she called in the fucking marines."

When I realized he was staring toward the parking lot, I gave a silent cheer. Even if Tabitha Vandekamp had called in the marines, that wasn't what we were hearing.

"The engines are heading away," one of the other men said. "That's not backup. It's deserters!"

Actually, it was the very creatures they'd been sent out to kill, currently stealing their cars in order to escape.

"Let's go!" the leader shouted, and his men fell back into two lines. When they'd passed me, I stood and peeked around the corner of the building, wishing I'd kept one of the electric batons for myself as I watched the men jog toward the next building.

Shivering in the fall air, I crept behind them into the next unlit patch of grass.

"Stop right where you are!" one of the men shouted, and I went still, terrified for a second that I'd been caught. But the men were all aiming their rifles in the opposite direction—at a satyr and a nymph, frozen in the beam of someone's flashlight.

Gunfire rang into the night, and I gasped as the defenseless cryptids were shot where they stood. Then the squad of handlers moved on with their mission, heading east across the compound, while I stood shaking in the shadows.

It took at least a minute for me to regain control of my trembling legs and press on, avoiding even a glance at the bodies of my fellow captives as I passed them.

I was a good fifteen feet from the infirmary entrance, still hidden by shadows, when a great, angry screech split the night. The thunder of heavy hooves shook the ground beneath me, and I froze again, my heart pounding.

Human screams rang out from the east, then several were suddenly silenced.

The stampede got louder by the second until a manticore rounded the corner of the arena, its scorpion tail arching ten feet in the air, spiky lion's mane blowing in the late night breeze. A black-clad human arm was speared on the beast's stinger, still dripping blood in an arcing pattern as it swayed over the creature's back.

I backed up until my spine hit the wall of the infirmary, as deep into the shadows as I could get, and I could only watch as beast after beast followed the lion-scorpion hybrid toward the courtyard and the topiary garden.

Three giants and an ogre alternately swapped blows as they fled the arena, and when the ogre got in too good of a punch, one of the giants uprooted a small tree from near the dormitory and swatted him with it.

The ogre flew backward and smashed into the side of the infirmary, on the other side of the entrance. Glass shattered and bricks crumbled down around him, but he was up in a second, brushing chunks of stone from his head and shoulders as he jumped back into the fray.

From near the end of the stampede, a phoenix tried to take flight, holding the corpse of a handler in its claws, but only made it ten feet into the air before its clipped wings brought it crashing to the ground again. It landed on a large lizard of some kind, which opened its mouth as if to screech, but breathed fire instead, singeing the poor bird in a weak imitation of the damage the phoenix would do to itself, at the end of its molting cycle.

From the other direction, voices shouted. Another small squad of handlers rounded the corner of one of the buildings, guns drawn, and began firing. The beasts charged, a bizarre parade of hooves, wings and huge feet. The cacophony was deafening.

As I stared, huddled in the shadows, I heard a familiar voice shouting from the cluster of handlers and recognized Bowman's profile, lit by a fixture mounted on the corner of the infirmary's roof. He lifted his rifle and charged into the fray, firing at the manticore.

I clamped one hand over my own mouth to hold back a scream of warning when I saw a terrifying silhouette rise out of the darkness behind him. With a great grunt, the giant swung the tree he'd uprooted.

The tangle of limbs struck Bowman in the chest with a sickening crack of bone and the splintering of wood. His padded body flew into the side of the dormitory fifty feet away, then crumpled to the ground.

Crisp leaves rained all around, ripped free by the force of the blow. I ran for the infirmary entrance, desperate to both escape the slaughter and to avoid seeing any more of it.

The door closed behind me and I leaned against it in the darkened foyer, my eyes closed, panting from my sprint after weeks of inadequate exercise. Between the noise from outside and the pounding of my heart in my ears, I didn't hear the approaching footsteps until they were almost upon me.

"Freeze, freak! Get down on the ground!"

I opened my eyes to find three handlers standing on the other end of the infirmary foyer, aiming automatic rifles at me in what light poured from the open manager's office. The rest of the building was dark and quiet. Had Gallagher already evacuated it?

"Really?" I said, trying to slow my pulse. "Have you been outside? I'm the least of your problems right now."

"On the floor, facedown!" the one on the left shouted. "Hands behind your back! We *will* shoot!"

I exhaled slowly, steeling my nerve. "The more time you waste with me, the less time you have to get away from what's happening out there."

From the courtyard, a man screamed, but the sound ended in a wet gurgle.

The handlers glanced at one another. Two of them were visibly sweating, and the third's gun shook in his grip.

"You can shoot me and hope the sound doesn't draw attention from the stampede of griffins, giants and manticores outside, or you can sneak quietly out the back door and live to see the—"

"Shoot her." Tabitha stepped out of the office and stood behind the men aiming guns at me, backlit by light pouring through the open door. She wore a satin robe, but her feet were bare and her hair hung down to her shoulders.

"Tabitha? If you kill me, the baby will—"

"Shoot her." Mrs. Vandekamp stepped into the light, and I saw that her face was red and streaked with tears. "Her lover killed my husband, and he *will* know the pain he's caused."

Vandekamp was dead. Joyful relief exploded deep inside me like a star at the end of its life, lighting me on fire from the inside out. I caught my breath on the tail of a sob.

"I found my husband in seven pieces, scattered around his office floor. But there wasn't a single drop of blood. Your lover feasted on the blood he spilled—"

"I'm sure he didn't *feast*…"

"—and I want to know if he'll feed from yours, as well." Her voice faltered beneath the weight of her grief. "Does he truly care about you, or will his brutish nature prevail?" She laid one hand on the shoulder of the handler closest to her. "Shoot her."

The handler's gaze was focused on the wall behind me, through which we could still hear the slaughter going on.

"We don't want to draw their attention until the system's up and running again."

"The system is destroyed," Tabitha snapped. "All of Willem's hard work—years and years of research and design—gone."

"Destroyed?" The handler on the left frowned, and his aim began to falter. "Then how are we supposed to…?"

"I've called in the National Guard." She pulled a handkerchief from a pocket of her robe and blotted at her eyes. "They're going to set up a perimeter and bomb the entire compound."

"Fuck!" the handler on the right whispered. "I'm outta here."

"No!" Tabitha shouted, when all three lowered their aim and turned toward the rear of the building. "Shoot her first! Then you can take my car!"

They brushed past her without even a glance at me over their shoulders.

"Wait!" Tabitha chased after them.

I headed in the opposite direction, toward Claudio's room, as fast as I could go in the dark hallway. The rooms were all empty; anyone who could walk had already fled, because even when they were locked, the infirmary doors could still be opened from the inside. But Claudio couldn't move well under his own power.

His room was empty. Two cuffs still hung from the bedposts, and his sheet was on the floor. Pagano's pale arm stuck out from under the bed.

"You did this."

Startled, I turned to find Woodrow, the gamekeeper, standing in the doorway, blocking my way into the hall. He had a pistol aimed at my chest.

Deep in my belly, the *furiae* stirred. She wanted him. Lost in the trove of information I'd stolen from myself there must have been a memory of Woodrow doing something very, very bad.

"Vandekamp started this," I said. "Gallagher and I are finishing it. And we're getting plenty of help, in case you haven't noticed." I tilted my head as another monstrous screech echoed from outside.

My fingertips began to itch and I resisted the urge to reach for him. If he saw my beast emerging, he would shoot.

"Where is he?" Woodrow demanded, and suddenly I understood.

"You want Gallagher? Are you suicidal?"

"Thanks to you, I'm unemployed. But there's a lab out west offering a cool million for the only redcap ever captured. Vandekamp turned it down, but he's not in charge anymore."

I indulged a bitter laugh. "You better hope you never find Gallagher. You're on his list." But he was on the *furaie's* list now too.

"Even the mighty *fear dearg* can't stop a bullet." Woodrow tossed me a set of handcuffs. "Put those on."

I bent to pick up the handcuffs, to keep him from seeing my eyes, as my vision became suddenly sharp and clear, even in the dark.

When my wrists were bound in front of me and my hair was just beginning to lift from my shoulders, Woodrow reached forward and grabbed my arm in his gloved hand. "Gallagher's the puppet and you're the string. Let's go make the big guy dance."

As he tugged me toward the door, I twisted and grabbed his forearm with both my hands.

Woodrow froze as rage poured from me into him. His arm fell to his side and the pistol clattered to the floor.

"Look beneath the flesh..." the *furiae* murmured through my lips. "See what really matters."

I let Woodrow go, and as my vision returned to normal, my hair still settling around my shoulders, the gamekeeper pulled a knife from his belt and made a long cut down the back of his left forearm. Then he began to peel back his own skin.

Horrified, I pushed past him into the hall, trying not to hear the soft patter of blood as each droplet hit the tile. "Claudio!" I called, as I ran toward the back of the building. "Claudio, where…?"

"She won't wake up."

I whirled toward the voice to find the werewolf standing in the hall behind me, holding his daughter's limp body in both arms.

"She won't wake up, and I can't carry her." Beneath Genevieve's thin, dangling arms and matted hair, blood had soaked through her father's bandage. He'd reopened his stitches.

"Oh no." She'd been fine an hour earlier, asleep in her hospital bed. And now she was…

Her chest rose.

"Let me see her." I jogged down the hall and felt Genni's forehead. Her skin was cool, but not cold. Her breathing was smooth and regular.

I pulled back her eyelids and her eyes dilated. "She's sedated. She must have fought the doctor. She'll wake up soon and be fine, but we have to get you both out of here. Give her to me."

But then I shook my head and took a step back. "Wait, I'm not supposed to lift anything." Among the things I remembered from the CVS procedure was the doctor telling Tabitha not to let me strain. "I'll find a wheelchair."

Yet as I turned to head for the supply room, heavy footsteps clomped toward us from around the corner. The walls shook with each one.

One of the beasts had gotten into the infirmary.

"Shit!" I whispered. "Go back the other way."

"Wait!" Claudio cried, as I tried to tug him along. "I can't—"

The footsteps stomped closer, and a shadow fell onto the tiles at the end of the hall. My heart leapt into my throat and I stepped in front of Claudio, shielding him and Genni out of instinct, before I realized I was actually putting my baby in harm's way.

The beast stepped around the corner, and I nearly fainted with relief. "Eryx!"

The minotaur couldn't speak, nor could he smile with his bull's mouth, but his outstretched arms spoke volumes.

"Give Genni to him!" I stepped out of the way so the werewolf could get by.

As the minotaur relieved Claudio of his daughter's limp weight, Rommily stepped around the corner, her long dark hair hanging half in her face, her eyes wide and completely, opaquely white.

"The cradle will fall," she said, and a chill traveled down my spine. But I didn't have time to worry about what that might mean.

"Okay, go! Find a car big enough for Eryx. Look for a van. Claudio, can you drive?" The werewolf nodded, and I wrapped my arm around him for support as we headed for the back door. "Has anyone seen Gal—"

Sound exploded from the other end of the hall, and I stumbled backward as pain stabbed at my left side. Rommily screamed.

I pressed my hand to my side, trying to find the source of the pain, and my fingers came away warm and wet. And red.

Stunned, I looked up to see Tabitha aiming a pistol from the other end of the hallway. "Now he'll know," she mumbled. "Now you'll all know."

"Go!" I shouted, but my voice carried little volume. I

couldn't draw a deep breath. Each beat of my heart somehow hurt deep inside. But they didn't go. "Claudio, get them out of here."

I fell against the wall, and my hand left a bloody print.

Tabitha lifted the gun again, as I fell to my knees. "Run!" I tried to shout. Then the world lost focus.

DELILAH

Something rushed out of the darkness of an open doorway, and Tabitha disappeared. I blinked, and my eyelids felt heavy. Tabitha's legs stuck out of the dark room, her bare feet turned in by their own limp weight.

I heard a wet thunk and forced my eyes open. Tabitha's head rolled to a stop next to her left ankle, her hair obscuring most of her face but little of the open wound her neck had become. Her arm flew out of the darkness to smack the wall to my left.

Gallagher stepped out of the room. He dropped Tabitha's other arm and his gaze landed on me. Fury and pain swam in his eyes.

Gallagher lifted me like a child and cradled me in both arms.

"Press here." He laid something over my wound and positioned my hands on top of it, and I realized he wasn't wearing a shirt.

He pressed with his hands on top of mine. I screamed as pain ripped through my stomach.

"I know it hurts, but you have to keep pressure on it."

I flew down the hall, bouncing in Gallagher's grip. Claudio limped as fast as he could ahead of us, while Rommily helped with one arm around his shoulders. Ahead of them, Eryx ran for the door with Genni in his arms. Every step he took shattered the tile beneath his feet.

We burst through the door into the night, and the cold night air shocked me awake, in spite of both pain and blood loss. Behind us, the roars and thuds of the beasts' battle still raged, punctuated by the occasional shout or rapid burst of gunfire.

"Head for the parking lot!" Gallagher shouted ahead to Eryx.

My eyes closed again, and sounds floated around me. Footsteps. An engine. The squeal of brakes.

Zyanya shouted something.

I opened my eyes as Gallagher wrenched open the rear door of a transport truck with one hand. He laid me inside, on the floor, and everyone else piled in around me. Zyanya and Lenore were in the cab.

The truck bounced as it drove, rocking crazily, but Gallagher kept pressure on my side. "Don't worry," he said, when I looked up into his eyes. "I've treated many battle wounds."

Tears filled my eyes, and his face blurred. We both knew I'd need more than stitches. "Aaron."

"What?" Gallagher said.

"Take me to Senator Aaron's house." I gasped from the effort it took to speak. "His wife's a surgeon. She owes me a favor."

"I don't know where that is," Zyanya called from the front seat.

I gave her the address I'd read on the mailbox at the end of the long driveway. Paper rustled as Lenore dug a map from the glove box.

"Only Gallagher goes in with me," I insisted.

No one argued.

In the distance, an explosion split the night, and the pressure rocked the van.

And that's when the world went black.

I woke up on a dining room table, staring up at a tray ceiling and a massive chandelier. I rolled my head to the left and found Gallagher snoozing on the floor. When I rolled my head to the other direction, I found Dr. Sarah Aaron sitting on a padded window seat, sipping from a glass of ice water. The early-morning sunlight pouring in from behind her pierced my head like spears through my eyes.

She noticed my movement and looked up. Then she stood. "You got lucky. The bullet broke your rib, but missed your lung. Your biggest problem was blood loss. Fortunately, I'm O positive."

I frowned, trying to understand.

"You now have a pint of my blood," she explained. "You're going to be fine. But you have to leave. Now."

I tried to sit up, and pain shot through my left side. I gasped, and froze.

"Wait, let me help." The floor creaked as Gallagher stood, then shook with each step as he rounded the table. He slid one arm beneath my back and set me upright. Slowly.

"Give her two of these a day, with plenty of water." She handed him a brown pill bottle. "They'll keep her from getting an infection. Give her Tylenol for the pain, every four hours, as needed. The stitches will dissolve on their own, but don't let her lift anything until that happens. And make sure she gets plenty of rest."

"The baby?" I asked, and my voice broke on the question. My throat was *so* dry.

Dr. Aaron gave me a small smile. "The heartbeat is strong. If you rest and stay hydrated, I'd say you've got a good shot."

Her face blurred beneath my tears. "So I'm still pregnant?"

"Yes. But I'm serious. Let Daddy, over there, take care of you. He looks like he's up for the challenge."

"Daddy?" I followed her gaze to Gallagher, who was clutching an envelope that had practically been pressed into the shape of his fist.

"I found it on his desk." He pulled a folded sheet of paper from the envelope and handed it to me.

I unfolded it with trembling hands and scanned the writing until I got to the bottom.

Fetal species: *fae* of indeterminate origin.

I burst into tears, then gasped at the pain in my side. Then I laughed, and cried again from the pain. After that, I was just crying.

"Thank you," Gallagher said to the doctor, while I sniffled and wiped tears from my face. He helped me toward the edge of the table, and I flinched at the pain in my side.

"Tylenol only," Dr. Aaron reminded us. "If she has any complications, you're going to have to find another doctor. You can't come back here."

"I understand." Gallagher stuffed the pill bottle into his pants pocket, then lifted me in both arms. He still wore no shirt. His chest and pants were still stained with my blood.

Gallagher carried me out of the kitchen and down the back steps toward the van. The rear doors opened just as Dr. Aaron closed her door behind us. I could see her watching through the sheer curtain over the window. But she would not open her home for us again.

She and I were even.

Zyanya started the engine as soon as Claudio closed the van doors. "Well?" he said as Gallagher laid me carefully on the floor.

"Delilah's going to be fine."

"And we're going to be parents," I added.

Genni sat in the front corner of the truck, right behind the driver's seat. Her leg was wrapped in a large bandage. *"Un bébé?"* she said, her golden eyes wide.

"Oui," I told her with a smile as Zyanya turned us out of the Aarons' neighborhood.

Lenore had her map open. She didn't look at me, and I wasn't hurt by that. Her loss was too fresh.

Crowded against the rear of the van, Rommily and Eryx sat side by side, their hands interlocked. She laid her head against his arm and smiled at me.

"Where to?" Zyanya asked as she pulled out of the driveway and onto the street.

"Away," I said as I stared through the windshield at the empty highway stretching before us. "We need to regroup. Recuperate. Then we'll find the others."

"Delilah, we need to lie low," Gallagher said, with a pointed glance at my stomach.

"I know. But I gave them my word. And my word is my honor."

★ ★ ★ ★ ★

ACKNOWLEDGMENTS

Thanks first and foremost to Lauren Smulski and Michelle Meade, the two amazing MIRA editors without whose guidance *SPECTACLE* would be just a shadow of the book it is now. Thanks also to Rinda Elliott and Jennifer Lynn Barnes, for endless advice and patient ears. You are my two most consistent and generous sounding boards, and I'm not sure I could function without your friendship and advice. Thanks, as always to my husband, daughter and son, who put up with my erratic and often long hours, as well as my tendency to actually be thinking about the book, even when I'm talking about something else. I'm sorry now and in advance for all the nights I'll spend in bed with my laptop, when the words flow better, for no reason I can seem to pin down.

Also, a huge thanks to the MIRA art department for the gorgeous cover of this book, and for all the hours spent to get it to this point. I love it! Thanks also to everyone in editorial, production, sales, marketing and publicity, who turned this story into a book and gave it to the world. You make me look good, in ways I don't completely understand, even ten years into my career.

And last but not least, thank you to Merrilee Heifetz, Alexandra Levick and everyone else at Writers House who represent my interests. I am so thankful to have you at my back!